Masterpieces

OF

Mystery

Masterpieces
OF
Mystery

The Forties

Selected by ELLERY QUEEN

COPYRIGHT NOTICES AND ACKNOWLEDGMENTS

Grateful acknowledgment is hereby made for permission to reprint the following:

His Heart Could Break by Craig Rice; copyright 1943 by The American Mercury, Inc., renewed; reprinted by permission of Scott Meredith Literary Agency, Inc.

The Man in the Velvet Hat by Jerome and Harold Prince; copyright 1944 by The American Mercury, Inc., renewed; reprinted by permission of the authors.

Chinoiserie by Helen McCloy; copyright 1946 by Helen McCloy, renewed; reprinted by permission of the author.

Malice Domestic by Philip MacDonald; copyright 1946 by The American Mercury, Inc., renewed; reprinted by permission of the author.

The Adventure of the Dead Cat by Ellery Queen; copyright © 1946, 1952 by Ellery Queen, renewed; reprinted by permission of Scott Meredith Literary Agency, Inc.

You Can't Hang Twice by Anthony Gilbert; copyright 1946 by The American Mercury, Inc., renewed; reprinted by permission of John Cushman Associates, Inc.

Love Comes to Miss Lucy by Q. Patrick; copyright 1947 by Q. Patrick, renewed; reprinted by permission of Curtis Brown, Ltd.

Challenge to the Reader by Hugh Pentecost; copyright 1947 by Judson Philips, renewed; reprinted by permission of Brandt & Brandt.

The House-in-Your-Hand Murder by Roy Vickers; copyright 1947 by The American Mercury, Inc., renewed; reprinted by permission of John Cushman Associates, Inc.

Don't Look Behind You by Fredric Brown; copyright 1947 by The American Mercury, Inc., renewed 1975 by Estate of Fredric Brown; reprinted by permission of Scott Meredith Literary Agency, Inc.

Fingerprints Don't Lie by Stuart Palmer; copyright 1947 by The American Mercury, Inc., renewed 1975 by Estate of Stuart Palmer; reprinted by permission of Scott Meredith Literary Agency, Inc.

The Garden of Forking Paths by Jorge Luis Borges; copyright 1948 by Jorge Luis Borges, renewed; reprinted by permission of Curtis Brown, Ltd.

The Lady and the Tiger by Jack Moffitt; copyright 1948 by The American Mercury, Inc., renewed; reprinted by permission of Mrs. Jack Moffitt.

A Study in White by Nicholas Blake; copyright © 1949 by Nicholas Blake, renewed; reprinted by permission of Harold Matson Company, Inc.

The Cat's-Paw by Stanley Ellin; copyright © 1949 by Stanley Ellin, renewed; reprinted by permission of Curtis Brown, Ltd.

Lacrimae Rerum by Edmund Crispin; copyright 1949 by The American Mercury, Inc., renewed; reprinted by permission of the author.

Double Exposure by Ben Hecht; copyright 1949 by The American Mercury, Inc., renewed; reprinted by permission of Rose C. Hecht.

The Arrow of God by Leslie Charteris; from THE SAINT ON THE SPANISH MAIN by Leslie Charteris; copyright 1949 by Leslie Charteris; reprinted by permission of Doubleday & Company, Inc.

Dust to Dust by Wilbur Daniel Steele; copyright © 1949 by Wilbur Daniel Steele, copyright © 1977 by Peter Steele; reprinted by permission of Harold Matson Company, Inc.

C O N T E N T S

PHOTOGRAPH CREDITS: p. 30, Les Armstrong (Harold Prince); p. 49, Van Dyke Studios, Boston; p. 73, Milestone Portraits; p. 92, Marc and Evelyne Bernheim; p.110, Ellis Sykes; p. 223, Flatté of Hollywood; pp.252, 299, The New York Public Library; p. 287, Nicholas Horne Ltd.; p. 310, Geroge W. Vassar for *The American Magazine*.

INTRODUCTION

DEAR READER:

Annexation of Estonia, Latvia, and Lithuania ... Four Freedoms proclaimed by President Franklin D. Roosevelt ... Atlantic Charter announced by Churchill and Roosevelt ... Pearl Harbor attacked December 7, 1941 ... first nuclear chain reaction ... race riots in Detroit and Harlem ... Yalta Conference ... death of President Roosevelt ... suicide of Hitler ... United Nations ... first atomic bomb ... Philippine independence ... Nuremberg trial ... Truman Doctrine ... Marshall Plan ... India and Pakistan independence ... Gandhi assassination ... Berlin blockade and airlift ... Free State of Israel ... Alger Hiss trials ... North Atlantic Treaty ... Tokyo Rose sentenced ...

The Forties—the War Years and Post-War Years for the United States, and against this background of momentous events and of struggle for survival, life went on and the detective-crime-mystery story continued to be written—in its own fashion. At the start of the decade, in 1941, Philip Van Doren Stern published an article cleverly titled "The Case of the Corpse in the Blind Alley." In it Mr. Stern wrote: "The great need of the mystery story today is not novelty of apparatus but novelty of approach. The whole genre needs overhauling, a return to first principles, a realization that murder has to do with human emotion and deserves serious treatment. Mystery story writers need to know more about life and less about death—more about the way people think and feel and act, and less about how they die."

Mystery-story writers listened, and if they didn't actually read Mr. Stern's warning, the strong hint of danger and its consequences was in the air for them to think about and feel and react to. So they turned away from some of the character-

6

istics of The Golden Age—rather, they modified and changed them, and adopted a new approach, taking Mr. Stern's words to heart. And in the 19 stories in this volume you will see clear evidence of these modifications and changes—the beginning of a new Golden Age, or perhaps, more accurately, of a Renaissance.

Happy reading!

ELLERY QUEEN

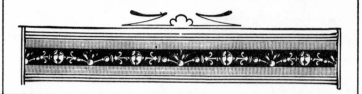

HIS HEART COULD BREAK

BY CRAIG RICE

Craig Rice was born Georgiana Ann Randolph in Chicago on June 5, 1908. She wrote under several names. Among her novels, *To Catch a Thief* (written as by Daphne Sanders) was published in 1943 and *Home Sweet Homicide* (written as by Craig Rice) the following year. In Hollywood, she wrote several movie scripts, one in collaboration with Stuart Palmer. They later combined their detectives, her John J. Malone and his Hildegarde Withers, in a series of stories collected in *The People vs. Withers and Malone*. She edited several fact-crime anthologies and was the subject of a cover and profile story in *Time* magazine in 1946. She died in 1957.

"As I passed by the ol' state's prison,
Ridin' on a streamline' train—"

JOHN J. MALONE SHUDDERED. He wished he could get the insidious melody out of his mind—or remember the rest of the words. It had been annoying him since three o'clock that morning, when he'd heard it sung by the janitor of Joe the Angel's City Hall Bar.

It seemed like a bad omen, and it made him uncomfortable. Or maybe it was the cheap gin he'd switched to between two and four A.M. that was making him uncomfortable. Whichever it was, he felt terrible.

"I bet your client's happy today," the guard said cordially, leading the way towards the death house.

"He ought to be," Malone growled. He reminded himself that he too ought to be happy. He wasn't. Maybe it was being in a prison that depressed him. John J. Malone, criminal lawyer, didn't like prisons. He devoted his life to keeping his clients out of them.

"Then the warden told me gently—"

That song again! How did the next line go?

"Well," the guard said, "they say you've never lost a client yet." It wouldn't do any harm, he thought, to get on the good side of a smart guy like John J. Malone.

"Not yet," Malone said. He'd had a close call with this one, though.

"You sure did a wonderful job, turning up the evidence to get a new trial," the guard rattled on. Maybe Malone could get him a better appointment, with his political drag. "Your client sure felt swell when he heard about it last night, he sure did."

"That's good," Malone said noncommittally. It hadn't been evidence that had turned the trick, though. Just a little matter of knowing some interesting facts about the judge's private life. The evidence would have to be manufactured before the trial, but that was the least of his worries. By that time, he might even find out the truth of what had happened. He

9

hummed softly under his breath. Ah, there were the next lines!

> *"Then the warden told me gently,*
> *He seemed too young, too young to die,*
> *We cut the rope and let him down—"*

John J. Malone tried to remember the rhyme for "die." By, cry, lie, my and sigh. Then he let loose a few loud and indignant remarks about whoever had written that song, realized that he was entering the death house, and stopped, embarrassed. That particular cell block always inspired him with the same behavior he would have shown at a high-class funeral. He took off his hat and walked softly.

And at that moment hell broke loose. Two prisoners in the block began yelling like banshees. The alarms began to sound loudly, causing the outside siren to chime in with its hideous wail. Guards were running through the corridor, and John J. Malone instinctively ran with them toward the center of disturbance, the fourth cell on the left.

Before the little lawyer got there, one of the guards had the door open. Another guard cut quickly through the bright new rope from which the prisoner was dangling, and eased the limp body down to the floor.

The racket outside was almost deafening now, but John J. Malone scarcely heard it. The guard turned the body over, and Malone recognized the very young and rather stupid face of Paul Palmer.

"He's hung himself," one of the guards said.

"With me for a lawyer?" Malone said angrily. "Hung himself . . ." He started to say "hell," then remembered he was in the presence of death.

"Hey," the other guard said excitedly. "He's alive. His neck's broke, but he's breathing a little."

Malone shoved the guard aside and knelt down beside the dying man. Paul Palmer's blue eyes opened slowly, with an expression of terrible bewilderment. His lips parted.

"It wouldn't break," Paul Palmer whispered. He seemed to recognize Malone, and stared at him, with a look of frightful urgency. *"It wouldn't break,"* he whispered. Then he died.

"You're damned right I'm going to sit in on the investigation," Malone said angrily. He gave Warden Garrity's wastebasket a vicious kick. "The inefficient way you run your prison

10

has done me out of a client." Out of a fat fee, too, he reminded himself miserably. He hadn't been paid yet, and now there would be a long tussle with the lawyer handling Paul Palmer's estate, who hadn't wanted him engaged for the defense in the first place. Malone felt in his pocket, found three crumpled bills and a small handful of change. He wished now that he hadn't got into that poker game last week.

The warden's dreary office was crowded. Malone looked around, recognized an assistant warden, the prison doctor—a handsome gray-haired man named Dickson—the guards from the death house, and the guard who had been ushering him in—Bowers was his name, Malone remembered, a tall, flat-faced, gangling man.

"Imagine him hanging himself," Bowers was saying incredulously. "Just after he found out he was gonna get a new trial."

Malone had been wondering the same thing. "Maybe he didn't get my wire," he suggested coldly.

"I gave it to him myself," Bowers stated positively. "Just last night. Never saw a man so happy in my life."

Doctor Dickson cleared his throat. Everyone turned to look at him.

"Poor Palmer was mentally unstable," the doctor said sadly. "You may recall I recommended, several days ago, that he be moved to the prison hospital. When I visited him last night he appeared hilariously—hysterically—happy. This morning, however, he was distinctly depressed."

"You mean the guy was nuts?" Warden Garrity asked hopefully.

"He was nothing of the sort," Malone said indignantly. Just let a hint get around that Paul Palmer had been of unsound mind, and he'd never collect that five thousand-dollar fee from the estate. "He was saner than anyone in this room, with the possible exception of myself."

Dr. Dickson shrugged his shoulders. "I didn't suggest that he was insane. I only meant he was subject to moods."

Malone wheeled to face the doctor. "Say. Were you in the habit of visiting Palmer in his cell a couple of times a day?"

"I was," the doctor said, nodding. "He was suffering from a serious nervous condition. It was necessary to administer sedatives from time to time."

Malone snorted. "You mean he was suffering from the effect

11

of being sober for the first time since he was sixteen."

"Put it any way you like," Dr. Dickson said pleasantly. "You remember, too, that I had a certain personal interest."

"That's right," Malone said slowly. "He was going to marry your niece."

"No one was happier than I to hear about the new trial," the doctor said. He caught Malone's eye and added, "No, I wasn't fond enough of him to smuggle in a rope. Especially when he'd just been granted a chance to clear himself."

"Look here," Warden Garrity said irritably. "I can't sit around listening to all this stuff. I've got to report the result of an investigation. Where the hell did he get that rope?"

There was a little silence, and then one of the guards said, "Maybe from the guy who was let in to see him last night."

"What guy?" the warden snapped.

"Why—" The guard paused, confused. "He had an order from you, admitting him. His name was La Cerra."

Malone felt a sudden tingling along his spine. Georgie La Cerra was one of Max Hook's boys. What possible connection could there be between Paul Palmer, socialite, and the big gambling boss?

Warden Garrity had recognized the name too. "Oh yes," he said quickly. "That must have been it. But I doubt if we could prove it." He paused just an instant, and looked fixedly at Malone, as though daring him to speak. "The report will read that Paul Palmer obtained a rope, by means which have not yet been ascertained, and committed suicide while of unsound mind."

Malone opened his mouth and shut it again. He knew when he was licked. Temporarily licked, anyway. "For the love of Mike," he said, "leave out the unsound mind."

"I'm afraid that's impossible," the warden said coldly.

Malone had kept his temper as long as he could. "All right," he said, "but I'll start an investigation that'll be a pip." He snorted. "Letting a gangster smuggle a rope in to a guy in the death house!" He glared at Dr. Dickson. "And you, foxy, with two escapes from the prison hospital in six months." He kicked the wastebasket again, this time sending it halfway across the room. "I'll show you from investigations! And I'm just the guy who can do it, too."

Dr. Dickson said quickly, "We'll substitute 'temporarily depressed' for the 'unsound mind.' "

12

But Malone was mad now. He made one last, loud comment regarding the warden's personal life and probably immoral origin, and slammed the door so hard when he went out that the steel engraving of Chester A. Arthur over the warden's desk shattered on the floor.

"Mr. Malone," Bowers said in a low voice as they went down the hall, "I searched that cell, after they took the body out. Whoever smuggled in that rope smuggled in a letter, too. I found it hid in his mattress, and it wasn't there yesterday because the mattress was changed." He paused, and added, "And the rope couldn't of been there last night either, because there was no place he could of hid it."

Malone glanced at the envelope the guard held out to him —pale gray expensive stationery, with "Paul Palmer" written across the front of it in delicate, curving handwriting.

"I haven't any money with me," the lawyer said.

Bowers shook his head. "I don't want no dough. But there's gonna be an assistant warden's job opening up in about three weeks."

"You'll get it," Malone said. He took the envelope and stuffed it in an inside pocket. Then he paused, frowned, and finally added, "And keep your eyes open and your mouth shut. Because there's going to be an awful stink when I prove Paul Palmer was murdered."

The pretty, black-haired girl in Malone's anteroom looked up as he opened the door. "Oh, Mr. Malone," she said quickly. "I read about it in the paper. I'm so sorry."

"Never mind, Maggie," the lawyer said. "No use crying over spilled clients." He went into his private office and shut the door.

Fate was treating him very shabbily, evidently from some obscure motive of personal spite. He'd been counting heavily on that five thousand-buck fee.

He took a bottle of rye out of the filing cabinet marked "Personal," poured himself a drink, noted that there was only one more left in the bottle, and stretched out on the worn red leather davenport to think things over.

Paul Palmer had been an amiable, stupid young drunk of good family, whose inherited wealth had been held in trust for him by an uncle considered to be the stingiest man in Chicago. The money was to be turned over to him on his

13

thirtieth birthday—some five years off—or on the death of the uncle, Carter Brown. Silly arrangement, Malone reflected, but rich men's lawyers were always doing silly things.

Uncle Carter had cramped the young man's style considerably, but he'd managed pretty well. Then he'd met Madelaine Starr.

Malone lit a cigar and stared dreamily through the smoke. The Starrs were definitely social, but without money. A good keen eye for graft, too. Madelaine's uncle was probably making a very good thing out of that political appointment as prison doctor.

Malone sighed, wished he weren't a lawyer, and thought about Madelaine Starr. An orphan, with a tiny income which she augmented by modeling in an exclusive dress shop—a fashionable and acceptable way of making a living. She had expensive tastes. (The little lawyer could spot expensive tastes in girls a mile away.)

She'd had to be damned poor to want to marry Palmer, Malone reflected, and damned beautiful to get him. Well, she was both.

But there had been another girl, one who had to be paid off. Lillian Claire by name, and a very lovely hunk of girl, too. Lovely, and smart enough to demand a sizable piece of money for letting the Starr-Palmer nuptials go through without a scandalous fuss.

Malone shook his head sadly. It had looked bad at the trial. Paul Palmer had taken his bride-to-be nightclubbing, delivering her back to her kitchenette apartment just before twelve. He'd been a shade high, then, and by the time he'd stopped off at three or four bars, he was several shades higher. Then he'd paid a visit to Lillian Claire, who claimed later at the trial that he'd attempted—unsuccessfully—to talk her out of the large piece of cash money, and had drunk up all the whiskey in the house. She'd put him in a cab and sent him home.

No one knew just when Paul Palmer had arrived at the big, gloomy apartment he shared with Carter Brown. The manservant had the night off. It was the manservant who discovered, next morning, that Uncle Carter had been shot neatly through the forehead with Paul Palmer's gun, and that Paul Palmer had climbed into his own bed, fully dressed, and was snoring drunk.

14

Everything had been against him, Malone reflected sadly. Not only had the jury been composed of hard-working, poverty-stricken men who liked nothing better than to convict a rich young wastrel of murder, but worse still, they'd all been too honest to be bribed. The trial had been his most notable failure. And now, this.

But Paul Palmer would never have hanged himself. Malone was sure of it. He'd never lost hope. And now, especially, when a new trial had been granted, he'd have wanted to live.

It had been murder. But how had it been done?

Malone sat up, stretched, reached in his pocket for the pale gray envelope Bowers had given him, and read the note through again.

> My dearest Paul:
>   I'm getting this note to you this way because I'm in terrible trouble and danger. I need you—no one else can help me. I know there's to be a new trial, but even another week may be too late. Isn't there *any* way?
>
> Your own
>
> *M.*

"M," Malone decided, would be Madelaine Starr. She'd use that kind of pale gray paper too.

He looked at the note and frowned. If Madelaine Starr had smuggled that note to her lover, would she have smuggled in a rope by the same messenger? Or had someone else brought in the rope?

There were three people he wanted to see. Madelaine Starr, Lillian Claire, and Max Hook.

He went out into the anteroom, stopped halfway across it and said aloud, "But it's a physical impossibility. If someone smuggled that rope into Paul Palmer's cell and then Palmer hanged himself, it isn't murder. But it must have been murder." He stared at Maggie without seeing her. "Damn it, though, no one could have got into Paul Palmer's cell and hanged him."

Maggie looked at him sympathetically, familiar from long experience with her employer's processes of thought. "Keep on thinking and it'll come to you."

"Maggie, have you got any money?"

"I have ten dollars, but you can't borrow it. Besides, you haven't paid my last week's salary yet."

15

The little lawyer muttered something about ungrateful and heartless wenches, and flung himself out of the office.

Something had to be done about ready cash. He ran his mind over a list of prospective lenders. The only possibility was Max Hook. No, the last time he'd borrowed money from the Hook, he'd got into no end of trouble. Besides, he was going to ask another kind of favor from the gambling boss.

Malone went down Washington Street, turned the corner, went into Joe the Angel's City Hall Bar, and cornered its proprietor at the far end of the room.

"Cash a hundred-dollar check for me, and hold it until a week from—" Malone made a rapid mental calculation— "Thursday?"

"Sure," Joe the Angel said. "Happy to do you a favor." He got out ten ten-dollar bills while Malone wrote the check. "Want I should take your bar bill out of this?"

Malone shook his head. "I'll pay next week. And add a double rye to it."

As he set down the empty glass, he heard the colored janitor's voice coming faintly from the back room.

> *"They hanged him for the thing you done*
> *You knew it was a sin,*
> *You didn't know his heart could break—"*

The voice stopped suddenly. For a moment Malone considered calling for the singer and asking to hear the whole thing, all the way through. No, there wasn't time for it now. Later, perhaps. He went out on the street, humming the tune.

What was it Paul Palmer had whispered in that last moment? *"It wouldn't break!"* Malone scowled. He had a curious feeling that there was some connection between those words and the words of that damned song. Or was it his Irish imagination, tripping him up up again? *"You didn't know his heart could break."* But it was Paul Palmer's neck that had been broken.

Malone hailed a taxi and told the driver to take him to the swank Lake Shore Drive apartment-hotel where Max Hook lived.

The gambling boss was big in two ways. He took in a cut from every crooked gambling device in Cook County, and most of the honest ones. And he was a mountain of flesh, over six feet tall and three times too fat for his height. His pink

16

head was completely bald and he had the expression of a pleased cherub.

His living room was a masterpiece of the gilt-and-brocade school of interior decoration, marred only by a huge, battle-scarred roll-top desk in one corner. Max Hook swung around from the desk to smile cordially at the lawyer.

"How delightful to see you! What will you have to drink?"

"Rye," Malone said, "and it's nice to see you too. Only this isn't exactly a social call."

He knew better, though, than to get down to business before the drinks had arrived. (Max Hook stuck to pink champagne.) That wasn't the way Max Hook liked to do things. But when the rye was down, and the gambling boss had lighted a slender, tinted (and, Malone suspected, perfumed) cigarette in a rose quartz holder, he plunged right in.

"I suppose you read in the papers about what happened to my client, Palmer," he said.

"I never read the papers," Max Hook told him, "but one of my boys informed me. Tragic, wasn't it?"

"Tragic is no name for it," Malone said bitterly. "He hadn't paid me a dime."

Max Hook's eyebrows lifted. "So?" Automatically he reached for the green metal box in the left-hand drawer. "How much do you need?"

"No, no," Malone said hastily, "that isn't it. I just want to know if one of your boys—Little Georgie La Cerra—smuggled the rope in to him. That's all."

Max Hook looked surprised, and a little hurt. "My dear Malone," he said at last, "why do you imagine he'd do such a thing?"

"For money," Malone said promptly, "if he did do it. I don't care, I just want to know."

"You can take my word for it," Max Hook said, "he did nothing of the kind. He did deliver a note from a certain young lady to Mr. Palmer, at my request—a bit of a nuisance, too, getting hold of that admittance order signed by the warden. I assure you, though, there was no rope. I give you my word, and you know I'm an honest man."

"Well, I was just asking," Malone said. One thing about the big gangster, he always told the truth. If he said Little Georgie La Cerra hadn't smuggled in that rope, then Little Georgie hadn't. Nor was there any chance that little Georgie had en-

17

gaged in private enterprises on the side. As Max Hook often remarked, he liked to keep a careful watch on his boys. "One thing more, though," the lawyer said, "if you don't mind. Why did the young lady come to you to get her note delivered?"

Max Hook shrugged his enormous shoulders. "We have a certain—business connection. To be exact, she owes me a large sum of money. Like most extremely mercenary people she loves gambling, but she is not particularly lucky. When she told me that the only chance for that money to be paid was for the note to be delivered, naturally I obliged."

"Naturally," Malone agreed. "You didn't happen to know what was in the note, did you?"

Max Hook was shocked. "My dear Malone! You don't think I read other people's personal mail!"

No, Malone reflected, Max Hook probably didn't. And not having read the note, the big gambler probably wouldn't know what kind of "terrible trouble and danger" Madelaine Starr was in. He decided to ask, though, just to be on the safe side.

"Trouble?" Max Hook repeated after him. "No, outside of having her fiancé condemned to death, I don't know of any trouble she's in."

Malone shrugged his shoulders at the reproof, rose and walked to the door. Then he paused, suddenly. "Listen, Max. Do you know the words to a tune that goes like this?" He hummed a bit of it.

Max Hook frowned, then nodded. "Mmm—I know the tune. An entertainer at one of my places used to sing it." He thought hard, and finally came up with a few lines.

> "He was leaning against the prison bars,
>   Dressed up in his new prison clothes—"

"Sorry," Max Hook said at last, "that's all I remember. I guess those two lines stuck in my head because they reminded me of the first time I was in jail."

Outside in the taxi, Malone sang the two lines over a couple of times. If he kept on, eventually he'd have the whole song. But Paul Palmer hadn't been leaning against the prison bars. He'd been hanging from the water pipe.

Damn, and double damn that song!

It was well past eight o'clock, and he'd had no dinner, but

he didn't feel hungry. He had a grim suspicion that he wouldn't feel hungry until he'd settled this business. When the cab paused for the next red light, he flipped a coin to decide whether he'd call first on Madelaine Starr or Lillian Claire, and Madelaine won.

He stepped out of the cab in front of the small apartment building on Walton Place, paid the driver, and started across the sidewalk just as a tall, white-haired man emerged from the door. Malone recognized Orlo Featherstone, the lawyer handling Paul Palmer's estate, considered ducking out of sight, realized there wasn't time, and finally managed to look as pleased as he was surprised.

"I was just going to offer Miss Starr my condolences," he said.

"I'd leave her undisturbed, if I were you," Orlo Featherstone said coldly. He had only one conception of what a lawyer should be, and Malone wasn't anything like it. "I only called myself because I am, so to speak and in a sense, a second father to her."

If anyone else had said that, Malone thought, it would have called for an answer. From Orlo Featherstone, it sounded natural. He nodded sympathetically and said, "Then I won't bother her." He tossed away a ragged cigar and said "Tragic affair, wasn't it?"

Orlo Featherstone unbent at least half a degree. "Distinctly so. Personally, I cannot imagine Paul Palmer doing such a thing. When I visited him yesterday, he seemed quite cheerful and full of hope."

"You—visited him yesterday?" Malone asked casually. He drew a cigar from his pocket and began unwrapping it with exquisite care.

"Yes," Featherstone said, "about the will. He had to sign it, you know. Fortunate for her," he indicated Madelaine Starr with a gesture toward the building, "that he did so. He left her everything, of course."

"Of course," Malone said. He lighted his cigar on the second try. "You don't think Paul Palmer could have been murdered, do you?"

"Murdered!" Orlo Featherstone repeated, as though it was an obscene word. "Absurd! No Palmer has ever been murdered."

Malone watched him climb into a shiny 1928 Rolls-Royce,

19

then started walking briskly toward State Street. The big limousine passed him just as he reached the corner, it turned north on State Street and stopped. Malone paused by the newsstand long enough to see Mr. Orlo Featherstone get out and cross the sidewalk to the corner drug store. After a moment's thought he followed and paused at the cigar counter, from where he could see clearly into the adjacent telephone booth.

Orlo Featherstone, in the booth, consulted a little notebook. Then he took down the receiver, dropped a nickel in the slot, and began dialling. Malone watched carefully. D-E-L—9-6-O—It was Lillian Claire's number.

The little lawyer cursed all soundproof phone booths, and headed for a bar on the opposite corner. He felt definitely unnerved.

After a double rye, and halfway through a second one, he came to the heartening conclusion that when he visited Lillian Claire, later in the evening, he'd be able to coax from her the reason why Orlo Featherstone, of all people, had telephoned her, just after leaving the late Paul Palmer's fiancée. A third rye braced him for his call on the fiancée herself.

Riding up in the self-service elevator to her apartment, another heartening thought came to him. If Madelaine Starr was going to inherit all the Palmer dough—then it might not be such a trick to collect his five thousand bucks. He might even be able to collect it by a week from Thursday.

And he reminded himself, as she opened the door, this was going to be one time when he wouldn't be a sucker for a pretty face.

Madelaine Starr's apartment was tiny, but tasteful. Almost too tasteful, Malone thought. Everything in it was cheap, but perfectly correct and in exactly the right place, even to the Van Gogh print over the midget fireplace. Madelaine Starr was in exactly the right taste, too.

She was a tall girl, with a figure that still made Malone blink, in spite of the times he'd admired it in the courtroom. Her bronze-brown hair was smooth and well-brushed, her pale face was calm and composed. Serene, polished, suave. Malone had a private idea that if he made a pass at her, she wouldn't scream. She was wearing black rayon house-pajamas. He wondered if they were her idea of mourning.

Malone got the necessary condolences and trite remarks out

20

of the way fast, and then said, "What kind of terrible trouble and danger are you in, Miss Starr?"

That startled her. She wasn't able to come up with anything more original than, "What do you mean?"

"I mean what you wrote in your note to Paul Palmer," the lawyer said.

She looked at the floor and said, "I hoped it had been destroyed."

"It will be," Malone said gallantly, "if you say so."

"Oh," she said. "Do you have it with you?"

"No," Malone lied. "It's in my office safe. But I'll go back there and burn it." He didn't add when.

"It really didn't have anything to do with his death, you know," she said.

Malone said, "Of course not. You didn't send him the rope too, did you?"

She stared at him. "How awful of you."

"I'm sorry," Malone said contritely.

She relaxed. "I'm sorry too. I didn't mean to snap at you. I'm a little unnerved, naturally." She paused. "May I offer you a drink?"

"You may," Malone said, "and I'll take it."

He watched her while she mixed a lot of scotch and a little soda in two glasses, wondering how soon after her fiancé's death he could safely ask her for a date. Maybe she wouldn't say Yes to a broken-down criminal lawyer, though. He took the drink, downed half of it, and said to himself indignantly, "Who's broken-down?"

"Oh, Mr. Malone," she breathed, "you don't believe my note had anything to do with it?"

"Of course not," Malone said. "That note would have made him want to live, and get out of jail." He considered bringing up the matter of his five thousand-dollar fee, and then decided this was not the time. "Nice that you'll be able to pay back what you owe Max Hook. He's a bad man to owe money to."

She looked at him sharply and said nothing. Malone finished his drink, and walked to the door.

"One thing, though," he said, hand on the knob. "This—terrible trouble and danger you're in. You'd better tell me. Because I might be able to help, you know."

"Oh, no," she said. She was standing very close to him, and her perfume began to mingle dangerously with the rye and

21

scotch in his brain. "I'm afraid not." He had a definite impression that she was thinking fast. "No one can help, now." She looked away, delicately. "You know—a girl—alone in the world—"

Malone felt his cheeks reddening. He opened the door and said, "Oh." Just plain Oh.

"Just a minute," she said quickly. "Why did you ask all these questions?"

"Because," Malone said, just as quickly, "I thought the answers might be useful—in case Paul Palmer was murdered."

That, he told himself, riding down in the self-service elevator, would give her something to think about.

He hailed a cab and gave the address of the apartment building where Lillian Claire lived, on Goethe Street. In the lobby of the building he paused long enough to call a certain well-known politician at his home and make sure that he was there. It would be just as well not to run into that particular man at Lillian Claire's apartment, since he was paying for it.

It was a nice apartment, too, Malone decided, as the slim mulatto maid ushered him in. Big, soft modernistic divans and chairs, panelled mirrors, and a built-in bar. Not half as nice, though, as Lillian Claire herself.

She was a cuddly little thing, small, and a bit on the plump side, with curly blonde hair and a deceptively simple stare. She said, "Oh, Mr. Malone, I've always wanted a chance to get acquainted with you." Malone had a pleasant feeling that if he tickled her, just a little, she'd giggle.

She mixed him a drink, lighted his cigar, sat close to him on the biggest and most luxurious divan, and said, "Tell me, how on earth did Paul Palmer get that rope?"

"I don't know." Malone said. "Did you send it to him, baked in a cake?"

She looked at him reprovingly. "You don't think I wanted him to kill himself and let that awful woman inherit all that money?"

Malone said, "She isn't so awful. But this is tough on you, though. Now you'll never be able to sue him."

"I never intended to," she said. "I didn't want to be paid off. I just thought it might scare her away from him."

Malone put down his glass; she hopped up and refilled it. "Were you in love with him?" he said.

"Don't be silly." She curled up beside him again. "I liked

22

him. He was much too nice to have someone like that marry him for his money."

Malone nodded slowly. The room was beginning to swim—not unpleasantly—before his eyes. Maybe he should have eaten dinner after all.

"Just the same," he said, "you didn't think that idea up all by yourself. Somebody put you up to asking for money."

She pulled away from him a little—not too much. "That's perfect nonsense," she said unconvincingly.

"All right," Malone said agreeably. "Tell me just one thing—"

"I'll tell you this one thing," she said. "Paul never murdered his uncle. I don't know who did, but it wasn't Paul. Because I took him home that night. He came to see me, yes. But I didn't put him in a cab and send him home. I took him home, and got him to his own room. Nobody saw me. It was late—almost daylight." She paused and lit a cigarette. "I peeked into his uncle's room to make sure I hadn't been seen, and his uncle was dead. I never told anybody because I didn't want to get mixed up in it worse than I was already."

Malone sat bolt upright. "Fine thing," he said, indignantly and a bit thickly. "You could have alibied him and you let him be convicted."

"Why bother?" she said serenely. "I knew he had you for a lawyer. Why would he need an alibi?"

Malone shoved her back against the cushions of the davenport and glared at her. "A'right," he said. "But that wasn't the thing I was gonna ask. Why did old man Featherstone call you up tonight?"

Her shoulders stiffened under his hands. "He just asked me for a dinner date," she said.

"You're a liar," Malone said, not unpleasantly. He ran an experimental finger along her ribs. She did giggle. Then he kissed her.

All this time spent, Malone told himself reprovingly, and you haven't learned one thing worth the effort. Paul Palmer hadn't killed his uncle. But he'd been sure of that all along, and anyway it wouldn't do any good now. Madelaine Starr needed money, and now she was going to inherit a lot of it. Orlo Featherstone was on friendly terms with Lillian Claire.

23

The little lawyer leaned his elbows on the table and rested his head on his hands. At three o'clock in the morning, Joe the Angel's was a desolate and almost deserted place. He knew now, definitely, that he should have eaten dinner. Nothing, he decided, would cure the way he felt except a quick drink, a long sleep, or sudden death.

He would probably never learn who had killed Paul Palmer's uncle, or why. He would probably never learn what had happened to Paul Palmer. After all, the man had hanged himself. No one else could have got into that cell. It wasn't murder to give a man enough rope to hang himself with.

No, he would probably never learn what had happened to Paul Palmer, and he probably would never collect that five thousand-dollar fee. But there was one thing that he could do. He'd learn the words of that song.

He called for a drink, the janitor, and the janitor's guitar. Then he sat back and listened.

"As I passed by the ol' State's prison,
Ridin' on a streamline' train—"

It was a long, rambling ballad, requiring two drinks for the janitor and two more for Malone. The lawyer listened, remembering a line here and there.

"When they hanged him in the mornin',
His last words were for you,
Then the sheriff took his shiny knife
An' cut that ol' rope through."

A sad story, Malone reflected, finishing the second drink. Personally, he'd have preferred "My Wild Irish Rose" right now. But he yelled to Joe for another drink, and went on listening.

"They hanged him for the thing you done,
You knew it was a sin,
How well you knew his heart could break,
Lady, why did you turn him in—"

The little lawyer jumped to his feet. That was the line he'd been trying to remember! And what had Paul Palmer whispered? *"It wouldn't break."*

Malone knew, now.

He dived behind the bar, opened the cash drawer, and scooped out a handful of telephone slugs.

"You're drunk," Joe the Angel said indignantly.

"That may be," Malone said happily, "and it's a good idea too. But I know what I'm doing."

He got one of the slugs into the phone on the third try, dialed Orlo Featherstone's number, and waited till the elderly lawyer got out of bed and answered the phone.

It took ten minutes, and several more phone slugs to convince Featherstone that it was necessary to get Madelaine Starr out of bed and make the three-hour drive to the state's prison, right now. It took another ten minutes to wake up Lillian Claire and induce her to join the party. Then he placed a long-distance call to the sheriff of Statesville County and invited him to drop in at the prison and pick up a murderer.

Malone strode to the door. As he reached it, Joe the Angel hailed him.

"I forgot," he said, "I got sumpin' for you." Joe the Angel rummaged back of the cash register and brought out a long envelope. "That cute secretary of yours was looking for you all over town to give you this. Finally she left it with me. She knew you'd get here sooner or later."

Malone said "Thanks," took the envelope, glanced at it, and winced. "First National Bank." Registered mail. He knew he was overdrawn, but—

Oh, well, maybe there was still a chance to get that five thousand bucks.

The drive to Statesville wasn't so bad, in spite of the fact that Orlo Featherstone snored most of the way. Lillian snuggled up against Malone's left shoulder like a kitten, and with his right hand he held Madelaine Starr's hand under the auto robe. But the arrival, a bit before seven A.M., was depressing. The prison looked its worst in the early morning, under a light fog.

Besides, the little lawyer wasn't happy over what he had to do.

Warden Garrity's office was even more depressing. There was the warden, eyeing Malone coldly and belligerently, and Madelaine Starr and her uncle, Dr. Dickson, looking a bit annoyed. Orlo Featherstone was frankly skeptical. The sheriff of Statesville County was sleepy and bored, Lillian Claire was

25

sleepy and suspicious. Even the guard, Bowers, looked bewildered.

And all these people, Malone realized, were waiting for him to pull a rabbit out of his whiskers.

He pulled it out fast. "Paul Palmer was murdered," he said flatly.

Warden Garrity looked faintly amused. "A bunch of pixies crawled in his cell and tied the rope around his neck?"

"No," Malone said, lighting a cigar. "This murderer made one try—murder by frame-up. He killed Paul Palmer's uncle for two reasons, one of them being to send Paul Palmer to the chair. It nearly worked. Then I got him a new trial. So another method had to be tried, fast, and that one did work."

"You're insane," Orlo Featherstone said. "Palmer hanged himself."

"I'm not insane," Malone said indignantly, "I'm drunk. There's a distinction. And Paul Palmer hanged himself because he thought he wouldn't die, and could escape from prison." He looked at Bowers and said "Watch all these people, someone may make a move."

Lillian Claire said, "I don't get it."

"You will," Malone promised. He kept a watchful eye on Bowers and began talking fast. "The whole thing was arranged by someone who was mercenary and owed money. Someone who knew Paul Palmer would be too drunk to know what had happened the night his uncle was killed, and who was close enough to him to have a key to the apartment. That person went in and killed the uncle with Paul Palmer's gun. And, as that person had planned, Paul Palmer was tried and convicted and would have been electrocuted, if he hadn't had a damn smart lawyer."

He flung his cigar into the cuspidor and went on, "Then Paul Palmer was granted a new trial. So the mercenary person who wanted Paul Palmer's death convinced him that he had to break out of prison, and another person showed him how the escape could be arranged—by pretending to hang himself, and being moved to the prison hospital—*watch her, Bowers!*"

Madelaine Starr had flung herself at Doctor Dickson. "Damn you," she screamed, her face white. "I knew you'd break down and talk. But you'll never talk again—"

There were three shots. One from the little gun Madelaine

26

had carried in her pocket, and two from Bowers' service revolver.

Then the room was quite still.

Malone walked slowly across the room, looked down at the two bodies, and shook his head sadly, "Maybe it's just as well," he said. "They'd probably have hired another defense lawyer anyway."

"This is all very fine," the Statesville County sheriff said. "But I still don't see how you figured it. Have another beer?"

"Thanks," Malone said. "It was easy. A song tipped me off. Know this?" He hummed a few measures.

"Oh, sure," the sheriff said. "The name of it is 'The Statesville Prison.' " He sang the first four verses.

"Well, I'll be double-damned," Malone said. The bartender put the two glasses of beer on the table. "Bring me a double gin for a chaser," the lawyer told him.

"Me too," the sheriff said. "What does the song have to do with it, Malone?"

Malone said, "It was the crank on the adding machine, pal. Know what I mean? You put down a lot of stuff to add up to what you want to know. See how simple it is?"

"I don't," the sheriff said, "but go on."

"I had all the facts," Malone said, "I knew everything I needed to know, but I couldn't add it up. I needed one thing, that one thing." He spoke almost reverently, downing his gin. "Paul Palmer said, '*It wouldn't break*'—just before he died. And he looked terribly surprised. For a long time, I didn't know what he meant. Then I heard that song again, and I did know." He sang a few lines. " '*The sheriff took his shiny knife, and cut that ol' rope through.'* " Then he finished his beer, and sang on " '*They hanged him for the thing you done, you knew it was a sin. You didn't know his heart could break, Lady, why did you turn him in.'* " He ended on a blue note.

"Very pretty," the sheriff said. "Only I heard it, '*You knew that this poor heart could break.'* "

"Same thing," Malone said, waving a hand. "Only, that song was what turned the crank on the adding machine. When I heard it again, I knew what Palmer meant by '*it wouldn't break.*' "

"His heart?" the sheriff said helpfully.

"No," Malone said, "the rope."

27

He waved at the bartender and said "Two more of the same." Then to the sheriff, "He expected the rope to break. He thought it would be artfully frayed so that he would drop to the floor unharmed. Then he could have been moved to the prison hospital—from which there had been two escapes in the past six months. He had to escape, you see, because his sweetheart had written him that she was in terrible trouble and danger—the same sweetheart whose evidence had helped convict him at the trial.

"Madelaine Starr wanted his money," Malone went on, "but she didn't want Paul. So her murder of his uncle served two purposes. It released Paul's money, and it framed him. Using poor old innocent Orlo Featherstone, she planted in Lillian Claire's head the idea of holding up Paul for money, so Paul would be faced with a need for ready cash. Everything worked fine, until I gummixed up the whole works by getting my client a new trial."

"Your client shouldn't of had such a smart lawyer," the sheriff said, over his beer glass.

Malone tossed aside the compliment with a shrug of his cigar. "Maybe he should of had a better one. Anyway, she and her uncle, Dr. Dickson, fixed it all up. She sent that note to Paul, so he'd think he had to break out of the clink. Then her uncle, Dickson, told Paul he'd arrange the escape, with the rope trick. To the world, it would have looked as though Paul Palmer had committed suicide in a fit of depression. Only he did have a good lawyer, and he lived long enough to say '*It wouldn't break.*'"

Malone looked into his empty glass and lapsed into a melancholy silence.

The phone rang—someone had hijacked a truck over on Springfield Road—and the sheriff was called away. Left by himself, Malone cried a little into his beer. Lillian Claire had gone back to Chicago with Orlo Featherstone, who really had called her up for a date, and no other reason.

Malone reminded himself he hadn't had any sleep, his head was splitting, and what was left of Joe the Angel's hundred dollars would just take him back to Chicago. And there was that letter from the bank, probably threatening a summons. He took it out of his pocket and sighed as he tore it open.

"Might as well face realities," Malone said to the bartender.

28

"And bring me another double gin."

He drank the gin, tore open the envelope, and took out a certified check for five thousand dollars, with a note from the bank to the effect that Paul Palmer had directed its payment. It was dated the day before his death.

Malone waltzed to the door, waltzed back to pay the bartender and kiss him good-bye.

"Do you feel all right?" the bartender asked anxiously.

"All right!" Malone said. "I'm a new man!"

What was more, he'd just remembered the rest of that song. He sang it, happily, as he went up the street toward the railroad station.

> *"As I passed by the ol' State's prison,*
> *Ridin' on a streamline' train*
> *I waved my hand, and said out loud,*
> *I'm never comin' back again,*
> *I'm never comin' back a—gain!"*

THE MAN IN THE VELVET HAT

BY JEROME AND HAROLD PRINCE

Jerome Prince (left) was born in New York City on August 26, 1907, and educated at the City College of New York and Brooklyn Law School. He is the author of numerous books on the laws of evidence, Dean and Professor Emeritus of Brooklyn Law School, and collaborator with his brother Harold (right) on a number of mystery short stories, of which *The Man in the Velvet Hat* was first. Harold Prince, a prolific ghostwriter with two best sellers to his credit, received his Master's degree from Columbia University and is former Editor-in-Chief of Curtis Publications' Books for Better Living Division. His series of guides to retirement living is regarded as a classic.

THERE WERE NO SEARCHLIGHTS that night. Far down at the
end of the corridor, black, no moonlight through the long
open windows, voices, low then loud, slipped through the
concrete from the office behind the walls, loud then low, a
mumble, a chatter, a senility of sounds. Then a block of light
crashed into the hallway—the door of the office was swinging
back—and the sounds became laughter, voices, a clarinet's
tune—*Come on along, Come on along, Alexander's Ragtime
Band*—and the doorknob cracked hard against a retaining
wall. Shadows, three-dimensional, bulged into the doorway;
the block of light was veined with moving strata of black, of
gray—*It's the best band in the land*—someone, soprano, was
singing; voices were hiccoughing, saying, good-bye, merry
Christmas, good-bye, merry Christmas, good-bye, good-bye.
Good-bye, a deep voice answered, good-bye, good-bye, good-
bye—*played in ragtime, Come on along, Come on along, Alexander's Ragtime Band*—merry Christmas. Then the shadows
stumbled back from the doorway; the man, alone in the corridor, the light upon him, wobbled, grinned, wiped lipstick
from his face, straightened his tie, his hat. The office door
clicked shut. There was no light now, and only a whispered
jazz tune growing fainter; and the man's footsteps sounded
loud as they moved up the corridor, sounded louder as they
moved more rapidly, seemed one burst of noise as the man
began to run. And then there was no sound at all.

When the police found his body in the alley two hours
later, there was something ugly where his head had been.
The short investigation that followed was decisive. Within
an hour, the police had learned that the dead man was a
boiler salesman, John Mongon; that he was twenty-six years
old, had no enemies; and that his death could not possibly
have resulted from foul play. Both the plainclothesmen as-
signed to the case and the local uniformed officer agreed that
Mongon, drunk, or, at least, strongly under the influence of
liquor, had left his company's Christmas party at eleven P.M.
on Monday, December seventeenth, during the height of a
practice blackout; that, unable to find his way in the dark,
he had walked by the elevator shaft, and, then, somehow,

had slipped and plunged through an open casement window. It was death by accident, and so far as the police were concerned, the case was closed, despite the morning mail which brought the same letter to Magruder as it did to Reynolds.

Magruder probably never saw the letter that day—it must have been pigeonholed by that clerical machine which is efficient because it has learned not to discriminate—or, if he did see the letter, he had seen so many like it in his long career as a police official that he must have returned it summarily for the clerical machine to pigeonhole. But Reynolds had to see the letter; he had to read it; it was his job. For years now, as a feature writer of that New York daily, as a contributor to the smartest of the slick magazines, he had made a reputation by describing, as Stevenson and Arthur Machen had once done, the romance lurking just beyond the pavement: the unusual, the macabre which rubbed elbows with you in the Polo Grounds, on the B.M.T., along the Bowery, in the middle of Central Park. His early works—he was very young then—were brilliant fantasies, derivatives of James Stephens, Lord Dunsany, Charles Fort, with, if you can imagine it, a strong dose of Ben Hecht and a good deal of O. Henry. But, as he, and his bank account, grew fatter, the rigid discipline which is necessary for the creation of the unreality which is real, was, after a small struggle, forgotten, and his poetry became fact, his dreams, articles. People had come to him—all sorts of queer people—telling him queer tales; and letters from Massilon, Ohio, and others with strange stamps and stranger scripts had brought the *outré* into his study. Most of those yarns—the identity of Hitler's wife, the man who was Crater, the route to Shangri-La—were, Reynolds had found, amateurish and scarcely original lies; but he had been surprised to learn that some of the stories were true and he had been even more surprised to learn that the publication of these stories, whether true or not, earned him more money than he had ever made before. It became his practice thereafter to listen closely to his visitors, to read his mail carefully, and whenever something interested him, to place a large red-crayon check on the relevant documents; and sometimes he would investigate these documents before publication, and sometimes he would not.

Check. *My dear Mr. Reynolds, It was My whim two hours ago to take home with Me to Eternity, My son, known in this*

32

life as John Mongon. Monday, December 18th. It was post-marked 1:00 A.M.

Check. *My dear Mr. Reynolds, In a swift chariot, I have taken Edward Tucker home to Glory.* Tuesday, December 19th.

Check. *My dear Mr. Reynolds, Five have been purified by flames, and are at peace within My heart.* Wednesday, December 20th.

Check. *My dear Mr. Reynolds, I have said love little children, and so I have taken her from suffering to Eternal Happiness.* Thursday, December 21st.

Check. *My dear Mr. Reynolds, Let he who is without sin cast the first stone, so she, too, now knows her God.* Friday, December 22nd.

Check. *My dear Mr. Reynolds, I saw Peter Savitcky to-day and I knew he was a good man. Peter Savitcky is no longer with you, but with Me in Celestial Happiness; and you must not, John Reynolds, hope that I shall come for you, for I have not willed it, and your time is not yet come. Nor will I be pleased if you seek me out, even though you cannot. You cannot. You cannot find Me, John Reynolds, and do not ask your police to help you. They find criminals, John Reynolds, here they must find a crime.* By special delivery, Saturday, December 23rd.

Check. *And on the Seventh Day He rested.* By telegram, Sunday, December 24th.

It was with the arrival of the seventh message on Christmas Eve that the events crystallized for Reynolds—and this he reported later—into a Mendeleyev chart of crime, with gaps in the future for events that must occur, with gaps in the past for events that had occurred but had not been observed. It was then that he decided to investigate the incidents of the last week and to find the unknown that he knew must exist. He acted immediately. A telephone call to the office of Western Union brought him no results: the telegram had been dictated from a pay station in the Borough Hall section of Brooklyn; yes, it was a man; no, I couldn't identify the voice; yes, I'm sure. Another call to the local police station wasted a nickel. And the woman who answered the telephone at Magruder's apartment was polite, but nothing could make her admit Magruder was at home. Reynolds dialed another number.

33

Then without shaving: from lounging pajamas into tweed, a camel's-hair coat, the Hudson on his left, cold wind against his cheeks, the lights of George Washington Bridge growing nearer, behind him now, the screech of his tires on dirty snow, snowflakes on his collar as he stepped from the car. The man was waiting for him, wanting to hear more; but when he heard what Reynolds had to say, he laughed quietly; and when Reynolds continued, excited now, insisting, the man was impatient; and when Reynolds began to argue, his red hair falling over his eyes, constantly being brushed back with a tic-like gesture, the man said, "Listen, mister, I don't know if you are who you say you are, and I don't care. But get this straight. Peter Savitcky was my brother. If anyone knows anything about him, I know, and I'm telling you this for the last time: my brother died of pneumonia and nothing else."

Then the car again, down a Broadway slippery with ice, across town, under an El, over car tracks and cobblestones, dark tenements on both sides of him, then a small brownstone house, shades pulled down on the windows, stained curtains over a large glass door. She answered the bell—her kimono was clinging tightly to her body . . . "What you want white man," she said; and Reynolds talked, as bluntly as to Peter Savitcky's brother, as he knew he must talk; but she just laughed, "Ain't worth worrying about, mister," she said; and when Reynolds muttered something in a low voice, "I ain't afraid. She was a no-good woman and she got what was coming to her. I saw the streetcar cut her in two, and it was nobody's fault but her own. I swear to God"—she kissed the tip of her small finger and held it high in the air—"I swear to God."

He walked now, a few blocks south to a four-story building of the old type. There was black crepe, already dirty and torn, hanging in the vestibule; the stairs were rotten, insects scurried across the walls; there was black crepe, dirty, too, and torn, hanging on a wooden door two flights up. Inside, it was cold: there was no steam, no stove. An old woman sat on a wooden box, staring in front of her, moaning, softly. When Reynolds spoke to her she whimpered. A neighbor said, "Don't. She's almost out of her mind"; and when Reynolds turned to him questioning, "You're crazy. Her grandmother told her to stay off the ice. A six-year-old girl don't listen. And what could an old lady do?"

34

He drove across town again, then down the highway, the snow falling more heavily now, the East River dull white, the sound of his tires a soporific crunch; then slush under his wheels as he turned back into the city, pushcarts, delicatessens, slums, a thin red house, skeletal, charred, and a fireman bending his face down to the car window, talking rapidly, and Reynolds answering, arguing, trying to win his point by logic, curses, until the fireman laughed and Reynolds heard him say what the others had said. "But don't you understand," Reynolds still insisted, "that a man smoking in bed could *not* have caused this fire"; but the fireman only smiled, "I don't know anything about that," he said. "Maybe the five guys who were toasted in this litle barbecue could tell you more"; and Reynolds shifted gears, cried, "Merry Christmas."

If he were to have continued his journey back into time, his next stop would have been the Coliseum in the Bronx; but the case of Edward Tucker who had made his living driving midget racing cars and who had met his death in one, was more blatantly accidental than any of the others; and, besides, it was now nearly eleven. Instead, Reynolds drove west, stopping at a drugstore near Fulton Street and Broadway. He waited until a phone booth cleared, then spoke into the mouthpiece for several minutes. When he came out, he was sweating, and the night air made him shudder, but he walked up the block to the bookstore on the corner, slumped, tired, against the wall of the building, waited. In five minutes, a boy-sized young man wearing an incipient mustache of indeterminate color—pants pegged tightly about his ankles, topcoat hugging his waist, mushrooming widely over his shoulders, low-crowned, all-brim hat perching on the back of his head—approached Reynolds uneasily, finally held out his hand.

"Mr. Reynolds? I'm Larry."

Reynolds took his hand, made the customary remarks, then spoke rapidly.

"Gee, no, Mr. Reynolds. Gee whiz, no!"

For the next few minutes, his back turned to Larry, Reynolds read a hundred titles in the bookstore window and remembered none; then, facing Larry again, he said quietly,

"Larry, this is more important to you than it is to me, or anybody else. Tell me, on the night Mongon fell through the window did you take anybody up to the party who didn't belong there?" He gave the boy a long, level look.

"No, sir."

"Larry, are you sure?"

"Sure, I'm sure."

"Now, listen, Larry, you know who I am, don't you? That's right. I can make you a pretty famous fellow, Larry—your picture in the paper, everybody talking about you—if you can remember what you saw last Monday night."

"I don't get you, Mr. Reynolds. I told you I saw nobody else."

"Are you sure, Larry? Could you swear to it if you had to in court—particularly if somebody else knew you were mistaken? Larry, our memories are curious things; they play us tricks. Larry, try to remember if you brought anybody else up in the elevator that night—somebody you never saw before."

"Mr. Reynolds, you got me all mixed up. I don't know what you mean."

"Larry! You know what I mean. Oh, all right, we'll pay you fifty dollars for your story. Now tell me what happened when you saw him."

Larry said, "Maybe you mean the tall guy who came in at a quarter to eleven?"

Reynolds said, "Of course. Now let's have it."

Larry moistened his lips.

"He comes in—it's pretty late. I say, 'Floor, please?' He says, 'Twelve.' I say, 'There ain't nobody on twelve.' He don't say a word. I say, 'The party's on sixteen.' He just ignores me. So I take him up."

"You never saw him before?"

"Never."

"Now what did he look like, besides being tall?"

"You got me there, Mr. Reynolds. I—"

"You must have seen his face. That's a pretty bright light in your elevator. Unless . . . he had his hat pulled down so you couldn't see his face. Was that it, Larry? Did he have his hat pulled down over his face?"

"Sure. That's what it was. He had his hat pulled down over his face."

"What kind of hat was it?"

"Black."

"Black? That's all?"

"Well, an ordinary hat. Old, though. Fuzzy."

"Fuzzy? Like old velvet?"

"If you say so."

"Not if I say so. Was it?"

"O.K., Mr. Reynolds, O.K. It was like you say—velvet. He wore a raincoat," Larry added.

"Good. What color?"

"Pretty dark. Brown. Dark brown."

"That's fine, Larry. Now one thing more, and be very careful that you remember this properly: what time did he come down?"

Larry's face was expressionless.

"He never did come down," he said.

Reynolds opened his wallet.

The remainder of that night was, as Reynolds reported it, an adventure in Freudian psychology: an attempt to restore to the consciousness the memory of the man in the velvet hat which was lost in the hinterland of many minds. (*Now, relax, Bessie. Put your head back on the pillow. Close your eyes—and talk, Bessie. Talk about anything that comes into your mind, Bessie, anything at all. How she walked, Bessie. How she walked when the streetcar hit her. Anything, Bessie, anything that comes into your mind.* a tall man black *Anything, Bessie, no matter how small it is, no matter how silly it sounds.* velvet raincoat a tall man black *No matter how silly it sounds, Savitcky, let me know.* a tall man a velvet hat *No matter how silly.* tall black a velvet hat *Here, grandmother, let me fix the pillow under your head. Just relax, rest, rest, rest.* tall black a velvet hat *Rest.* atallman abrownraincoat avelvethat *Head back on the pillow.* abrownraincoatavelvet

Slowly. Slowly. atallmanatallatallmanabrownraincoat a velvet hat. . . . *A dozen people have sworn that they saw this man talking to the doctor during your brother's crisis. Savitcky, I don't give a damn one way or another, but the police are going to be mighty unpleasant if you deny that you saw him. That suits me, Bessie, but I don't have to remind you that the police and my newspaper might be interested in the business you do. A hundred dollars now; the rest, grandmother, when you find that picture of your daughter. The others swore that they saw this man, surely you're not going to be the only exception?*) And by the morning of Christmas

37

day, Reynolds had in his possession the written testimony of seven witnesses; and by the evening of Christmas day, he said later, he had completed his pattern, and had finished what was to be the first of a series of articles.

In that story which appeared early on the afternoon of December 26th, Reynolds sketched the death scenes of the eight men, the woman, the child, introduced the contents of the letters, stressing the apparent God-substitution schizophrenia; and then made it impossible for the reader to doubt the existence of some agency behind each of the noncriminal acts. How he had searched for that agency and how he had finally identified it as the man in the black velvet hat, he then told in a sequence of exclamation points, culminating in an accusation of murder. "But if murder has been done, and if this man is a murderer"—and now Reynolds was writing as he had a hundred times before—"he is a murderer such as the world has never known, or perhaps, such as the world has always known, but never seen. There is no motive for any of his crimes. no evidence of lust or of envy, of passion or of gain. He kills by caprice, through kindness, by whim, or by some deep underlying necessity. Certainly, if this man is not a God, he has not only successfully adopted the posturings of one, but the psychic attributes as well. Where he walks, death walks—and this man may be Death himself."

There was no comment on the yarn from Magruder, nothing about it in the later editions of the other evening papers, just a casual reference to it by an obscure radio newscaster; but dozens of people came to see Reynolds, others telegraphed or telephoned, and each swore that he had seen the man in the black velvet hat just before or just after a death by accident or by suicide or by disease. Reynolds remembered particularly an old Italian woman—her face was a tapestry of hard gray threads—who crossed herself as she talked, about her son: dying, slowly, screams clinging to the house, the Blessed Saints and prayer, kissing a silver crucifix as she talked, prayer on bony knees in damp churches, again and again and again, then convalescence in the sunlight, laughter in the sunlight, a blanket over his knees, gay in a wheelchair, laughing, she laughing, too, then a tall man walking in the sunlight, a brown raincoat close to his rib-thin body, a black velvet hat pulled down hard over his eyes, we, laughing in the sunlight, Holy Mother how we laughed in the sunlight, a lean shadow down the street, a lean shadow falling on her son, a silent passing—she kissed the crucifix again—and death. Others remembered that story, too: it was dramatized on several radio news programs almost immediately after its publication under Reynolds's byline; it appeared, rewritten, in several current news magazines, in every other paper in New York; it served to introduce the man in the black velvet hat to seven million New Yorkers, and to create, if nothing else, a sense of expectation which was the prelude to the change which came over the city after the eighth letter was made public on Thursday night.

My dear Mr. Reynolds, it read, Do not deceive yourself. I have been silent, but I have never rested, nor have I ever rested. I shall continue to choose as I have always chosen, as the whim strikes me; and as the whim strikes me, so shall I tell. You will not always know, John Reynolds, how merciful I have been.

On the following morning, many newspapers began the practice of publishing a daily list of accidental—they printed it "accidental"—deaths in a black-lined box on their front pages; but there was, apparently, no excitement, except in the voices of radio announcers; no panic, except for those few who had seen the man in the velvet hat; no fear, except for the quasi-supernatural warnings of Reynolds and the paraphrases of his colleagues. New York seemed to go about its affairs with its customary indifference; but on that Friday night business began to boom in the night clubs, and flop shows dusted off the standing-room-only signs. The Broadway area during the next few days was so crowded that it often took an hour to walk from Fifty-ninth to Forty-second Street. At the Stork Club, at the Famous Door, at 21, at Fefe's Monte Carlo more people were turned away in one week than had been admitted in the previous six. Eight new jazz bands were imported: six from Chicago, two from New Orleans. The waiting lines to the larger motion picture houses were often as long as two city blocks. There were no cabs to be had at all in the midtown area. At Macy's, in five other department stores, the Bible topped all book sales. Restaurants placed their chairs back to back; and a local comic added to his act a sketch of Casper Milquetoast trying to drink a brimming glass of milk at Dinty Moore's. But on January 5th, all that stopped.

By curtain time of that day, four men and two women had already died, and of the six others at the Polyclinic Hospital, only two were to survive. Most reporters, including Reynolds, credited the first scream ("I did it to warn the others," she said) to a small upholstered woman of about forty; others placed the blame on a middle-aged male neurasthenic, on an unemployed salesman, on a high school girl. But the official report submitted to Magruder spoke of the cause of the panic as a simultaneity of shouts and screams, and of the impossible task of fixing responsibility on any known person: by the time the police had arrived, there was no trace of the man in the black velvet hat, and no one had seen him enter the Radio Building, and no one had seen him leave. But more than two hundred people of the studio audience swore that they had rushed by him just after the first screams—and all New York knew that Reynolds must have received that ninth letter, even though he did not publish it. His column of the next day, denying receipt of the letter, stridently proving—and this was not at all in Reynolds's style—that there could be no connection between the incidents at the radio station and the man in the velvet hat, was met by New York with the same cynicism with which it meets all mollifying propaganda—and it was after that, late on Sunday night, that Reynolds and Magruder came face to face for the first time.

They sat opposite each other, across a small round table, lamplight hushing the ugliness of the room, steam hissing fitfully from a radiator, an old electric clock wheezing, ticking loudly, Reynolds, Magruder, watching each other, listening to the Mayor's footsteps as he walked on the thinly carpeted floor, Magruder a bludgeon, a roll of fat curving over the Mayor's high white stiff collar like a half-baked doughnut, walking, Reynolds sweating, the Mayor talking on and on, pacing up and down, Magruder's eyes hard on Reynolds, on and on, Magruder *Listen, Reynolds, I've been a policeman for forty years. I've seen them come and go. Tricks don't fool me.* Across the room, his hands behind his back, mop of hair in his eyes, shouting, hands on the table, his face close to theirs, walking again, Magruder saying nothing, Reynolds blinking the sting of a sweat-drop from his eye, Magruder *I've walked beats on nights so cold that fat body of yours would have shriveled. I have a bullet buried somewhere in my chest.* The steam screeching from the radiator, the Mayor's

40

words drowned in it, weather strips along the windows, fog liquefying against the panes, the Mayor smashing his pudgy fist on the table, asking a question, quiet now.

"Maybe there isn't any murderer," Magruder said. "Not in the ordinary sense."

Reynolds tried to say, then said, "I believe there is."

Magruder went on talking. "The letters that Reynolds got came to us, too. You know that. We checked each one—different typewriter, different stationery, no fingerprints. I don't know if one man wrote them. Or, if he did, he's the cleverest crank I've ever come across. And even if it is the work of one man, there's nothing to connect the writer of the letters with murder. Except for that little picnic at the radio station, every death was accidental or natural as sure as we three are in this room."

The Mayor dragged a small armchair from a corner of the room, forced himself into it, formed a triangle around the table. The clock was ticking more loudly than ever.

Magruder said, "I'd like to put the screws on some of those people who saw the man in the velvet hat. I'd like to bet he'd disappear just like—" He snapped his fingers.

Reynolds stood up. The perspiration on his body had turned cold. The Mayor talked directly to Magruder.

"Forget it." His shrill voice was always pitched to a key of anger. It hid, perhaps, what may have been other emotional states. "You couldn't prove it if you had until Doomsday to do it, and if you did no one would believe you. To them, the man in the velvet hat is real, and there's panic."

Magruder lit his pipe, blew out the match. "That's not so. Not in New York. There never will be panic in New York."

"Magruder! Magruder, you think a panic is what happened at the radio station. Somebody screams, 'He's here!' and people lose their heads and trample each other to death. You can't imagine the whole city acting like that. I can't either. But a panic in New York is a cold thing. Listen to me. How's show business? Did you ever see Times Square as empty as you did last night? What was the attendance at the basketball carnival? People are avoiding crowds. They won't admit it. They won't even think it, but what happened at the radio station, they're afraid will happen again. And they're not just afraid. They're scared blue, Magruder."

Reynolds sat down, unbuttoned his vest, straightened his

41

tie, then buttoned his vest. He said,

"Why don't you catch him?"

The Mayor grasped Magruder's coat lapel. "I want to stop all this. Show them that we can stop it—if there is no man in the velvet hat, invent one, and get him."

"That won't help." Reynolds's voice was louder than the ticking of the clock. "He'll murder again. It will be worse."

"I won't do it," said Magruder. "That's not my style."

The Mayor drummed with his child-sized fingers on the liquor-stained, coffee-stained surface of the table; Reynolds looked from one to the other, trying to catch an expression on their averted faces; the steam began to hammer and sizzle in the risers. Magruder knocked ashes from his pipe, a dying cinder glowing on the rug.

"The way I see it," Magruder's tone was speculative, his voice low, "the thing is either a hoax, or there is a man in the velvet hat—perhaps a crank, perhaps a murderer. If we can prove the hoax, or catch our man, the panic, such as it is, disappears. I think we can do it—with Reynolds's co-operation. . . . I'm going to challenge the man in the velvet hat—and Reynolds is going to publish that challenge. I'm going to say that I don't think he's a god, and I don't think he's a good criminal. I'm going to say, I don't even think he *is* a criminal—anybody can boast of a murder after it's happened, but only a master criminal can boast of a murder before it's happened—and get away with it."

The Mayor smiled; his whole face became a series of semi-circles curving upwards.

"You see the implications," Magruder went on, as slowly as before. "If he doesn't accept the challenge, or if he does accept the challenge and doesn't show up—" He made a gesture indicating finality. "And if he accepts the challenge and tries to succeed, we'll nab him. In either case, the thing is done. Can I count on Reynolds's help?"

The Mayor said, "Yes."

Reynolds had picked up his hat and cane. He was on his feet, walking to the door. He stopped, turned about.

"My own guess is—" he was trying to make himself heard above the banging of the steam, the ticking of the clock—"that he will accept the challenge, and that when he does, you will not nab him."

And then it was night again, the Times Building a pale

42

shadow across the street, sounds centrifuged at him, amoeba-forms of clouds tasting and disgorging a full white moon, hints of rain slapping his cheeks, jazz from the dance hall overhead, a drunken clown shouting, "Nine o'clock and all's well." *Come on along, Come on along, Alexander's Ragtime Band.* The illuminated dial of his watch told Magruder that it was only three minutes to nine, three more minutes, three minutes to nine. *it's the bestest band what am* Simon and Thompson were in front of the Times Building. Burke and LaMantia were in the lobby. Rowan was across the street on Seventh Avenue. The homicide squad was scattered over the theatrical district. He wanted to, but he didn't dare increase the uniformed police force. No one else knew—only Reynolds, himself, his asistant, Kuchatsky, and the man who wrote the note—written this time in medieval script, delicate colors on yellow parchment. *if you want to hear the Swanee River* Two minutes, two minutes more, two minutes. Anyway, it's over with. After tonight . . . *At nine o'clock, precisely, on Wednesday night, January tenth, a man will die, poisoned, in front of the Times Building. After this I will move again in silence, for only those without faith need signs.* There was a glinting sheet of rain in front of him now. *honey lamb honey lamb* Kuchatsky slipped under the awning dripping wet, a stream of water running from his hat. We thought we had him, Chief. In front of the Majestic, fit the description to a T, turned out to be one of our own boys from Staten Island. They laughed. Another minute, one more minute, less now, less than a minute. *Alexander's Ragtime Band.* Keep your eyes open. Cars were sliding on the water-smooth asphalt. The traffic cops cursed. I see by the clock, Chief, that it's nine o'clock. Done. We'll stick around, maybe his watch is slow. They laughed. Another plainclothesman elbowed his way through to the awning. He was sweating, but he was grinning. Overhead they were beginning to jam it, bass fiddle throbbing, traps coughing out hoarse subliminals. A man was standing on the Seventh Avenue curb, watching the cars. *ragtime ragtime ragtime* The man was wearing no hat; he was carrying a coat under his arm. He was watching the sliding cars carefully. *come on come on come on along* A trumpet pleading.

The man leapt. Magruder started forward. The man was avoiding the cars, weaving like a basketball player, running hard. Somebody called him a damn fool. He was running toward the wedge-end of the Times Building, drenched to the skin.

come on along bugle call in the land in the land

The man was more than halfway across. The traffic cop was shouting at him. Magruder was waving at Simon and Thompson in the lobby of the Times Building. They didn't see him. The man's coat in the dimout blackness could have been any color, but it was cloth, tweed.

The man had reached the sidewalk in front of the Times Building. There was some light on him. He was tall and thin. He fumbled in his pocket.

It was the clarinet's lick now. He was warming up, playing it straight for a few bars. *it's the best band in the land if you want to hear* The man was raising his hand to his mouth, gulping out of a tiny bottle—and then he began to crumble, liquidly, like a trick shot from a motion picture.

Magruder began to sprint. Kuchatsky blew his whistle. Thompson and Simon were already bending over the man. The others were running, too. The traffic cop was trying to hold off the crowd.

Magruder said, "Take him to a hospital."

Simon said, "He's dead as a doornail."

Then Magruder looked at the man. He knew he had never seen that pain-distorted face before, drops of water pounding on open eyes. He knelt and closed the eyelids. Then he picked up the man's coat, held it in his hand. It was light, too light. He shook it. Oilskin glistened where lining should have been. He turned the coat inside out. It was a raincoat, now, and brown. Out of one pocket jutted a crumpled black velvet hat.

Kuchatsky tugged at Magruder's sleeve. "Look, Chief, the boys say he dropped it just before he kicked off." Folded vellum, tied with a string; Magruder, automatically untying the string, blocked Gothic letters, in red, in blue, rain covering them with a wavering film—*And God*, it read, *so loved this world that He gave His only begotten Son.*

Traffic had stopped; there was an excited crowd-whisper all about, but across the street, the jazzmen were taking a rest. Magruder began to whistle softly. The tune was "Alexander's Ragtime Band."

Then the Mayor said, seesawing on the swivel chair behind Magruder's desk, "This is thanks—" winter sunlight breaking against Venetian blinds, the room soft shadows, Magruder leaning under a photograph, Reynolds grinning—"man to man, this is thanks." And Magruder, irritated, playing with the tassels of the blinds, sucking on a long-cold pipe, saying, "Yes, yes, we have a good deal to thank Reynolds for." Reynolds, easy on the leather lounge, his red hair parted, smooth, the points of his white handkerchief distinct against the brown covert of his suit, bland, happy, saying the proper things—"So, Reynolds, this is thanks, but you surprised me." "When he died that way, even *I* thought the thing was supernatural. 'Don't have to give me odds,' I said, 'that Reynolds will play it up for all he's worth, and leave us in a worse mess than we were before.' Not surprised?" Magruder's head pivoting in negation.

"Why should you be surprised?" asked Reynolds. "I admit, I'd fancy a supernatural ending to a natural one. After all, that's my trade. But when Magruder told me about the suicide—about his being insane, I mean, what could I think? It was clear then that he couldn't have been associated with the crimes in that inexplicable manner I dreamt of. Actually, there were no crimes; he must have attached his mad ego to each death after the fact. How he got the information so quickly, I don't know; but Magruder says it's easy enough. And once he knew, he appeared at or near the scene of the death in that striking costume, and then he posted the letters. That some witnesses swore he appeared before the deaths, well, that's a human failing, isn't it?

"He was a true psychopath; there's no doubt about that. In his own diseased brain, he was a death-dealing but merciful God, taking to rest those who were 'heavy laden,' or rewarding the Good of the earth with the joys of Paradise; and even to the end, he was madly consistent, sacrificing himself rather than admit his inability to accept Magruder's challenge. . . . There was no other way to see it, agreed? That's what I wrote."

"It was enough," said the Mayor. "It brought us back to normalcy." And Magruder striding to his desk, standing over the Mayor, "I have work to do," he said. They, arising, making apologies, the Mayor, his back to Magruder, chuckling, the Mayor, walking to the door, outside in the corridor, Reynolds still in the room, at the door, the Mayor turning to Reynolds, winking, Reynolds adjusting his scarf, the Mayor poking Reynolds in the rubs with his elbow, shouting, "Listen, Magruder. Congratulations to you, too. That challenge idea—it was brilliant," laughing silently; and Magruder, head bent over his desk, reports scattered about him, answering softly, "Was it? It amazes me that a hundred lunatics didn't show up, not just one." The Mayor laughing freely now, Magruder head low, footsteps fainter, the glass door closing with a quiver, Magruder busy, reading, annotating, scribbling on a small white pad, yawning, stretching, looking up. Reynolds was standing in front of him.

"Yes?"

Staccato, "It was a queer case, Magruder, wasn't it? Not really knowing . . . All that . . ."

"Yes?"

"I had the right hunch from the beginning. . . . Kept it to myself, you know. . . . Interesting study . . . Lunacy . . ."

"Yes."

"Funny thing, though. About the lunatic, I mean. You never did find out who he really was, did you?"

"Look here, Reynolds, I had you pegged from the start." He turned again to his paper-disarrayed desk.

Reynolds stood where he was. "What do you mean," he asked, " 'pegged from the start'?"

Magruder looked up.

"Interested?"

"Yes."

"Why?"

"I don't know precisely. Curiosity. Was it because you thought I had easy access to the information—my being a newspaperman, I mean?"

"Maybe."

"Do you think I gave the information to the man in the velvet hat?"

"No. . . . I never thought there was a man in the velvet hat. I thought you wrote the letters."

"I? *You* had as easy access to the information as I had. Why didn't *you* write the letters?"

"I had no motive."

"Motive! What motive could I have?"

Magruder said, "I'm an old-fashioned cop, Reynolds, and I always ask, 'Who gains?' You gained—in more ways than one. Do you remember what you wrote after that Orson Welles broadcast. 'If he had done that deliberately,' you said—oh, I don't know if I'm quoting you exactly—you said, 'then it would have been the grimmest but the most satisfactory of literary achievements.'"

"That!"

"Not only that. You had access; you had motive; and it was you who supplied the witnesses and interviewed them before anyone else. It would have been easy for you to have fixed the details of the man in the velvet hat in their minds by coercion, by bribery—"

Magruder said, "Maybe we found the typewriters. Maybe we didn't; but if we didn't you can be sure that we will. Maybe I was so sure because I knew beforehand what you'd do after the panic at the radio station. You never could have anticipated the screams of an exhibitionist female—and homicide frightened you. I knew you'd claim there was no letter; I knew you'd deny any connection between the man in the velvet hat and the deaths at the radio station, because the game was getting out of hand, and your wind was up."

Reynolds said, "So that is what you thought."

"That is what I think."

And Reynolds, wiping his face with his pocket handkerchief, "A beautiful theory, Magruder, but spoiled by an ugly fact—" Magruder tilting back in his swivel chair, Reynolds waving good-bye, "There was a man in the velvet hat, Magruder—" Magruder filling his pipe, Reynolds, back to Magruder, walking to the door—"and you have him," scarf adjusted, hat set right, hand on the doorknob.

Magruder saying, "But we haven't the man in the velvet hat."

And Reynolds stopping, turning on one foot, facing Magruder, Magruder puffing on his pipe, Reynolds walking slowly again toward the desk, "How do you know?" Magruder laughing.

"Because the man we found dead was released from an asylum *only two days before* you published my challenge. He couldn't have been the man in the velvet hat all those other times—not while he was *in* the asylum."

And Reynolds sober, then resting his palms flat on Magruder's desk, his body leaning over the desk, Magruder swinging forward to meet him, Reynolds, Magruder, faces inches apart, Magruder shouting, "You wrote your script.

Then you got some poor diseased brain—bribery, coercion, again—to play your principal role."

Reynolds trying to say something, the door opening behind him, a little fat man, perspiring, Kuchatsky, happy, shoving the little man in front of him, Kuchatsky, "Here he is, Chief. From a second-hand typewriter store in Flatbush."

Then Kuchatsky pointing to Reynolds, the second-hand dealer squinting, nodding, "That's him!," nodding, nodding, "That's the man, that's the man!"

And Reynolds blurting, "For God's sake, Magruder, listen to me. When I began, I never dreamt—"

Magruder spoke slowly. "I talked to the D.A. this morning," he said. "He didn't think we could make a charge of homicide stick. . . . But that was this morning, Reynolds, that was this morning."

CHINOISERIE

BY HELEN McCLOY

Helen McCloy was born in New York on June 6, 1904, and received her first check for writing when she was fourteen. After nearly ten years as an art critic in Paris, she returned to the United States to write fiction. She became the first woman president of the Mystery Writers of America in 1950 and in 1971 she founded that organization's Boston chapter. She was married to mystery writer Brett Halliday and has a daughter and a granddaughter. Her most recent novel is *The Impostor*. Her first, *Dance of Death* (1938), and many of her subsequent books and stories have featured psychiatrist-detective Dr. Basil Willing.

THIS IS THE STORY OF Olga Kyrilovna and how she disappeared in the heart of old Pekin.

Not Peiping, with its American drugstore on Hatamen Street. Pekin, capital of the Manchu Empire. Didn't you know that I used to be language clerk at the legation there? Long ago. Long before the Boxer Uprising. Oh, yes, I was young. So young I was in love with Olga Kyrilovna. . . . Will you pour the brandy for me? My hand's grown shaky the last few years. . . .

When the nine great gates of the Tartar City swung to at sunset, we were locked for the night inside a walled, medieval citadel, reached by camel over the Gobi or by boat up the Pei-ho, defended by bow and arrow and a painted representation of cannon. An Arabian Nights city where the nine gate towers on the forty-foot walls were just ninety-nine feet high so they would not impede the flight of air spirits. Where palace eunuchs kept harems of their own to "save face." Where muscians were blinded because the use of the eye destroys the subtlety of the ear. Where physicians prescribed powdered jade and tigers' claws for anemia brought on by malnutrition. Where mining operations were dangerous because they opened the veins of the Earth Dragon. Where felons were slowly sliced to death and beggars were found frozen to death in the street every morning in the winter.

It was into this world of fantasy and fear that Olga Kyrilovna vanished as completely as if she had dissolved into one of the air spirits or ridden away on one of the invisible dragons that our servants saw all around us.

It happened the night of a New Year's Eve ball at the Japanese Legation.

When I reached the Russian Legation for dinner, a Cossack of the Escort took me into a room that was once a Tartar General's audience hall. Two dozen candle flames hardly pierced the bleak dusk. The fire in the brick stove barely dulled the cutting edge of a North China winter. I chafed my hands, thinking myself alone. Someone stirred and sighed in the shadows. It was she.

Olga Kyrilovna . . . How can I make you see her as I saw her that evening? She was pale in her white dress against walls of tarnished gilt and rusted vermilion. Two smooth, shining wings of light brown hair. An oval face, pure in line, delicate in color. And, of course, unspoiled by modern cosmetics. Her eyes were blue. Dreaming eyes. She seemed to live and move in a waking dream, remote from the enforced intimacies of our narrow society. More than one man had tried vainly to wake her from that dream. The piquancy of her situation provoked men like Lucien de l'Orges, the French *chargé*.

She was just seventeen, fresh from the convent of Smolny. Volgorughi had been Russian minister in China for many years. After his last trip to Petersburg, he had brought Olga back to Pekin as his bride, and . . . Well, he was three times her age.

That evening she spoke first. *"Monsieur* Charley . . .*"*

Even at official meetings the American minister called me "Charley." Most Europeans assumed it was my last name.

"I am glad you are here," she went on in French, our only common language. "I was beginning to feel lonely. And afraid."

"Afraid?" I repeated stupidly. "Of what?"

A door opened. Candle flames shied and the startled shadows leaped up the walls. Volgorughi spoke from the doorway, coolly. "Olga, we are having sherry in the study . . . oh!" His voice warmed. *"Monsieur* Charley, I didn't see you. Good evening."

I followed Olga's filmy skirts into the study, conscious of Volgorughi's sharp glance as he stood aside to let me pass. He always seemed rather formidable. In spite of his grizzled hair, he had the leanness of a young man and the carriage of a soldier. But he had the weary eyes of an old man. And the dry, shrivelled hands, always cold to the touch, even in summer. A young man's imagination shrank from any mental image of those hands caressing Olga. . . .

In the smaller room it was warmer and brighter. Glasses of sherry and vodka had been pushed aside to make space on the table for a painting on silk. Brown, frail, desiccated as a dead leaf, the silk looked hundreds of years old. Yet the ponies painted on its fragile surface in faded pigments were the same lively Mongol ponies we still used for race meetings outside the city walls.

"The Chinese have no understanding of art," drawled Lucien de l'Orges. "Chinese porcelain is beginning to enjoy a certain vogue in Europe, but Chinese painters are impossible. In landscape they show objects on a flat surface, without perspective, as if the artist were looking down on the earth from a balloon. In portraits they draw the human face without shadows or thickness, as untutored children do. The Chinese artist hasn't enough skill to imitate nature accurately."

Lucien was baiting Volgorughi. "Pekin temper" was as much a feature of our lives as "Pekin throat." We got on each other's nerves like a storm-stayed house party. An unbalanced party where men outnumbered women six to one.

Volgorughi kept his temper. "The Chinese artist doesn't care to 'imitate' nature. He prefers to suggest or symbolize what he sees."

"But Chinese art is heathen!" This was Sybil Carstairs, wife of the English Inspector-General of Maritime Customs. "How can heathen art equal art that's inspired by Christian morals?"

Her husband's objection was more practical. "You're wastin' money, Volgorughi. Two hundred Shanghai *taels* for a daub that will never fetch sixpence in any European market!"

Incredible? No. This was before Hirth and Fenellosa made Chinese painting fashionable in the West. Years later I saw a fragment from Volgorughi's collection sold in the famous *Salle Six* of the *Hôtel Drouot*. While the *commissaire-priseur* was bawling: *On demande quatre cent mille francs . . .* I was seeing Olga again, pale in a white dress against a wall of gilt and vermilion in the light of shivering candle flames. . . .

Volgorughi turned to her just then. "Olga, my dear, you haven't any sherry." He smiled as he held out a glass. The brown wine turned to gold in the candlelight as she lifted it to her lips with an almost childish obedience.

I had not noticed little Kiada, the Japanese minister, bending over the painting. Now he turned sleepy slanteyes on Volgorughi and spoke blandly. "This is the work of Han Kan, greatest of horse painters. It must be the finest painting of the T'ang dynasty now in existence."

"You think so, Count?" Volgorughi was amused. He seemed to be yielding to an irresistible temptation as he went on. "What would you say if I told you I knew of a T'ang painting

52

infinitely finer—a landscape scroll by Wang Wei himself?"

Kiada's eyes lost their sleepy look. He had all his nation's respect for Chinese art, tinctured with jealousy of the older culture. "One hears rumors now and then that these fabulous masterpieces still exist, hidden away in the treasure chests of great Chinese families. But I have never seen an original Wang Wei."

"Who, or what, is Wang Wei?" Sybil sounded petulant.

Kiada lifted his glass of sherry to the light. "Madame, Wang Wei could place scenery extending to ten thousand *li* upon the small surface of a fan. He could paint cats that would keep any house free from mice. When his hour came to Pass Above, he did not die. He merely stepped through a painted doorway in one of his own landscapes and was never seen again. All these things indicate that his brush was guided by a god."

Volgorughi leaned across the table, looking at Kiada. "What would you say if I told you that I had just added a Wang Wei to my collection?"

Kiada showed even, white teeth. "Nothing but respect for your excellency's judgment could prevent my insisting that it was a copy by some lesser artist of the Yüan dynasty—possibly Chao Meng Fu. An original Wang Wei could not be bought for money."

"Indeed?" Volgorughi unlocked a cabinet with a key he carried on his watch chain. He took something out and tossed it on the table like a man throwing down a challenge. It was a cylinder in an embroidered satin cover. Kiada peeled the cover and we saw a scroll on a roller of old milk-jade.

It was a broad ribbon of silk, once white, now ripened with great age to a mellow brown. A foot wide, sixteen feet long, painted lengthwise to show the course of a river. As it unrolled, a stream of pure lapis, jade and turquoise hues flowed before my enchanted eyes, almost like a moving picture. Born in a bubbling spring, fed by waterfalls, the river wound its way among groves of tender, green bamboo, parks with dappled deer peeping through slender pine trees, cottages with curly roofs nestling among round hills, verdant meadows, fantastic cliffs, strange wind-distorted trees, rushes, wild geese, and at last, a foam-flecked sea.

Kiada's face was a study. He whispered brokenly. "I can hear the wind sing in the rushes. I can hear the wail of the wild geese. Of Wang Wei truly is it written—his pictures were unspoken poems."

"And the color!" cried Volgorughi, ecstasy in his eyes.

Lucien's sly voice murmured in my ear. "A younger man, married to Olga Kyrilovna, would have no time for painting, Chinese or otherwise."

Volgorughi had Kiada by the arm. "This is no copy by Chao Meng Fu! Look at that inscription on the margin. Can you read it?"

Kiada glanced—then stared. There was more than suspicion in the look he turned on Volgorughi. There was fear. "I must beg your excellency to excuse me. I do not read Chinese."

We were interrupted by a commotion in the compound. A gaunt Cossack, in fullskirted coat and sheepskin cap, was coming through the gate carrying astride his shoulders a young man, elegantly slim, in an officer's uniform. The Cossack knelt on the ground. The rider slipped lightly from his unconventional mount. He sauntered past the window and a moment later he was entering the study with a nonchalance just this side of insolence. To my amazement I saw that he carried a whip which he handed with his gloves to the Chinese boy who opened the door.

"Princess, your servant. Excellency, my apologies. I believe I'm late."

Volgorughi returned the greeting with the condescension of a Western Russian for an Eastern Russian—a former officer of *Chevaliers Gardes* for an obscure Colonel of Oussurian Cossacks. Sometimes I wondered why such a bold adventurer as Alexei Andreitch Liakoff had been appointed Russian military *attaché* in Pekin. He was born in Tobolsk, where there is Tartar blood. His oblique eyes, high cheekbones and sallow, hairless skin lent color to his impudent claim of descent from Genghis Khan.

"Are Russian officers in the habit of using their men as saddle horses?" I muttered to Carstairs.

Alexei's quick ear caught the words. "It may become a habit with me." He seemed to relish my discomfiture. "I don't like Mongol ponies. A Cossack is just as sure-footed. And much more docile."

Olga Kyrilovna roused herself to play hostess. "Sherry, Colonel Liakoff? Or vodka?"

"Vodka, if her excellency pleases." Alexei's voice softened as he spoke to Olga. His eyes dwelt on her face gravely as he took the glass from her hand.

The ghost of mockery touched Volgorughi's lips. He despised vodka as a peasant's drink.

Alexei approached the table to set down his empty glass. For the first time, his glance fell on the painting by Wang Wei. His glass crashed on the marble floor.

"You read Chinese, don't you?" Volgorughi spoke austerely. "Perhaps you can translate this inscription?"

Alexei put both hands wide apart on the table and leaned on them studying the ideographs. "*Wang Wei.* And a date. The same as our 740 A.D."

"And the rest?" insisted Volgorughi.

Alexei looked at him. "Your excellency really wishes me to read this? Aloud?"

"By all means."

Alexei went on. "*At an odd moment in summer I came across this painting of a river course by Wang Wei. Under its influence I sketched a spray of peach blossom on the margin as an expression of my sympathy for the artist and his profound and mysterious work. The Words of the Emperor. Written in the Lai Ching summerhouse, 1746.*"

Kiada had been frightened when he looked at that inscription. Alexei was angry. Why I did not know.

Carstairs broke the silence. "I don't see anything 'mysterious' about a picture of a river!"

"Everything about this picture is . . . mysterious." Kiada glanced at Volgorughi. "May one inquire how your excellency obtained this incomparable masterpiece?"

"From a pedlar in the Chinese City." Volgorughi's tone forbade further questions. Just then his Number One Boy announced dinner.

There was the usual confusion when we started for the ball at the Japanese Legation. Mongol ponies had to be blindfolded before they would let men in European dress mount and even then they were skittish. For this reason it was the custom for men to walk and for women to drive in hooded Pekin carts. But Sybil Carstairs always defied this convention, exclaiming: "Why should I be bumped black and blue in a springless cart just because I am a woman?" She and her husband were setting out on foot when Olga's little cart clattered into the compound driven by a Chinese groom. Kiada had gone on ahead to welcome his early guests. Volgorughi lifted Olga into the cart. She was quite helpless in a Siberian cloak of blue fox paws and clumsy Mongol socks of white felt over her dancing slippers. Her head drooped against Volgorughi's shoulder drowsily as he put her down in the cart. He drew the fur cloak around her in a little gesture that seemed tenderly possessive. She lifted languid eyes.

"Isn't Lady Carstairs driving with me?"

"My dear, you know she never drives in a Pekin cart. You are not afraid?" Volgorughi smiled. "You will be quite safe, Olga Kyrilovna. I promise you that."

Her answering smile wavered. Then the hood hid her face from view as the cart rattled through the gateway.

Volgorughi and Lucien walked close behind Olga's cart. Alexei and I followed more slowly. Our Chinese lantern boys ran ahead of us in the darkness to light our way like the linkmen of medieval London. Street lamps in Pekin were lighted only once a month—when the General of the Nine Gates made his rounds of inspection.

The lantern light danced down a long, empty lane winding between high, blank walls. A stinging Siberian wind threw splinters of sleet in my face. We hadn't the macadamized roads of the Treaty Ports. The frozen mud was hard and slippery as glass. I tried to keep to a ridge that ran down the middle of the road. My foot slipped and I stumbled down the slope into a foul gutter of sewage frozen solid. The lanterns turned a corner. I was alone with the black night and the icy wind.

I groped my way along the gutter, one hand against the wall. No stars, no moon, no lighted windows, no other pedestrians. My boot met something soft that yielded and squirmed. My voice croaked a question in mandarin: "Is this the way to the Japanese Legation?" The answer came in sing-song Cantonese. I understood only one word: "Alms . . ."

Like heaven itself I saw a distant flicker of light coming nearer. Like saints standing in the glow of their own halos I recognized Alexei and our lantern boys. "What happened?" Alexei's voice was taut. "I came back as soon as I missed you."

"Nothing. I fell. I was just asking this—"

Words died on my lips. Lantern light revealed the blunted

lion-face, the eyeless sockets, the obscene, white stumps for hands—"mere corruption, swaddled man-wise." A leper. And I had been about to touch him.

Alexei's gaze followed mine to the beggar, hunched against the wall. "She is one of the worst I've ever seen."

"She?"

"I think it's a woman. Or, shall I say, it was a woman?" Alexei laughed harshly. "Shall we go on?"

We rounded the next corner before I recovered my voice. "These beggars aren't all as wretched as they seem, are they?"

"What put that idea into your head, Charley?"

"Something that happened last summer. We were in a market lane of the Chinese City—Sybil Carstairs and Olga Kyrilovna, Lucien and I. A beggar, squatting in the gutter, stared at us as if he had never seen Western men before. He looked like any other beggar—filthy, naked to the waist, with tattered, blue cotton trousers below. But his hands were toying with a little image carved in turquoise matrix. It looked old and valuable."

"He may have stolen it."

"It wasn't as simple as that," I retorted. "A man in silk rode up on a mule leading a white pony with a silver embroidered saddle. He called the beggar 'elder brother' and invited him to mount the pony. Then the two rode off together."

Alexei's black eyes glittered like jet beads in the lantern light. "Was the beggar the older of the two?"

"No. That's the queer part. The beggar was young. The man who called him 'elder brother' was old and dignified. . . . Some beggars at home have savings accounts. I suppose the same sort of thing could happen here."

Again Alexei laughed harshly. "Hold on to that idea, Charley, if it makes you feel more comfortable."

We came to a gate where lanterns clustered like a cloud of fireflies. A piano tinkled. In the compound, lantern boys were gathering outside the windows of a ballroom, tittering as they watched barbarian demons "jump" to Western music.

Characteristically, the Japanese Legation was the only European house in Pekin. Candle flames and crystal prisms. Wall mirrors and a polished *parquet* floor. The waltz from *Traviata*. The glitter of diamonds and gold braid. Punch *à la Romaine*.

"Where is Princess Volgorughi?" I asked Sybil Carstairs.

"Didn't she come with you and Colonel Liakoff?"

"No. Her cart followed you. We came afterward."

"Perhaps she's in the supper room." Sybil whirled off with little Kiada.

Volgorughi was standing in the doorway of the supper room with Lucien and Carstairs. "She'll be here in a moment," Carstairs was saying.

Alexei spoke over my shoulder. "Charley and I have just arrived. We did not pass her excellency's cart on the way."

"Perhaps she turned back," said Lucien.

"In that case she would have passed us," returned Alexei. "Who was with her?"

Volgorughi's voice came out in a hoarse whisper. "Her groom and lantern boy. Both Chinese. But Kiada and the Carstairs were just ahead of her; *Monsieur* de l'Orges and I, just behind her."

"Not all the way," amended Lucien. "We took a wrong turning and got separated from each other in the dark. That was when we lost sight of her."

"My fault." Volgorughi's mouth twisted bitterly. "I was leading the way. And it was I who told her she would be . . . safe."

Again we breasted the wind to follow lanterns skimming before us like will-o'-the-wisps. Vainly we strained our eyes through glancing lights and broken shadows. We met no one. We saw nothing. Not even a footprint or wheel rut on that frozen ground. Once something moaned in the void beyond the lights. It was only the leper.

At the gate of the Russian Legation, the Cossack guard sprang to attention. Volgorughi rapped out a few words in Russian. I knew enough to understand the man's reply. "The *baryna* has not returned, excellency. There has been no sign of her or her cart."

Volgorughi was shouting. Voices, footfalls, lights filled the compound. Alexei struck his forehead with his clenched hand. "Fool that I am! The leper!"

He walked so fast I could hardly keep up with him. The lantern boys were running. A Cossack came striding after us. Alexei halted at the top of the ridge. The leper had not moved. He spoke sharply in mandarin. "Have you seen a cart?" No answer. "When she asked me for alms, she spoke Cantonese," I told him. He repeated his question in Cantonese. Both Volgorughi and Alexei spoke the southern dialects. All the rest of us were content to stammer mandarin.

Still no answer. The Cossack stepped down into the gutter. His great boot prodded the shapeless thing that lay there. It toppled sidewise.

Alexei moved down the slope. "Lights!" The lanterns shuddered and came nearer. The handle of a knife protruded from the leper's left breast.

Alexei forced himself to drop on one knee beside that obscene corpse. He studied it intently, without touching it.

"Murdered . . . There are many knives like that in the Chinese City. Anyone might have used it—Chinese or European." He rose, brushing his knee with his gloved hand.

"Why?" I ventured.

"She couldn't see." His voice was judicious. "She must have heard . . . something."

"But what?"

Alexei's Asiatic face was inscrutable in the light from the paper lanterns.

Police? Extra-territorial law courts? That was Treaty Port stuff. Like pidgin English. We had only a few legation guards. No gunboats. No telegraph. No railway. The flying machine was a crank's daydream. Even cranks hadn't dreamed of a wireless telegraphy. . . . Dawn came. We were still searching. Olga Kyrilovna, her cart and pony, her groom and lantern boy, had all vanished without trace as if they had never existed.

As character witnesses, the Chinese were baffling. "The Princess' groom was a Manchu of good character," Volgorughi's Number One Boy told us. "But her lantern boy was a Cantonese with a great crime on his conscience. He caused his mother's death when he was born, which the Ancients always considered Unfilial."

At noon some of us met in the smoking room of the Pekin Club. "It's curious there's been no demand for ransom," I said.

"Bandits? Within the city walls?" Carstairs was skeptical. "Russia has never hesitated to use *agents provocateurs*. They say she's going to build a railway across Siberia. I don't believe it's practical. But you never can tell what those Russians will do. She'll need Manchuria. And she'll need a pretext for taking it. Why not the abduction of the Russian minister's wife?"

Kiada shook his head. "Princess Volgorughi will not be found until The River is restored to its companion pictures, The Lake, The Sea, and The Cloud."

"What do you mean?"

Kiada answered me patiently as an adult explaining the obvious to a backward child. "It is known that Wang Wei painted this series of pictures entitled Four Forms of Water. Volgorughi has only one of them—The River. The separation of one painting from others in a series divinely inspired is displeasing to the artist."

"But Wang Wei has been dead over a thousand years!"

"It is always dangerous to displease those who have Passed Above. An artist as steeped in ancient mysteries as the pious Wang Wei has power over men long after he has become a Guest On High. Wang Wei will shape the course of our lives into any pattern he pleases in order to bring those four paintings together again. I knew this last night when I first saw The River and—I was afraid."

"I wonder how Volgorughi did get that painting?" mused Carstairs. "I hope he didn't forget the little formality of payment."

"He's not a thief!" I protested.

"No. But he's a collector. All collectors are mad. Especially Russian collectors. It's like gambling or opium."

Lucien smiled unpleasantly. "Art! Ghosts! Politics! Why go so far afield? Olga Kyrilovna was a young bride. And Volgorughi is . . . old. Such marriages are arranged by families, we all know. Women, as Balzac said, are the dupes of the social system. When they consent to marriage, they have not enough experience to know what they are consenting to. Olga Kyrilovna found herself in a trap. She has escaped, as young wives have escaped from time immemorial, by taking a lover. Now they've run off together. *Sabine a tout donné, sa beauté de colombe, et son amour . . .*"

"*Monsieur* de l'Orges."

We all started. Alexei was standing in the doorway. His eyes commanded the room. "What you say is impossible. Do I make myself clear?"

"Of course, Alexei. I—I was only joking." Lucien sounded piteous.

But Alexei had no pity. "A difference of taste in jokes has broken many friendships. . . . Charley, will you come back to the Russian Legation with me?"

The Tartar General's audience hall had never seemed more shabby. Volgorughi sat staring at the garish wall of red and gilt. He was wearing an overcoat, carrying hat and gloves.

"News, excellency?" queried Alexei.

Volgorughi shook his head without looking up. "I've been to the *Tsungli Yamên.*" He spoke like a somnambulist. "The usual thing. Green tea. Melon seeds. A cold stone pavilion. Mandarins who giggle behind satin sleeves. I asked for an audience with the Emperor himself. It was offered—on the usual terms. I had to refuse—as usual. By the time a gunboat gets to the mouth of the Pei-ho, they may agree to open another seaport to Russian trade by way of reparation, but . . . I shall never see Olga Kyrilovna again. Sometimes I think our governments keep us here in the hope that something will happen to give them a pretext for sending troops into China. . . ."

We all felt that. The *Tsungli Yamên* or Foreign Office assumed that our legations were vassal missions to their Emperor like those from Thibet. The Emperor would not receive us unless we acknowledged his sovereignty by kowtowing, the forehead to strike the floor audibly nine times. Even if we had wished to go through this interesting performance for the sake of peace and trade, our governments would not let us compromise their sovereignty. But they kept us there, where we had no official standing, where our very existence was doubted. "It may be there are as many countries in the West as England, France, Germany and Russia," one mandarin had informed me. "But the others you mention—Austria, Sweden, Spain and America—they are all lies invented to intimidate the Chinese."

Alexei was not a man to give up easily. "Excellency, I shall find her."

Volgorughi lifted his head. "How?"

Alexei shouted. The study door opened. An old man in workman's dress came in with a young Chinese. I knew the old man as Antoine Billot, one of the Swiss clockmakers who were the only Western tradesmen allowed in Pekin.

"Charley," said Alexei. "Tell Antoine about the fingering piece you saw in the hands of a beggar last summer."

"It was turquoise matrix, carved to represent two nude figures embracing. The vein of brown in the stone colored their heads and spotted the back of the smaller figure."

"I have seen such a fingering piece," said Antoine. "In the Palace of Whirring Phoenixes. It is in that portion of the Chinese City known as the Graveyard of the Wu Family, in the Lane of Azure Thunder."

"It is the Beileh Tsai Heng who lives there," put in Antoine's Chinese apprentice. "Often have we repaired his French clocks. Very fine clocks of Limoges enamel sent to the Emperor Kang Hsi by Louis XIV. The Beileh's grandmother was the Discerning Concubine of the Emperor Tao Kwang."

"An old man?" asked Alexei.

"The Beileh has not yet attained the years of serenity. Though the name Heng means 'Steadfast' he is impetuous as a startled dragon. He memorialized the late Emperor for permission to live in a secluded portion of the Chinese City so that he could devote his leisure to ingenious arts and pleasures."

I looked at Alexei. "You think the beggar who stared at us was a servant of this prince?"

"No. Your beggar was the prince himself. 'Elder Brother' is the correct form for addressing a Manchu prince of the third generation."

"It is the latest fad among our young princes of Pekin," explained the apprentice, "to haunt the highways and taverns dressed as beggars, sharing the sad life of the people for a few hours. They vie with each other to see which can look the most dirty and disreputable. But each one has some little habit of luxury that he cannot give up, even for the sake of disguise. A favorite ring, a precious fan, an antique fingering piece. That is how you can tell them from the real beggars."

Alexei turned to me. "When a taste for the exquisite becomes so refined that it recoils upon itself and turns into its opposite—a taste for the ugly—we call that decadence. Prince Heng is decadent . . . bored, curious, irresponsible, ever in search of a new sensation." Alexei turned back to the apprentice. "Could the Beileh be tempted with money?"

"Who could offer him anything he does not already possess?" intoned the young Chinese. "His revered father amassed one hundred thousand myriad snow-white *taels* of silver from unofficial sources during his benevolent reign as Governor of

Kwantung. In the Palace of Whirring Phoenixes even the wash bowls and spitting basins are curiously wrought of fine jade and pure gold, for this prince loves everything that is rare and strange."

Alexei hesitated before his next question. "Does the Beileh possess any valuable paintings?"

"His paintings are few but priceless. Four landscape scrolls from the divine brush of the illustrious Wang Wei."

Volgorughi started to his feet. "What's this?"

"You may go, Antoine." Alexei waited until the door had closed. "Isn't it obvious, sir? Your Wang Wei scroll was stolen."

Volgorughi sank back in his chair. "But . . . I bought it. From a pedlar in the Chinese City. I didn't ask his name."

"How could a nameless pedlar acquire such a painting from such a prince honestly?" argued Alexei. "Your pedlar was a thief or a receiver. Such paintings have religious as well as artistic value to the Chinese. They are heirlooms, never sold even by private families who need the money. Last night, the moment I saw the marginal note written by the Emperor Ch'ien Lung I knew the picture must have been stolen from the Imperial Collection. I was disturbed because I knew that meant trouble for us if it were known you had the painting. That's why I didn't want to read the inscription aloud. It's easy to see what happened. The thief was captured and tortured until he told Heng you had the painting. Heng saw Olga Kyrilovna with Charley and Lucien in the Chinese City last summer. He must have heard then that she was your wife. When he found you had the painting, he ordered her abduction. Now he is holding her as hostage for the return of the painting. All this cannot be coincidence."

Volgorughi buried his face in his hands. "What can we do?"

"With your permission, excellency, I shall go into the Chinese City tonight and return the painting to Heng. I shall bring back Olga Kyrilovna . . . if she is still alive."

Volgorughi rose, shoulders bent, chin sunk on his chest. "I shall go with you, Alexei Andreitch."

"Your excellency forgets that special circumstances make it possible for me to go into the Chinese City after dark when no other European can do so with safety. Alone, I have some chance of success. With you to protect, it would be impossible."

"You will need a Cossack escort."

"That would strip the legation of guards. And it would antagonize Heng. Olga Kyrilovna might be harmed before I could reach her. I prefer to go alone."

Volgorughi sighed. "Report to me as soon as you get back. . . . You are waiting for something?"

"The painting, excellency."

Volgorughi walked with a shuffling step into the study. He came back with the scroll in its case. "Take it. I never want to see it again."

At the door I looked back. Volgorughi was slumped in his seat, a figure of utter loneliness and despair.

Alexei glanced at me as we crossed the compound. "Something is puzzling you, Charley. What is it?"

"If this Beileh Heng is holding Olga Kyrilovna as a hostage for the painting, he wants you to know that he has abducted her. He has nothing to conceal. Then why was the leper murdered? If not to conceal something?"

Alexei led the way into a room of his own furnished with military severity. "I'm glad Volgorughi didn't think of that question, Charley. It has been troubling me too."

"And the answer?"

"Perhaps I shall find it in the Palace of Whirring Phoenixes. Perhaps it will lead me back to one of the men who dined with us yesterday evening. Except for the Carstairs, we were all separated from each other at one time or another in those dark streets—even you and I. . . ."

Alexei was opening a cedar chest. He took out a magnificent robe of wadded satin in prismatic blues and greens. When he had slipped it on he turned to face me. The Tartar cast of his oblique eyes and sallow skin was more pronounced than I had ever realized. Had I passed him wearing this costume in the Chinese City I should have taken him for a Manchu or a Mongol.

He smiled. "Now will you believe I have the blood of Temudjin Genghis Khan in my veins?"

"You've done this before!"

His smile grew sardonic. "Do you understand why I am the only European who can go into the Chinese City after dark?"

My response was utterly illogical. "Alexei, take me with you tonight!"

He studied my face. "You were fond of Olga Kyrilovna, weren't you?"

"Is there no way?" I begged.

"Only one way. And it's not safe. You could wear the overalls of a workman and carry the tools of a clockmaker. And stay close to me, ostensibly your Chinese employer."

"If Antoine Billot will lend me his clothes and tools . . ."

"That can be arranged." Alexei was fitting a jewelled nail shield over his little finger.

"Well? Is there any other objection?"

"Only this." He looked up at me intently. His pale face and black eyes were striking against the kingfisher blues and greens of his satin robe. "We are going to find something ugly at the core of this business, Charley. You are younger than I and . . . will you forgive me if I say you are rather innocent? Your idea of life in Pekin is a series of dances and dinners, race meetings outside the walls in spring, charades at the English Legation in winter, snipe shooting at Hai Tien in the fall. Your government doesn't maintain an Intelligence Service here. So you can have no idea of the struggle that goes on under the surface of this pleasant social life. Imperialist ambitions and intrigues, the alliance between politics and trade, even the opium trade—what do you know of all that? Sometimes I think you don't even know much about the amusements men like Lucien find in the Chinese City. . . . Life is only pleasant on the surface, Charley. And now we're going below the surface. Respectability is as artificial as the clothes we wear. What it hides is as ugly as our naked bodies and animal functions. Whatever happens tonight, I want you to remember this: under every suit of clothes, broadcloth or rags, there is the same sort of animal."

"What are you hinting at?"

"There are various possibilities. You said Heng stared at your party as if he had never seen Western men before. Are you sure he wasn't staring at Olga Kyrilovna as if he had never seen a Western woman before?"

"But our women are physically repulsive to Chinese!"

"In most cases. But the Chinese are not animated types. They are individuals, as we are. Taste is subjective and arbitrary. Individual taste can be eccentric. Isn't it possible that there are among them, as among us, men who have romantic fancies for the exotic? Or sensual fancies for the experimental?

65

I cannot get those words of Antoine's apprentice out of my mind: *this prince loves everything that is rare and strange. . . ."*

A red sun was dipping behind the Western Hills when we passed out a southern gate of the Tartar City. In a moment all nine gates would swing shut and we would be locked out of our legations until tomorrow's dawn. It was not a pleasant feeling. I had seen the head of a consul rot on a pike in the sun. That was what happened to barbarian demons who went where they were not wanted outside the Treaty Ports.

The Chinese City was a wilderness of twisting lanes, shops, taverns, theatres, tea-houses, opium dens, and brothels. Long ago conquering Manchu Tartars had driven conquered Chinese outside the walls of Pekin proper, or the Tartar City, to this sprawling suburb where the conquered catered to the corruption of the conqueror. The Chinese City came to life at nightfall when the Tartar City slept behind its walls. Here and there yellow light shone through blue dusk from a broken gateway. Now and then we caught the chink of porcelain cups or the whine of a *yuehkin* guitar.

Alexei seemed to know every turn of the way. At last I saw why he was Russian military *attaché* at Pekin. Who else would learn so much about China and its people as this bold adventurer who could pass for a Manchu in Chinese robes? When we were snipe-shooting together, he seemed to know the Pei-chih-li plain as if he carried a military map of the district in his head. Years afterward, when the Tsar's men took Port Arthur, everyone learned about Russian Intelligence in China. I learned that evening. And I found myself looking at Alexei in his Chinese dress as if he had suddenly become a stranger. What did I know of this man whom I had met so casually at legation parties? Was he ruthless enough to stab a beggar already dying of leprosy? Had he had any reason for doing so?

We turned into a narrower lane—a mere crack between high walls. Alexei whispered: "The Lane of Azure Thunder."

A green-tiled roof above the dun-colored wall proclaimed the dwelling of a prince. Alexei paused before a gate, painted vermilion. He spoke Cantonese to the gate-keeper. I understood only two words—"Wang Wei." There were some moments of waiting. Then the gate creaked open and we were ushered through that drab wall into a wonderland of fantastic parks and lacquered pavilions blooming with all the colors of Sung porcelain.

I was unprepared for the splendor of the audience hall. The old palaces we rented for legations were melancholy places, decaying and abandoned by their owners. But here rose, green and gold rioted against a background of dull ebony panels, tortured by a cunning chisel into grotesquely writhing shapes. There were hangings of salmon satin embroidered with threads of gold and pale green, images of birds and flowers carved in jade and coral and malachite. The slender rafters were painted a poisonously bright jade-green and on them tiny lotus buds were carved and gilded. There was a rich rustle of satin and the Beileh Heng walked slowly into the room.

Could this stately figure be the same rude fellow I had last seen squatting in the gutter, half naked in the rags of a beggar? He moved with the deliberate grace of the grave religious dancers in the Confucian temples. His robe was lustrous purple—the "myrtle-red" prescribed for princes of the third generation by the Board of Rites. It swung below the paler mandarin jacket in sculptured folds, stiff with a sable lining revealed by two slits at either side. Watered in the satin were the Eight Famous Horses of the Emperor Mu Wang galloping over the Waves of Eternity. His cuffs were curved like horseshoes in honor of the cavalry that set the Manchu Tartars on the throne. Had that cavalry ridden west instead of south, Alexei himself might have owed allegiance to this prince. Though one was Chinese and one Russian, both were Tartar.

Heng's boots of purple satin looked Russian. So did his round cap faced with a band of sable. His skin was a dull ivory, not as yellow as the southern Chinese. His cheeks were lean; his glance, searching and hungry. He looked like a purebred descendant of the "wolf-eyed, lantern-jawed Manchus" of the Chinese chronicles. A conquerer who would take whatever he wanted, but who had learned from the conquered Chinese to want only the precious and fanciful.

Something else caught my eye. There was no mistake. This was the beggar. For, pale against his purple robe, gleamed the fingering piece of turquoise matrix which his thin, neurotic fingers caressed incessantly.

No ceremonial tea was served. We were being received as

67

enemies during a truce. But Alexei bowed profoundly and spoke with all the extravagance of mandarin politeness.

"An obscure design of destiny has brought the property of your highness, a venerable landscape scroll painted by the devout Wang Wei, into the custody of the Russian minister. Though I appear Chinese in this garb, know that I am Russian and my minister has sent me in all haste and humility to restore this inestimable masterpiece to its rightful owner."

Heng's eyes were fixed on a point above our heads for, Chinese or barbarian, we were inferiors, unworthy of his gaze. His lips scarcely moved. "When you have produced the scroll, I shall know whether you speak truth or falsehood."

"All your highness's words are unspotted pearls of perpetual wisdom." Alexei stripped the embroidered case from the jade roller. Like a living thing the painted silk slipped out of his grasp and unwound itself at the Beileh's feet.

Once again a faery stream of lapis, jade and turquoise hues unrolled before my enchanted eyes. Kiada was right. I could hear the wind sing in the rushes and the wail of the wild geese, faint and far, a vibration trembling on the outer edge of the physical threshold of sound.

The hand that held the fingering piece was suddenly still. Only the Beileh's eyeballs moved, following the course of Wang Wei's river from its bubbling spring to its foam-flecked sea. Under his cultivated stolidity, I saw fear and, more strangely, sorrow.

At last he spoke. "This painting I inherited from my august ancestor the ever-glorious Emperor Ch'ien Lung who left his words and seal upon the margin. How has it come into your possession?"

Alexei bowed again. "I shall be grateful for an opportunity to answer that question if your highness will first condescend to explain to my mean intelligence how the scroll came to leave the Palace of Whirring Phoenixes."

"Outside Barbarian, you are treading on a tiger's tail when you speak with such insolence to an Imperial Clansman. I try to make allowances for you because you come of an inferior race, the Hairy Ones, without manners or music, unversed in the Six Fine Arts and the Five Classics. Know then that it is not your place to ask questions or mine to answer them. You may follow me, at a distance of nine paces, for I have something to show you."

He looked neither to right nor left as he walked soberly through the audience hall, his hands tucked inside his sleeves. At the door he lifted one hand to loosen the clasp of his mandarin jacket, and it slid from his shoulders. Before it had time to touch the ground, an officer of the Coral Button sprang out of the shadows to catch it reverently. The Beileh did not appear conscious of this officer's presence. Yet he had let the jacket fall without an instant's hesitation. He knew that wherever he went at any time there would always be someone ready to catch anything he let fall before it was soiled or damaged.

We followed him into a garden, black and white in the moonlight. We passed a pool spanned by a crescent bridge. Its arc of stone matched the arc of its reflection in the ice-coated water, completing a circle that was half reality, half illusion. We came to another pavilion, its roof curling up at each corner, light filtering through its doorway. Again we heard the shrill plaint of a guitar. We rounded a devil-screen of gold lacquer and the thin sound ended on a high, feline note.

I blinked against a blaze of lights. Like a flight of particolored butterflies, a crowd of girls fluttered away from us, tottering on tiny, mutilated feet. One who sat apart from the rest, rose with dignity. A Manchu princess, as I saw by her unbound feet and undaunted eyes. Her hair was piled high in the lacquered coils of the Black Cloud Coiffure. She wore hairpins, earrings, bracelets and tall heels of acid-green jade. Her gown of sea-green silk was sewn with silver thread worked in the Pekin stitch to represent the Silver Crested Love Birds of Conjugal Peace. But when she turned her face, I saw the sour lines and sagging pouches of middle age.

Princess Heng's gaze slid over us with subtle contempt and came to rest upon the Beileh with irony. "My pleasure in receiving you is boundless and would find suitable expression in appropriate compliments were the occasion more auspicious. As it is, I pray you will forgive me if I do not linger in the fragrant groves of polite dalliance, but merely inquire why your highness has seen fit to introduce two male strangers, one a barbarian, into the sanctity of the Inner Chamber?"

Heng answered impassively. "Even the Holy Duke of Yen neglected the forms of courtesy when he was pursued by a tiger."

A glint of malice sparkled in the eyes of the Beileh's Principal Old Woman. "Your highness finds his present situation equivalent to being pursued by a tiger? To my inadequate understanding that appears the natural consequence of departing from established custom by attempting to introduce a barbarian woman into the Inner Chamber."

Heng sighed. "If the presence of these far-travelled strangers distresses you and my Small Old Women you have permission to retire."

Princess Heng's jade bangles clashed with the chilly ring of ice in a glass as she moved towards the door. The Small Old Women, all girls in their teens, shimmered and rustled after the Manchu princess who despised them both as concubines and as Chinese.

Heng led us through another door.

"Olga!"

The passion in Alexei's voice was a shock to me. In my presence he had always addressed her as "excellency" or "princess" . . . She might have been asleep as she lay there on her blue fox cloak, her eyes closed, her pale face at peace. her slight hands relaxed in the folds of her white tulle skirt. But the touch of her hands was ice and faintly from her parted lips came the sweet, sickish odor of opium.

Alexei turned on Heng. "If you had not stolen her, she would not have died!"

"Stolen?" It was the first word that had pierced Heng's reserve. "Imperial Clansmen do not steal women. I saw this far-travelled woman in a market lane of the Chinese City last summer. I coveted her. But I did not steal her. I offered money for her, decently and honorably, in accord with precepts of morality laid down by the Ancients. Money was refused. Months passed. I could not forget the woman with faded eyes. I offered one of my most precious possessions. It was accepted. The painting was her price. But the other did not keep his side of the bargain. For she was dead when I lifted her out of her cart."

The lights were spinning before my eyes. "Alexei, what is this? Volgorughi would not . . ."

Alexei's look stopped me.

"You . . ." Words tumbled from my lips. "There was a lover. And you were he. And Volgorughi found out. And he watched you together and bided his time, nursing his hatred and planning his revenge like a work of art. And finally he

70

punished you both cruelly by selling her to Heng. Volgorughi knew that Olga would drive alone last night. Volgorughi had lived so long in the East that he had absorbed the Eastern idea of women as well as the Eastern taste in painting. The opium must have been in the sherry he gave her. She was already drowsy when he lifted her into the cart. No doubt he had planned to give her only a soporific dose that would facilitate her abduction. But at the last moment he commuted her sentence to death and let her have the full, lethal dose. He gave her goodbye tenderly because he knew he would never see her again. He promised her she would be safe because death is, in one sense, safety—the negation of pain, fear and struggle . . .

"There was no pedlar who sold him the painting. That was his only lie. He didn't prevent your coming here tonight because he wanted you to know. That was your punishment. And he saw that you could make no use of your knowledge now. Who will believe that Olga Kyrilovna, dead of a Chinese poison in the Chinese City, was killed by her own husband? Some Chinese will be suspected—Heng himself, or his jealous wife, or the men who carry out his orders. No European would take Heng's story seriously unless it were supported by at least one disinterested witness. That was why the leper had to die last night, while Volgorughi was separated from Lucien through a wrong turning that was Volgorughi's fault. The leper must have overheard some word of warning or instruction from Volgorughi to Olga's lantern boy that revealed the whole secret. That word was spoken in Cantonese. Olga's lantern boy was Cantonese. Volgorughi spoke that dialect. The leper knew no other tongue. And Lucien, the only person who walked with Volgorughi, was ignorant of Cantonese as all the rest of us, save you."

Heng spoke sadly in his own tongue. "The treachery of the Russian minister in sending this woman to me dead deserves vengeance. But one thing induces me to spare him. He did not act by his own volition. He was a blind tool in the skillful hand of the merciless Wang Wei. Through this woman's death The River has been restored to its companion pictures, The Lake, The Sea, and The Cloud. And I, who separated the pictures so impiously, have had my own share of suffering as a punishment. . . ."

71

. . . Yes, I'll have another brandy. One more glass. Olga? She was buried in the little Russian Orthodox cemetery at Pekin. Volgorughi was recalled. The breath of scandal clung to his name the rest of his life. The Boxer Uprising finally gave the West its pretext for sending troops into China. That purple satin Epicurean, the Beileh Heng, was forced to clean sewers by German troops during the occupation and committed suicide from mortification. The gay young bloods of Pekin, who had amused themselves by playing beggar, found themselves beggars in earnest when the looting was over. Railways brought Western business men to Pekin and before long it was as modern as Chicago.

Alexei? He became attentive to the wife of the new French minister, a woman with dyed hair who kept a Pekinese sleeve dog in her bedroom. I discovered the distraction that can be found in study of the early Chinese poets. When I left the service, I lost track of Alexei. During the Russian revolution, I often wondered if he were still living. Did he join the Reds, as some Cossack officers did? Or was he one of the Whites who settled in Harbin or Port Arthur? He would have been a very old man then, but I think he could have managed. He spoke so many Chinese dialects. . . .

The scroll? Any good reference book will tell you that there are no Wang Wei scrolls in existence today, though there are some admirable copies. One, by Chao Meng Fu, in the British Museum, shows the course of a river. Scholars have described this copy in almost the same words I have used here tonight to describe the original. But they are not the same. I went to see the copy. I was disappointed. I could no longer hear the song of the wind in the rushes or the wail of the wild geese. Was the change in the painting? Or in me?

MALICE DOMESTIC

BY PHILIP MacDONALD

Philip MacDonald was born in the British Isles on November 5, 1900. He served with the British cavalry in Mesopotamia during World War I. His first detective novel, *The Rasp* (1924), introduced Colonel Anthony Gethryn, and like all of his mysteries since it was scrupulously fair to the reader. In 1931 MacDonald and his wife, novelist F. Ruth Howard, went to Hollywood, where he wrote the scenario of Daphne du Maurier's *Rebecca,* several Charlie Chan movies, and a number of other screenplays. His short stories have won several awards from *Ellery Queen's Mystery Magazine* as well as an Edgar from the Mystery Writers of America.

CARL BORDEN CAME OUT of Seaman's bookstore into the sun-drenched, twisting little main street of El Morro Beach. He looked around to see if his wife were in view, and then, as she wasn't, walked to the bar entrance of Eagles' and went in. He was a big, loosely-built, rambling sort of a man, with untidy blond hair and a small, somehow featureless face which was redeemed from indistinction by his eyes, which were un-expectedly large, vividly blue and always remarkably alive. He was a writer of some merit, mediocre sales and—at least among the wordier critics—considerable reputation.

He sat on the first stool at the bar and nodded to the real estate man, Dockweiler, who had once been a Hollywood actor; to Dariev, the Russian who did the murals; then—vaguely—to some people in booths. He didn't smile at all, not even at the barman when he ordered his beer—and Dock-weiler said to old Parry beside him, "Catch that Borden, will you! Wonder whatsa matter. . . ."

The barman, who was always called Hiho for some reason everyone had forgotten, brought Carl's drink and set it down before him and glanced at him and said, "Well, Mr. Borden—and how've you been keeping?"

Carl said, "Thanks, Hiho—oh, all right, I guess. . . ." He took a long swallow from the cold glass.

Hiho said, "And how's Mrs. Borden? Okay?"

"Fine!" Carl said, and then again, "Fine!" He put a dollar bill on the bar and Hiho picked it up and went back to the cash-register.

Carl put his elbows on the bar and dropped his face into his hands; then sat quickly upright as Hiho returned with his change. He pocketed it and swallowed the rest of his beer and stood up. He nodded to Hiho without speaking and walked out into the street again.

His wife was standing by the car with her arms full of packages. He said, "Hey, Annette—hold it!" and quickened his pace to a lumbering trot.

She smiled at him. A brief, wide smile which was just a little on the toothy side. She looked slim and straight and cool and soignée, as she always did. She was a blonde Norman woman of thirty-odd, and she had been married to Carl for nine years. They were regarded, by everyone who did not know them well, as an "ideal couple." But their few intimates, of late, had been vaguely unsure of this.

Carl opened the door of the car and took the parcels from Annette's arms and stowed them away in the back. She said, "Thank you, Carlo," and got into the seat beside him as he settled himself at the wheel. She said, "Please—go around by Beatons. I have a *big* package there."

He drove down to Las Ondas Road and parked, on the wrong side of the street, outside a white-fenced little building over which a sign announced, BEATON AND SON—NURSERIES.

He went into the shop, and the girl gave him a giant paper sack, stuffed overfull with a gallimaufry of purchases. He picked it up—and the bottom tore open and a shower of the miscellany sprayed to the floor.

Carl swore beneath his breath, and the girl said "Oh, drat!" and whipped around to help him. He put the things he had saved on the counter, then, stooping, retrieved a thick pamphlet called *The Rose-Grower's Handbook* and a carton labeled KILLWEED in white lettering above a red skull-and-crossbones design.

The girl had everything else. Apologizing profusely, she put the whole order into two fresh sacks. Carl put one under each arm and went out into the sunny street again, and saw Dr. Wingate walking along it, approaching the car. Carl called out, "Hi, Tom!" and smiled his first smile of the morning as the other turned and saw him.

"Hi yourself!" Wingate said. He was a man in the middle forties, a little dandiacal as to dress, and he wore—unusual in a medico—a small neatly-trimmed imperial which some people thought distinguished, others merely caprine. He turned to the car and raised his hat to Annette, wishing her good-morning a trifle formally. He opened the rear door for Carl and helped him put the two packages in with the others. He looked at Carl, and for a moment his gaze became sharply professional. He said, "How's the book going?" and Carl hesitated before he answered, "Fine! Tough sledding, of course—but it'll be all right, I think."

"Well—" said Wingate, "don't go cold on it. It's too good."

Carl shrugged. Annette said, impatiently, "We must get

back, Carlo," and he got into the car and started the engine and waved to his friend.

He drove back through the town and then branched inland up into the hills and came in five minutes to the narrow, precipitous road which led up to his house, standing alone on its little bluff. It was a sprawling, gray-shingled building, with tall trees behind it and, in front, a lawn which surrounded a rose-bed. Beside the lawn a graveled driveway, with traces of devil-grass and other weeds showing through its surface, ran down to the garage.

As he stopped the car, an enormous dog appeared around the corner of the house and bounded towards them. Annette got out first, and looked at the animal and said, "Hello," and put out her hand as if to fondle it.

The dog backed away. It stood with its head up and stared at her. It was a Giant Schnauser, as big as a Great Dane, and it was called G.B. because something about its bearded face and sardonic eye had always made Carl think of Shaw.

Annette looked at it; then, with a quick little movement of her head, at her husband. She said sharply, "The dog! Why does he look at me like that?"

Carl was getting out of the car. "Like what?" he said—and then it was upon him, its tail-stump wagging madly, its vast mouth open in a wet, white-and-scarlet smile.

"Hi there, G.B.!" Carl said—and the creature rose up on its hind legs and put its forepaws on his shoulders and tried to lick his face. Its head was almost on a level with Carl's.

Annette said, "It is—peculiar. He does not like me lately." She was frowning.

Carl said, "Oh, that's your imagination," and the dog dropped upon all fours again and stood away while the packages were taken out of the car.

Carl carried most of them, Annette the rest. They stood in the kitchen, and Annette began to put her purchases away. Carl stood and watched her. His blue eyes were dark and troubled, and he looked like a Brobdingnagian and bewildered little boy who has found himself in trouble for some reason he cannot understand.

Annette wanted to get to the icebox, and he was in her way. She pushed at his arm, and said sharply, "Move! You are too big for this kitchen!"

But he put his long arms around her and pulled her close

76

to him. He said, "Annette! What's the matter, darling? What is it? What have I done?"

She strained back against his arms—but he tightened their pressure and drew her closer still and buried his face in the cool, firm flesh of her throat.

"Carl!" she said. She sounded amazed.

He went on talking, against her neck. His voice sounded almost as if there were tears in it. He said, "Don't tell me there isn't something wrong! Just tell me what it *is*! Tell me what I've *done*! It's been going on for weeks now—maybe months. Ever since you came back from that trip. You've been—different. . . ."

His wife stood motionless. She said, slowly, "But Carlo— that is what I have been feeling about you."

He raised his head and looked at her. He said, "It's almost as if you were—suspicious of me. And I don't know what it's about!"

She frowned. "I—" she said, "I—" and then stopped for a long moment.

She said, "Do you know what I think? I think we are two very stupid people." The lines were leaving her face, the color coming back to it.

"Two stupid people!" she said again. "People who are not so young as they were. People who do not see enough other people—and begin to imagine things . . ."

She broke off as there drifted through the open window the sound of a car, old and laboring, coming up the hill. She said, "Ah!" and put her hands on Carl's shoulders and kissed him at the corner of his mouth. She said, "The mail—I will get it," and went quickly out of the side door.

He made no attempt to follow her, no suggestion that he should do the errand. Annette had always been very jealous about her letters, and seemed to be growing even more so.

He stood where he was, his big shoulders sagging, the smile with which he had met her smile slowly fading from his face. He shook his head. He drew in a deep breath. He shambled away, through the big living-room and through that again into his study. He sat down in front of his typewriter and stared at it for a long time.

He began to work—at first slowly but finally with a true and page-devouring frenzy. . . .

It was dusk, and he had already switched on his desk light,

when there came a gentle sound behind him. He dragged himself back to the world which he did not control and turned in his chair and saw his wife just inside the door. She was very slim, almost boyish, in her gardening overalls. She said, "I do not want to interrupt, Carlo—just to know about dinner." Her face was in shadow, and she might have been smiling.

He stood up and threw his arms wide and stretched. "Any time you like," he said, and then, as she moved to leave the room, "Wait a minute!"

He crossed to her and took her by the shoulders and looked down at her. For a moment she was rigid; then suddenly she put her arms around his neck and molded her slim strong softness against him and tilted her face up to his.

It was a long and passionate kiss—and it was only broken by the sound of a jarring, persistent thudding at the french windows.

Annette pulled abruptly away from his clasp. She muttered something which sounded like, "*Sacré chien!* . . ." and went quickly out through the door behind her.

Except for the pool of light upon the desk, the room was very dark now, and after a moment Carl reached out and snapped on the switch of the overhead light. Slowly, he walked over to the windows and opened them and let in the big dog.

It stood close to him, its head more than level with his waist, and he stroked it and pulled gently at its ears. He shut the window then, and went out of the study and upstairs to his own room, the animal padding heavily beside him. He took a shower and changed his clothes, and when he had finished, could still hear his wife in her own room. He said, "Come on, G.B." and went downstairs again and out of the house.

He put the car away and shut the garage—and was still outside when Annette called him in to dinner.

This was, like all Annette's dinners, a complete and rounded work of art—and it was made all the more pleasant because, during it, she seemed almost her old self. She was bright, talkative, smiling—and although the dog lay directly in the way of her path to the kitchen and would not move for her, she made no complaint but walked around him.

As usual, they had coffee in the living room. After his

second cup, Carl got up, and stretched. He snapped his fingers at G.B., who went and stood expectantly by the door. Carl stood over his wife, smiling down at her. He started to speak—but she was first, looking up at him in sudden concern.

She said, "Carlo—you do not look well! . . . You work, I think, too hard! . . . You should not go out, perhaps."

But Carl pooh-poohed her. "Feel fine!" he said and bent over and kissed her on the forehead and crossed to the door and was gone.

Whistling, and with G.B. bounding ahead of him, he walked down the steep slant of their own road and onto the gentler slopes of Paseo Street.

He had gone less than quarter of a mile when his long, measured stride faltered. He took a few uneven steps, then stopped altogether. He swayed. He put a hand up to his forehead and found it covered with clammy sweat. He wobbled to the edge of the road and sat down upon a grass bank. He dropped his face into both his hands. A vast, black bulk appeared out of the darkness and thrust a damp nose at him. He mumbled something and took his hands away from his face and clapped them to his stomach and bent his head lower, down between his knees, and began to vomit. . . .

Old Parry was sitting in his living room, a book on his knee, a glass on the table beside him. He heard a scratching at the porch door; then a series of short, deep, demanding barks. He stood up creakily and went to the door and pulled it open. He bowed and said, "I am honored, Mr. Shaw!"—and then had his high-pitched giggle cut off short as the enormous dog seized the edge of his jacket between its teeth and began to tug at it with gentle but imperious sharpness.

"Something the matter, boy?" said Parry—and went the way he was being told and in a moment found the sick man by the roadside.

Carl had stopped vomiting now, and was sitting straighter. But he was badly shaken and weak as a kitten. In answer to Parry's shocked inquiries he mumbled, ". . . all right now . . . sorry . . . just my stomach upset . . ." He tried to laugh—a ghastly little sound. "I'm not drunk," he said. "Be all right in a minute—don't bother yourself. . . ."

But Parry did bother himself: he had seen Carl's face—pinched and drawn and of a strange, greenish pallor shining with an oily film. Somehow, he got the big man to his feet;

79

somehow, under the watchful yellow eye of the Schnauser, managed to pilot him into the house and settle him, half-seated, half-sprawling upon a sofa.

"Thanks," Carl muttered. "Thanks . . . that's fine. . . ." He sank back on the cushions and closed his eyes.

"Just a minute now—" said old Parry—and went out into his little hallway and busied himself at the telephone to such effect that in less than fifteen minutes, a car pulled up outside and Dr. Thomas Wingate, bag in hand, walked in upon them.

Carl protested. He was much better already, and his face was pale with a more normal pallor. He was embarrassed and shy. He was grateful to old Parry, and yet plainly annoyed by all this fuss. He sat up very straight, G.B. at his feet, and said firmly, "Look, I'm all right now! Just a touch of ptomaine or something." He looked from his host to the doctor. "Awfully good of you to take so much trouble, Parry. And thanks for turning out, Tom. But—"

"But nothing!" Wingate said, and sat down beside him and took hold of his wrist and felt the pulse. "What you been eating?"

Carl managed a grin. "Better dinner than you'll ever get," he said—and then, "Oh—I had lunch out, maybe *that* was it! Annette and I went to the Hickory Nut, and I had fried shrimps—a double order! Tom, I bet that's what it was!"

Wingate let go of his wrist. "Could be," he said. He looked at Carl's face again and stood up. "That's a trick tummy of yours anyway." He turned to Parry. "I'll just run him home," he said.

Carl got up too. He thanked Parry all over again, and followed Wingate to his car. They put G.B. in the back and he sat immediately behind Carl, breathing protectively down his neck.

Wingate slowed down almost to a crawl as they reached Carl's driveway. He said, with the abruptness of discomfort, "Look now, I know you pretty well, both as a patient and a fellow human being: this—call it 'attack'—may not have been caused by bad food at all. Or bad food may have been only a contributing factor. In other words, my friend, what everyone insists on calling 'nerves' may be at the bottom of it." They were in the driveway now, and he stopped the car. But he made no move to get out. He looked at Carl's face in the

80

dimness and said, "Speaking purely as a doctor, Carl, have you been—worried at all lately?" He paused, but Carl said nothing. "You haven't seemed like yourself the past few weeks. . . ."

Carl opened the door on his side. "I don't know what the hell you're talking about," he said curtly.

As he stepped out of the car the front door of the house opened and Annette came out onto the porch. She peered through the darkness at the car. She called, "Who is there? Who is it?" Her voice was high-pitched, sharp.

"Only me, dear," Carl said. "Tom Wingate drove me home." He opened the rear door and G.B. jumped out, then followed his master and Wingate up the steps to the house.

Annette stood just inside the door as they entered. Her face was in shadow, but she seemed pale. She acknowledged Wingate's formal greeting with a stiff little bow, and Carl looked harassed and uncomfortable. He tried to stop Wingate from saying what had happened, but to no purpose. Annette was told the whole story, firmly, politely and incisively—and Annette was given instructions.

She was most distressed. She said that Carl had not looked well after dinner, and she had not wanted him to go out. She was extremely polite to Dr. Wingate, and repeated his instructions carefully and asked for reassurance that the attack had been nothing serious. But all the time she was rigid and unbending, with frost in her manner. Only when Wingate had gone—and that was very soon—did she thaw. It was a most complete thaw, however. She rushed at Carl and fussed over him and got him upstairs and nursed him and mothered him. And when he was comfortably in bed, she kissed him with all the old tenderness.

"Carlo, *mon pauvre!*" she said softly, and then, "I am sorry I was not nice to your doctor, *chéri*. But—but—*eh bien*, you know that I do not like him."

He patted her shoulder, and she kissed him again—and he was very soon asleep. . . .

It was ten days after this that he had the pains again. They struck late at night. He was in his study, working. It was after one, and Annette had been in bed since before midnight.

They were much worse this time. They were agonizing.

They started with painful cramps in his thighs—and when he stood up to ease this there was a terrible burning in the pit of his stomach. And then a faintness came over him and he dropped back into his chair. He doubled up, his hands clutching desperately at his belly. Great beads of cold sweat burst out all over his head and neck. He began to retch. Desperately, he swung his chair around until his hanging head was over the big metal wastebasket. He vomited hideously, and for what seemed an eternity. . . .

At last, momentarily, the convulsions ceased. He tried to raise his head—and everything in the room swam before his eyes. Outside, G.B. scratched on the french windows, and a troubled whining came from his throat. Carl pulled a weak hand across his mouth and his fingers came away streaked with blood. He rested his forehead upon the table-top and with tremendous effort reached out for the telephone and managed to pull it towards him. . . .

In exactly ten minutes, a car came to a squealing halt in the driveway—and Wingate jumped out of it and raced up the steps. The front door was unlocked, and he was halfway across the living room when Annette appeared at the top of the stairs. She was in a night-gown and was fumbling to get her arms into a robe. She said, wildly, "What is it? What is the matter?"

Wingate snapped, "Where's Carl?"—and then heard a sound from the study and crossed to it in three strides and burst in.

Carl was on his hands and knees, near the door of the toilet. He raised a ghastly face to Wingate and tried to speak. The room was a shambles—and beside his master, near the leaf of the french window he had broken open, stood G.B.

Carl tried to stand and could not. "Steady now!" Wingate said. "Take it easy. . . ." He crossed quickly to the sick man and half-dragged, half-lifted him to a couch and began to work over him. G.B. stopped whining and lay down. Annette came into the room and stood at Wingate's shoulder. Her hair was in tight braids and her pallid face shone beneath a layer of cream. Her eyes were wide, their pupils dilated. A curious sound—perhaps a scream strangled at birth—had come from her as she entered, but now she seemed in control of herself, though her hands were shaking. She started to speak but Wingate cut her short, almost savagely.

"Hot water," he snapped. "Towels. Glass."

She ran out of the room—and was quickly back with the things he wanted; then stayed with him, an efficient and self-effacing helper, while for an hour and more he labored.

By three o'clock, though weak and languid and gaunt in the face, Carl was himself again and comfortable in his own bed. He smiled at Wingate, who closed his bag with a snap.

"Thanks, Tom . . ." he said—and then, "Sorry to be such a nuisance."

"You're okay." Wingate smiled back at him with tired eyes —and turned to Annette.

"You go to bed, Mrs. Borden," he said, "He'll sleep—he's exhausted." He turned towards the door, stopped with his fingers on the handle. "I'll call by at eight thirty. If he wants anything—don't give it to him."

Annette moved towards him but he checked her. "Don't bother—I'll let myself out," he said—and was gone.

Very slowly, Annette moved back to the bed and stood beside it, looking down at her husband. The mask of cold cream over her face had broken into glistening patches which alternated with islands of dryness which showed the skin tight and drawn, its color a leaden gray.

Carl reached out and took her hand. He said, "Did I scare you, darling? . . . I'm awfully sorry!"

Stiffly, she bent over him. She kissed him. "Go to sleep," she said. "You will be all well in the morning. . . ."

And indeed he was, save for a great lassitude and a painful tenderness all around his stomach. He barely waked when Wingate came at eight thirty, and was asleep again the instant he left five minutes later.

At twelve—like a child about to surprise a household—he got up and washed himself and dressed. He was a little tired when he finished—but less so than he had expected. He opened his door quietly, and quietly went downstairs. As he reached the study door, Annette came out of it. She was in her usual houseworking clothes, and carried a dustpan and broom. Under the gay bandana which was tied around her head, her face seemed oddly thin and angular.

She gave a little exclamation at the sight of him. "Carlo!" she said. "You should not be up! You should have called me!"

He laughed at her tenderly. He pinched her cheek and then kissed it. "I'm fine," he said. "Sort of sore around the mid-section—but that's nothing." He slid his arm around her waist and they went into the study together. She fussed over him, and was settling him in the big chair beside the desk when the telephone rang.

Carl reached out and picked it up and spoke into it. He said, "Hello? . . . Oh, hello, Tom. . . ."

"So you're up, huh?" said Wingate's voice over the wire. "How d'you feel?"

"Fine," said Carl. "Hungry, though. . . ."

"Eaten yet?" The voice on the telephone was suddenly sharp.

"No. But I—"

"Good. Don't. Not until you've seen me. I want to examine you—run a test or two—while that stomach's empty. Can you get down here to the office? That'd be better. Or do you want me to come up?" Wingate's voice wasn't sharp any more: it seemed even more casual than it normally was.

Carl said, "Sure I can come down. When?"

"Right away," said the telephone. "I'll fit you in. G'bye."

Carl hung up. He looked at his wife and smiled ruefully. "Can't eat yet," he said. "Tom Wingate wants to examine me first." He put his hands on the arms of the chair and levered himself to his feet.

Annette stood stock still. "I am coming too," she announced. "I will drive you."

"Oh, phooey!" Carl said. "You know you hate breaking off halfway through the chores." He patted her on the shoulder. "And I'm perfectly all right, darling. Really! Don't you think I've caused enough trouble already?"

"Oh, Carlo—you are foolish!" Her face was very white—and something about the way her mouth moved made it seem as if she were about to cry.

Carl put an arm around her shoulders. "You must be played out, sweet," he said.

"I am very well," she snapped. "I am not tired at all." And then, with effort, she managed to smile. "But perhaps I am," she said. "Do not mind because I am cross. Go and see your Doctor Wingate. . . ."

She hooked her arm in his and walked through the living room with him, and at the front door she kissed him.

"Take care of yourself, Carlo," she said. "And come back quickly." She shut the door behind him.

As he entered the garage, G.B. came racing up—and the

84

moment Carl opened the car door, leapt neatly in to sit enormous in the seat beside the driver's. His tongue was hanging out and he was smiling all around it.

Carl laughed at him; then winced as the laughter hurt his sore stomach muscles. He said, "All right, you bum," and got in behind the wheel and started the car and backed out.

He drove slowly, but in a very few minutes was parking outside Wingate's office. He left G.B. in charge of the car and walked around to the back door—entrance for the favored few.

Wingate was standing by his desk. The light was behind him and Carl couldn't see his face very well, but he seemed older than usual, and tired. Even the little beard looked grayer. He waved Carl to a chair and then came and stood over him, feeling his pulse and making him thrust out his tongue to be looked at.

Carl grinned at him. "Goddam professional this morning," he said.

But Wingate didn't answer the smile, or the gibe. He sat down in his swivel chair and stared at Carl and said, "You were pretty sick last night, my friend," and then, after Carl had thrown in a "You're telling me!", added sharply, "You're lucky not to be dead."

Carl's grin faded slowly—and he gave a startled "Huh?"

"You heard what I said." Wingate had taken a pencil from the desk and was rolling it around in his fingers. He was looking at the pencil and not at Carl.

He said, "By the way, there's some property of yours there," and pointed with the pencil to a bulky, cylindrical package, roughly wrapped in brown paper, which stood upon a side-table. "Want to take it with you?"

Carl looked bewildered. "What? . . ." He stared uncomprehendingly. "What you talking about?"

"That's your wastebasket." Wingate still kept his eyes on the twirling pencil. "From your study. I took it with me last night. . . ."

"Why? . . . Oh—you mean to get it cleaned. . . ." Carl was floundering. He burst out, "What the hell *is* all this? What're you driving at, Tom?"

Wingate looked at him, and drew in a deep breath. He said, in a monotone, "You'll find out very soon. Where did you eat yesterday?"

"At home, of course. What's—"

"Be quiet a minute. So you ate at home. What was the last thing you had? Probably around midnight."

"Nothing. . . . Wait a second, though—I'd forgotten. I had a bowl of soup—Annette's onion soup. She brought it to me before she went to bed. But that couldn't—"

"Wait! So you had this soup, at about twelve. And around an hour later, you have cramps in the legs and stomach, faintness, nausea, acute pain in the intestines. And you vomit, copiously. A lot of it, but by no means all, was in that metal wastebasket. And the contents of the basket, analyzed, show you must have swallowed at least a grain and a half of arsenic. . . ."

He let his voice fade into silence, then stood up to face Carl, who had jumped to his feet. He put his hand on Carl's arm and pushed him back into his chair. He unconsciously repeated the very words he had used the night before. "Steady now!" he said. "Take it easy!"

Carl sat down. His pallor had increased. He pulled a shaking hand across his forehead and then tried to smile.

"Narrow squeak," he said—and after that, "Grain and a half, huh? That's quite a dose, isn't it?"

"Could be fatal," Wingate said. "And you had more, maybe."

Carl said, "How in hell d'you suppose I picked it up?" He wasn't looking at Wingate, but past him. "Vegetables or something? They spray 'em, don't they?"

"Not in that strength." Wingate went back to his own chair and sat in it. "And you had that other attack ten days ago. Same thing—but not so much." His voice was absolutely flat. "And you at home, both times."

Carl shot out of his chair again. His face was distorted, his blue eyes blazing.

"For God's sake!" he shouted. "Have you gone out of your mind! What are you hinting at?"

"I'm not hinting anything." Wingate's voice was still toneless. "I'm stating something. You have twice been poisoned with arsenic during the last ten days. The second time provably."

Carl flung his big body back into the chair again. He started to speak, but all that came from him was a muffled groan.

Wingate said, "You don't imagine I like doing this, do you?

86

But you have to face it, man! Someone is feeding you arsenic. The odds against accident are two million to one."

Carl's hands gripped the arms of his chair until his knuckles shone white. He said, hoarsely, "If I didn't know you so well, I'd break your neck!" His voice began to rise. "Can't you see the whole thing must have been some weird, terrible accident! Don't you *know* that what's in your mind is completely, utterly impossible!" He stopped abruptly. He was panting, as if he had been running.

Wingate sat motionless. His face was shaded by the hands which propped it. He spoke as if Carl had been silent.

"Arsenic's easy to get," he said. "Especially for gardeners— ant paste, Paris green, rose-spray, weed-killer—"

"God blast you!" Carl crashed his fist down upon the chair-arm. "There *is* weed-killer in the house—but *I* told her to get it!"

He got to his feet and towered over Wingate. He said, "I'm going. And I'm not coming back. I don't think you're lying about the arsenic, but I know you're making a monstrous, evil mistake about how I got it—a mistake which oughtn't to be possible to a man of your intelligence!"

He started for the door, turned back. "And another thing," he said. "I can't stop you from thinking your foul thoughts—" his voice was shaking with suppressed passion—"but I *can* stop you from voicing them—and I will! If you so much as breathe a word of this to anyone—I'll half kill you, and then I'll ruin you! And don't forget that—because I mean it!"

He stood over the other man for a long moment—but Wingate did not move, did not so much as look at him—and at last Carl went back to the door and opened it and passed out of the room. He got out into the air again and made his way to the car. He was very white. He opened the car and slumped into the driving seat. He put his arms down on the wheel and rested his head upon them. He was breathing in long shuddering gasps. G.B. made a little whimpering sound and licked at his master's ear—and two women passing by looked at the tableau with curiosity.

Perhaps Carl felt their gaze, for he raised his head and saw them. He straightened in his seat, and pushed the dog's great head aside with a gentle hand.

He drove home very slowly. Annette heard the car and opened the front door as he climbed up the steps. She said at once, "What did he say, Carlo? Did he know what is the matter with you?" Her haggard, worn look seemed to have intensified.

Carl looked at her—and then he shook his head. He stepped through the door and sank into the nearest chair. He said, slowly, "No . . . No, he didn't. I don't think he knows much about it. . . ."

He said, "God, I'm tired! . . . Come and give me a kiss, darling."

She came and sat upon the arm of his chair and kissed him. She pulled his head against her breast and stroked his hair. He could not see her face as she spoke.

"But, *chéri*," she said, "he must know *something*."

Carl sighed. "Oh, he used a lot of medical jargon—all beginning with *gastro* . . . But I don't think he really knows any more than I do—which is that I happen to have a nervous stomach." He leaned back in the chair and looked up at her. "I tell you—maybe you're right about Tom Wingate. I don't mean as a man—but as a doctor. I think another time—well, I might go to that new man . . ."

Annette jumped up. "That is quite enough talk about doctors," she said. "And I, I am very bad! Here is my poor man here, white and weak because he has no food! Wait one little moment, Carlo. . . ."

She hurried off to the kitchen. She seemed to have shed her fatigue, her tenseness.

Carl sat where he was. He stared straight ahead with eyes which did not look as if they saw what was in front of them.

In a very little while Annette came back. She was carrying a small tray upon which were a spoon, a napkin and a bowl which steamed, gently and fragrantly.

She said, "*Voilà!*—" and set the tray on his knees and put the spoon in his hand and stood back to watch him.

He looked at her for a long unwavering moment—and when she said, "Hurry now and drink your soup!" he did not seem to hear.

He said, very suddenly, "Annette: do you love me?"—and kept on looking at her.

She stared. She said, after an instant, "But yes—but of *course*, Carlo!"

And then she laughed and said, "Do not be a baby! Take your soup—it is not very hot."

He looked at the spoon in his hand and seemed surprised to find it there. He set it down upon the tray and picked up the bowl and looked at his wife over the edge of it.

"*Santé!*" he said—and put the china to his lips and began to drink in great gulps. . . .

He did not have the pains that night.

A week went by and he did not have them—a week in which he had not spoken to, nor seen, nor heard any word of Dr. Thomas Wingate.

It was past eleven at night, and he was walking with G.B. up the last slope of Paseo Street. Behind him, old Parry called a last good-night, and he half-turned and waved a valedictory hand. He had been returning from a longer walk than usual and had met Parry at the mail-box; a meeting which had somehow led to drinks in Parry's house and a long talk upon Parry's favorite topic, which was that of the world's declining sanity.

He reached his own steep little road and shortened his stride for the climb and whistled for G.B., who came at once and padded beside him.

He was humming as he strode down the drive and up the steps. He opened the front door and let the dog ahead of him and then went in himself.

He said, "*Oh, my God!*"

He stood motionless for an instant which might have been a century.

Annette was lying on the floor, twisted into a strange and ugly shape—and all around her prostrate and distorted body the room was dreadfully befouled.

G.B. stared, then pushed through the half-open door to the kitchen. There was a thump as he lay down.

Carl dropped to his knees beside the prostrate woman. He raised her head and it lolled against his arm. Her eyes were closed and her stained and swollen mouth hung open. She was breathing, but lightly, weakly—and when he felt for her heart its beat was barely perceptible. . . .

Somehow, he was in the study, at the telephone . . . As if automatically, his shaking fingers dialed a number . . .

He was speaking to Wingate. "Tom!" he said, on a harsh high note. "Tom! This is Carl. Come at once! *Hurry!*"

His hand put back the phone. His feet took him out into

the living room again. His knees bent themselves once more and once more he held his wife in his arms. . . .

He was still holding her when Wingate came.

Wingate examined her and shook his head. He made Carl get up—and took him into the study. He said, "You've got to face it, Carl . . . She's dead."

Carl was shaking all over—his hands, his body, his head, all of him.

Wingate said, "Sit there—and don't move," and went out into the living room again.

He looked at the dead woman; at the foulness around her; at everything in the room. He was staring at the two coffee cups which stood on the top of the piano when G.B. came in from the kitchen, paced over to the study and disappeared.

Wingate picked up the cups, one after the other. They were small cups, and each held the heavy, pasty remains of Turkish coffee. He dipped a dampened fingertip into each cup in turn, each time touching the finger to his tongue. The second test gave him the reaction he wanted—and, his face clearing, he strode back to the study.

Carl had not moved, but his trembling had increased. The dog sat beside him, looking into the face.

Wingate put a hand on the shaking shoulder. Carl tried to speak—but his teeth started to chatter and no words came out of him.

Wingate said: "You know, don't you? She tried again . . . You wouldn't let *me* look after you—but the Fates did!"

Carl mumbled, "I—I—I d-don't understand . . ."

Wingate said, "She was over-confident. And something went wrong—some little thing to distract her attention." He lifted his shoulders. "And—well, she took the wrong cup."

Carl said, "*God! . . .*" He covered his face with his hands, the fingers digging into his temples. He said: "Tom—I almost wish it *had* been me!"

"Come on, now!" Wingate took him by the arm. "Stop thinking—just do what I tell you!"

He hauled Carl to his feet and led him out of the study and up the stairs and into his own room. G.B. came close behind them, and lay watchful while Wingate got Carl out of his clothes and into bed and finally slid a hypodermic needle into his arm.

"There!" he said. "You'll be asleep in five minutes. . . ."

He was turning away when Carl reached out and caught his hand and held it.

Carl said, "Don't go . . ." And then he said, "About what I said in your office—I'm sorry, Tom . . ."

Wingate did not try to release his hand. "Forget it," he said. "I have."

And then he started talking—slowly, quietly, his casual voice a soothing monotone. He said, "All you have to do now is go to sleep . . . I'll see to everything else . . . In a little while, all this will just be a nightmare you've half-forgotten . . . And don't go worrying yourself about publicity and scandal and things like that, Carl . . . There won't be any . . . You see, I was *sure*—and in spite of what you said I told Chief Nichols . . . He and I will explain it all to the Coroner . . ."

He let his voice trail off into silence—Carl Borden was asleep.

It was three weeks before Carl permitted himself to smile— and then he was not in El Morro Beach. He was in San Francisco—and Lorna was waiting for him.

When he smiled, he was driving up Market Street, G.B. erect beside him.

"Tell you something, boy," he murmured. "I nearly took too much that second time!"

The smile became a chuckle.

THE ADVENTURE OF THE DEAD CAT

BY ELLERY QUEEN

The collaboration between Manfred B. Lee, right, (b. January 11, 1905; d. April 3, 1971) and Frederic Dannay, left, (b. October 20, 1905), which began with *The Roman Hat Mystery* in 1929, has been a predominant influence on the detective story. As Ellery Queen, they have contributed a sizeable literature of novels, short stories, novelets, and scholarly works, and conspicuously to radio, television, films, and the theater as well. Of *Ellery Queen's Mystery Magazine,* which they initiated in 1941, Julian Symons has said, "It is not too much to say that the continuation of the crime story as we know it seems largely dependent upon *EQMM.*"

THE SQUARE-CUT ENVELOPE was a creation of orange ink on black notepaper; by which Ellery instantly divined its horrid authorship. Behind it leered a bouncy hostess, all teeth and enthusiastic ideas, who spent large sums of some embarrassed man's money to build a better mousetrap.

Having too often been one of the mice, he was grateful that the envelope was addressed to "Miss Nikki Porter."

"But why to me at your apartment?" wondered Nikki, turning the black envelope over and finding nothing.

"Studied insult," Ellery assured her. "One of those acid-sweet women who destroy an honest girl's reputation at a stroke. Don't even open it. Hurl it into the fire, and let's get on with the work."

So Nikki opened it and drew out an enclosure cut in the shape of a cat.

"I am a master of metaphor," muttered Ellery.

"What?" said Nikki, unfolding the feline.

"It doesn't matter. But if you insist on playing the mouse, go ahead and read it." The truth was, he was a little curious himself.

"*Fellow Spook*," began Nikki, frowning.

"Read no more. The hideous details are already all too clear—"

"Oh, shut up," said Nikki. "*There is a secret meeting of The Inner Circle of Black Cats in Suite 1313, Hotel Chancellor, City, Oct. 31.*"

"Of course," said Ellery glumly. "That follows logically."

"*You must come in full costume as a Black Cat, including domino mask. Time your arrival for 9:05 P.M. promptly. Till the Witching Hour.* Signed—*G. Host.* How darling!"

"No clue to the criminal?"

"No. I don't recognize the handwriting. . . ."

"Of course you're not going."

"Of course I *am*!"

"Having performed my moral duty as friend, protector, and employer, I now suggest you put the foul thing away and get back to our typewriter."

"What's more," said Nikki, "you're going, too."

Ellery smiled his Number Three smile—the toothy one. "Am I?"

"There's a postscript on the cat's—on the reverse side. *Be sure to drag your boss-cat along, also costumed.*"

Ellery could see himself as a sort of overgrown Puss-in-Boots plying the sjambok over a houseful of bounding tabbies all swilling Scotch. The vision was tiring.

"I decline with the usual thanks."

"You're a stuffed shirt."

"I'm an intelligent man."

"You don't know how to have fun."

"These brawls inevitably wind up with someone's husband taking a poke at a tall, dark, handsome stranger."

"Coward."

"Heavens, I wasn't referring to myself—!"

Whence it is obvious that Ellery had already lost the engagement.

Ellery stood before a door on the thirteenth floor of the Hotel Chancellor, cursing the Druids.

For it was Saman at whose mossy feet must be laid the origins of our recurrent October silliness. True, the lighting of ceremonial bonfires in a Gaelic glade must have seemed natural and proper at the time, and a Gallic grove fitting rendezvous for an annual convention of ghosts and witches; but the responsibility of even pagan deities must surely be held to extend beyond temporal bounds, and the Druid lord of death should have foreseen that a bonfire would be out of place in a Manhattan hotel suite, not to mention disembodied souls, however wicked.

Then Ellery recalled that Pomona, goddess of fruits, had contributed nuts and apples to the burgeoning Hallowe'en legend, and he cursed the Romans, too.

There had been Inspector Queen at home, who had intolerably chosen to ignore the whole thing; the taxi driver, who had asked amiably: "Fraternity initiation?"; the dread chorus of miaows during the long, long trek across the Chancellor lobby; and, finally, the reeking wag in the elevator who had tried to swing Ellery around by his tail, puss-pussying obscenely as he did so.

Cried Ellery out of the agony of his mortification: "Never, *never* again will I—"

94

"Stop grousing and look at this," said Nikki, peering through her domino mask.

"What is it? I can't see through this damned thing."

"A sign on the door. *If You Are a Black Cat, Walk In!!!!!* With five exclamation points."

"All right, all right. Let's go in and get it over with."

And, of course, when they opened the unlocked door of 1313, darkness.

And Silence.

"Now what do we do?" giggled Nikki, and jumped at the snick of the door behind them.

"I'll tell you what," said Ellery enthusiastically. "Let's get the hell out of here."

But Nikki was already a yard away, black in blackness.

"Wait! Give me your hand, Nikki."

"*Mister* Queen. That's not my hand."

"Beg your pardon," muttered Ellery. "We seem to be trapped in a hallway . . ."

"There's a red light down there! Must be at the end of the hall—*eee!*"

"Think of the soup this would make for the starving." Ellery disentangled her from the embrace of some articulated bones.

"Ellery! I don't think that's funny at all."

"I don't think *any* of this is funny."

They groped toward the red light. It was not so much a light as a rosy shade of darkness which faintly blushed above a small plinth of the raven variety. "The woman's cornered the Black Paper Market," Ellery thought disagreeably as he read the runes of yellow fire on the plinth:

TURN LEFT!!!!!

"And into, I take it," he growled, "the great unknown." And, indeed, having explored to the left, his hand encountered outer space; whereupon, intrepidly, and with a large yearning to master the mystery and come to grips with its diobolical authoress, Ellery plunged through the invisible archway, Nikki bravely clinging to his tail.

"Ouch!"

"What's the matter?" gasped Nikki.

"Bumped into a chair. Skinned my shin. What would a chair be doing—?"

"Pooooor Ellery," said Nikki, laughing. "Did the dreat bid man hurt his—*Ow!*"

"Blast this—Ooo!"

"Ellery, where are you? Ooch!"

"Ow, my foot," bellowed Ellery from somewhere. "What is this—a tank-trap? Floor cluttered with pillows, hassocks—"

"Something cold and wet over here. Feels like an ice bucket . . . Owwwww!" There was a wild clatter of metal, a soggy crash, and silence again.

"Nikki! What happened?"

"I fell over a rack of fire tongs, I think," Nikki's voice came clearly from floor level. "Yes. Fire tongs."

"Of all the stupid, childish, unfunny—"

"Oop."

"Lost in a madhouse. Why is the furniture scattered every which way?"

"How should I know? Ellery, where *are* you?"

"In Bedlam. Keep your head now, Nikki, and stay where you are. Sooner or later a St. Bernard will find you and bring—"

Nikki screamed.

"Thank God," said Ellery, shutting his eyes.

The room was full of blessed Consolidated Edison light, and various adult figures in black-cat costumes and masks were leaping and laughing and shouting: "Surpriiiise!" like idiot phantoms at the crisis of a delirium.

O Hallowe'en.

"Ann! Ann Trent!" Nikki was squealing. "Oh, Ann, you fool, how ever did you find me?"

"Nikki, you're looking *wonderful*. Oh, but you're famous, darling. The great E. Q.'s secretary . . ."

Nuts to you, sister. Even bouncier than predicted. With that lazy, hippy strut. And chic, glossy chic. Lugs her sex around like a sample case. Kind of female who would be baffled by an egg. Looks five years older than she is, Antoine notwithstanding.

"But it's not Trent any more, Nikki—Mrs. John Crombie. Johnnnny!"

"Ann, you're *married*? And didn't invite me to the wedding!"

"Spliced in dear old Lunnon. John's British—or was.

Johnny, stop flirting with Edith Baxter and come here!"

"Ann darlin'—this exquisite girl! Scotch or bourbon, Nikki? Scotch if you're the careful type—but bourbon works faster."

John Crombie, Gent. Eyes of artificial blue, slimy smile, sunlamp complexion, Olivier chin. British Club and Fox and Hounds—he posts even in a living room. He will say in a moment that he loathes Americah. Exactly. Ann Trent Crombie must have large amounts of the filthy. He despises her and patronizes her friends. He will fix me with the superior British smile and flap a limp brown hand . . . *Quod erat demonstrandum.*

"I warn you, Nikki," Ann Crombie was saying. "I'm hitched to a man who tries to jockey every new female he meets." Blush hard, prim Nikki. Friends grow in unforeseen directions. "Oh, Lucy! Nikki, do you remember my kid sister Lu—?"

Squeal, squeal. "Lucy Trent! This isn't *you?*"

"Am I grown up, Nikki?"

"Heavens!"

"Lucy's done *all* the party decorating, darling—spent the whole sordid day up here alone fixing things up. Hasn't she done an *inspired* job? But then I'm so useless."

"Ann means she wouldn't help, Nikki. Just a lout."

Uncertain laugh. Poor Lucy. Embarrassed by her flowering youth, trying hard to be New York . . . There she goes re-filling a glass—emptying an ashtray—running out to the kitchen—for a tray of fresh hot pigs-in-blankets?—bong! . . . the unwanted and gauche hiding confusion by making herself useful. Keep away from your brother-in-law, dear; that's an upstanding little bosom under the Black Cat's hide.

"Oh, Ellery, do come here and meet the Baxters. Mrs. Baxter—Edith—Ellery Queen . . ."

What's this? A worm who's turned, surely! The faded-fair type, hard-used by wedlock. Very small, a bit on the spready side—she'd let herself go—but now she's back in harness again, all curried and combed, with a triumphant lift to her pale head, like an old thoroughbred proudly prancing in a paddock she had never hoped to enter again. And that glitter of secret pleasure in her blinky brown eyes, almost malice, whenever she looked at Ann Crombie . . .

"Jerry Baxter, Edith's husband. Ellery Queen."

"Hiya, son!"

97

"Hi yourself, Jerry."

Salesman, or advertising-agency man, or Broadway agent. The life of the party. Three drinks and he's off to the races. He will be the first to fall in the apple tub, the first to pin the tail on Lucy or Nikki instead of on the donkey, the first to be sick and the first to pass out. Skitter, stagger, sweat, and whoop. Why do you whoop, Jerry Baxter?

Ellery shook hot palms, smiled with what he hoped was charm, said affably: "Yes, isn't it?" "Haven't we met somewhere?" "Here, here, that's fine for now," and things like that, wondering what he was doing in a hotel living-room festooned with apples, marshmallows, nuts, and criss-crossing crêpe-paper twists, hung with grinning pumpkins and fancy black-and-orange cardboard cats, skeletons, and witches, and choked with bourbon fumes, tobacco smoke, and Chanel No. 5. Some Chinese lanterns were reeking, the noise was maddening, and merely to cross the room required the preparations of an expedition, for the overturned furniture and other impedimenta on the floor—cunningly plotted to trap groping Black Cats on their arrival—had been left where they were.

So Ellery, highball in hand, wedged himself in a safe corner and mentally added Nikki to the Druids and the Romans.

Ellery accepted the murder game without a murmur. He knew the futility of protest. Wherever he went, people at once suggested a murder game, apparently on the theory that a busman enjoys nothing so much as a bus. And, of course, he was to be the detective.

"Well, well, let's get started," he said gaily, for all the traditional Hallowe'en games had been played, Nikki had slapped Jerry Baxter laughingly once and British Johnny—not laughingly—twice, the house detective had made a courtesy call, and it was obvious the delightful evening had all but run its course. He hoped Nikki would have sense enough to cut the *pièce de résistance* short, so that a man might go home and give his thanks to God; but no, there she was in a whispery, giggly huddle with Ann Crombie and Lucy Trent, while John Crombie rested his limp hand on her shoulder and Edith Baxter splashed some angry bourbon into her glass.

Jerry was on all fours, being a cat.

"In just a minute," called Nikki, and she tripped through

the archway—kitchen-bound, to judge from certain subsequent cutlery sounds—leaving Crombie's hand momentarily suspended.

Edith Baxter said: "Jerry, get up off that floor and stop making a darned fool of yourself!"—furiously.

"Now we're all set," announced Nikki, reappearing. "Everybody around in a circle. First I'll deal out these cards, and whoever gets the ace of spades *don't let on!*—because you're the Murderer."

"Ooh!"

"Ann, you stop peeking."

"Who's peeking?"

"A tenner says I draw the fatal pasteboard," laughed Crombie. "I'm the killer type."

"*I'm* the killer type!" shouted Jerry Baxter. "Gack-gack-gack-gack!"

Ellery closed his eyes.

"Ellery! Wake up."

"Huh?"

Nikki was shaking him. The rest of the company were lined up on the far side of the room from the archway, facing the wall. For a panicky moment he thought of the St. Valentine's Day Massacre.

"You go on over there with the others, smartypants. You mustn't see who the murderer is, either, so you close your eyes, too."

"Fits in perfectly with my plans," said Ellery, and he dutifully joined the five people at the wall.

"Spread out a little there—I don't want anyone touching anyone else. That's it. Eyes all shut? Good. Now I want the person who drew the ace of spades—Murderer—to step quietly away from the wall—"

"Not cricket," came John Crombie's annoying alto. "*You'll* see who it is, dear heart."

"Yes," said Edith Baxter nastily. "The light's on."

"But I'm running the assassination! Now stop talking, eyes closed. Step out, Murderer—that's it . . . quietly! No talking there at the wall! Mr. Queen is *very* bright and he'd get the answer in a shot just by eliminating voices—"

"Oh, come, Nikki," said Mr. Queen modestly.

"Now, Murderer, here's what you do. On the kitchen table you'll find a full-face mask, a flashlight, and a bread-knife.

99

Wait! Don't start for the kitchen yet—go when I switch off the light in here; that will be your signal to start. When you get to the kitchen, put on the mask, take the flashlight and knife, steal back into the room, and—pick a victim!"

"Oooh."

"Ahhhh!"

"Ee!"

Mr. Queen banged his forehead lightly against the wall. How long, O Lord?

"Now remember, Murderer," cried Nikki, "you pick anyone you want—except, of course, Ellery. He has to live long enough to solve the crime. . . ."

If you don't hurry, my love, I'll be dead of natural causes.

"It'll be dark, Murderer, except for your flash, so even I won't know what victim you pick—"

"May the detective inquire the exact purpose of the knife?" asked the detective wearily of the wall. "Its utility in this amusement escapes me."

"Oh, the knife's just a prop, goopy—atmosphere. Murderer, you just tap your victim on the shoulder. Victim, whoever feels the tap, turn around and let Murderer lead you out of the living room to the kitchen."

"The kitchen, I take it, is the scene of the crime," said Mr. Queen gloomily.

"Uh-huh. And Victim, as soon as Murderer gets you into kitchen, scream like all fury as if you're being stabbed. Make it realistic! Everybody set? Ready? . . . All right, Murderer, soon's I turn this light off go to the kitchen, get the mask and stuff, come back, and pick your victim. Here goes!"

Click went the light switch. Being a man who checked his facts, Ellery automatically cheated and opened one eye. Dark, as advertised. He shut the eye, and then jumped.

"Stop!" Nikki had shrieked.

"What, what?" asked Ellery excitedly.

"Oh, I'm not talking to you, Ellery. Murderer, I forgot something! Where are you? Oh, never mind. Remember, after you've supposedly stabbed your victim in the kitchen, come back to this room and quickly take your former place against the wall. Don't make a sound; don't touch anyone. I want the room to be as quiet as it is this minute. Use the flash to help you see your way back, but as soon as you reach the wall turn the flash off and throw flash and mask into the middle of the living room—thus, darling, getting rid of the evidence. Do you see? But, of course, you *can't.*" You're in rare form, old girl. "Now even though it's dark, people, *keep your eyes shut.* All right, Murderer—get set—*go!*"

Ellery dozed. . . .

It seemed a mere instant later that he heard Nikki's voice saying with incredible energy: "Murderer's tapping a victim —careful with that flashlight, Murderer!—we mustn't tempt our Detective *too* much. All right, Victim? Now let Murderer lead you to your doom . . . the rest of you keep your eyes closed . . . don't turn ar . . ."

Ellery dozed again.

He awoke with a start at a man's scream.

"Here! What—"

"Ellery Queen, you asleep again? That was Victim being carved up in the kitchen. Now . . . yes! . . . here's Murderer's flash back . . . that's it, to the wall quietly . . . now flash *off!*— fine!—toss it and your mask away . . . Boom. Tossed. Are you turned around, face to the wall, Murderer, like everybody else? Everybody ready? Lllllights!"

"Now—" began Ellery briskly.

"Why, it's John who's missing," laughed Lucy.

"Pooooor John is daid," sang Jerry.

"My poor husband," wailed Ann. "Jo-hon, come back to me!"

"Ho, John!" shouted Nikki.

"Just a moment," said Ellery. "Isn't Edith Baxter missing, too?"

"My wiff?" shouted Jerry. "Hey, wiff! Come outa the wood-work!"

"Oh, darn," said Lucy. "There mustn't be two victims, Nikki. That spoils the game."

"Let us repair to the scene of the crime," proclaimed Miss Porter, "and see what gives."

So, laughing and chattering and having a hell of a time, they all trooped through the archway, turned left, crossed the foyer, and went into the Crombie kitchen and found John Crombie on the floor with his throat cut.

When Ellery returned to the kitchen from his very inter-esting telephone chat with Inspector Queen, he found Ann

101

Crombie being sick over the kitchen sink, her forehead supported by the greenish hand of a greenish Lucy Trent, and Nikki crouched quietly in a corner, as far away from the covered thing on the floor as the architect's plans allowed, while Jerry Baxter raced up and down weeping: "Where's my wife? Where's Edith? We've got to get out of here."

Ellery grabbed Baxter's collar and said: "It's going to be a long night, Jerry—relax. Nikki—"

"Yes, Ellery." She was trembling and trying to stop it and not succeeding.

"You know who was supposed to be the murderer in that foul game—the one who drew the ace of spades—you saw him or her step away from the living-room wall while the lights were still on in there. Who was it?"

"Edith Baxter. Edith got the ace. Edith was supposed to be the murderer."

Jerry Baxter jerked out of Ellery's grasp. "You're lying!" he yelled. "You're not mixing my wife up in this stink! You're a lying—"

Ann crept away from the sink, avoiding the mound. She crept past them and went into the foyer and collapsed against the door of a closet just outside the kitchen. Lucy crept after Ann and cuddled against her, whimpering. Ann began to whimper, too.

"Edith Baxter was Murderer," said Nikki drearily. "In the game, anyway."

"You lie!—you lying—"

Ellery slapped his mouth without rancor and Baxter started to cry again. "Don't let me come back and find any other throats cut," said Ellery, and he went out of the kitchen.

It was tempting to assume the obvious, which was that Edith Baxter, having drawn the ace of spades, decided to play the role of murderer in earnest, and did so, and fled. Her malice-dipped triumph as she looked at John Crombie's wife, her anger as she watched Crombie pursue Nikki through the evening, told a simple story; and it was really unkind of fate—if fate was the culprit—to place Edith Baxter's hand on John Crombie's shoulder in the victim-choosing phase of the game. In the kitchen, with a bread-knife at hand, who could blame a well-bourboned woman if she obeyed that impulse and separated Mr. Crombie's neck from his British collar?

But investigation muddled the obvious. The front door of

102

the suite was locked—nay, even bolted—on the inside. Nikki proclaimed herself the authoress thereof, having performed the sealed-apartment act before the game began (she said) in a moment of "inspiration."

Secondly, escape by one of the windows was out of the question, unless, like Pegasus, Edith Baxter possessed wings.

Thirdly, Edith Baxter had not attempted to escape at all: Ellery found her in the foyer closet against which the widow and her sister whimpered. Mrs. Baxter had been jammed into the closet by a hasty hand, and she was unconscious.

Inspector Queen, Sergeant Velie & Co. arrived just as Edith Baxter, with the aid of ammonium carbonate, was shuddering back to life.

"Guy named Crombie's throat slit?" bellowed Sergeant Velie, without guile.

Edith Baxter's eyes rolled over and Nikki wielded the smelling salts once more, wearily.

"Murder games," said Inspector Queen gently. "Hallowe'en," said Inspector Queen. Ellery blushed. "Well, son?"

Ellery told his story humbly, in penitential detail.

"Well, we'll soon find out," grumbled his father, and he shook Mrs. Baxter until her chin waggled and her eyes flew open. "Come, come, Madam, we can't afford these luxuries. What the hell were you doing in that closet?"

Edith screamed, "How should I know, you old man?" and had a convulsion of tears. "Jerry Baxter, how can you sit there and—?"

But her husband was doubled over, holding his head.

"You received Nikki's instructions, Edith," said Ellery, "and when she turned off the light you left the living room and went to the kitchen. Or started for it. What did happen?"

"Don't third-degree me, you detective!" screeched Mrs. Baxter. "I'd just passed under the archway, feeling my way, when somebody grabbed my nose and mouth from behind and I must have fainted because that's all I knew till just now and Jerry Baxter, if you don't get up on your two feet like a man and defend your own wife, I'll—I'll—"

"Slit his throat?" asked Sergeant Velie crossly, for the Sergeant had been attending his own Hallowe'en Party with the boys of his old precinct and was holding three queens full when the call to duty came.

103

"The murderer," said Ellery glumly. "The real murderer, dad. At the time Nikki first put out the lights, while Edith Baxter was still in the room getting Nikki's final instructions, one of us lined up at that wall stole across the room, passed Edith Baxter in the dark, and ambushed her—"

"Probably intended to slug her," nodded the Inspector, "but Mrs. Baxter obliged by fainting first."

"Then into the closet and away to do the foul deed?" asked the Sergeant poetically. He shook his head.

"It would mean," mused Inspector Queen, "that after stowing Mrs. Baxter in the foyer closet, the real killer went into the kitchen, got the mask, flash, and knife, came back to the living room, tapped John Crombie, led him out to the kitchen, and carved him up. That part of it's okay—Crombie must have thought he was playing the game—but how about the assault on Mrs. Baxter beforehand? Having to drag her unconscious body to the closet? Wasn't there any noise, any sound?"

Ellery said apologetically: "I kept dozing off."

But Nikki said: "There was no sound, Inspector. Then or at any other time. The first *sound* after I turned the light off was John screaming in the kitchen. The only other *sound* was the murderer throwing the flash into the middle of the room after he . . . she . . . whoever it was . . . got back to the wall."

Jerry Baxter raised his sweating face and looked at his wife.

"Could be," said the Inspector.

"Oh, my," said Sergeant Velie. He was studying the old gentleman as if he couldn't believe his eyes—or ears.

"It could be," remarked Ellery, "or it couldn't. Edith's a very small woman. Unconscious, she *could* be carried noiselessly the few feet in the foyer to the closet . . . by a reasonably strong person."

Immediately Ann Crombie and Lucy Trent and Jerry Baxter tried to look tiny and helpless, while Edith Baxter tried to look huge and heavy. But the sisters could not look less tall or soundly made than Nature had fashioned them, and Jerry's proportions, even allowing for reflexive shrinkage, were elephantine.

"Nikki," said Ellery in a very thoughtful way, "you're sure Edith was the only one to step away from the wall while the light was still on?"

"Dead sure, Ellery."

"And when the one you thought was Edith came back from the kitchen to pick a victim, that person had a full mask on?"

"You mean after I put the light out? Yes. I could see the mask in the glow the flash made."

"Man or woman, Miss P?" interjected the Sergeant eagerly. "This could be a pipe. If it was a man—"

But Nikki shook her head. "The flash was pretty weak, Sergeant. And we were all in those Black Cat outfits."

"Me, I'm no Fancy Dan," murmured Inspector Queen unexpectedly. "A man's been knocked off. What I want to know is not who was where when, but—who had it in for this character?"

It was a different sort of shrinkage this time, a shrinkage of four throats. Ellery thought: They *all* know.

"Whoever," he began casually, "whoever knew that John Crombie and Edith Baxter were—"

"*It's a lie!*" Edith was on her feet, swaying, clawing the air. "There was nothing between John and me. Nothing. Nothing! Jerry, don't believe them!"

Jerry Baxter looked down at the floor again. "Between?" he mumbled. "I guess I got a head. I guess this has got me." And, strangely, he looked not at his wife but at Ann Crombie. "Ann . . . ?"

But Ann was jelly-lipped with fear.

"Nothing!" screamed Jerry's wife.

"That's not true." And now it was Lucy's turn, and they saw she had been shocked into a sort of suicidal courage. "John was a . . . a . . . John made love to every woman he met. John made love to *me*—"

"To you." Ann blinked and blinked at her sister.

"Yes. He was . . . disgusting. I . . . ." Lucy's eyes flamed at Edith Baxter with scorn, with loathing, with contempt. "But *you* didn't find him disgusting, Edith."

Edith glared back, giving hate for hate.

"You spent four weekends with him. And the other night, at that dinner party, when you two stole off—you thought I didn't hear—but you were both tight . . . You begged him to marry you."

"You nasty little blabbermouth," said Edith in a low voice.

"I heard you. You said you'd divorce Jerry if he'd divorce

Ann. And John kind of laughed at you, didn't he?—as if you were dirt. And I saw your eyes, Edith, I saw your eyes . . ."

And now they, too, saw Edith Baxter's eyes—as they really were.

"I never told you, Ann. I couldn't. I couldn't . . ." Lucy began to sob into her hands.

Jerry Baxter got up.

"Here, where d'ye think you're going?" asked the Sergeant, not unkindly.

Jerry Baxter sat down again.

"Mrs. Crombie, did you know what was going on?" asked Inspector Queen sympathetically.

It was queer how she would not look at Edith Baxter, who was sitting lumpily now, no threat to anyone—a soggy old woman.

And Ann said, stiff and tight: "Yes, I knew." Then her mouth loosened again and she said wildly: "I knew, but I'm a coward. I couldn't face him with it. I thought if I shut my eyes—"

"So do I," said Ellery tiredly.

"What?" said Inspector Queen, turning around. "You what, son? I didn't get you."

"I know who cut Crombie's throat."

They were lined up facing the far wall of the living room—Ann Crombie, Lucy Trent, Edith Baxter, and Jerry Baxter—with a space the breadth of a man, and a little more, between the Baxters. Nikki stood at the light switch, the Inspector and Sergeant Velie blocked the archway, and Ellery sat on a hassock in the center of the room, his hands dangling listlessly between his knees.

"This is how we were arranged a couple of hours ago, dad, except that I was at the wall, too, and so was John Crombie . . . in that vacant space."

Inspector Queen said nothing.

"The light was still on, as it is now. Nikki had just asked Murderer to step away from the wall and cross the room—that is, towards where you are now. Do it, Edith."

"You mean—"

"Please."

Edith Baxter backed from the wall and turned and slowly picked her way around the overturned furniture. Near the

106

archway, she paused, an arm's length from the Inspector and the Sergeant.

"With Edith about where she is now, Nikki, in the full light, instructed her about going to the kitchen, getting the mask, flash, and knife there, coming back in the dark with the flash, selecting a victim, and so on. Isn't that right?"

"Yes."

"Then you turned off the light, Nikki—didn't you?"

"Yes. . . ."

"Do it."

"D-do it, Ellery?"

"Do it, Nikki."

When the darkness closed down, someone at the wall gasped. And then the silence closed down, too.

And after a moment Ellery's voice came tiredly: "It was at this point, Nikki, that you said 'Stop!' to Edith Baxter and gave her a few additional instructions. About what to do after the 'crime.' As I pointed out a few minutes ago, dad—it's during this interval, with Edith standing in the archway getting Nikki's afterthoughts, and the room in darkness, that the real murderer must have stolen across the living room from the wall, got past Nikki and Edith and into the foyer, and waited there to ambush Edith."

"Sure, son," said the Inspector. "So what?"

"How did the murderer manage to cross this room in pitch darkness without making any noise?"

At the wall, Jerry Baxter said hoarsely: "Y'know, I don't have to stand here. I don't have to!"

"Because, you know," said Ellery, reflectively, "there wasn't any noise. None at all. In fact, Nikki, you actually remarked in that interval: 'I want the room to be as quiet as it is this minute.' And only a few moments ago you corroborated yourself when you told dad that the first sound after you turned off the light was John screaming in the kitchen. You said the only other sound was the sound of the flashlight landing in the middle of the room after the murderer got back to the wall. So I repeat: How did the murderer cross this room in darkness without making a sound?"

Sergeant Velie's disembodied bass complained from the archway that he didn't get it at all, at all.

"Well, Sergeant, you've seen this room—it's cluttered crazily with overturned furniture, pillows, hassocks, miscellaneous

107

objects. Do you think *you* could cross it in darkness without sounding like the bull in the china shop? Nikki, when you and I first got here and blundered into the living room—"

"In the dark," cried Nikki. "We bumped. We scraped. I actually fell—"

"Why didn't the murderer?"

"I'll tell you why," said Inspector Queen suddenly. "*Because no one did cross this room in the dark.* It can't be done without making a racket, or without a light—and there was no light at that time or Nikki'd have seen it."

"Then how's it add up, Inspector?" asked the Sergeant pathetically.

"There's only one person we know crossed this room, the one Nikki saw cross while the light was on, the one they found in the closet in a 'faint,' Velie. *Edith Baxter!*"

She sounded nauseated. "Oh, no," she said. "No."

"Oh, yes, Mrs. Baxter. It's been you all the time. You did get to the kitchen. You got the mask, the flash, the knife. You came back and tapped John Crombie. You led him out to the kitchen and there you sliced him up—"

"No!"

"Then you quietly got into that closet and pulled a phoney faint, and waited for them to find you so you could tell that cock-and-bull story of being ambushed in the foyer, and—"

"Dad," sighed Ellery.

"Huh?" And because the old gentleman's memory of similar moments—many similar moments—was very green, his tone became truculent. "Now tell me I'm wrong, Ellery!"

"Edith Baxter is the one person present tonight who couldn't have killed John Crombie."

"You see?" moaned Edith. They could hear her panting.

"Nikki actually saw somebody with a flash *return* to the living room after Crombie's death-scream, go to the wall, turn off the flash, and she heard that person hurl it into the middle of the room. Who was it Nikki saw and heard? We've deduced that already—the actual murderer. Immediately after that, Nikki turned up the lights.

"If Edith Baxter were the murderer, wouldn't we have found her *at the wall with the rest of us* when the lights went on? But she wasn't. She wasn't in the living room at all. We found her in the foyer closet. So she *had* been attacked. She *did* faint. She *didn't* kill Crombie."

They could hear her sobbing in a great release.

"Then who did?" barked the Inspector. His tone said he was tired of this fancy stuff and give him a killer so he could book the rat and go home and get to sleep.

"The one," replied Ellery in those weary tones, "who was able to cross the room in the dark without making any noise. For if Edith is innocent, only one of those at the wall could have been guilty. And that one had to cross the room."

There is a maddening unarguability about Ellery's sermons.

"But how, son, how?" bellowed his father. "It couldn't be done without knocking *something* over—making *some* noise!"

"Only one possible explanation," said Ellery tiredly; and then he said, not tiredly at all, but swiftly and with the slashing finality of a knife, "I thought you'd try that. That's why I sat on the hassock, so very tired. That's why I staged this whole . . . silly . . . scene . . ."

Velie was roaring: "Where the hell are the lights? Miss Porter, turn that switch on, will you?"

"I can't find the—the damned thing!" wept Nikki.

"The rest of you stay where you are!" shouted the Inspector.

"Now drop the knife," said Ellery, in the slightly gritty tones of one who is exerting pressure. "Drop it. . . ." There was a little clatter, and then a whimper. "The only one who could have passed through this jumbled maze in the dark without stumbling over anything," Ellery went on, breathing a bit harder than usual, "would be someone who'd *plotted a route through this maze in advance of the party* . . . someone, in fact, who'd plotted the maze. In other words, the clutter in this room is not chance confusion, but deliberate plant. It would require photographing the details of the obstacle-course on the memory, and practice, plenty of practice—but we were told you spent the entire day in this suite *alone*, my dear, fixing it up for the party."

"Here!" sobbed Nikki, and she jabbed the light switch.

"I imagine," said Ellery gently to the girl in his grip, "you felt *someone* had to avenge the honor of the Trents, Lucy."

YOU CAN'T HANG TWICE

BY ANTHONY GILBERT

Anthony Gilbert (Lucy Beatrice Malleson) was born in England in 1899. Her mother wanted her to be a schoolteacher but she turned to mystery writing instead, with *The Tragedy at Treyne* (1927). For many years she kept her identity a secret. Her detective, Arthur Crook, was an enormous success from his first appearance in *Murder by Experts* in 1936. "You Can't Hang Twice," the only Crook short story, won second prize ten years later in *Ellery Queen's Mystery Magazine*'s contest. Her non-series stories have received criticism for straining credibility but far more often have received high praise for their poignancy, skill, and perception. She died in 1973.

THE MIST THAT HAD been creeping up from the river during the early afternoon had thickened into a gray blanket of fog by twilight, and by the time Big Ben was striking nine and people all over England were turning on their radio sets for the news, it was so dense that Arthur Crook, opening the window of his office at 123 Bloomsbury Street and peering out, felt that he was poised over chaos. Not a light, not an outline, was visible; below him, the darkness was like a pit. Only his sharp ears caught, faint and far away, the uncertain football of benighted pedestrians and the muffled hooting of a motorist ill-advised enough to be caught abroad by the weather.

"An ugly night," reflected Arthur Crook, staring out over the invisible city. "As bad a night as I remember." He shut the window down. "Still," he added, turning back to the desk where he had been working for the past twelve hours, "it all makes for employment. Fogs mean work for the doctor, for the ambulance driver, for the police and the mortician, for the daring thief and the born wrong 'un."

Yes, and work, too, for men like Arthur Crook, who catered specially for the lawless and the reckless and who was known in two continents as the Criminals' Hope and the Judges' Despair.

And even as these thoughts passed through his mind, the driver was waiting unaware of what the night was to hold, the victim crept out under cover of darkness from the rabbit-hutch-cum-bath that he called his flat, and his enemy watched unseen but close at hand.

In his office, Mr. Crook's telephone began to ring.

The voice at the other end of the line seemed a long way off, as though that also were muffled by the fog, but Crook, whose knowledge of men was wide and who knew them in all moods, realized that the fellow was ridden by fear.

"Mr. Crook," whispered the voice and he heard the pennies fall as the speaker pressed Button B. "I was afraid it woud be too late to find you. . . ."

"When I join the forty-hour-a-week campaign I'll let the world know," said Crook, affably. "I'm one of those chaps you read about. Time doesn't mean a thing to me. And in a fog like this it might just as well be nine o'clock in the morning as nine o'clock at night."

"It's the fog that makes it possible for me to call you at all," said the voice mysteriously. "You see, in the dark, one hopes he isn't watching."

Hell, thought Crook disappointedly. Just another case of persecution mania, but he said patiently enough, "What is it? Someone on your trail?"

His correspondent seemed sensitive to his change of mood. "You think I'm imagining it? I wish to Heaven I were. But it's not just that I'm convinced I'm being followed. Already he's warned me three times. The last time was tonight."

"How does he warn you?"

"He rings up my flat and each time he says the same thing. 'Is that you, Smyth? Remember—silence is golden' and then he rings off again."

"On my Sam," exclaimed Crook, "I've heard of better gags at a kids' party. Who is your joking friend?"

"I don't know his name," said the voice, and now it sounded further away than ever, "but—he's the man who strangled Isobel Baldry."

Everyone knows about quick-change artists, how they come onto the stage in a cutaway coat and polished boots, bow, go off and before you can draw your breath they're back in tinsel tights and tinfoil halo. You can't think how it can be done in the time, but no quick-change artist was quicker than Mr. Crook when he heard that. He became a totally different person in the space of a second.

"Well, now we are going places," he said, and his voice was as warm as a fire that's just been switched on. "What did you say your name was?"

"Smyth."

"If that's the way you want it . . . ."

"I don't. I'd have liked a more distinguished name. I did the best I could spelling it with a Y, but it hasn't helped much. I was one of the guests at the party that night. You don't remember of course. I'm not the sort of man people do remember. She didn't. When I came to her house that night she thought I'd come to check the meter or something. She'd never expected me to turn up. She'd just said, 'You must come in one evening. I'm always at home on Fridays,'

112

and I thought she just meant two or three people at most . . ."

"Tête-a-tête with a tigress," said Crook. "What are you any-how? A lion-tamer?"

"I work for a legal firm called Wilson, Wilson and Wilson. I don't know if it was always like that on Fridays, but the house seemed full of people when I arrived and—they were all the wrong people, wrong for me, I mean. They were quite young and most of them were either just demobilized or were waiting to come out. Even the doctor had been in the Air Force. They all stared at me as if I had got out of a cage. I heard one say, He looks as if he had been born in a bowler hat and striped p-pants. They just thought I was a joke."

And not much of one at that, thought Mr. Crook unsym-pathetically.

"But as it happens, the joke's on them," continued the voice, rising suddenly. "Because I'm the only one who knows that Tom Merlin isn't guilty."

"Well, *I* know," Mr. Crook offered mildly, "because I'm defendin' him, and I only work for the innocent. And the young lady knows or she wouldn't have hauled me into this—the young lady he's going to marry, I mean. And of course the real murderer knows. So that makes four of us. Quite a team. Suppose you tell us how you know?"

"Because I was behind the curtain when *he* came out of the Turret Room. He passed me so close I could have touched him, though of course I couldn't see him because the whole house was dark, because of this game they were playing, the one called Murder. I didn't know then that a crime had been committed, but when the truth came out I realized he must have come out of the room where she was, because there was no other place he could have come from."

"Look," said Mr. Crook, "just suppose I've never heard this story before." And probably he hadn't heard this one, he reflected. "Start from page one and just go through to the end. Why were you behind the curtain?"

"I was hiding—not because of the game, but because I—oh, I was so miserable. I ought never to have gone. It wasn't my kind of party. No one paid any attention to me except to laugh when I did anything wrong. If it hadn't been for Mr. Merlin I wouldn't even have had a drink. And he was just sorry for me. I heard him say to the doctor, Isobel ought to remember everyone's human, and the doctor—Dr. Dunn—said, it's a bit late in the day to expect that."

"Sounds a dandy party," said Crook.

"It was—terrible. I couldn't understand why all the men seemed to be in love with her. But they were. She wasn't specially goodlooking, but they behaved as though there was something about her that made everyone else unimportant."

Crook nodded over the head of the telephone. That was the dead woman's reputation. A courtesan manquée—that's how the press had described her. Born in the right period she'd have been a riot. As it was, she didn't do so badly, even in 1945.

"It had been bad enough before," the voice went on. "We'd had charades, and of course I'm no good at that sort of thing. The others were splendid. One or two of them were real actors on the stage, and even the others seemed to have done amateur theatricals half their lives. And how they laughed at me—till they got bored because I was so stupid. They stopped after a time, though I offered to drop out and just be audience; and then I wanted to go back, but Miss Beldry said how could I when she was three miles from a station and no one else was going yet? I could get a lift later. Murder was just as bad as the rest, worse in a way, because it was dark, and you never knew who you might bump into. I bumped right into her and Tom Merlin once. He was telling her she better be careful, one of these days she'd get her neck broken, and she laughed and said, Would you like to do it, Tom? And then she laughed still more and asked him if he was still thinking of that dreary little number—that's what she called her—he'd once thought he might marry. And asked him why he didn't go back, if he wanted to? It was most uncomfortable. I got away and found a window onto the flat roof, what they call the leads. I thought I'd stay there till the game was over. But I couldn't rest even there, because after a minute Mr. Merlin came out in a terrible state, and I was afraid of being seen, so I crept round in the shadows and came into the house through another window. And that's how I found myself in the Turret Room."

"Quite the little Lord Fauntleroy touch," observed Crook, admiringly. "Well?"

"Though, of course, all the lights were out, the moon was quite bright and I could see the blue screen and I heard a sound and I guessed Miss Baldry was hidden there. For a minute I thought I'd go across and find her and win the game, but another second and I realized that there was some-one—a man—with her."

"But you don't know who?"

"No."

"Tough," said Crook. "Having a good time, were they?"

"I don't know about a good time. I think the fact is every-one had been drinking rather freely, and they were getting excited, and I never liked scenes—I haven't a very strong stomach, I'm afraid—so I thought I'd get out. They were so much engrossed in one another—You have it coming to you, Isobel, I heard him say. I got out without them hearing me —I did fire-watching, you know, and one learns to move quietly."

"Quite right," assented Crook. "No sense startling a bomb. Well?"

"I went down a little flight of stairs and onto a landing, and I thought I heard feet coming up, so I got behind the curtain. I was terrified someone would discover me, but the feet went down again and I could hear whispers and laughter —everything you'd expect at a party. They were all enjoying themselves except me."

"And Isobel, of course," suggested Crook.

"She had been—till then. Well, I hadn't been behind the curtain for very long when the door of the Turret Room shut very gently, and someone came creeping down. He stopped quite close to me as if he were leaning over the stair-case making sure no one would see him come down. I scarcely dared breathe—though, of course, I didn't know then there had been a murder—and after a minute I heard him go down. The next thing I heard was someone coming up, quickly, and going up the stairs and into the Turret Room. I was just getting ready to come out when I heard a man call-ing, Norman! Norman! For Pete's sake . . . and Dr. Dunn— he was the R.A.F. doctor, but of course you know that— called out, I'm coming. Where are you? And the first man— it was Andrew Tatham, the actor, who came out of the Army after Dunkirk—said, Keep the women out. An appalling thing's happened."

"And, of course, the women came surgin' up like the sea washin' round Canute's feet?"

"A lot of people came up, and I came out from my hiding-place and joined them, but the door of the Turret Room was shut, and after a minute Mr. Tatham came out and said, We'd better all go down. There's been an accident, and Dr. Dunn joined him and said, What's the use of telling them that? They'll have to know the truth. Isobel's been murdered, and we're all in a spot."

"And when did it strike you that you had something to tell the police?" enquired Crook drily.

"Not straight away. I—I was very shocked myself. Everyone began to try and remember where they'd been, but, of course, in the dark, no one could really prove anything. I said, I was behind that curtain. I wasn't really playing, but no one listened. I might have been the invisible man. And then one of the girls said, Where's Tom? and Mr. Tatham said, That's queer. Hope to Heaven he hasn't been murdered, too. But he hadn't, of course. He joined us after a minute and said, A good time being had by all? and one of the girls, the one they called Phoebe, went into hysterics. Then Mr. Tatham said, Where on earth have you been? and he said he was on the leads. He wasn't playing either. They all looked either surprised or—a bit disbelieving, and Dr. Dunn said, But if you were on the leads you must have heard something, and he said, Only the usual row. Why? Have we had a murder? And Mr. Tatham said, Stop it, you fool. And then he began to stare at all of us, and said, Tell me, what is it? Why are you looking like that? So then they told him. Some of them seemed to think he must have heard noises, but Dr. Dunn said that if whoever was responsible knew his onions there needn't be enough noise to attract a man at the farther end of the flat roof, particularly as he'd expect to hear a good deal of movement and muttering and so on."

"And when the police came—did you remember to tell them about the chap who'd come out of the Turret Room? or did you have some special reason for keeping it dark?"

"I—I'm afraid I rather lost my head. You see, I was planning exactly what I'd say when it occurred to me that nobody else had admitted going into that room at all, and I hadn't an atom of proof that my story was true, and—it isn't as if I knew who the man was. . . ."

"You know," said Crook, "it looks like I'll be holding your baby when I'm through with Tom Merlin's."

"I didn't see I could do any good," protested Mr. Smyth.
"And then they arrested Mr. Merlin and I couldn't keep silent any longer. Because it seemed to me that though I couldn't tell them the name of the murderer or even prove that Mr. Merlin was innocent, a jury wouldn't like to bring in a verdict of guilty when they heard what I had to say."

"Get this into your head," said Crook, sternly. "They won't bring in a verdict of guilty in any circumstances. I'm lookin' after Tom Merlin, so he won't be for the high jump this time. But all the same, you and me have got to get together. Just where do you say you are?"

"On the Embankment—in a call-box."

"Well, what's wrong with you coming along right now?"

"In this fog?"

"I thought you said the fog made it safer."

"Safer to telephone, because the box is quite near my flat."
He broke suddenly into a queer convulsive giggle. "Though as a matter of fact I began to think the stars in their courses were against me, when I found I only had one penny. Luckily, there was one in my pocket—I keep one there for an evening paper—"

"Keep that bit for your memoirs," Crook begged him.
"Now all you've got to do is proceed along the Embankment . . . "

"The trams have stopped."

"Don't blame 'em," said Crook.

"And I don't know about the trains, but I wouldn't dare travel by Underground in this weather, and though I think there was one taxi a little while ago . . ."

"Listen!" said Crook. "You walk like I told you till you come to Charing Cross. You can't fall off the Embankment and if there's no traffic nothing can run you down. The tubes are all right, and from Charing Cross to Russell Square is no way at all. Change at Leicester Square. Got that? You can be in my office within twenty-five minutes. I'm only three doors from the station."

"Wouldn't tomorrow . . . ?" began Smyth, but Crook said, "Not it. You might have had another warning by tomorrow and this time it might be a bit more lethal than an anonymous telephone message. Now, don't lose heart. It's like going to the dentist. Once it's done, it's over for six months. So long as X. thinks you're huggin' your guilty secret to your own

117

buzoom you're a danger to him. Once you've spilt the beans you're safe."

"It's a long way to Charing Cross," quavered the poor little rabbit.

"No way at all," Crook assured him. "And never mind about the trams and the taxi-cabs. You might be safer on your own feet at that."

Thus is many a true word spoken in jest.

"And now," ruminated Mr. Crook, laying the telephone aside and looking at the great pot-bellied watch he drew from his pocket, "first, how much of that story is true? and second, how much are the police going to believe? If he was a pal of Tom Merlin's, that's just the sort of story he would tell, and if it's all my eye and Betty Martin, he couldn't have thought of a better. It don't prove Tom's innocent, but as he says, it's enough to shake the jury."

It was also, of course, the sort of story a criminal might tell, but in that case he'd have told it at once. Besides, even the optimistic Mr. Crook couldn't suspect Mr. Smyth of the murder. He wasn't the stuff of which murderers are made.

"No personality," decided Crook. "Black tie, wing collar, umbrella and brief-case, the eight-ten every week-day—Yes, Mr. Brown. Certainly, Mr. Jones. I will attend to that, Mr. Robinson. Back on the six-twelve regular as clockwork, a news-reel or pottering with the window-boxes on Saturday afternoons, long lie-in on Sunday"—that was his program until the time came for his longest lie-in of all.

And at that moment neither Mr. Smyth nor Arthur Crook had any notion how near that was.

Crook looked at his watch. "Five minutes before the balloon goes up," he observed. It went up like an actor taking his cue. At the end of five minutes the telephone rang again.

As he made his snail's pace of a way towards Charing Cross Mr. Smyth was rehearsing feverishly the precise phrases he would use to Mr. Crook. He was so terrified of the coming interview that only a still greater terror could have urged him forward. For there was nothing of the hero about him. The services had declined to make use of him during the war, and it had never occurred to him to leave his safe employment and volunteer for anything in the nature of war work. Fire-watching was compulsory.

118

"The fact is, I wasn't born for greatness," he used to assure himself. "The daily round, the common task . . . I never wanted the limelight." But it looked as though that was precisely what he was going to get. For the hundredth time he found himself wishing he had never met Isobel Baldry, or, having met her, had never obeyed the mad impulse which made him look up the number she had given him and virtually invite himself to her party. The moment he arrived he knew she had never meant him to accept that invitation.

The darkness seemed full of eyes and ears. He stopped suddenly to see whether he could surprise stealthy footsteps coming after him, but he heard only the endless lapping of black water against the Embankment, the faint noise of the police launch going downstream, and above both these sounds, the frenzied beating of his own heart. He went on a little way, then found to his horror that he could not move. In front of him the darkness seemed impenetrable; behind him the atmosphere seemed to close up like a wall, barring his retreat. He was like someone coming down the side of a sheer cliff who suddenly finds himself paralyzed, unable to move a step in either direction. He didn't know what would have happened, but at that moment a car came through the fog travelling at what seemed to him dangerous speed. It was full of young men, the prototype of those he had met at Isobel Baldry's ill-starred party. They were singing as they went. That gave him a fresh idea, and without moving he began to call "Taxi! Taxi!" Someone in the car heard him and leaned out to shout, "No soap, old boy," but now panic had him in its grip. And it seemed as if then his luck changed. Another vehicle came more slowly through the darkness.

"Taxi!" he called, and to his relief he heard the car stop.

Relief panted in his voice. "I want to go to Bloomsbury Street. Number one-twenty-three. Do you know it?"

"Another client for Mr. Cautious Crook." The driver gave a huge chuckle. "Well, well."

"You—you mean you know him?"

"All the men on the night shift know about Mr. Crook. Must work on a night shift 'imself, the hours 'e keeps."

"You mean—his clients prefer to see him at night?" He was startled.

"Yerss. Not so likely to be reckernized by a rozzer, see? Oh, 'e gets a queer lot. Though this is the first time I've bin asked to go there in a fog like this." His voice sounded dubious. "Don't see 'ow it can be done, guvnor."

"But you must. It's most important. I mean, he's expecting me."

"Sure? On a night like this? You should worry."

"But—I've only just telephoned him." Now it seemed of paramount importance that he should get there by hook or crook.

"Just like that. Lumme, you must be in a 'urry."

"I am. I—I don't mind making it worth your while . . ." It occurred to him that to the driver this sort of conversation might be quite an ordinary occurrence. He hadn't realized before the existence of a secret life dependent on the darkness.

"Cost yer a quid," the driver said promptly.

"A pound?" He was shocked.

"Mr. Crook wouldn't be flattered to think you didn't think 'im worth a quid," observed the driver.

Mr. Smyth made up his mind. "All right."

"Sure you've got it on you?"

"Yes. Oh, I see." He saw that the man intended to have the pound before he started on the journey, and he fumbled for his shabby shiny note-case and pulled out the only pound it held and offered it to the driver. Even in the fog the driver didn't miss it. He snapped on the light inside the car for an instant to allow Mr. Smyth to get in, then put it off again, and his fare sank sprawling on the cushions. The driver's voice came to him faintly as he started up the engine.

"After all, guvnor, a quid's not much to save yer neck."

He started. His neck? His neck wasn't in danger. No one thought he'd murdered Isobel Baldry. But the protest died even in his heart within a second. Not his neck but his life— that was what he was paying a pound to save. Now that the car was on its way he knew a pang of security. He was always nervous about journeys, thought he might miss the train, get into the wrong one, find there wasn't a seat. Once the journey started he could relax. He thought about the coming interview; he was pinning all his faith on Arthur Crook. He wouldn't be scared; the situation didn't exist that could scare such a man. And perhaps, he reflected, lulling himself into a false security, Mr. Crook would laugh at his visitor's fears. That's just what I wanted, he'd say. You've solved the whole case for me, provided the missing link. Justice should be grateful to you, Mr. Smyth. . . . He lost himself in a maze of prefabricated dreams.

Suddenly he realized that the cab, which had been crawling for some time, had now drawn to a complete standstill. The driver got down and opened the door.

"Sorry, sir, this perishin' fog. Can't make it, after all."

"You mean, you can't get there?" He sounded incredulous.

"It's my neck as well as yours," the driver reminded him.

"But—I must—I mean are you sure it's impossible? If we go very slowly . . ."

"If we go much slower we'll be proceedin' backwards. Sorry, guvnor, but there's only one place we'll make tonight if we go any further and that's Kensal Green. Even Mr. Crook can't help you once you're there."

"Then—where are we now?"

"We ain't a 'undred miles from Charing Cross," returned the driver cautiously. "More than that I wouldn't like to say. But I'm not taking the cab no further in this. If any mug likes to try pinchin' it 'e's welcome."

Reluctantly Mr. Smyth crawled out into the black street; it was bitterly cold and he shivered.

"I'll 'ave to give you that quid back," said the driver, wistfully.

"Well, you didn't get me to Bloomsbury Street, did you?" He supposed he'd have to give the fellow something for his trouble. He put out one hand to take the note and shoved the other into the pocket where he kept his change. Then it happened, with the same shocking suddennes as Isobel Baldry's death. His fingers had just closed on the note when something struck him with appalling brutality. Automatically he grabbed harder, but it wasn't any use; he couldn't hold it. Besides, other blows followed the first. A very hail of blows in fact, accompanied by shock and sickening pain and a sense of the world ebbing away. He didn't really appreciate what had happened; there was too little time. Only as he staggered and his feet slipped on the wet leaves of the gutter, so that he went down for good, he thought, the darkness closing on his mind for ever, "I thought it was damned comfortable for a taxi."

It was shortly after this that Arthur Crook's telephone rang for the second time, and a nervous voice said, "This is Mr.

Smyth speaking. I'm sorry I can't make it. I—this fog's too thick. I'll get lost. I'm going right back."

"That's all right," said Crook heartily. "Don't mind me. Don't mind Tom Merlin. We don't matter."

"If I get knocked down in the fog and killed it won't help either of you," protested the voice.

"Come to that, I daresay I won't be any worse off if you are."

"But—you can't do anything tonight."

"If I'm goin' to wait for you I shan't do anything till Kingdom Come."

"I—I'll come tomorrow. It won't make any difference really."

"We've had all this out before," said Crook. "I was brought up strict. Never put off till tomorrow what you can do today."

"But I can't—that's what I'm telling you. I'll come—I'll come at nine o'clock tomorrow."

"If he lets you," said Crook darkly.

"He?"

"He might be waiting for you on the doorstep. You never know. Where are you, by the way?"

"In a call-box."

"I know that. I heard the pennies drop. But where?"

"On the Embankment."

"What's the number?"

"It's a call-box, I tell you."

"Even call-boxes have numbers."

"I don't see . . ."

"Not trying to hide anything from me, Smyth, are you?"

"Of course not. It's Fragonard fifteen double one."

"That's the new Temple exchange. You must have overshot your mark."

"Oh? Yes. I mean, have I?"

"You were coming from Charing Cross. You've walked a station too far."

"It's this fog. I thought—I thought it was Charing Cross just over the road."

"No bump of locality," suggested Crook, kindly.

"I can't lose my way if I stick to the Embankment. I'm going straight back to Westminster and let myself into my flat, and I'll be with you without fail at nine sharp tomorrow."

"Maybe," said Crook pleasantly. "Happy dreams." He rang

122

off. "Picture of a gentleman chatting to a murderer," he announced. "Must be a dog's life, a murderer's. So damned lonely. And dangerous. You can't trust anyone, can't confide in anyone, can't even be sure of yourself. One slip and you're finished. One admission of something only the murderer can know and it's the little covered shed for you one of these cold mornings. Besides, you can't guard from all directions at once, and how was the chap who's just rung me to know that Smyth only had two coppers on him when he left his flat tonight, and so he couldn't have put through a second call?"

The inference was obvious. Someone wanted Mr. Crook to believe that Smyth had gone yellow and that was why he hadn't kept his date. Otherwise—who knew?—if the mouse wouldn't come to Mahomet, Mahomet might go looking for the mouse. And later, when the fog had dispersed, some early workman or street cleaner, perhaps even a bobby, would stumble over a body on the Embankment, and he—Crook—would come forward with his story and it would be presumed that the chap had been bowled over in the dark—or even manhandled for the sake of any valuable he might carry. Crook remembered his earlier thought—work for the doctor, for the ambulance driver, for the mortician—and for Arthur Crook. Somewhere at this instant Smyth lay, deprived forever of the power of passing on information, rescuing an innocent man, helping to bring a guilty one to justice, somewhere between Temple Station and Westminster Bridge.

"And my bet 'ud be Temple Station," Crook told himself.

It was a fantastic situation. He considered for a moment ringing the police and telling them the story, but the police are only interested in crimes after they've been committed, and a murder without a corpse just doesn't make sense to them at all. So, decided Mr. Crook, he'd do all their spadework for them, find the body and then sit back and see how they reacted to that. He locked his office, switched off the lights and came tumbling down the stairs like a sack of coals. It was his boast that he was like a cat and could see in the dark, but even he took his time getting to Temple Station. Purely as a precaution he pulled open the door of the telephone booth nearby and checked the number. As he had supposed, it was Fragonard 1511.

There was a chance, of course, that X. had heaved the body over the Embankment, but Crook was inclined to think not.

123

To begin with, you couldn't go dropping bodies into the Thames without making a splash of some sort, and you could never be sure that the Thames police wouldn't be passing just then. Besides, even small bodies are heavy, and there might be blood. Better on all counts to give the impression of a street accident. Crook had known of cases where men had deliberately knocked out their victims and then ridden over them in cars. Taking his little sure-fire pencil torch from his pocket Crook began his search. His main fear wasn't that he wouldn't find the body, but that some interfering constable would find him before that happened. And though he had stood up to bullets and blunt instruments in his time, he knew that no career can stand against ridicule. He was working slowly along the Embankment, wondering if the fog would ever lift, when the beam of his torch fell on something white a short distance above the ground. This proved to be a handkerchief tied to the arm of one of the Embankment benches. It was tied hard in a double knot, with the ends spread out, as though whoever put it there wanted to be sure of finding it again. He looked at it for a minute before its obvious significance occurred to him. Why did you tie a white cloth to something in the dark? Obviously to mark a place. If you didn't, on such a night, you'd never find your way back. What he still didn't know was why whoever had put out Smyth's light should want to come back to the scene of the crime. For it was Smyth's handkerchief. He realized that as soon as he had untied it and seen the sprawling letters "Smyth" in one corner. There was something peculiarly grim about a murderer taking his victim's handkerchief to mark the spot of the crime. After that it didn't take him long to find the body. It lay in the gutter, the blood on the crushed forehead black in the bright torchlight, the face dreadful in its disfigurement and dread. Those who talked of the peace of death ought to see a face like that; it might quiet them a bit, thought Mr. Crook grimly. He'd seen death so often you'd not have expected him to be squeamish, but he could wish that someone else had found Mr. Smyth.

Squatting beside the body like a busy little brown elephant, he went through the pockets. He'd got to find out what the murderer had taken that he had to return. Of course, someone else might have found the body and left the handkerchief but an innocent man, argued Crook, would have left his own.

124

You'd have to be callous to take things off the body of a corpse. There wasn't much in the dead man's pockets, a note-case with some ten-shilling notes in it, a season ticket, some loose cash, an old-fashioned turnip watch—that was all. No matches, no cigarettes, of course no handkerchief.

"What's missing?" wondered Mr. Crook, delving his hands into his own pockets and finding there watch, coin-purse, note-case, identity card, tobacco pouch, latch-key. . . . "That's it," said Mr. Crook. "He hasn't got a key. But he talked of going back and letting himself in, so he had a key. . . ." There was the chance that it might have fallen out of his pocket, but though Crook sifted through the damp sooty leaves he found nothing; he hadn't expected to, anyhow. There were only two reasons why X. should have wanted to get into the flat. One was that he believed Smyth had some evidence against him and he meant to lay hands on it; the other was to fix an alibi showing that the dead man was alive at, say, 10:30, at which hour, decided Mr. Crook, the murderer would have fixed an alibi for himself. He instantly cheered up. The cleverest criminal couldn't invent an alibi that an even cleverer man couldn't disprove.

He straightened himself, and as he did so he realized that the corpse had one of its hands folded into a fist; it was a job to open the fingers, but when he had done so he found a morsel of tough white paper with a greenish blur on the torn edge. He recognized that all right, and in defiance of anything the police might say he put the paper into his pocket-book. The whole world by this time seemed absolutely deserted; every now and again a long melancholy hoot came up from the river and some benighted tug or the sirens at the mouth of the estuary echoed faintly through the murk; but these were other-worldly sounds that increased rather than dispelled the deathlike atmosphere. As to cause of death, his guess would be a spanner. A spanner is a nice anonymous weapon, not too difficult to procure, extraordinarily difficult to identify. Only fools went in for fancy weapons like sword-sticks and Italian knives and loaded riding-crops, all of which could be traced pretty easily to the owners. In a critical matter like murder it's safer to leave these to the backroom boys and stick to something as common as dirt. Crook was pretty common himself, and, like dirt, he stuck.

"The police are going to have a treat tonight," he told

himself, making a bee-line for the telephone. His first call was to the dead man's flat, and at first he thought his luck was out. But just when he was giving up hope he could hear the receiver being snatched off and a strained, breathless voice said, "Yes?"

"Mr. Smyth? Arthur Crook here. Just wanted to be sure you got back safely."

"Yes. Yes. But only just. I decided to walk after all."

"Attaboy!" said Mr. Crook. "Don't forget about our date tomorrow."

"Nine o'clock," said the voice. "I will be there."

Mr. Crook hung up the receiver. What a liar you are, he said, and then at long last he dialed 999.

The murderer had resolved to leave nothing to chance. After his call to Mr. Crook's office he came back to the waiting car and drove as fast as he dared back to the block of flats where he lived. At this hour the man in charge of the car park would have gone off duty, and on such a night there was little likelihood of his encountering anyone else. Carefully he ran the car into an empty space and went over it carefully with a torch. He hunted inside in case there should be any trace there of the dead man, but there was none. He had been careful to do all the opening and closing of doors, so there was no fear of fingerprints, but when he went over the outside of the car his heart jumped into his mouth when he discovered blood-marks on the right-hand passenger-door. He found an old rag and carefully polished them off, depositing the rag in a corner at the further end of the car park. This unfortunately showed up the stains of mud and rain on the rest of the body, but he hadn't time to clean all the paintwork; there was still a lot to be done and, as he knew, there is a limit to what a man's nervous system can endure. Locking the car he made his way round to the entrance of the flats. The porter was just going off; there wasn't a night porter, labor was still scarce, and after ten thirty the tenants looked after themselves.

"Hell of a night, Meadows," he observed, drawing a long breath. "I was beginning to wonder if I'd be brought in feet first."

The porter, a lugubrious creature, nodded with a sort of morbid zest.

"There'll be a lot of men meeting the Recording Angel in

126

the morning that never thought of such a thing when they went out tonight," he said.

His companion preserved a poker face. "I suppose a fog always means deaths. Still, one man's meat. It means work for doctors and undertakers and ambulance-men. . . ." He didn't say anything about Arthur Crook. He wasn't thinking of Arthur Crook. Still under the man's eye he went upstairs, unlocked the door of his flat, slammed it and, having heard the man depart, came stealing down again, still meeting no one, and gained the street. So far all had gone according to plan.

It took longer to get to Westminster than he had anticipated, because in the fog he lost his way once, and began to panic, which wasted still more time. His idea was to establish Smyth alive and talking on his own telephone at, say, ten thirty P.M. Then, if questions should be asked, Meadows could testify to his own return at ten thirty. On his way back, he would return the key to the dead man's pocket, replace the handkerchief, slip home under cover of darkness. . . . He had it worked out like a B.B.C. exercise.

Luck seemed to be with him. As he entered the flats the hall was in comparative darkness. It was one of those houses where you pushed a button as you came in and the light lasted long enough for you to get up two floors; then you pushed another button and that took you up to the top. There wasn't any lift. As he unlocked the door of the flat the telephone was ringing and when he unshipped the receiver there was Arthur Crook, of all the men on earth, calling up the dead man. He shivered to think how nearly he'd missed that call. He didn't stay very long; there was still plenty to do and the sooner he got back to his own flat the more comfortable he'd feel. And how was he to guess that he would never walk inside that flat again?

He congratulated himself on his foresight in tying the handkerchief to the arm of the bench; in this weather he might have gone blundering about for an hour before he found the spot where Smyth lay in the gutter, his feet scuffing up the drenched fallen leaves. As it was he saw his landmark, by torchlight, without any trouble. It was then that things started to go wrong. He was level with the seat when he heard the voice of an invisible man exclaim, "Hey there!" and he jumped back, automatically switching off his torch, and muttering, "Who the devil are you?"

127

"Sorry if I startled you," said the same voice, "but there's a chap here seems to have come to grief. I wish you'd take a look at him."

This was the one contingency for which he had not prepared himself, but he knew he dared not refuse. He couldn't afford at this stage to arouse suspicion. Besides, he could offer to call the police, make for the call-box and just melt into the fog. Come what might, he had to return the dead man's key. He approached the curb and dropped down beside the body. Crook watched him like a lynx. This was the trickiest time of all; if they weren't careful he might give them the slip yet.

"Have you called the police?" enquired the newcomer, getting to his feet. "If not, I . . ." But at that moment both men heard the familiar sound of a door slamming and an inspector with two men hovering in the background came forward saying, "Now then, what's going on here?"

"Chap's got himself killed," said Crook.

X. thought like lightning. He made a slight staggering movement, and as Crook put out his hand to hold him he said, "Silly—slipped on something—don't know what it was." He snapped on his torch again, and stooping, picked up a key. "Must have dropped out of his pocket," he suggested. "Unless," he turned politely to Crook, "unless it's yours."

Crook shook his head.

"Which of you was it called us up?" the Inspector went on.

"I did," said Crook. "And then this gentleman came along and . . ." he paused deliberately and looked at the newcomer. It was a bizarre scene, the men looking like silhouettes against the grey blanket of fog with no light but the torches of the civilians and the bulls-eyes of the force. "Seeing this gentleman's a doctor. . ." As he had anticipated there was an interruption.

"What's that you said?"

"Penalty of fame," said Crook. "Saw your picture in the papers at the time of the Baldry case. Dr. Noel Dunn, isn't it? And p'raps I should introduce myself. I'm Arthur Crook, one of the three men living who *know* Tom Merlin didn't kill Miss Baldry, the others bein' Tom himself and, of course, the murderer."

"Isn't that a coincidence?" said Dr. Dunn.

"There's a bigger one coming," Crook warned him. "While I was waitin' I had a looksee at that little chap's identity card,

128

and who do you think he is? Mr. Alfred Smyth, also interested in the Baldry case."

The doctor swung down his torch. "So that's where I'd seen him before? I had a feeling the face was familiar in a way, only . . ."

"He is a bit knocked about, isn't he?" said Crook. "What should you say did that?"

"I shouldn't care to hazard a guess without a closer examination. At first I took it for granted he'd been bowled over by a car . . ."

"In that case we ought to be able to trace the car. He can't have gotten all that damage and not left any of his blood on the hood."

There was more noise and a police ambulance drove up and spewed men all over the road. Crook lifted his head and felt a breath of wind on his face. That meant the fog would soon start to lift. Long before morning it would have gone. The inspector turned to the two men.

"I'll want you to come with me," he said. "There's a few things I want to know."

"I can't help you," said Dunn sharply, but the inspector told him, "We'll need someone to identify the body."

"Mr. Crook can do that. He knows him."

"Always glad to learn," said Crook.

"But you . . ." He stopped.

"You don't know the police the way I do," Crook assured him. "Just because a chap carries an identity card marked Alfred Smyth—that ain't proof. I never set eyes on him before."

"Mr. Crook's right," said the inspector. "We want someone who saw him when he was alive."

They all piled into the car, Crook and Dunn jammed together, and no one talked. Dunn was thinking hard. Sold for a sucker, he thought. If I hadn't tried so hard for an alibi—perhaps, though, they won't touch Meadows. Meadows will remember, all the same. He'll think it's fishy. And the car. Of course there was blood on the car. If they examine it they'll notice it's washed clean in one place. They'll want to know why. No sense saying I was coming back from the pictures. Meadows can wreck that. Besides, Baron, the man who looks after the cars, may remember mine hadn't come in when he went off duty. Round and round like a squirrel in its cage went his tormented mind. There must be some way out, he was thinking, as thousands have thought before him. They've no proof, no actual proof at all. Outwardly he was calm enough, maintaining the attitude that he couldn't imagine why they wanted him. But inside he was panicking. He didn't like the station surroundings, he didn't like the look on the inspector's face, most of all he feared Crook. The police had to keep the rules, Crook had never heard of Queensberry. To him a fair fight was gouging, shoving, and kicking in the pit of the stomach. A terrible man. But he stuck to it, they hadn't got anything on him that added up to murder. He'd had the forethought to get rid of the spanner, dropped it in one of those disused pig buckets that still disfigured London's streets; but he'd had to use the one near his own flats, because in the dark he couldn't find any others. He thought now the river might have been safer.

He tried to seem perfectly at ease, pulled off his burberry and threw it over the back of a chair, produced his cigarette case.

"Of course, our own doctor will go over the man," the inspector said, "but how long should you say he'd been dead, Dr. Dunn?"

He hesitated. "Not so easy. He was a little chap and it's a bitter cold night. But not long."

"But more than twenty minutes?" the Inspector suggested.

"Yes, more than that, of course."

"That's screwy," said the inspector. "I mean, Mr. Crook was talking to him on the telephone in his flat twenty minutes before you happened along."

He couldn't think how he'd forgotten that telephone conversation. That, intended for his prime alibi, was going to ball up everything.

"I don't see how he could," he protested. "Not unless the chap's got someone doubling for him."

"You know all the answers," agreed Crook. "Matter of fact, the same chap seems to be making quite a habit of it. He rang me a bit earlier from Fragonard fifteen double one to tell me Smyth couldn't keep an appointment tonight. Well, nobody knew about that but Smyth and me, so how did X. know he wasn't coming, if he hadn't made sure of it himself?"

"Don't ask me," said Dunn.

"We are asking you," said the inspector deliberately.

The doctor stared. "Look here, you're on the wrong tack if you think I know anything. It was just chance. Why don't you send a man round to Smyth's flat and see who's there?"

"We did think of that," the inspector told him. "But there wasn't anyone. . . ."

"Then—perhaps this is Mr. Crook's idea of a joke."

"Oh no," said Crook looking shocked. "I never think murder's a joke. A living perhaps, but not a joke."

Dunn made a movement as though to rise. "I'm sorry I can't help you. . . ."

"I wouldn't be too sure about that," drawled Crook.

"What does that mean?"

"There's just one point the inspector hasn't mentioned. When I found that poor little devil tonight he'd got a bit of paper in his hand. All right, inspector. I'll explain in a minute. Just now, let it ride." He turned back to Dr. Noel Dunn. "It was a bit of a treasury note, and it seemed to me that if we could find the rest of that note, why then we might be able to lay hands on the murderer."

"You might. And you think you know where the note is?"

"I could make a guess."

"If you think I've got it . . ." Dunn pulled out his wallet and threw it contemptuously on the table. "You can look for yourself."

"Oh, I don't expect it would be there," replied Crook, paying no attention to the wallet. "But—every murderer makes one mistake, Dunn. If he didn't, God help the police. And help innocent men, too. And a man with murder on his hands is like a chap trying to look four ways at once. Now that note suggested something to me. You don't go round carrying notes in a fog, as if they were torches. You'd only get a note out if you were going to pay somebody, and who's the only person you're likely to want to pay in such circumstances? I'm talking like a damned politician," he added disgustedly. "But you do see what I'm drivin' at?"

"I'm only a doctor," said Dunn. "Not a professional thought-reader."

"You'd pay a man who drove you to your destination—or tried to. There was some reason why Smyth had a note in his hand, and my guess is he was tryin' to pay some chap off. That would explain his bein' at Temple Station. On his own feet he wouldn't have passed Charing Cross, not a chap as fright-

131

ened of the dark as he was. While he was offerin' the note, X. knocked him out, and realizin' that funny questions might be asked if the note was found with him, he'd remove it. You agree so far?"

"I don't know as much about murder as you do, Mr. Crook," said Dunn.

"That's your trouble," Mr. Crook agreed. "That's always the trouble of amateurs setting up against pros. They're bound to lose. Let's go on. X. removes the note. So far, so good. But he's got a lot to remember and not much time. He can't be blamed if he don't remember it's trifles that hang a man. If I was asked, I'd say X. shoved that note into his pocket, meanin' to get rid of it later, and I'd say it was there still."

"You're welcome to search my pockets," Dunn assured him. "But I warn you, Crook, you're making a big mistake. Your reputation's not going to be worth even the bit of a note you found in Smyth's hand when this story breaks."

"I'll chance it," said Crook.

At a nod from the inspector the police took up Dunn's burberry and began to go through the pockets. During the next thirty seconds you could have heard a pin drop. Then the man brought out a fist like a ham, and in it was a crumpled ten-shilling note with one corner missing!

"Anything to say to that?" enquired Crook.

Dunn put back his head and let out a roar of laughter. "You think you're smart, don't you? You planted that on me, I suppose, when we were coming. But, as it happens, Smyth's note was for a pound, not ten shillings. You didn't know that, did you?"

"Oh, yes," said Crook, "I did—because I have the odd bit of the note in my wallet. One of the old green ones it was. What I'm wondering is—*how did you?*"

"That was highly irregular, Mr. Crook," observed the inspector, drawing down the corners of his mouth, after the doctor had been taken away.

"It beats me how the police even catch as many criminals as they do," returned Crook frankly. "Stands to reason if you're after a weasel you got to play like a weasel. And a gentleman—and all the Police Force are gentlemen—don't know a thing about weasels."

132

"Funny the little things that catch 'em," suggested the inspector, wisely letting that ride.

"I reckoned that if he saw the wrong note suddenly shoved under his nose he wouldn't be able to stop himself. It's what I've always said. Murderers get caught because they're yellow. If they just did their job and left it at that, they might die in their beds at ninety-nine. But the minute they've socked their man they start feverishly buildin' a little tent to hide in, and presently some chap comes along, who might never have noticed them, but gets curious about the little tent. When you start checking up his story I bet you'll find he's been buildin' alibis like a beaver buildin' a dam. And it's his alibis are goin' to hang him in the end."

His last word in this case was to Tom Merlin and the girl Tom was still going to marry.

"Justice is the screwiest thing there is," he told them. "You're not out of chokey because Noel Dunn killed the Baldry dame, though he's admitted that, too. Well, why not? We know he got Smyth, and you can't hang twice. But it was his killing Smyth that put you back on your feet. If he hadn't done that, we might have had quite a job straightenin' things out. Y'know the wisest fellow ever lived? And don't tell me Solomon."

"Who, Mr. Crook?" asked Tom Merlin's girl, hanging on Tom's arm.

"Br'er Rabbit. And why? Becos he lay low and said nuffin. And then they tell you animals are a lower order of creation!"

LOVE COMES TO MISS LUCY

BY Q. PATRICK

Q. Patrick is the pseudonym used by two English-born writers, Hugh Wheeler (photograph above) and Richard Webb, who also wrote together as Patrick Quentin and Jonathan Stagge. They wrote some 30 mystery novels, 20 novelets, and 100 short stories. Webb was born in 1901 and attended Cambridge. Wheeler was born in 1912 and attended London University. Both became American citizens and served in the U.S. Army during World War II. Webb left the collaboration in the 1950s to spend his last years in the South of France. Wheeler continued to write as Patrick Quentin until 1965 when he turned his talent, with great success, to the stage and movies.

THEY SAT AROUND THE breakfast table, their black coats hanging sleevelessly from their shoulders in the Mexican tourist fashion. They looked exactly what they were—three middle-aged ladies from the most respectable suburbs of Philadelphia.

"*Mas cafe,*" demanded Miss Ellen Yarnell from a recalcitrant waitress. Miss Ellen had traveled before and knew how to get service in foreign countries.

"And *mas* hot—*caliente,*" added Mrs. Vera Truegood who was the oldest of the three and found the mornings in Mexico City chilly.

Miss Lucy Bram didn't say anything. She looked at her watch to see if it was time for Mario to arrive.

The maid dumped a tin pot of lukewarm coffee on the table.

"Don't you think, Lucy," put in Ellen, "that it would be a good idea if we got Mario to come earlier in the morning? He could take us out somewhere so we could get a nice hot breakfast."

"Mario does quite enough for us already." Miss Lucy flushed slightly as she spoke of the young Mexican guide. She flushed because her friends had teased her about him, and because she had just been thinking of his strong, rather cruel Mexican legs as she had seen them yesterday when he rowed them through the floating gardens of Xochimilco.

Miss Lucy Bram had probably never thought about a man's legs (and certainly not at breakfast time) in all her fifty-two years of polite, Quakerish spinsterhood. This was another disturbing indication of the change which had taken place in her since her cautious arrival in Mexico a month before. The change, perhaps, had in fact happened earlier, when the death of an ailing father had left her suddenly and bewilderingly rich, both in terms of bonds and a release from bondage. But Miss Lucy had only grown aware of it later, here in Mexico—on the day when she had found Mario in Taxco.

It had been an eventful day for Miss Lucy. Perhaps the most eventful of all these new Mexican days. Her sense of freedom, which still faintly shocked her sedate soul, had awakened with her in her sunny hotel bedroom. It had hovered over her patio breakfast with her two companions (whose expenses she was discreetly paying). It had been quenched neither by Vera's complaints of the chill mountain air nor by Ellen's travel-snobbish remark that Taxco was sweet, of course, but nowhere near as picturesque as the hill towns of Tuscany.

To Miss Lucy, with only Philadelphia and Bar Harbor behind her, Taxco's pink weathered roofs and pink, feathery-steepled churches was the impossible realization of a dream. "A rose-red city half as old as time. . . ."

The raffish delight of "foreignness," of being her own mistress, had reached a climax when she saw The Ring.

She saw it one of the little silversmith shops below the leafy public square. It caught her attention while Vera and Ellen were haggling with the proprietor over a burro pin. It wasn't a valuable ring. To her Quaker eyes, severely trained against the ostentatious, it was almost vulgar. A large, flamboyant white sapphire on a slender band of silver. But there was something tempting in its brash sparkle. She slipped it on her finger and it flashed the sunlight back at her. It made her mother's prim engagement ring, which was worth certainly fifty times as much, fade out of the picture. Miss Lucy felt unaccountably gay, and then self-conscious. With a hurried glance at the stuffy black backs of Vera and Ellen, she tried to take it off her finger.

It would not come off. And while she was still struggling Vera and Ellen joined her, inspecting it with little cries of admiration.

"My, Lucy, it's darling."

"Pretty as an engagement ring."

Miss Lucy flushed. "Don't be foolish. It's much too young for me. I just tried it on. I don't seem to be able . . ."

She pulled at the ring again. The Mexican who owned the shop hovered at her side, purring compliments.

"Go on, Lucy," said Ellen daringly. "Buy it."

"Really, it's annoying. But since I can't seem to get it off, I suppose I'll have to . . ."

Miss Lucy bought the white sapphire ring for a sum which was higher than its value, but which was still negligible to her. While Ellen, who handled all the financial aspects of the trip because she was "so clever" at those things, settled with the proprietor, Miss Lucy said to Vera:

136

"I'll get it off with soap and water back at the hotel."

But she didn't take it off. Somehow her new disturbing happiness had become centered in it.

In Taxco Miss Lucy's energy seemed boundless. That evening, before dinner, while Vera and Ellen were resting aching feet in their rooms, she decided upon a second trip to the Church of Santa Prisca which dominated the public square. Her first visit had been marred by the guidebook chatter of her companions. She wanted to be alone in that cool, tenebrous interior, to try to get the feeling of its atmosphere, so different from the homespun godliness of her own Quaker meeting-house at home.

As she stepped through the ornate wooden doors, the fantastic Churrigueresque altar of gold-leaf flowers and cherubs gleamed richly at her. An ancient peasant woman, sheathed in black, was offering a guttering candle to an image of the Virgin. A mongrel dog ran past her into the church, looked around and ran out again. The splendor and the small humanities of the scene had a curious effect upon Miss Lucy. This stood for all that was "popish" and alien and yet it seemed to call her. On an impulse which she less than half understood, she dropped to her knees, in imitation of the peasant woman, and crossed herself, the sapphire ring flashing with some of the exotic quality of the church itself.

Miss Lucy remained kneeling only a short time, but before she rose she was conscious of a presence close to her on the right. She glanced around and saw that a Mexican youth in a spotless white suit had entered the church and was kneeling a few yards away, the thick hair shining on his reverently bent head. As she got up, his gaze met hers. It was only a momentary glance, but she retained a vivid impression of his face. Honey-brown skin and the eyes—particularly the eyes—dark and patient with a gentle, passive beauty. Somehow that brief contact gave her the sensation of seeing a little into the mind of this strange city of strange people. Remembering him, her spontaneous genuflection seemed somehow the right thing to have done. Not, of course, that she would ever speak of it to Vera and Ellen.

She left the church, happy and ready for dinner. The evening light had faded, and as she passed from the crowded Xocalo into the deserted street which led to the hotel, it was almost night. Her footsteps echoed unfamiliarly against the

137

rough cobblestones. The sound seemed to emphasize her loneliness. A single male figure, staggering slightly, was coming up the hill now toward her. Miss Lucy was no coward, but with a tingle of alarm she realized that the oncomer was drunk. She looked around. There was no one else in sight. A weak impulse urged her to return to the Xocalo, but she suppressed it. After all, she was an American, she would not be harmed. She marched steadfastly on.

But the seeds of fear were there, and when she came abreast of the man, he peered at her and swung toward her. He was bearded and shabby and his breath reeked of tequila. He started a stream of Spanish which she couldn't understand. She knew he was begging and, trained to organized charities, Miss Lucy had no sympathy for street beggars. She shook her head firmly and tried to move on. But a dirty hand grabbed her sleeve, and the soft whining words continued. She freed her arm more violently than she intended. Anger glinted in the man's eyes. He raised his arm in an indignant gesture.

Although he was obviously not intending to strike her, Miss Lucy recoiled instinctively and as she did so, caught her high heel in the uneven cobbles and fell rather ungracefully on the ground. She lay there, her ankle twisted underneath her while the man stood threateningly, it seemed, over her.

For a moment, Miss Lucy felt panic—blind overwhelming terror completely unjustified by the almost farcical unpleasantness of the situation.

And then from the shadows, another man appeared. A slight man in a white suit. Miss Lucy could not see his face but she knew that it was the boy from the church. She was conscious of his white-sleeved arm flashing toward the beggar and pushing him away.

She saw the beggar reel backwards and shuffle mutteringly off. Then she was aware of a young face close to her own, and a strong arm was helping her to rise. She could not understand all her rescuer said, but his voice was gentle and concerned.

"*Qué malo,*" he said, grinning in the direction of the departing beggar. "*Malo Mexicano.*" The teeth gleamed white in the moonlight. "Me Mario, from the church, yes? Me help the señora, no?"

He almost carried Miss Lucy, who had twisted her ankle

painfully, back to the hotel and right into her room where she was turned over to the flustered administrations of Vera and Ellen.

As Mario hovered solicitously around, Ellen grabbed at her pocket book with a whispered: "How much, Lucy?"

But here Miss Lucy showed a will of her own. "No. Money would be an insult."

And Mario, who seemed to understand, said *"Gracias, Señora."* And after several sentences, in which Miss Lucy understood only the word *"madre,"* he picked up Miss Lucy's left hand—the one with the new sapphire ring—kissed it and then bowed himself smilingly out.

That was how Mario had come into their lives. And having come in, it was apparent that he intended to stay. Next morning he came to the hotel to inquire for Miss Lucy and she saw him squarely for the first time. He was not really handsome. His long-lashed eyes were perhaps a shade too close together. His slight mustache above the full-lipped mouth was perhaps too long. But his figure, though slight, was powerful, and there was something about him that inspired both affection and confidence.

He was, he explained, a student anxious to make a little money on vacation. He wanted to be a guide to the Señoras, and since Miss Lucy could not walk with her twisted ankle, he suggested that he hire a car and act as their chauffeur. The fee he requested was astonishingly small and he stubbornly refused to accept more.

The next day he hired a car at a low price which more than satisfied even the parsimonious Miss Ellen and from then on he drove the ladies around to points of interest with as much care and consideration as if they had been his three *"madres."*

His daily appearances, always in spotless white, were a constant delight to Miss Lucy—indeed, to all three of them. He was full of plans for their entertainment. One day he drove them around the base of Mount Popocatepetl and for several hours they were able to rhapsodize over what is certainly one of the most beautiful and mysterious mountains in the world. And for a moment when they happened to be alone together, staring at the dazzling whiteness of the mountain's magnificent summit, Miss Lucy felt her hand taken in Mario's firm brown one and softly squeezed.

139

It was of course, his way of telling her, despite the difficulties of language, that they were sharing a great Mexican experience and he was glad they were sharing it together. Under his touch the large sapphire in the ring pressed into her finger painfully, but another feeling, different from pain, stirred in her.

After the Popocatepetl trip, Miss Lucy decided that it was time to leave Taxco and take up their quarters in Mexico City.

She instructed Ellen to dismiss Mario—to give him an extra hundred pesos and to let him know politely yet firmly that his services were terminated. But Ellen might as well have tried to dispel Popocatepetl or bid it remove itself into the sea. Mario just laughed at her, waved away the hundred pesos, and referred himself directly to Miss Lucy. There were bad Mexicans in Mexico City. He threw out his strong, honeygold hands. He would take care of them. No, of no importance was the money of Señora Ellen (the other two women were always Señora to him, Miss Lucy alone was Señorita). The important thing was that he should show them everything. Here the strong arms waved to embrace the sun, the sky, the mountains, all of Mexico. And the dark eyes with the too-thick lashes embraced Miss Lucy too.

And Miss Lucy, acting against some deeply rooted instinct, yielded.

Mario went with them to Mexico City.

It was the second week of their stay in Mexico City and they had decided upon a trip to the Pyramids at Teotihuacan. As usual Miss Lucy sat in front with Mario. He was an excellent driver and she loved to watch his profile as he concentrated on the road; loved his occasional murmurs to himself when something pleased or displeased him. She liked it less when he turned to her, flashing his dark eyes caressingly on her face and lowering them to her breast.

His gaze embarrassed her and today something prompted her to say to him laughingly in English:

"Mario, you are what in America we call a flirt. I imagine you are very popular with the girls here in Mexico."

For a moment he did not seem to understand her remark. Then he burst out:

"Girls—*muchachas. Para me, no.*" His hand went into his breast pocket and he brought out a small battered photograph. *"Mi muchacha.* My girl, *mi unica muchacha . . . Una sola . . ."*

Miss Lucy took the photograph. It was of a woman older than herself with gray hair and large sad eyes. There were lines of worry and illness in her face.

"Your mother?" said Miss Lucy gently. "Tell me about her."

Mario rattled on, not in the slow careful Spanish which he generally reserved for the ladies, but in a rapid monologue of which Miss Lucy understood but part. She gathered that Mario's mother was terribly poor, that she had devoted her life in a tiny Guerreros village to raising fatherless children, and was a saint on earth. It was obvious that Mario felt the almost idolatrous love for his mother that is so frequent in young Mexican males.

While he talked excitedly, Miss Lucy reached a decision. Somehow, before her vacation was over, she'd get from Mario his mother's address and she'd write and send her money, enough money to finance Mario at college. A mother surely would accept it even though her son might be too proud to yield to persuasion.

"Is that one of the pyramids?" It was Ellen's disappointed voice that broke the chain of Miss Lucy's thought. "Why, it's nothing compared to the pyramids in Egypt!"

Miss Lucy was thrilled, however, by the pyramids of the Sun and the Moon. And as she gazed at their somber, ancient magnificence, she felt that strange inner elation, which she had felt on the morning when she had genuflected and crossed herself in the church at Taxco.

"I'm not going to climb up those crumbly steps," said Ellen peevishly. "I'm too old and it's too hot."

And Vera, though never too hot, was far too old. She stood at the foot of the pyramid, her coat hanging sleevelessly over her shoulders, the inevitable cigarette held in her clawlike hand. "You go, Lucy—you're young and active."

Lucy went.

With Mario's help she climbed to the very top of the Pyramid of the Sun and she was hardly out of breath when she reached the summit, so great was her sense of mystic exaltation.

They sat alone and close together on the summit, this cultivated woman past fifty with a degree from Bryn Mawr, and this almost ignorant boy from an adobe hut in the hinterland of Guerreros. They looked over the vast design of the square where the ancient village had been with its Temple of Quetzalcoatl of the Plumed Serpents, gazing down at the Road of the Dead which led from the Temple to the Pyramid of the Moon.

Mario started to tell her of the sacrificial rites of the feast of Toxcatl which, in ancient days, took place once a year.

As he talked, Miss Lucy half-closed her eyes and visualized the scene: the assembled public hushed in the huge square beneath them; the priests, each in his appointed place on the steps of the Pyramid; the spotless youth who was, of course, Mario.

And because it was Mario who was being sacrificed in her mind, sacrificed to the futility of life and beauty, she felt a warm human pity for him and instinctively her hand went out—the hand with the cheap sapphire ring that would not come off—and it found his, and was held fast in his warm brown fingers.

Miss Lucy was hardly aware of it when Mario's arm slipped round her, and his dark head dropped against her breast. It was not until she became conscious of a smell like warm brown sugar, which was his skin, and a smell of flowery oil which he used on his hair, that all Philadelphia came rushing back. She jumped up hastily—jumping out of the centuries to this practical moment when two friends would be waiting at the base of the pyramid, hungry for lunch—and there were a great many steps to descend.

On the way home Miss Lucy decided that she and Vera would take the back seat, so Ellen sat in front and argued with the sulky Mario.

When they reached the pension, Miss Lucy said quickly:

"It's a Sunday tomorrow, Mario. You'd better take a holiday."

He began to protest. When Lucy repeated, "No, not tomorrow, Mario," his face fell like a disappointed child's. Then his expression changed, and his dark eyes looked squarely, challengingly into hers.

As she turned into the house, Miss Lucy felt her heart pounding. The intimacy of that glance had brought into the open the thing which she had not dared to contemplate before. She was quite certain of it now.

142

Somehow—for some reason that she did not understand and in some way that her simple mind had never dreamed of—Mario desired her.

He desired her physically.

That night, before she went to bed, Miss Lucy did something she had never done in her life before. She stood in her plain cotton nightgown for several minutes before the long Venetian mirror in the sumptuous room and took stock of herself as a woman.

She saw nothing new or startling—nothing external to balance the startling changes which were going on inside her. Her face was not beautiful. It never had been, even in youth, and now it was uncompromisingly middle-aged. Her hair was almost white but not white enough. It was soft and plentiful and sat rather prettily on her forehead. Her eyes were clear and pleasing in themselves, but surrounded by the lines and shadows natural to her age. Her breasts were firm beneath the cotton nightgown but her figure was in no way remarkable. In fact, there was nothing externally desirable either about her face or her body. And yet she was desired. She knew it. For some reason a handsome Mexican youth found her desirable. Miss Lucy was sure of that.

There was no nonsense about Miss Lucy and she knew that young men often make up to rich older women in the hopes of eventually obtaining money from them. But Mario, apart from the fact that he'd refused all financial offers, did not even know that Miss Lucy was by far the richest of the three ladies. Only a Philadelphia lawyer or a member of their old Quaker family could possibly know how rich Miss Lucy really was. No, if Mario had wanted money, he would have concentrated on Ellen who held the purse strings and never for a moment let it be known to anyone that it was Miss Lucy's money she was dispensing.

There was nothing about Miss Lucy, drab, black-clad Miss Lucy, to suggest wealth. True, her mother's engagement ring had a rather valuable diamond in it. But only an expert jeweler would recognize that. As for the flashy white sapphire ring, that wasn't worth anyone's time or energy and Miss Lucy would have gladly given it to Mario out of gratitude if only she could have got it off her finger.

No, there were thousands of other women in Mexico City with far more obvious signs of wealth. There were young, beautiful women and any one of them might have been pleased and proud to have Mario as an escort and—yes, Miss Lucy faced it uncompromisingly—as something else.

And yet . . . suddenly Miss Lucy became frightened at the illogicality of it all.

Some virginal instinct stirred in her and warned her of—danger.

And because there was no nonsense about Miss Lucy, she decided that she must do something final about it. Lying there quietly beneath the sheets, she came to her great resolution.

Miss Lucy and Vera were waiting at the bus station. Both of them hugged their coats around them as if cold. Vera was always cold, of course. But today Miss Lucy was cold, too, despite the splendid warmth of the spring sunshine. Her eyes —and her nose—were red.

They were waiting for Ellen who had been left behind to deliver the final *coup de grâce* to Mario. The bus for Patz-cuaro was leaving in twenty minutes.

At last Ellen appeared. Her nose was red too.

"You shouldn't have done it, Lucy," she snapped. "It was cruel." She thrust two one-hundred-peso bills into Lucy's hands. "I thought he was going to hit me when I gave him these." She sniffed. "And he burst into tears like a child when he read your letter."

Miss Lucy did not speak. In fact, she spoke very little dur-ing the entire length of the tiring bus journey to Patzcuaro.

The three women had been sitting since dinner around their table on the veranda overlooking the serene expanse of Lake Patzcuaro. Ellen restlessly voluble, was discussing possible plans for the next day. Miss Lucy was, apparently, paying no attention. Her eyes studied the evening gray-green waters of the lake with its clustering islands and its obscene bald-headed vultures that squawked and fought greedily over scraps of carrion on the lake shore.

After a short time she rose, saying: "It's getting a bit cold. I think I'll go up to my room. Goodnight."

Miss Lucy's room, with its small veranda, commanded a view of the lake from another angle. Below her, in the grow-ing darkness, the fishermen were pottering with their boats, talking in low, sibilant voices or singing snatches of Michoa-can songs.

Miss Lucy sat watching them. She was thinking of Mario,

missing him with an intensity that was almost painful. She had thought of him constantly since she left Mexico City and now was appalled at her harshness in dismissing him by proxy through Ellen. She should have spoken to him herself. She would hate to have him think . . . The thoughts went on with a goading persistence. She had done him a wrong, hurt him. . . .

At some indeterminate stage of her reverie she became conscious of a white-clad figure moving among the fishermen below. Miss Lucy's gaze rested on him and then her heart turned over. She strained forward and peered into the darkness. Surely, surely, there was something familiar about those light, graceful movements—that small, compact form.

But it couldn't be Mario! She had left him hundreds of miles away in Mexico City, and Ellen had been particularly instructed not to tell him where they were going.

The figure in white moved away from the lake shore towards her window. He passed through a shaft of light from an open door. There was no doubt about it now.

It was Mario.

She bent over the balcony, her heart fluttering like a foolish bird. He was only about fifteen feet below her.

"Oh, Miss Lucy, I have found you." He spoke in the slow careful Spanish which he reserved for her. "I knew I would find you."

"But, Mario, how . . . ?"

"The bus company told me you had come here. I got a ride and I have been waiting."

She saw his teeth gleaming as he smiled at her. "Miss Lucy, why did you go away without saying *adios?*"

She did not answer.

"But I am back now to take care of you. And tomorrow you and I—we will go on the lake. Before the other two ladies are up. You and I alone together. There will be a moon and then the sunrise."

"Yes . . ."

"At five o'clock in the morning I come. I will have a boat. Before even the birds awake I will be waiting here."

"Yes, yes . . ."

"Goodnight, *carissima.*"

Miss Lucy went back into her room. Her hands were trembling as she undid her dress and slipped into bed.

145

And she was still trembling when—in the middle of the night, it seemed—a low whistle beneath her window told her that Mario had come for her.

She dressed swiftly, patted her soft gray hair into place, threw a coat over her shoulders and hurried downstairs. The hotel was very quiet. No one saw her as she made her way through the deserted lobby and no one saw her as she went down the slope to where Mario was waiting for her with the boat.

He took her hand and pressed it to his lips. Then he drew her gently towards the boat.

She did not resist. It was as though he were Destiny leading her onwards towards the inevitable.

Mario had been right. There was a moon—full and lemon-white, it shed a weird light on the opaque waters of the lake.

Miss Lucy was in the bottom of the boat, lying on her coat. It was cold, but she did not seem to notice it. She was watching Mario as he stood up in the boat, guiding it skillfully past the other craft into the deep waters of the lake. He had rolled his trousers up beyond his knees and his legs looked strong and somehow cruel in the moonlight. He was singing.

Miss Lucy had not realized before what a beautiful voice he had. The song seemed sweet and ineffably sad. Mario's eyes caressed her as his gaze travelled downward from her face and rested on her hands which lay impassive on her lap. The cheap sapphire sparkled in the moonlight.

Miss Lucy was not conscious of time or place as the boat moved slowly toward the secret heart of the lake with its myriad islets. She was not conscious of the dimming stars and the moon paling before the dawn. She felt only a deep, utter tranquility, as though this gentle, almost imperceptible motion must go on forever. She started at the sound of Mario's voice:

"Listen, the birds."

She heard them in the cluster of small islands that were all around her, but she could see only the vultures that hovered silently overhead.

Mario rested from his rowing and produced a parcel. It contained *tortas*, butter, and goat cheese. He also brought out a bottle of red Mexican wine.

He spread butter on a *torta* with his large clasp knife and handed it to Miss Lucy. Suddenly she realized that she was

146

very hungry. She ate wolfishly and drank from the bottle of the sweet Mexican wine. It went to her head and made her feel girlish and happy. She laughed at everything Mario said and he laughed too while his eyes still caressed her.

And so they breakfasted like honeymoon lovers, as a sunrise splashed red gold over the lake, miles away now from anyone, with only the visible vultures and the invisible songsters to witness them.

When the last *torta* was eaten and the bottle drained, Mario took up his paddle again and propelled the boat deeper into the heart of the lake, on and on without speaking.

As soon as she saw the island, Miss Lucy knew it was the one Mario had chosen. It looked more solitary, more aloof than the rest of them, and there was a fringe of high reeds around its edges.

He steered the boat carefully through the reeds which were so tall that they were completely hidden in a little world of their own. When they reached the shore, he took her hand and raised her gently with the one word: "Come."

She followed him like a child. He found a dry spot and spread out her coat for her. Then, as she lay down, he sat with her head in his lap. She could see his face above hers very close; could see those dark eyes set a little too close together; could feel the warm breath, wine-scented, that came from his lips.

She closed her eyes knowing that this was the moment to which everything had been leading—ever since the day in the church of Santa Prisca when she had first met Mario. She could feel his hands caressing her hair, her face, gently, gently. She felt him take her hand, felt him touch the sapphire ring.

The moment he touched the ring, she knew. She could feel it in his fingers, an outflowing, obsessive desire. The whole pattern which had seemed so complex was plain.

His hands moved upward. His fingers, still gentle, reached her throat. She didn't scream. She wasn't even frightened.

As his hands tightened their grasp, the full mouth came down upon hers, and their lips met in their first and only kiss.

Mario threw the bloodstained knife away. He hated the sight of blood and it had disgusted him that he had had to cut off a finger to get the ring.

He hadn't even bothered about the engagement ring that had belonged to Miss Lucy's mother. It was a plain, cheap affair, and for weeks now the great beauty of the sapphire had blinded him to anything else.

He spread the coat carefully over Miss Lucy's body. For a moment he considered putting it in the reeds, but it might float away and be discovered by the fishermen.

Here, on the island, it could be years before anyone came, and by that time—he glanced up at the vultures hovering eternally overhead. . . .

Without looking back Mario went to the boat and rowed towards the deserted mainland shore. There he landed, overturned the boat, and pushed it free so that it would drift into deep water.

An American woman had gone out in a boat on the lake with an inexperienced boatman. They had both been drowned. The officials would never drag so big a lake to find the bodies.

Mario made his way in the direction of the railroad track. He could board a freight car and tomorrow perhaps he would be in Guerreros.

He was sure his mother would like the ring.

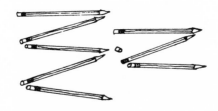

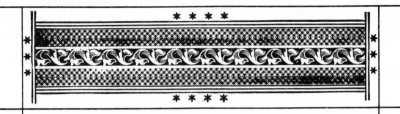

CHALLENGE TO THE READER

BY HUGH PENTECOST

Hugh Pentecost (Judson Pentecost Philips) was born in Massachusetts on August 10, 1903. He traveled widely as a child and while a sophomore at Columbia University he wrote his first short story, "Room Number Twenty-three." He wrote for the pulp magazines and is a founding member of the Mystery Writers of America, for whom he served as third president and from whom he received the Grand Master Award in 1973. He also founded the Sharon, Connecticut, Playhouse. Notable among his series characters are artist John Jericho, public-relations man Julian Quist, hotel manager Pierre Chambrun, and (as written by Judson Philips) magazine columnist Peter Styles.

THE BLOND MAN LAY on his stomach on the lawn near the edge of the lake, a newspaper spread out on the grass in front of him. A large picture of Nancy Bradford and her small daughter, Sybil, stared up at him. Of course the picture showed Nancy Bradford and her child as they had looked *before* the murder, not afterwards.

The blond man's hair and heavy eyebrows were bleached almost white, probably by the bright August sunshine. Those eyebrows were drawn together in a concentrated frown as he read the newspaper story. It was a Sunday supplement with many pictures and a long rehash of the Bradford case written by the paper's leading crime reporter. The article purported to give all the known facts in the particularly brutal and sadistic killing of the lovely actress and her small daughter. They had been beaten to death, almost out of human semblance, with a heavy iron poker. It was the opinion of the medical examiner that the murderous beating had gone on, violently, long after both mother and child were dead. It was called a crime of passion—black, turbulent, sick passion.

The murderer had been described in the usual confusing fashion by the doorman in Nancy Bradford's apartment—described as a tall, short, fair, dark, fat, thin man who wore blue-tinted glasses, a tweed topcoat in July, and a dark-gray snap-brim hat. He had come into the foyer and asked for Nancy Bradford. The doorman had pointed to the house phone, and the tall, short, fair, dark, fat, thin man had called Nancy Bradford's apartment. The doorman heard him speak. He said: "Hello, darling. It's me." He was evidently invited up because he went directly to the automatic elevator and the doorman watched the indicator needle rise to Nancy's floor.

An hour later a certain Mrs. Carpenter, whose job it was to sit with small Sybil Bradford if Nancy went out for the evening, arrived and went up to the apartment. She reappeared in the foyer presently, screaming hysterically and making no sense whatever. The doorman phoned the police after he was able to distinguish the word "murder" amidst the jumble of Mrs. Carpenter's ravings. The doorman did *not* go upstairs. He justified this on the ground of duty. But there was a result from it. The doorman could swear that the tall, short, fair, dark, fat, thin man with the blue glasses and the tweed topcoat had never left the building. He hadn't come down in the elevator and he hadn't come down the inside fire stairs which also opened into the lobby, and there wasn't any other way out. The papers had made a lot of this, but the police were not overly concerned by this mystery angle. Whatever the testimony, the man was gone—perhaps like Chesterton's postman, perhaps by magic. The puzzle of *how* was not important. The important thing was that he must be found.

There wasn't much to go on. There had been money and jewelry in the apartment. The jewelry had been taken but the money—several hundred dollars—had been left. The police were of two minds about it. The jewelry had been stolen as a blind for the real motive—or it had been a gift from the murderer which he now took back. Outside of this one clue? Well, on the floor of the Bradford apartment were two extinguished lives, two dreadfully mutilated bodies, and—two pine needles.

The blond man raised his eyes from the newspapers and turned his head toward the hotel which was set back about a hundred yards from the lake. Back of the hotel was the dark green mystery of a heavy pine forest. He stared for a long time as if he hoped somehow to penetrate the brooding darkness of the wood to some bright point of clarification. Finally he lowered his eyes to the newspaper once more.

The blond man's concentration was so intense that he was not aware of the approach of the fat man. The fat man came from the direction of the boathouse. He wore faded khaki pants, a corduroy hunting coat with deep, bulging pockets, and a battered gray hat with fishing flies stuck in the band. He was reaming out the bowl of a short, black pipe with the blade of a penknife. The operation completed, he put the stem of the pipe in his mouth and blew hard to clear it. Then he paused, his gray eyes blinking through the lenses of his steel-rimmed spectacles at the newspaper reader. He moved quietly across the grass until he stood directly over the blond man.

"Pretty gruesome business—the Bradford case," he said.

The blond man moved as if someone had jabbed a pin into him. He rolled over onto his side, braced half-upright on his elbow, staring up at the fat man, his eyes dilated, his whole attitude defensive.

151

"Sorry if I startled you," the fat man said. His smile was slow and friendly.

"I—I didn't hear you coming," the blond man said. He fished for cigarettes in the breast pocket of his blue denim shirt.

"My name is Doyle," the fat man said. "I noticed you in the hotel dining room last night. You just arrived?"

"Yes. I'm Jerry Hartman—radio writer."

Doyle grinned. "You mean—'Love that soap!'?"

"I write dramatic shows. The agencies handle the commercials."

Doyle's mild eyes moved back to the newspaper on the grass. "Maybe you knew Nancy Bradford. I understand she did a lot of radio acting."

"I never happened to meet her," Hartman said.

That seemed to end it. Doyle looked out at the shimmering expanse of the lake. "I was going out to try to catch a few bass," he said. "It's pretty sunny but there are some shady spots along the shore."

"I have a license," Hartman said, "but I don't know one fish from another."

"Same here," Doyle said. "It's just getting out and relaxing that counts. Steep in a little sun. Want to join me?"

Hartman had difficulty lighting the match for his cigarette. He finally managed and dragged the smoke deep into his lungs. "I—I don't know," he said. "I haven't any equipment. I—"

"I've got extra stuff," Doyle said. "We probably won't catch anything anyway. I just thought a little company—But if you feel like being alone—"

"I—I think I'd like it," Hartman said. He scrambled up to his feet and then bent down to pick up the paper. He rolled it up and stuck it under his arm.

"I've rented one of the rowboats," Doyle said. "You ready to start now?"

"Yes. Yes, I'm all ready if you've got some extra tackle."

"Let's go," Doyle said.

The rowboat was chained to the platform inside the boathouse. Doyle's tackle was in the back of the boat along with a small wicker hamper.

"I've got some sandwiches and a thermos of iced tea in there," Doyle said. "If you want some liquor—"

"I don't drink," Hartman said.

"And you in the radio business?" Doyle chuckled.

Hartman seemed to force a smile. "Maybe that's why. I'm on my second ulcer."

"Get in," Doyle said. "I'll row. I know a place where we might have some luck."

Hartman climbed into the back of the boat, balancing himself unsteadily. Doyle unfastened the chain and then climbed in and sat down in the middle seat. He reached out and pushed off with his hand. The boat moved slowly out of the boathouse shade into the bright sun. Once clear, Doyle fitted the oars into the oarlocks and began rowing. He used short but very powerful strokes that shot the boat forward in the water. He was the first one to speak.

"It seems impossible he could have got away without leaving a clearer trail," he said.

"Who could have got away from what?" Hartman asked.

"The Bradford murderer."

"Oh," Hartman said.

"I've toyed with the idea that the man with the blue glasses wasn't the murderer at all."

"Oh?" Hartman tossed his cigarette stub out onto the water. He watched it bob up and down in the boat's wake.

Doyle kept rowing steadily as he talked. "Suppose you were a friend of Nancy Bradford's. You went upstairs and walked into that shambles. *My* impulse would be to get away—not to be involved."

"But that couldn't have been the way it was," Hartman said.

Doyle stopped rowing, leaning forward on the oars. The boat continued to move slowly through the water. "Why not?"

"He spoke to her on the house phone," Hartman said. He tapped the newspaper which lay on the seat beside him. "The doorman heard him say 'Hello, darling. It's me.' He went right up. She must have been alive then, you see."

"Maybe the man in the glasses was bluffing."

Hartman shook his head. "If he was bluffing then he was involved anyway. No, it must have been that guy all right. Only the description of him just isn't any use. He wouldn't wear those blue glasses again. You can bank on that."

Doyle nodded slowly. "I guess you're right," he said. He began rowing again.

153

"Those pine needles," Hartman said, after a moment.

"What about 'em?"

"Well, he must have come from some place where he'd walked in pine needles. They stuck to his shoes—or maybe to the bottom of his trousers." Hartman looked back across the lake toward the pine forest behind the hotel. "Here, perhaps."

Doyle laughed. "Pleasant idea! The Bradford murderer may have been around here all the time I've been vacationing."

"It's quite possible," Hartman said. "There's the brooch."

Doyle stopped rowing. His gray eyes were fixed, unblinking, on Hartman's pale face. It was odd that Hartman's hair should be so bleached by the sun and yet his face was neither sunburned nor brown.

"What brooch?" Doyle asked.

"Why, Nancy Bradford's brooch," Hartman said. "It was found in a path in the woods here. Some local kid picked it up and turned it over to the cops."

"They found it *here*?"

"That's right. A day or two after the murder."

"How do you know that?" Doyle's voice was on a curious dead level.

"Why—I guess I read it somewhere," Hartman said.

"That's funny. I thought I'd read everything about the case and I never saw anything about the brooch."

Hartman moistened his lips. "Well, I must have read it somewhere," he said. "I wouldn't have any other way of knowing."

"No," Doyle said, slowly. "No, I suppose not." He started rowing again, the rhythm a little slower than before. "If they found the brooch here you'd think the place would be swarming with detectives."

Hartman's smile was forced. "Maybe it is," he said. "They wouldn't necessarily come out in the open for fear of scaring off their man."

"Yes," Doyle said, "I suppose they would handle it that way. Since they have no way of identifying the man, they'd just lie low till he made a mistake."

"What kind of mistake?"

"I don't know," Doyle said. "Probably they don't either. They'd just wait and hope." He pulled on the right oar and headed the boat in toward the shore. "Good shady place over there," he said, nodding toward a clump of willows whose branches spread shadow well over the water. When he had his bearings he started pulling on the oars again. He smiled. "You wouldn't kid me, would you, Hartman? About being a radio writer?"

"Well, it's a secret," Hartman said, in a mock-confidential tone, "but I'm really a junior G-man."

They both laughed.

Doyle pulled the boat into the shade of the willows. Then he shipped his oars and climbed to the bow of the boat. He lowered an anchor which was fastened to the boat by a heavy chain. Hartman looked over the side at a colony of water bugs that flitted across the dark blue surface of the lake.

"Push that box of tackle forward and I'll bait a line for you," Doyle said.

There was a can of damp earth from which Doyle extracted worms. He fastened one to each hook on the two lines and handed one line to Hartman. They dropped the lines over the side and the little tan floats bobbed away from the side of the boat. Doyle hooked his line around one of the oarlocks and began filling his pipe.

"How would you go about it, Hartman, if you were a detective?" he asked.

Hartman shrugged. "There isn't much to go on. The doorman's description wouldn't give you any particular physical type to look for."

"Not much."

"About all you'd have to go on from the physical side is that he is extremely strong. It was a man of considerable strength who beat those two into a pulp."

Doyle held a match to the bowl of his pipe. "Not necessarily," he said, after the pipe was going. "I believe it's a medical fact that people who are worked into a homicidal rage often show evidence of strength far beyond their normal capacity. Something to do with the adrenal glands."

"I wouldn't know about that," Hartman said. He looked out across the water. "Say, looks like you have something."

The float on Doyle's line was ducking sharply below the surface. Doyle began to pull in the line. Rock bass don't put up much of a fight. For a moment the silver scales of the fish gleamed in the sunlight and then Doyle hauled it aboard.

"There was a kind of savage cruelty involved in that beating," Doyle said. "I think you could expect to see it crop up in the man in other directions." When Hartman didn't answer he glanced up. The blond man was staring at Doyle, who was holding the bass in one hand and wrenching at the hook in the fish's mouth with the other.

"Stuck good," Doyle said. He gave it another wrench and pulled it free, ripping out the side of the fish's mouth with it. Then he took a short piece of baling wire, jammed it through the fish's gill and out through the mouth. He twisted the wire together so that the fish hung from a loop. He attached the other end of the wire to an oarlock and dropped the fish over the side so that it dragged in the water and would keep fresh there. There had been a kind of ruthless efficiency about it. He looked up and saw the revulsion in Hartman's blue eyes.

"They don't feel anything," he said. "Cold-blooded." He rebaited his hook and dropped the line over the side. "You were saying you'd expect to see some evidence of a cruel streak in the man you'd be looking for—if you were a detective."

"Yes," Hartman said. "Yes—I think you could expect that."

"Not a nice guy to find yourself with alone," Doyle said.

"No . . . not nice at all."

They fished in silence for a long time. The fish weren't biting. Then Hartman glanced down the lake. The sky had taken on a peculiar copper hue. Doyle followed the direction of Hartman's glance and whistled. "Looks like a thunderstorm," he said. "Maybe we better think about getting in. Those things get pretty bad out here on the lake."

"Do you think we can make the hotel before it breaks?"

"We can try," Doyle said. "Here, I'll take in the lines and get things organized. You want to pull up the anchor and start rowing?"

"Okay," Hartman said. He squeezed past Doyle to the bow of the boat. He took hold of the anchor chain with both hands and pulled. Nothing happened. He stopped trying after a moment, breathing hard. "Seems to be caught in something," he said. He took a lower grip on the chain and tried pulling again. He looked back at Doyle. "I'm afraid I can't budge it," he said.

Doyle finished packing away the lines in the wicker hamper and closed the lid. "You come back here and I'll take a whack at it," he said.

156

The boat rocked slightly as Hartman made his way to the stern seat. Then Doyle worked his way forward and took hold of the anchor chain. As he began pulling at it, the cords stood out in his neck, the corduroy coat seemed to bulge at the shoulders. He didn't yank at the chain. He just applied a steady, powerful pressure. Suddenly he staggered back slightly, the anchor free. In the distance there was the deep, ominous rumble of thunder.

Doyle climbed back into the seat at the oars, grinning. There was a curious tense look about the corners of Hartman's mouth.

"I believe you said the murderer was a strong guy," Doyle said, and laughed. He put out the oars and began rowing back toward the hotel. A jagged streak of lightning split the sky.

Hartman fumbled for a cigarette and lit it. He kept glancing over his shoulder at the approaching storm. Doyle rowed with long, even, powerful strokes. The sun was still bright where they were, but the storm was coming rapidly. At the far end of the lake they could see sheets of rain.

"Of course the murderer would be smarter than that," Doyle said.

"Smarter than what?" Hartman's voice sounded tense, a little frightened.

"To show his strength—since that's what the police would be looking for."

"Oh."

"He might even pretend that he had no strength at all. Now, if I were the murderer I'd have done what you did."

"What I did?"

"Demonstrated that I couldn't do something—like lift an anchor."

"I see." Hartman took a deep drag on his cigarette. "That *would* be the clever thing."

Doyle rowed for a moment in silence. Then he smiled disarmingly. "That anchor wasn't stuck very tight," he said. "I made it look tougher than it was."

"Why?" Hartman asked, sharply.

"Just a gag, Hartman. The idea amuses me."

"What idea?"

"That we're both probably wondering a little bit about each other."

Lightning struck across the sky again and a sudden gust of

157

wind sent water chopping against the side of the boat.

Doyle was still smiling. "Do you ever wear tinted glasses, Hartman? Most blonds suffer from bright sunshine. Wrong pigmentation."

"Look," Hartman said, "I don't think this gag of yours is very funny."

"Sorry," Doyle said. His smile faded. "I'm afraid we're going to get good and soaked."

Hartman felt a faint spatter of rain against his face. They were still a good five hundred yards from shore. A fork of lightning shot down into the water not far from them and the clap of thunder set the boat vibrating. Doyle kept on with his rowing as if nothing had happened. Hartman's hands were gripping the sides of the boat, his knuckles white.

"Scared?" Doyle asked.

"Not really. But I don't like thunderstorms. Never did."

"Must be a little bit like what happened to the Bradford murderer," Doyle said. "A calm, sunny day—and then—the wrath of God!" He took a deep full stroke with the oars. "Why do you suppose he did it, Hartman? A beautiful woman —charming little girl—"

"Some people can't stand treachery," Hartman said.

The oars remained suddenly poised over the water—water that seemed to have begun to boil slightly. "Treachery?" Doyle said.

"That's the way some men would look at a turndown," Hartman said.

The oars dipped slowly again and Doyle continued his rowing. Lightning and thunder seemed suddenly to engulf them. The rain came—hard—almost painful in the sharpness of its drive. Doyle increased the rhythm of his rowing but he threw his head back, laughing.

"What's the joke?" Hartman shouted at him.

"Your hair!" Doyle shouted back.

"What about my hair?"

Doyle's laughter rang out over the noise of the storm. "I thought it was dyed. So help me, Hartman, I thought it was dyed. I thought the color would run when it got wet."

Hartman lifted his hand to his soaking hair and brought it away again, staring at it as if he, too, expected something odd.

"Everybody always says that . . ." he explained.

And then Doyle nosed the boat into the sanctuary of the

boathouse. They sat there, protected from the rain, wiping the water from their faces. Doyle took off his glasses and tried drying them with a damp handkerchief.

"Boy, that really came down!"

Hartman nodded.

"You said you didn't drink, Hartman, but after that soaking maybe you should have something—for medicinal purposes. I've got a bottle of old brandy up in my room."

"Really," Hartman said, "I don't think—"

"Do you good," Doyle said. "You don't want to get chilled."

"Well—"

They walked up across the lawn to the hotel. There was no point in hurrying. They'd never be any wetter than they were now. They crossed the wide porch and went into the big main hall. The water ran off their clothes and made little puddles on the floor. The corner of Hartman's mouth twitched.

"Suppose we each get a quick shower and rubdown before that drink," he said.

Doyle nodded. "Perhaps that's a good idea. But make it snappy. My room's Number Eleven on the second floor."

"See you," Hartman said.

Hartman went to his room. He stripped off his clothes and dropped them on the bathroom floor. He got under the hot shower in the tub and stood there till he was thoroughly warmed. Then he got out and dried himself with a rough bath towel. He walked, naked, into his room and opened the middle bureau drawer. He put on dry socks and underwear, a clean blue flannel shirt. From the closet he got dry trousers and shoes and a worn tweed jacket. Then he stood in front of the mirror and brushed his light blond hair. His mouth twitched again as he looked at his reflection. After he put down his brush and comb he held out his hands in front of him. They were shaking.

Then Hartman pulled open one of the top bureau drawers and moved a pile of handkerchiefs. Under them was a small thirty-two caliber revolver. He slipped it, along with a fresh package of cigarettes and matches, into the right-hand pocket of the tweed coat. Then he looked at his shaking hands once more and swore softly.

Hartman paused outside the door of Room Eleven and then knocked. He heard Doyle call out to him.

159

"Come on in!"

He opened the door and went in. He could hear water running in the bathtub.

"I got soaking wet here," Doyle called out through the half-open bathroom door. "It felt so good. Be with you in a minute."

"That's okay," Hartman said.

"The brandy's on the bureau. Help yourself."

"Thanks."

Hartman walked over to the bureau. The bottle of brandy and two water glasses stood on the white linen bureau cover. Hartman glanced toward the bathroom. The water was still running in the tub. He reached out—not toward the bottle but toward the top bureau drawer. He pulled the drawer open. He drew in his breath, sharply.

Lying on top of a stack of clean shirts were some photographs—theatrical photographs of Nancy Bradford. They'd been mutilated. Some of them were torn, some of them had been defaced with a heavy black crayon. Hartman picked them up. His hands shook so that the heavy photographic paper rattled in his fingers. Then he heard a faint squeaking noise. He dropped the pictures and swung around. His right hand dove into the pocket of his coat and came out holding the revolver.

"Well, well," Doyle said. He stood in the bathroom doorway, fully dressed. The sound of the water, still running in the tub, came from behind him. And he, too, was holding a gun, quite steadily, pointed at Hartman. "I had a feeling you'd snoop if you had the chance."

Hartman drew a deep breath. He spoke in a loud, very clear voice. "So you're the Bradford murderer," he said.

Doyle's mouth smiled, but the eyes behind the steel-rimmed spectacles were cold. "It won't work, Hartman," he said.

"I knew it," Hartman said, "when I saw you unhook that fish. I knew it when you pulled up that anchor. I knew it when you kept probing and probing to find out who I was. I knew it the way you reacted to my telling you about the brooch."

"It won't work, Hartman," Doyle said.

"How do you explain these pictures of Nancy Bradford in your bureau drawer?"

"They came from Nancy Bradford's apartment." Then Doyle said, still smiling, "The murderer had to destroy even

160

the symbols of Nancy Bradford. You must have hated her like hell, Hartman!"

"It was *you* who hated her," Hartman said. "Even after you'd murdered her you had to go on destroying everything that reminded you of her." His voice was loud, like an attorney addressing a courtroom.

"You ought to know," Doyle said. "You ought to know how the murderer felt. You even told me, Hartman. Some men would think of a turndown as treachery, you said."

"It was you, Doyle. You've been staying around here because you'd lost the brooch. You didn't know whether it had been found or not. No one knew that but the police."

"That's right, Hartman. No one knew but the police. You were fishing when you brought it up. You wanted to know if it *had* been found. You were trying to find out from me because you'd decided that maybe I was a cop looking for you. Well, you were right. I *was* looking for you."

Hartman laughed. "I'll bet you were," he said.

"The pretense that you weren't strong enough to lift the anchor. Your pretended squeamishness when I yanked that hook out of the bass's mouth. I did that on purpose—just to see how you'd behave. You're a good actor, Hartman."

"This isn't getting us anywhere," Hartman said. "You'd better drop that gun."

"You've been in the radio and theater business, Hartman. You knew how easy it would be to fool the doorman at Nancy Bradford's apartment. You made yourself noticeable going in and unnoticeable coming out."

"Drop that gun," Hartman said.

Doyle laughed. "Stop kidding," he said. "It won't work, Hartman." He took a step forward.

Suddenly thunder shook the room—the thunder of two guns fired almost simultaneously. The two men stood there, swaying, pulling the triggers of the two guns. Slowly Hartman slumped to his knees, a bewildered, frightened look on his face. The smoking gun fell out of his hand and he pitched forward on his face.

Doyle leaned against the door jamb. There were bright red stains spreading on the front of his white shirt. He coughed—a wet, choking cough.

There were excited voices in the hall outside and the sound of running feet. The door burst open and the clerk and the

161

hotel porter, in a blue uniform, burst into the room. They stopped just inside the door staring at the man on the floor—and at Doyle.

Doyle coughed. "He was the Bradford murderer," he said. He coughed again. "I'd been looking for him—special assignment."

The porter crossed the room and knelt beside Hartman. Presently he stood up. His face was very pale. "Dead," he said. He looked at Doyle. "You look as though you were pretty badly hurt," he said. "You better lie down on the bed while we get you a doctor." He walked over to Doyle.

"I—I feel a little sick at my stomach," Doyle said, smiling weakly.

The porter reached him. Then suddenly the porter's left hand knocked the gun from Doyle's flabby fingers and his right smashed squarely against Doyle's mouth in a pile-driving punch. Doyle staggered back and fell on the bathroom floor.

"Special assignment!" the porter shouted. "Special assignment for murder—you crazy killer!" He turned to the hotel clerk. From his pocket he took a small leather folder and opened it, disclosing a police badge. "There's your Bradford murderer," he said, pointing at Doyle. "Hartman was a homicide man. We worked as a team." His voice was bitter. "Why wasn't I around when they came in? He might have passed the tip to me. I might have saved him." He looked down at Hartman's body. "Poor guy! He was always scared as hell on a job like this—but he never flinched—never took a backward step."

The clerk's eyes moved from the body of Hartman to the still figure of Doyle.

"Why—why did he k-kill Nancy Bradford?" It was almost a whisper.

"He was her first husband," the homicide man said. "A paranoid killer. She'd been hiding from him—changed her name—remarried. Then he showed up—seemed all right—wanted to see his child. She thought he was cured—everything all right. Then—"

"Maybe—maybe I b-better get a d-doctor for him," the clerk said.

"Let the—let him die," the homicide man said, grimly. "It'll save the state a lot of dough."

THE HOUSE-IN-YOUR-HAND MURDER

BY ROY VICKERS

Roy Vickers was born in England in 1889 and attended
Oxford. A long-time journalist, court reporter, and editor
of *Novel Magazine,* he published his first novel as a serial
in the *Daily Mail.* His first fiction had little success in
America until Ellery Queen discovered one of his "in-
verted" detective stories, "The Rubber Trumpet," in an
old magazine and reprinted it in *Ellery Queen's Mystery
Magazine* in November 1943. This was followed by a
number of stories about the Department of Dead Ends.
Among his most successful novels is *The Girl in the News,*
published in 1938 and filmed by Carol Reed two years
later. Vickers died in 1965.

THE MURDER OF Albert Henshawk, headlined as the House-in-Your-Hand Mystery, became a test case for plainclothes constables who had put in for promotion. It is still used to emphasize that the most trivial remark of a murderer—such as a comment on a work of commercial art—may contain the raw material of a clue.

Henshawk, who specialized in financing the purchase of houses, had been running an advertisement showing, in an outstretched palm, a picturesque country cottage, with the slogan: *A House in Your Hand is Worth Two in the Clouds.* It is noteworthy that the picture in the advertisement was a photograph of a model. The whole model, including the outstretched hand, covered an area about equal to that of a pocket handkerchief. It was kept in Henshawk's office under a glass dome, flanked by the bronze statuette with which Henshawk was battered to death. It is an ironical comment on this amiable egotist that the statuette was the work of Henshawk, and the subject—Henshawk himself.

A tubby, chubby little man in the early forties, he was naïvely proud of himself and his not inconsiderable talent as an artist. "Neat bit of work, that model, eh! Supplied the idea myself," he would say, if you were a business acquaintance. Your attention would be directed to the seventeenth-century thatched cottage, to the oaks on one side of it, to the sloping meadow in which a cow drank at a sluggish brook, to a somewhat startling confusion of farm stock in the foreground.

"And, mind you, it isn't a studio fake, except for those pigs and things. Made from a drawing. A little effort of my own." You were urged to inspect a charcoal drawing—complete with farm stock but minus the outstretched palm—hung in a somewhat elaborate frame. "Of course, I'm only an amateur, but you can see it's drawn from life."

The last statement was confirmed, after the murder, by a number of experts, consulted independently. Each said, in his own words, that if the model had been a work of fancy it would have exhibited certain essential differences. Architects, also consulted independently, passed the house as structurally and historically correct; surveyors agreed that the layout of the land contained no absurdity.

The murder took place on February sixteenth, 1938, at about six forty-five, in Henshawk's office in Gorlay House, Westminster. After lunching at the Redmoon Restaurant, Henshawk had spent the afternoon at his club, discussing business with an official of a big investment trust, for which he was, in effect, an agent.

At a few minutes past six, when his staff had left, with the exception of his secretary, he entered his room by the private door, which opened directly on the corridor. In the wall on your right as you entered by this door was another door, now ajar, to the staff room, in which Miss Birdridge was waiting.

She heard his key, then his voice talking to a companion. Of the latter she had only an oblique view. But she was able to state that he was between forty and fifty, of medium height, regular features, and with an iron-gray mustache.

"I must have a word with my secretary—shan't be a minute," Henshawk was saying. "Suppose you look about until I get back. I think you'll be pleased." He went into the staff room, leaving the communicating door open.

"Miss Birdridge, I simply must get that report off tonight. So will you go and have a meal right away, and be back here at seven sharp." Henshawk had a booming voice: the other man must have overheard him. "Oh, and you might 'phone Mrs. Henshawk that I shan't be home till about ten and I'll eat in Town."

There was nothing unusual in this. Miss Birdridge was a middle-aged woman with no home ties, who appreciated a restaurant dinner at the firm's expense and the extra payment for late work. Henshawk lingered in the doorway while she reported an item of minor importance, but she noticed that his attention had shifted to the other room.

"Ah! It caught your eye at once, old man. Neat bit of work, eh! Made from that drawing of mine on the wall there."

Then the other man's voice: "But, my dear fellow, that damned cow spoils the whole thing! And why is it perched on a giant's hand? Makes it look like a cartoon."

"You're not far off. I've been using it for an advertisement display. I felt sure you wouldn't mind. After all—"

At that point the communicating door was closed. Miss Birdridge was sure that it was exactly at that point, and sure

165

that she had reported the exact words used by each man.

She went out to dinner, returning as Big Ben was striking seven. In the meantime the communicating door had been used and was again ajar. A couple of minutes later, having equipped herself for work on the report, she went into the inner office, to find Henshawk sprawling face downwards over his chair, patently murdered. She observed no more than this before rushing back into the outer office and calling the police.

By midnight, Detective Inspector Karslake had a clear outline. For about forty minutes, during which he had smoked four of Henshawk's cigarettes, the murderer had sat in the client's chair, with his back to both doors.

At about six forty, Henshawk's wife had knocked on the private door. Henshawk had opened the door but had stepped into the corridor to speak to her. He told her, she said, that he was engaged with a client, so could not take her home. He himself expected to be home late.

Over her husband's shoulder Mrs. Henshawk had seen a man sitting in the client's chair with his back towards her. She did not take particular notice of him, because, she said, being a client he was of no interest to her. She was somewhat hurt because her husband had apparently forgotten that he had asked her to call for him at the office.

After getting rid of his wife, Henshawk had probably sat down again in his chair. But a few minutes later he had got up and turned his back, whereupon the other had struck him on the back of the head with the statuette, causing almost instant death.

At the cupboard-toilette the murderer had washed bloodstains from his hands. He had not removed bloodstains from the soap well. He had left the statuette immersed in the basin.

Although his time was running perilously short, he had lingered in order to remove a drawing from its frame on the wall. As this drawing was the original from which the House-In-Your-Hand model was made, the incident gave emphasis to the remark, overheard by Miss Birdridge, seeming to connect the deceased with the cottage depicted in the model.

The murderer left by the outer office, within two minutes of seven o'clock, carrying the drawing loosely wrapped in tissue paper. In the hall he asked the porter to call him a taxi. He was getting into it when Miss Birdridge returned,

166

though she noticed no more than that a man was getting into a taxi, carrying something flat and loosely wrapped in tissue paper. He told the driver to take him to the Westminster Station of the Underground. Nothing further was known of his movements.

"The porter is no good, sir," said young Rawlings. "All he can do is a 'middle aged, middle height, middling well-dressed gentleman with a mustache'—which of course will be shaved off by now."

"Never mind his mustache—he has practically left us his address, hasn't he?" snorted Karslake. He had recently had several big successes and was becoming a trifle didactic.

"Yes, sir—that cottage!" said Rawlings, who had not yet learned how to handle seniors.

"I guessed that myself," snapped Karslake. "Where is that cottage? What's it called?"

Rawlings slunk away and woke Miss Birdridge by calling her on the telephone.

But Miss Birdridge did not know, had always thought the cottage was an imaginary one until she had overheard the murderer's reference to it. Next he rang Mrs. Henshawk, who was equally unhelpful. Her husband was a prolific amateur artist, but she knew nothing about art and he never talked to her about his hobby.

"All right then—we'll advertise for that cottage," said Karslake. "The papers will make a news story of it, with picture. Warn all stations in the U.K. to study that picture in the Press and report to us if the cottage is in their district."

In his Appreciation for the Chief, Karslake wrote: "An unpremeditated murder (cigarettes) by a man on familiar terms with deceased, who was urging Henshawk to do something important enough to make the latter forget his appointment with his wife (Mrs. Henshawk's admitted annoyance). Mrs. Henshawk's interruption broke the trend of their talk. Henshawk rejected the proposition, whereupon the other lost his temper and struck with the nearest object, not necessarily intending to kill. The murderer owns, or has some direct or indirect interest in, the cottage (theft of drawing: remark reported by Miss Birdridge—'I felt sure you wouldn't mind' i.e., use of cottage as advertisement). There should be little difficulty in tracing such a cottage."

Karslake had Miss Birdridge's report under his hand as he

167

wrote. Yet he missed the clue-value of that other remark about "that damned cow."

True, the murder was, in the legal sense, unpremeditated. But it might be argued that Harold Ledlaw had been unconsciously premeditating the murder for eighteen years, though he did not know that the victim would be Henshawk.

Ledlaw had been waiting outside Gorlay House expecting Henshawk to leave at the end of the office day. But he spotted him at once when he stepped out of the taxi that brought him from the club.

"Hullo, Albert! . . . Dammit, you've forgotten me!"

"I certainly have *not*—" a second's pause "—Harold Ledlaw, of course." He was pumping the other's hand. "You've changed a lot, old man, but I'd have known you at once anywhere. I suppose we shall both soon be what they call middle-aged. Well, I'm jiggered! We must fix something. Are you staying long?"

"I'm not going back to Canada. It has done me proud, but I'm back for keeps. I landed last week. Been getting acclimatized. I'm counting on you to give me the low-down on one thing and another."

"Look here, I'm rushed off my feet, but come up to the office for a few minutes and we'll fix something."

They ignored the lift and walked to the first floor, exchanging the commonplaces of an almost forgotten friendship, for Ledlaw had been in Canada for nearly eighteen years.

At the first pause, which occurred just outside Henshawk's private door, Ledlaw said:

"Whiddon Cottage! I heard some of the timber had been cut. Can you tell me anything about it?"

"It so happens I can tell you quite a lot about it—though I'm not in touch with—er—anyone." He unlocked the private door, said that he must speak to his secretary and, with a fatuous archness, invited the other to look about the office.

The first thing one noticed in that office was the model under its glass dome. Ledlaw stared at it, at first in confusion, then with full recognition.

"My God, what damned cheek, and what the hell does it mean!" he muttered under his breath, then warned himself that he must keep his temper. Albert Henshawk was braying at him from the doorway: he must say something in reply.

168

"But, my dear fellow, that damned cow spoils the whole thing!" Ledlaw heard his own voice making the protest, and asking what the hand meant, and Henshawk telling him it was a sort of advertisement.

"I felt sure you wouldn't mind. After all, a place like that belongs, at least in its artistic aspect—well, it belongs to England, don't you think! It symbolizes the urban Englishman's dream of home. And that's my line of business now, Harold—helping the hard-up middle-class to own their homes. I had to put those beastly animals in afterwards on the advice of the advertising experts. You see, the town dweller always fancies he'll do a spot of spare-time farming, the stock to look after itself and pay off the mortgage."

There was a good deal of it, but Ledlaw barely listened. He had already decided that they would not "fix something." He would find out the two things he had come to find out, and then he need never see Henshawk again.

"You were going to tell me about the timber, Albert."

"Ah! Wheels within wheels! I have not seen—er—Mrs. Ledlaw. But I heard last year through a mutual acquaintance—a woman you don't know—that your daughter, Harold, wants to be a doctor. Let's see, she's nearly eighteen now, isn't she? That's a seven-year course. Well—er—my informant said that you would not be asked to make any further contribution. So Mrs. Ledlaw decided to sell the timber in Swallowbath Rise. Mind you, it won't affect the look of the place, being the other side of the hill."

He had been speaking with some awkwardness which now slipped away.

"When I heard this, I thought perhaps Mrs. Ledlaw might want to sell the whole outfit, as I knew you had bought it outright for her. I went down to see her last year, but she was on holiday and the place was shut up. So I thought I'd sketch it. I wrote to her asking if it was in the market and got a reply, written in the third person, saying no. I don't suppose she remembers me. I haven't seen her since—well, *since*."

So that was that! He had the right to see that his daughter took her medical course in comfort. Now for that other question that must be approached circuitously. Twenty past six. He would have to hurry or he might fumble the showdown he had planned—if indeed it was to be a showdown, of which he was not yet certain.

169

"There's another thing I want to ask you, Albert. You perhaps remember that, when Ruth divorced me, I withdrew the defense I had previously entered denying infidelity. I then vamoosed to Canada. I want to know whether you believed what that Valerie Carmaen said—that I had been her lover?"

"Really, Harold, after all these years!" Henshawk was definitely embarrassed.

"You knew her. And you knew she was the kind of dirt I wouldn't touch if she were the only female left in the world."

"Yes, yes, Harold! Just as you say!"

"Then you believe she faked that bedroom incident—that my original pleading, which I showed you, stated the truth?"

"Of course, I believe it if you say so! Didn't I tell you at the time that I believed you! I wondered why you didn't go on with the defense." .

"I withdrew the defense because Ruth made it clear that, whatever was proved in court, she would believe me guilty. That broke me up, Albert. Ruth and I hadn't started too well. The first few months had been difficult. But we were just getting right. Life was going to be grand. And then this thing happened." .

"But it's more than eighteen years ago, old man!"

"To me it's as if it were yesterday. I know it's an obsession and not quite sane, and all that. But all these years, when I've not been actually working, I've felt much as I felt at the time—humiliated, washed up, finished."

Henshawk was making soothing noises. He looked sympathetic, not afraid. Perhaps, thought Ledlaw, there was no reason why he should be afraid. Perhaps the information he had received about Henshawk had been incorrect. He glanced at the clock—he would know in a few minutes.

"Have you any idea why that girl picked on me? I didn't like her, but I never insulted her. She had no reason to hate me."

"No, of course not! You shouldn't let your mind dwell on it, old man. What about seeing a good psychiatrist?"

"She didn't hate me. She just used me callously because she wanted to be divorced."

He was not thinking now of Henshawk. In the grip of his obsession, he repeated the words he had been repeating for eighteen years.

"She had an income in her own right and could have fixed

it with a professional co-respondent for a tenner and a little bother. But what she did to me is worse than positive cruelty, which at least has the excuse of malice or perversion. I think of that woman as the lowest moral type—a moral slug."

"You're working yourself up, Harold. It's bad for you, and it's very distressing for me—ah, excuse me!"

There had come a knock on the private door—the knock for which Ledlaw had been waiting. Both glanced at the clock. It was twenty-two minutes to seven.

Henshawk went to the door. Ledlaw remained still, his back—as Superintedent Karslake had inferred—to both doors. He would let her get well into the room before he turned and faced her. And if she were not *the* woman, he would just acknowledge the introduction and go.

"I am in conference," he heard Henshawk say.

Too late, Ledlaw turned round. Henshawk had stepped into the corridor and was speaking to her there. Ledlaw could see neither. He sprang up, intending to thrust himself into the corridor. But Henshawk had already returned alone and shut the door.

"Only an anxious client! Look here, I don't want to turn you out, old man, but I must get some work ready for my secretary who will be back presently. What about dining with me at the club tomorrow night?"

Ledlaw saw that a simple bluff would give him the answer he must have.

" 'An anxious client,' you said, Albert. Why did you say it?"

"I don't get you, old man."

"Was it your wife, Albert? I ask, because I sent Mrs. Henshawk a wire in your name asking her to call here at six-thirty. I 'phoned it from the Redmoon—where you were lunching. She was a little late." He paused, decided it was safe to add: "I saw her face, Albert. I must apologize for having called *your wife* a moral slug."

Ledlaw got up, actually intending to go. The love of self-torture that accompanies such an obsession as his had something new to feed on. Fate had used him even more vilely than he had known, for Henshawk had been his friend since school days.

But Henshawk, the frank egotist who had delighted in making a statuette of himself, could not endure the loss of face.

171

"I am sorry you saw Valerie. It can only deepen the tragedy for all three of us. To know all, Harold, is to forgive all. I want you to sit down again and let me explain."

"Go ahead." Ledlaw dropped back into the client's chair. "It might be amusing to hear why she smashed up my life to save herself a tenner. Why, surely, she could have got the tenner from you! And you'd have gladly taken all the bother off her hands."

"I didn't know what she was doing until she had done it," Henshawk began. "And I didn't know the man was you until you yourself told me. It all originated in my refusal to deceive her husband. I'm like that, as you know—I can't bear anything underhand. Well, I went to Carmaen and asked him to divorce her and let us marry. If ever there was a dog-in-the-manger it was Carmaen. He refused. But, being a beast, he gave Valerie to understand that, if it was anybody but myself, he would gladly divorce her. I happened to mention that I had recommended that hotel when you had to run down to Frensmouth for the night, and Valerie ran down too—but without my knowledge."

"But what about your knowledge when I showed you the writ and my defense? You didn't believe that I had been her lover?"

"No, of course not! Naturally, I put it to Valerie. And she refused to budge an inch. Said it was entirely her affair, and that I could take what attitude I pleased. What could I do? Telling you about it wouldn't have made any difference."

"Yet you married her! Built your marriage on the ruin of mine!"

"Ruin of my grandmother's aunt!" exploded Henshawk. Both were standing, glaring at each other across the table. "Can't you see you're pulling your own leg? Ever asked yourself why Ruth didn't believe you? Of *course* she believed you! Your marriage had crashed. D'you think I didn't know that much? Ruth couldn't stick you any longer, and she jumped at the chance of release which Valerie had given her."

To Ledlaw the words brought horrifying self-suspicion, the glimpse of an utterly unbearable truth. As Henshawk turned his back, Ledlaw snatched up the object nearest his hand and struck. He struck at the image of a self-pitying poltroon, at himself posing and strutting for eighteen years in order to hide from himself the truth that his wife had been unable to endure his affection—that she had been driven to a mean escape.

But what he had actually done was to kill Henshawk.

Returning clarity brought, not remorse, but renewed self-pity.

"Just my luck! I lost my head for half a second and now I shall be hanged."

Not death, but the dreadful ritual of trial and execution, awakened self-preservation. He remembered the danger of fingerprints. When he had washed his hands, he refilled the basin and put the statuette in it. With Henshawk's sponge he wiped the ashtray and the arms of the chair.

"That secretary may have heard him blithering to me about the cottage. I shall be hanged! Steady! I shall just have to bet she didn't hear—or that he hasn't told anybody where it is."

He stood over the model, wondering whether there would be any safety in smashing it.

"That damned cow!" Taut nerves and muscles suddenly relaxed, and he giggled like a schoolgirl. A moment later he had sobered and turned to the charcoal drawing on the wall.

"It looks more realistic without the hand. And the damned cow isn't so pronounced." About to pass on, he turned back on impulse, dipped his hands in the basin and removed the drawing from its frame.

"The outer office would be better—more people turn the handles." With hands still wet he opened the communicating door. In the outer office he caught up a piece of tissue paper and wrapped it loosely round the drawing.

Downstairs the porter was loafing about the hall. If he were to try to slink past, the fellow might think he had stolen the drawing. What was the most ordinary and natural thing to do?

"Get me a taxi, please."

In the taxi he checked his first impulse to leave the drawing under the mat. That drawing must be burned—the mill board was too stiff to be torn in small pieces. He re-wrapped it in the tissue paper.

At Westminster he traveled by Underground to Earl's Court. He was staying at the Teneriffe Hotel, near the station. He emptied a dispatch case and put the drawing in it. He would take it out to the countryside and burn it tomorrow. He had the illusion of forgetting Henshawk and his own peril. Active thought was suspended. He dined in the hotel,

173

and afterwards went back to the West End to a music hall.

The next morning the London editions carried the photograph of the model. When Ledlaw opened a paper over breakfast he instantly accepted failure.

With a certain coolness he worked out how arrest would come. Ruth would see the picture and the police appeal. As a respectable citizen, she would write to Scotland Yard. A detective would call, would learn from her that she had passed her childhood in the cottage, that her father had been compelled to sell it, that some years later, on her marriage, her husband had bought it and made it over to her, that they had lived in it for a short time. Then the divorce and his departure to Canada. They would hardly need to trace him through the bank. The shipping lists would show that he had arrived six days ago and put up at the Teneriffe Hotel.

At a guess, he would have about forty-eight hours—at worst, twenty-four, unless Ruth telephoned, which was improbable.

Before he died, he wanted to see his daughter. Even more than that, he wanted to know whether Henshawk's taunt had any foundation. In short, he would go at once to the cottage and see Ruth, whether she wanted to see him or not.

In his baggage were some things he had left in his will—a photograph album of snapshots he had taken during their first year, a packet of her letters to him before marriage, a rare edition of *Canterbury Tales* which her father had given him. In half an hour he had sorted them out.

He put them in the dispatch case on top of the drawing, which no longer had any importance. In his sense of defeat, he thought only that he had been a fool for his pains in bringing it away. He had forgotten that Ruth would be sure to recognize the photograph of the model at once. And she would remember Henshawk's name.

He would take no further precautions against arrest. He would not even shave his mustache.

By the middle of the morning, he was in the train for Hallery-on-Thames. There was no taxi at the little station and no car to be hired in the village, so he had to walk the half mile along the towpath and then tackle the stiff climb up the hillside.

He was hot when he arrived at Whiddon Cottage, and stopped to rest a minute by the oaks. While he was getting his breath, he reflected, with the self-conscious wistfulness of

174

one who believes that his days are numbered, that the beauty of Whidden was even greater than his memory of it. Set high on a hill on the edge of the Berkshire Downs, it had a clear view of undulating country for fifteen miles. To the rear of the cottage the downland sloped half a mile in a green carpet to the Thames. And now for Ruth.

She opened the door to him. She was a tall woman who had once been pretty and was now handsome, but with an air of masterfulness that was not romantically attractive. Yet at sight of him, he thought, she had looked afraid.

"Harold! Why have you come?" Her tone was reproachful, but not unfriendly.

"I want to see Aileen. I imagine you will not raise objections."

"Of course not! But she's away for a few days with friends."

"I also wanted to see you. May I?"

It was ridiculously formal, not in the least as he had planned. It chilled them both into small talk. She offered him lunch, and he said he had already lunched, which was untrue. They chattered about Canada and London. He congratulated her on her success as an author.

"Well, of course, only students read my books and only a few of those, though I get good reviews. Harold, is that man who has been murdered the Henshawk you used to know?"

"Yes. You've seen the paper, I gather. I rather took it for granted that you had already notified. Scotland Yard. I knew you must recognize the picture, in spite of the pigs and hens and that preposterous cow."

"*Harold?*"

"Yes, Ruth—I killed him." She had guessed before he said it. He added. "Did you know that he married Valerie Carmaen?"

She winced at the name. "No. But that was no reason for killing him."

"He knew that woman had borne false witness against me. I accused him of building his marriage on the ruin of mine. And I lost my temper when he said that you, too, knew it was false—that you had jumped at the chance of getting rid of me. Did you, Ruth?"

She was long in answering. His own tension had vanished. It was as if he were no longer interested in her answer.

"I believed her evidence at the time. But after a few years

I began to suspect I was wrong. It would be meaningless to say that I am sorry. As young lovers—well, we were not successful, Harold. In our maturity, I can feel deep friendship as well as gratitude for your generosity."

"Well, my dear, that's that! This case—" he placed the dispatch case by the side of the huge open hearth "—contains a few purely personal knicknacks you might like to keep. I'll leave it." He got up to go.

"Will you be caught, Harold?"

"Yes, I think so. Someone will bring them to this cottage, and then they're bound to find me. I wish I could have seen Aileen."

"If they come here I shall do everything I can to put them off. You may say you do not wish me to make sacrifices on your behalf. I am thinking of Aileen and—frankly—my public, small though it is. If you are tried, and if you give your reason for—doing what you did—the scandal will hurt us both. I want to do everything we can both do—to ensure your escape."

Three quarters of a mile away, the village police sergeant was advising Scotland Yard of the existence of the seventeenth-century cottage, known as Whiddon Cottage, identical in appearance with that in the published picture.

There are more seventeenth-century cottages in England than many Englishmen would believe. By midday, local police had reported eighty, of which thirty-three were "possibles." By the end of the week, the grand total for all Britain stood at one hundred and seventy-three "possibles."

In sorting, three features beside the cottage itself were deemed essential: oaks on left of cottage; contiguous, sloping meadow; brook from which it would be possible for an animal, such as a cow, to drink. Sixty of the hundred and seventy-three contained these essentials. But the balance included cottages, of the correct period and dimensions, whose oaks had been felled, whose meadow had been built over, whose brook had been diverted.

Within a week, the sixty "probables" had been inspected, without noteworthy result. In another fortnight, the balance of "possibles" had been eliminated. Detective Inspector Karslake felt that he had been handed a raw deal.

Within twenty-four hours identification of the cottage had become the solitary line of investigation. The comb had been run through all Henshawk's business and social acquaintances. The telegram to Mrs. Henshawk had been telephoned from a call box at the Redmoon Restaurant. This started new hope—until a client reported that he had lunched there with Henshawk, who had excused himself for a few minutes before lunch in order to telephone.

At the end of the month the Press, somewhat grudgingly, complied with the request to reprint the photograph of the model and the police appeal. They helped its news value and at the same time got their own back by writing up the absurdity of such a cottage being untraceable. The comic artists were allowed free play. There was a rather unkind picture of a cow goggling at a model of Scotland Yard on an outstretched palm.

In short, Karslake was unable to advance in any direction. At the end of April the case was allowed to drift into the Department of Dead Ends.

By its very nature it was impossible for the Department to originate any investigation. Cases sent there were, in effect, put into cold storage against the chance of some other case accidentally criss-crossing, the chance of some unrelated circumstance happening to throw a sidelight.

A day or so after the statuette of Henshawk, the model under its glass dome, and the empty picture frame had been sent to Detective Inspector Rason, Karslake made a perfunctory inquiry and received a somewhat more voluble answer than he had anticipated.

"Well, sir, since you ask me, I think that, instead of looking for the cottage, we ought to have looked for that cow."

It was a dangerous moment, for there had been a comic picture in the *Daily Record* rather in that sense.

"I mean, I think there's something funny about this case—something psychological, if you understand me."

"I don't," said Karslake.

"There's that remark in the girl's statement about what he calls 'that damned cow.' Why was it a 'damned' cow? And why should it spoil the whole thing? A cow is just what you'd look for in those surroundings. You'd miss it if it wasn't there. Now, suppose that man had been frightened by a cow when he was very little—too young to remember? All his life, though he doesn't know why—"

"Now look here, Rason, if you talk to the Press with a tale

of a man frightened of cows, there'll be trouble good and hot, and all of it for you."

"I was thinking of the mental hospitals—"

"So was I—only I don't mean what you mean. It's facts we want, Rason. And if you're lucky enough to find any, then we'll fix 'em up with a theory."

Lucky enough! Rason's past successes in linking apparently unconnected events, in perceiving method in that which seemed blind chance, had never earned him a pat on the back for anything but his "luck." Even when he found Harold Ledlaw, Karslake ungenerously asserted that success was thrown into his lap solely because he chanced to go to a particular picture theatre on a particular night with his sister-in-law.

He had invited his niece, whom he regarded, since his brother's death, as an honorary daughter; but her mother had come instead.

They had arrived too early and were afflicted with a "short," advertising a breakfast food, in which a spirit voice whispered to a young wife that her husband could not do a hard day's work on just tea or coffee. What, therefore, should she put in his cup, held in a slender bejeweled hand? Trick photography then showed a huge cow galloping into the picture and leaping into the breakfast cup.

"Sorry, Meg," said Rason. "I've got to go."

"Why, George, what is it?"

"That damned cow!" chuckled Rason, and left her.

That was not luck, in Karslake's sense. The whole of Scotland Yard might have seen that film without learning anything from its apparent irrelevance. But it was lucky that Ledlaw happened to be at Whiddon Cottage when Rason took Karslake there—though they would have caught him just the same if he had been elsewhere.

The day after his visit to Whiddon, Ledlaw had met his daughter. They had met as strangers and had approved of each other. When a month had gone by and the chances of his escape now seemed overwhelming, Mrs. Ledlaw consented to another meeting.

After the failure of the second Press campaign, Ledlaw was convinced that the trail was utterly lost, and Mrs. Ledlaw concurred. He reasoned that, if the police ever succeeded in finding the cottage, they would inevitably reach him through Mrs. Ledlaw. Therefore he risked nothing by taking his daughter home—which he did one evening in June. The efficient domesticity he witnessed awakened dormant longings.

"I have been thinking, Ruth," he said at the end of June, "that if anything were to happen—not that we need fear it now—but if it *were* to happen, you would be in a dangerous position for having shielded me. You would certainly go to prison. But if we were married, you could successfully plead that you acted under my domination—absurd, my dear, though it may sound."

On the understanding that it was to be a marriage of companionship only and on the further understanding that he would take steps to pursue his profession of engineering, Mrs. Ledlaw remarried him on July eleventh.

By this time he had long lost all sense of peril. Indeed his crime, when he thought of it, seemed no more than a bad dream, of which the details were already blurred.

In August there was a strike at the engineering works, leaving nothing for the supervising engineer to do. So Ledlaw was pottering in the garden when the car containing the detectives arrived towards the end of the morning. Mrs. Ledlaw, hearing the car, came out of the cottage.

Rason, carrying a largish bag, was in nominal charge. As they got out of the car, Karslake muttered: "It's not the place. It's not a bit like it, except for the cottage itself. It's no different from sixty others."

"Mr. Ledlaw?" asked Rason, having learned the name at the local police station. "We are from Scotland Yard. I believe you knew Albert Henshawk?"

"The fellow who was murdered? We wondered." He turned to his wife. "This is Mrs. Ledlaw. We knew an Albert Henshawk slightly some twenty years ago. But we lost touch. Anyhow, what did you want to ask us about him?"

"I want to know when you last saw Albert Henshawk, Mr. Ledlaw."

"But you aren't connecting my husband with the murder," boomed Mrs. Ledlaw, "because we live in a seventeenth-century cottage? The local sergeant told me he had reported this cottage at the time, and it was inspected by a Scotland Yard man."

"It isn't very like the one in the picture, you know," said

179

Ledlaw tolerantly. "True, there are somewhat similar oaks. But there—" he waved his hand at the half-mile of hillside sloping down to the Thames.

Karslake maintained a glum silence, wondering how they would explain Rason's ineptitude. Rason opened his bag, took out the original model of the cottage, and laid it on the ground.

"I admit it's not a bit like it," he said.

Ledlaw smiled, while Karslake looked glummer than ever. Rason continued:

"But that is because—*that damned cow spoils the whole thing*, Mr. Ledlaw."

Ledlaw's face was expressionless.

"I can't follow that," said Mrs. Ledlaw.

"Funny thing, Mrs. Ledlaw. I went to the pictures last night. Saw a film where a whopping big cow appears to jump into a tea cup. Clever bit of photography—messing about with perspective. Made me think of this cow. So I thought—well, look here!"

The last was addressed mainly to Karslake. As Rason spoke, he plucked the figure of the cow from the model.

"Good Lord!" muttered Karslake, gaping from the model to the landscape and back again at the model.

With the removal of the cow, *the meadow had vanished!* It became, in fact, a half-mile of sloping hillside, while the "brook" was instantly recognizable as the Thames, half a mile away in the valley below.

"No deception in this trick, ladies and gentlemen!" chirped Rason, and fitted the peg back into its socket—thus restoring the meadow, with a brook from which a cow was drinking.

"It's messing about with perspective. Got the idea from that cow jumping into the tea cup." he told them all over again. "That's what you meant when you told Henshawk the damned cow spoiled the whole thing, wasn't it, Mr. Ledlaw! I suppose you can account for your movements on the evening of February sixteenth?"

"I can, if he can't," said Mrs. Ledlaw. "He was here. I remember the date, because he was asking me to marry him."

"*Last* February, madam!" cut in Karslake. "We are informed that you have a grown-up daughter. And that she's known as 'Miss Ledlaw.' "

"Yes, but it's all quite simple, really," said Mrs. Ledlaw.

180

"You see, we were divorced some years ago. And then we thought better of it—you look as if you didn't believe me."

"It's of no great importance at the moment, Mrs. Ledlaw—"

"It is of great importance to me," retorted Mrs. Ledlaw. "I insist on your inspecting my marriage certificate. I will not keep you more than a couple of minutes."

When she had gone, Karslake spoke to Ledlaw.

"If you deny that you saw Henshawk that day, Mr. Ledlaw, are you willing to come back with us to London and let us see if Henshawk's secretary and the porter recognize you?"

"Certainly not. You've no case against me. You can darned well bring them down here, if you're so keen to waste your time."

Mrs. Ledlaw was coming from the house carrying his dispatch case, which had become hers.

With horror he suddenly remembered.

"The certificate is not in there, dear. I took it out last week. Don't you remember, Ruth?"

"Oh, of course! How stupid of me!"

But there had been altogether too much anxiety in Ledlaw's voice. Karslake strode forward.

"I'll have that opened, please, Mrs. Ledlaw!"

"Oh, very well, if you wish!" Mrs. Ledlaw did not know why her husband had shouted that nonsense about removing the certificate. It surely couldn't matter much when they remarried.

Inside the case were: a packet of Mrs. Ledlaw's letters, a photograph album, a rare edition of *Canterbury Tales*, the marriage certificate, a few other oddments and—Henshawk's drawing of the cottage, loosely wrapped in tissue paper.

181

DON'T LOOK BEHIND YOU

BY FREDRIC BROWN

Fredric Brown was born in Cincinnati, Ohio, on October 29, 1906, and attended Hanover College in Indiana. He worked at various occupations, from office boy to carnival worker, and it was while he was a proofreader with *The Milwaukee Journal* that he began to write for the pulps. His first novel, *The Fabulous Clipjoint,* won an Edgar from the Mystery Writers of America in 1947. He wrote over 300 mystery, detection, and science-fiction stories, some television scripts, and 28 novels. The last of his eight short-story collections, *Paradox Lost,* was published post-humously. He died on March 12, 1972, in Tucson, Arizona.

JUST SIT BACK AND RELAX, now. Try to enjoy this; it's going to be the last story you ever read, or nearly the last. After you finish it, you can sit there and stall a while, you can find excuses to hang around your house, or your room, or your office, wherever you're reading this; but sooner or later you're going to have to get up and go out. That's where I'm waiting for you: outside. Or maybe closer than that. Maybe in this room.

You think that's a joke, of course. You think this is just a story in a magazine, and that I don't really mean you. Keep right on thinking so. But be fair; admit that I'm giving you fair warning.

Harley bet me I couldn't do it. He bet me a diamond he's told me about, a diamond as big as his head. So you see why I've got to kill you. And why I've got to tell you how and why and all about it first. That's part of the bet. It's just the kind of idea Harley would have.

I'll tell you about Harley first. He's tall and handsome, and sauve and cosmopolitan. He looks something like Ronald Colman, only he's taller. He dresses like a million dollars, but it wouldn't matter if he didn't; I mean that he'd look distinguished in overalls. There's a sort of magic about Harley, a mocking magic in the way he looks at you; it makes you think of palaces and far-off countries and bright music.

It was in Springfield, Ohio, that he met Justin Dean. Justin was a funny-looking little runt who was just a printer. He worked for the Atlas Printing & Engraving Company. He was a very ordinary little guy, just about as different as possible from Harley; you couldn't pick two men more different. He was only thirty-five, but he was mostly bald already, and he had to wear thick glasses because he'd worn out his eyes doing fine printing and engraving. He was a good printer and engraver; I'll say that for him.

I never asked Harley how he happened to come to Springfield, but the day he got there, after he'd checked in at the Castle Hotel, he stopped in at Atlas to have some calling cards made. It happened that Justin Dean was alone in the shop at the time, and he took Harley's order for the cards;

Harley wanted engraved ones, the best. Harley always wants the best of everything.

Harley probably didn't even notice Justin; there was no reason why he should. But Justin noticed Harley all right, and in him he saw everything that he himself would like to be, and never would be, because most of the things Harley has, you have to be born with.

And Justin made the plates for the cards himself, and printed them himself, and he did a wonderful job—something he thought would be worthy of a man like Harley Prentice. That was the name engraved on the card, just that and nothing else, as all really important people have their cards engraved.

He did fine-line work on it, freehand cursive style, and used all the skill he had. It wasn't wasted, because the next day when Harley called to get the cards, he held one and stared at it for a while, and then he looked at Justin, seeing him for the first time. He asked, "Who did this?"

And little Justin told him proudly who had done it, and Harley smiled at him and told him it was the work of an artist, and he asked Justin to have dinner with him that evening after work, in the Blue Room of the Castle Hotel.

That's how Harley and Justin got together, but Harley was careful. He waited until he'd known Justin a while before he asked him whether or not he could make plates for five- and ten-dollar bills. Harley had the contacts; he could market the bills in quantity with men who specialized in placing them, and—most important—he knew where he could get paper with the silk threads in it, paper that wasn't quite the genuine thing, but was close enough to pass inspection by anyone but an expert.

So Justin quit his job at Atlas and he and Harley went to New York, and they set up a little printing shop as a blind, on Amsterdam Avenue south of Sherman Square, and they worked at the bills. Justin worked hard, harder than he had ever worked in his life, because besides working on the plates for the bills, he helped meet expenses by handling what legitimate printing work came into the shop.

He worked day and night for almost a year, making plate after plate, and each one was a little better than the last, and finally he had plates that Harley said were good enough. That night they had dinner at the Waldorf-Astoria to cele-

184

brate and after dinner they went the rounds of the best night clubs, and it cost Harley a small fortune, but that didn't matter because they were going to get rich.

They drank champagne, and it was the first time Justin ever drank champagne and he got disgustingly drunk and must have made quite a fool of himself. Harley told him about it afterwards, but Harley wasn't mad at him. He took him back to his room at the hotel and put him to bed, and Justin was pretty sick for a couple of days. But that didn't matter, either, because they were going to get rich.

Then Justin started printing bills from the plates, and they got rich. After that, Justin didn't have to work so hard, either, because he turned down most jobs that came into the print shop, told them he was behind schedule and couldn't handle any more. He took just a little work, to keep up a front. And behind the front, he made five- and ten-dollar bills, and he and Harley got rich.

He got to know other people whom Harley knew. He met Bull Mallon, who handled the distribution end. Bull Mallon was built like a bull, that was why they called him that. He had a face that never smiled or changed expression at all except when he was holding burning matches to the soles of Justin's bare feet. But that wasn't then; that was later, when he wanted Justin to tell him where the plates were.

And he got to know Captain John Willys of the Police Department, who was a friend of Harley's, to whom Harley gave quite a bit of the money they made, but that didn't matter, either, because there was plenty left and they all got rich. He met a friend of Harley's who was a big star of the stage, and one who owned a big New York newspaper. He got to know other people equally important but in less respectable ways.

Harley, Justin knew, had a hand in lots of other enterprises besides the little mint on Amsterdam Avenue. Some of these ventures took him out of town, usually over weekends. And the weekend that Harley was murdered, Justin never found out what really happened, except that Harley went away and didn't come back. Oh, he knew that he was murdered, all right, because the police found his body—with three bullet holes in his chest—in the most expensive suite of the best hotel in Albany. Even for a place to be found dead in, Harley Prentice had chosen the best.

185

All Justin ever knew about it was that a long distance call came to him at the hotel where he was staying, the night that Harley was murdered—it must have been a matter of minutes, in fact, before the time the newspapers said Harley was killed.

It was Harley's voice on the phone, and his voice was debonair and unexcited as ever. But he said, "Justin? Get to the shop and get rid of the plates, the paper, everything. Right away. I'll explain when I see you." He waited only until Justin said, "Sure, Harley," and then he said, "Atta-boy," and hung up.

Justin hurried around to the printing shop and got the plates and the paper and a few thousand dollars' worth of counterfeit bills that were on hand. He made the paper and bills into one bundle and the copper plates into another, smaller one, and he left the shop with no evidence that it had ever been a mint in miniature.

He was very careful and very clever in disposing of both bundles. He got rid of the big one first by checking in at a big hotel, not one he or Harley ever stayed at, under a false name, just to have a chance to put the big bundle in the in-cinerator there. It was paper and it would burn. And he made sure there was a fire in the incinerator before he drop-ped it down the chute.

The plates were different. They wouldn't burn, he knew, so he took a trip to Staten Island and back on the ferry, and somewhere out in the middle of the bay, he dropped the bundle over the side into the water.

Then, having done what Harley had told him to do, and having done it well and thoroughly, he went back to the hotel—his own hotel, not the one where he had dumped the paper and the bills—and went to sleep.

In the morning, he read in the newspapers that Harley had been killed, and he was stunned. It didn't seem possible. He couldn't believe it; it was a joke someone was playing on him. Harley would come back to him, he knew. And he was right; Harley did, but that was later, in the swamp.

But anyway, Justin had to know, so he took the very next train for Albany. He must have been on the train when the police went to his hotel, and at the hotel they must have learned he'd asked the desk about trains for Albany, because they were waiting for him when he got off the train there.

186

They took him to a station and they kept him there a long, long time, days and days, asking him questions. They found out, after a while, that he couldn't have killed Harley because he'd been in New York City at the time Harley was killed in Albany, but they knew, also, that he and Harley had been operating the little mint, and they thought that might be a lead to who killed Harley, and they were interested in the counterfeiting, too, maybe even more than in the murder.

They asked Justin Dean questions, over and over and over, and he couldn't answer them, so he didn't. They kept him awake for days at a time, asking him questions over and over. Most of all they wanted to know where the plates were. He wished he could tell them that the plates were safe where nobody could ever get them again, but he couldn't tell them that without admitting that he and Harley had been counterfeiting, so he couldn't tell them.

They located the Amsterdam shop, but they didn't find any evidence there, and they really had no evidence to hold Justin on at all, but he didn't know that, and it never occurred to him to get a lawyer.

He kept wanting to see Harley, and they wouldn't let him; then, when they learned he really didn't believe Harley could be dead, they made him look at a dead man they said was Harley, and he guessed it was, although Harley looked different dead. He didn't look magnificent, dead. And Justin believed, then, but still didn't believe. And after that he just went silent and wouldn't say a word, even when they kept him awake for days and days with a bright light in his eyes, and kept slapping him to keep him awake. They didn't use clubs or rubber hoses, but they slapped him a million times and wouldn't let him sleep. And after a while, he lost track of things and couldn't have answered their questions even if he'd wanted to.

For a while after that, he was in a bed in a white room, and all he remembers about that are nightmares he had, and calling for Harley and an awful confusion as to whether Harley was dead or not, and then things came back to him gradually and he knew he didn't want to stay in the white room; he wanted to get out so he could hunt for Harley. And if Harley was dead, he wanted to kill whoever had killed Harley, because Harley would do the same for him.

187

So he began pretending, and acting, very cleverly, the way the doctors and nurses seemed to want him to act, and after a while they gave him his clothes and let him go.

He was becoming cleverer, now. He thought, What would Harley tell me to do? And he knew they'd try to follow him because they'd think he might lead them to the plates, which they didn't know were at the bottom of the bay, and he gave them the slip before he left Albany, and he went first to Boston, and from there by boat to New York, instead of going direct.

He went first to the print shop, and went in the back way after watching the alley for a long time to be sure the place wasn't guarded. It was a mess; they must have searched it very thoroughly for the plates.

Harley wasn't there, of course. Justin left and from a phone booth in a drug store, he telephoned their hotel and asked for Harley and was told Harley no longer lived there; and to be clever and not let them guess who he was, he asked for Justin Dean, and they said Justin Dean didn't live there any more either.

Then he moved to a different drug store and from there he decided to call up some friends of Harley's, and he phoned Bull Mallon first and because Bull was a friend, he told him who he was and asked if he knew where Harley was.

Bull Mallon didn't pay any attention to that; he sounded excited, a little, and he asked, "Did the cops get the plates, Dean?" and Justin said they didn't, that he wouldn't tell them, and he asked again about Harley.

Bull asked, "Are you nuts, or kidding?" And Justin just asked him again, and Bull's voice changed and he said, "Where are you?" and Justin told him. Bull said, "Harley's here. He's staying under cover, but it's all right if you know, Dean. You wait right there at the drug store, and we'll come and get you."

They came and got Justin, Bull Mallon and two other men in a car, and they told him Harley was hiding out way deep in New Jersey and that they were going to drive there now. So he went along and sat in the back seat between two men he didn't know, while Bull Mallon drove.

It was late afternoon then, when they picked him up, and Bull drove all evening and most of the night and he drove fast, so he must have gone farther than New Jersey, at least into Virginia or maybe farther, into the Carolinas.

The sky was getting faintly gray with first dawn when they stopped at a rustic cabin that looked like it had been used as a hunting lodge. It was miles from anywhere, there wasn't even a road leading to it, just a trail that was level enough for the car to be able to make it.

They took Justin into the cabin and tied him to a chair, and they told him Harley wasn't there, but Harley had told them that Justin would tell them where the plates were, and he couldn't ever leave until he did tell.

Justin didn't believe them; he knew then that they'd tricked him about Harley, but it didn't matter, as far as the plates were concerned. It didn't matter if he told them what he'd done with the plates, because they couldn't get them again, and they wouldn't tell the police. So he told them, quite willingly.

But they didn't believe him. They said he'd hidden the plates and was lying. They tortured him to make him tell. They beat him, and they cut him with knives, and they held burning matches and lighted cigars to the soles of his feet, and they pushed needles under his fingernails. Then they'd rest and ask him questions and if he could talk, he'd tell them the truth again, and after a while they'd start to torture him again.

It went on for days and weeks—Justin doesn't know how long, but it was a long time. Once they went away for several days and left him tied up with nothing to eat or drink. They came back and started in all over again. And all the time he hoped Harley would come to help him, but Harley didn't come, not then.

After a while what was happening in the cabin ended, or anyway he didn't know any more about it. They must have thought he was dead; maybe they were right, or anyway not far from wrong.

The next thing he knows was the swamp. He was lying in shallow water at the edge of deeper water. His face was out of the water; it woke him when he turned a little and his face went under. They must have thought him dead and thrown him into the water, but he had floated into the shallow part before he had drowned, and a last flicker of consciousness had turned him over on his back with his face out.

I don't remember much about Justin in the swamp; it was a long time, but I just remember flashes of it. I couldn't

189

move at first; I just lay there in the shallow water with my face out. It got dark and it got cold, I remember, and finally my arms would move a little and I got farther out of the water, lying in the mud with only my feet in the water. I slept or was unconscious again and when I woke up it was getting gray dawn, and that was when Harley came. I think I'd been calling him, and he must have heard.

He stood there, dressed as immaculately and perfectly as ever, right in the swamp, and he was laughing at me for being so weak and lying there like a log, half in the dirty water and half in the mud, and I got up and nothing hurt any more.

We shook hands and he said, "Come on, Justin, let's get you out of here," and I was so glad he'd come that I cried a little. He laughed at me for that, and said I should lean on him and he'd help me walk, but I wouldn't do that, because I was coated with mud and filth of the swamp and he was so clean and perfect in a white linen suit, like an ad in a magazine. And all the way out of that swamp, all the days and nights we spent there, he never even got mud on his trouser cuffs, nor his hair mussed.

I told him just to lead the way, and he did, walking just ahead of me, sometimes turning around, laughing and talking to me and cheering me up. Sometimes I'd fall, but I wouldn't let him come back and help me. But he'd wait patiently until I could get up. Sometimes I'd crawl instead when I couldn't stand up any more. Sometimes I'd have to swim streams that he'd leap lightly across.

And it was day and night and day and night, and sometimes I'd sleep, and things would crawl across me. And some of them I caught and ate, or maybe I dreamed that. I remember other things, in that swamp, like an organ that played a lot of the time, and sometimes angels in the air and devils in the water, but those were delirium, I guess.

Harley would say, "A little farther, Justin; we'll make it. And we'll get back at them, at all of them."

And we made it. We came to dry fields, cultivated fields with waist-high corn, but there weren't ears on the corn for me to eat. And then there was a stream, a clear stream that wasn't stinking water like the swamp, and Harley told me to wash myself and my clothes and I did, although I wanted to hurry on to where I could get food.

190

I still looked pretty bad; my clothes were clean of mud and filth but they were mere rags and wet, because I couldn't wait for them to dry, and I had a ragged beard and I was barefoot.

But we went on and came to a little farm building, just a two-room shack, and there was a smell of fresh bread just out an oven, and I ran the last few yards to knock on the door. A woman, an ugly woman, opened the door and when she saw me she slammed it again before I could say a word.

Strength came to me from somewhere, maybe from Harley, although I can't remember him being there just then. There was a pile of kindling logs beside the door. I picked one of them up as though it were no heavier than a broomstick, and I broke down the door and killed the woman. She screamed a lot, but I killed her. Then I ate the hot fresh bread.

I watched from the window as I ate, and saw a man running across the field toward the house. I found a knife, and I killed him as he came in at the door. It was much better, killing with the knife; I liked it that way.

I ate more bread, and kept watching from all the windows, but no one else came. Then my stomach hurt from the hot bread I'd eaten and I had to lie down, doubled up, and when the hurting quit, I slept.

Harley woke me up, and it was dark. He said, "Let's get going; you should be far away from here before it's daylight."

I knew he was right, but I didn't hurry away. I was becoming, as you see, very clever now. I knew there were things to do first. I found matches and a lamp, and lighted the lamp. Then I hunted through the shack for everything I could use. I found clothes of the man, and they fitted me not too badly except that I had to turn up the cuffs of the trousers and the shirt. His shoes were big, but that was good because my feet were so swollen.

I found a razor and shaved; it took a long time because my hand wasn't steady, but I was very careful and didn't cut myself much.

I had to hunt hardest for their money, but I found it finally. It was sixty dollars.

And I took the knife, after I had sharpened it. It isn't fancy; just a bone-handled carving knife, but it's good steel. I'll show it to you, pretty soon now. It's had a lot of use.

Then we left and it was Harley who told me to stay away

191

from the roads, and find railroad tracks. That was easy because we heard a train whistle far off in the night and knew which direction the tracks lay. From then on, with Harley helping, it's been easy.

You won't need the details from here. I mean, about the brakeman, and about the tramp we found asleep in the empty reefer, and about the near thing I had with the police in Richmond. I learned from that; I learned I mustn't talk to Harley when anybody else was around to hear. He hides himself from them; he's got a trick and they don't know he's there, and they think I'm funny in the head if I talk to him. But in Richmond I bought better clothes and got a haircut and a man I killed in an alley had forty dollars on him, so I had money again. I went on to Philadelphia by bus, and Harley wanted me to stay there a while. So I got a job in a little printing shop. I got fired pretty quick, but the next job I held for a week. I wanted to go on to New York right away. I've got to find Bull Mallon, which will be easy, and the two men who helped him, which will be a little harder because I know only their first names.

But Harley keeps telling me to wait, that I need practice, that those fellows are big time and know their way around. Harley says we should travel around, too, and we've been doing that. Now we're here. I've learned a lot of things. I can hold a job down now, for one thing, and people don't think I'm too strange; they don't get scared when I look at them. I don't talk to Harley except in our room, and then only very quietly so the people in the next room won't think I'm talking to myself. And I've learned how to use the knife quickly and efficiently. You'll hardly feel it.

The bet I told you about came up because Harley kept telling me it's one thing to kill someone who isn't looking for it, and another thing to get a man who's on the alert, like Bull Mallon, and Harry and Carl. He said I wasn't ready for them yet, and I told him I bet I could warn a man I was going to use the knife on him, and tell him all about it, and why, and approximately when, and that I could still get away with it. And he bet me I couldn't.

That's where he's going to lose a bet, because I'm going to do just that. You see, I know you don't believe this. You think it's just another story in a magazine.

People are like that; you won't believe that this is the *only*

192

copy of this magazine that contains this story. Even when I tell you how it was done.

That's where I'm putting one over on Harley; he didn't think of doing it this way. He never thought how easy it will be for a good all-around printer to counterfeit one story in a magazine. I'm setting this up now on the Linotype late at night in the shop where I work days. I even have the boss' permission—told him I was going to set up a story a friend of mine had written as a surprise for him and that I'd melt the lead back once I'd taken a proof for him.

I know the magazine I'm going to use, picked it because this shop can match the type-face and size perfectly. We've got a paper stock here that will match closely enough that you can't tell the difference. I've got a copy of the current issue here.

When I've finished this, I'll make up the type in pages, and then pick out a story that takes up just that many pages in the magazine. I'll folio these pages to match the ones of the story I'll substitute it for. And run off one backed-up copy on the proof press. There'll be a minute difference in type size because of mat shrinkage, but you won't notice that unless you're a printer.

It'll be just as easy to print a new title page, and to write myself a blurb to fit the story. Not really necessary and maybe you think I'm going to a lot of trouble, but Harley will get a kick out of it if I do a really artistic job, and so will I.

I'll cut the new pages to fit and bind them in; you won't be able to tell the difference, even if a faint suspicion may cause you to look at it. Don't forget I made five- and ten-dollar bills you couldn't have told from the original, and this is kindergarten stuff compared to that job.

Tomorrow I'll go to some newsstand or drug store—you know which one by now—and plant this copy with the others like it. I'll be watching when you buy it.

The rest I can't tell you, yet. You can be sure I followed you wherever you went after you bought this magazine. You can be sure I know who you are by the time you're reading this.

The rest depends on circumstances I won't know until I follow you. Maybe—if it's possible—I'm in the house with you right now. Maybe I'm in this very room, hidden, watching until you finish the story. Maybe I'm sitting near you on the streetcar or train, if you're reading it there. Maybe I'm on a fire escape outside your hotel room. But I'll be with you, or near you; you can count on that.

That little shiver of cold running down your spine—maybe it's a window opening silently.

Don't look around; you'll be happier if you don't know, if you don't see the knife coming. I've killed people from behind and they don't seem to mind so much.

Go on, just a little while, thinking this is just another fiction story. Don't look behind you. Don't believe this—*until you feel the knife*.

FINGERPRINTS DON'T LIE

BY STUART PALMER

Stuart Palmer was born in Baraboo, Wisconsin, on June 21, 1905. After attending the Chicago Art Institute and the University of Wisconsin, he held various jobs, including iceman, seaman, newspaper reporter, and taxi driver. He sold his first story at the age of twenty. In 1931, his first mystery, *The Penguin Pool Murder,* introduced spinster detective Hildgarde Withers. The following year it was made into the first of a popular series of movies. He served in the Army in World War II. He wrote over 35 screenplays, most of them mysteries featuring the Falcon, the Lone Wolf, and Bulldog Drummond. He died in 1968.

THE TRAP—THOUGH THE policemen who were setting it would have called it a "stakeout"—was set around noon. It was a little before two in the afternoon when a soft knock came at the front door of the little adobe cottage, and then another.

Before either of the two detectives could make up his mind about answering, the knob started to turn—hopefully but without result. Then there was the sound of footsteps scrunching around through the bedraggled little cactus garden to the rear of the place.

Young Rankin snorted. "This is going to be good!" He was a beefy man who bulged his blue serge, and he had a way of speaking faster than he thought. "It says in the book—"

Detective Tom Macy had been on the Las Vegas force for twenty-one years, and for his money nothing was any good except keeping out of trouble, getting off duty, and going home for supper. "All right, all right. So it says in the book they always return to the scene of the crime. Relax, eager-beaver."

Yet he too was alert, his gnarled red hand hovering near his holster, as there came the soft sound of scratching at the lock of the kitchen door. He caught Rankin's arm and drew him into the hall closet. They listened as the kitchen door opened and closed. There was the creak of light, cautious steps on the linoleum, then tinware rattled and cupboard doors opened. After a while the footsteps came past the breakfast nook and into the living room, and then stopped.

"Now!" Macy said, and they pounced. Rankin had his lead-heavy sap in the air, and narrowly managed to bring it down without damaging their prisoner, who turned out to be an angular spinster of uncertain years. She had no other weapon than her tongue, and needed none.

"I am Miss Hildegarde Withers!" she announced. "Take your big clumsy hands off me at once! What if I did enter this place? I have as much right in this cottage as you have, and perhaps more."

Rankin said that they would see about that. But Macy elbowed him firmly aside. "Lady, we're listening. But give it straight. We're Las Vegas police."

"In that case," Miss Withers said acidly, "I shall try to speak clearly and in words of one syllable. I am here, having interrupted a train journey from New York to Los Angeles, because a girl named Eileen Travis is supposed to be living here. For more than five weeks she has been establishing residence for a Nevada divorce. Her family back East has considerable influence with the powers that be, and they called on the New York police at Centre Street. You see, they were very worried about her—"

"Oh, so you claim to be a policewoman?" Rankin cut in.

"Nothing of the kind. My I.Q. is much too high, for one thing. I am a schoolteacher. But once in a while I fall heir to problems which are too far off the beaten track for Centre Street to bother with. Some friends of mine at Headquarters knew that I was en route to California for a vacation, so after Eileen's mother put the pressure on, she was told to telegraph me, and—"

Macy cleared his throat noisily. "Just why was the girl's mother worried about her?"

"I don't quite know. It was about some threats that George Travis, the girl's husband, was supposed to have made. The Kings County Grand Jury recently indicted him for violation of OPA rules—some sort of black market practices—and he felt that his wife was rushing through the divorce so that she would be able legally to testify against him at his forthcoming trial. On top of that, Eileen's mother phoned her long distance last week, and the girl acted strangely—she refused to talk." Miss Withers sniffed again. "Now you know as much as I do. By the way, where is the body?"

"Ah, ha!" cried Rankin jubilantly. "How'd you know about that?"

"I didn't, until you told me. But I suspected it. There's an odor of perfume, stale alcohol, tobacco, and cordite in this room. Besides, why should there be two detectives lurking in the house?"

Macy sighed, and indicated the bedroom door. "She's in there. Around midnight last night, close as we can figure, somebody let her have it with a shotgun, right smack in her pretty face. We're waiting for the ambulance now—only two in town, and both pretty busy." He gestured. "Sorry, but you'll have to come down to the station."

"Illegal, but to be expected. Meanwhile, of course, the real

197

murderer is making tracks out of town. Never fear, I shall go quietly."

"I wish!" Rankin muttered fervently.

"But first," insisted the scholteacher, "I think I ought to look at the body. Or has it been identified?"

Macy hesitated, and then said "Come on."

In the bedroom there were the grotesquely pitiful remains of a plump, tanned girl in a black négligée, sprawled all akimbo on a white goatskin rug. A lightweight shotgun lay nearby.

"That her?" Macy demanded. "I mean as far as you can tell, without any face."

Miss Withers knelt over the body. "New nylons. Shoes from I. Miller, New York. Négligée from Altman's—the expensive kind that you can draw through a ring. And speaking of rings—"

"We want to know, is that her or isn't it?" Rankin cut in.

"She must have been pretty," Miss Withers said. "Once."

Rankin sighed. "Sure musta. Don't see a figure like that once in a coon's age, even in this town."

"He's an expert," Macy said dryly. "These bachelors! Sure you never were out with her, Rank?"

"No such luck." Rankin was oddly blushing. "Well, ma'am?"

"I don't know if it's Eileen Travis or not," the scholteacher admitted. "I never saw the girl. I just wanted to find out if there were any clues you'd missed."

Rankin looked angry, but Macy almost laughed. "And were there?"

"Only that her ring is missing." Miss Withers pointed to the narrow pale line around the ring-finger of the dead girl's left hand.

"Pretty sharp," Macy said. "Only there was a ring there when we found her. This one." From his pocket he produced a heavy white-gold wedding ring. "It says, 'From G T to E H Jan 20 '44.'"

"From George Travis to Eileen Hampton," Miss Withers said. "He gave himself top billing, as they used to say in vaudeville. That tells us something about George, does it not?"

"You mean because he put his own initials first?" Macy looked at her with a new respect.

"Uh-hmmm." The schoolteacher had opened the closet door and was looking at the rows of expensive clothes, the big leather bag of golf clubs—everything well cared-for and expensive.

"Nothing in here," Macy said, "but the shotgun. And that's just an ordinary sixteen-gauge, not new, not old."

"Everybody around here has one," Rankin put in. "We use 'em for shooting doves and prairie jacks. Jackrabbits, that is."

They went back into the living room, and Macy showed Miss Withers the bottle of Scotch, part-full, which had been found on the coffee table, beside two glasses. There was also an ashtray with some cigarette butts and ashes, and a half-smoked perfecto, unchewed and still bearing the band decorated with the head and plump bust of a señorita.

"A fifty-center," Rankin said. "Boy, could I go for a box of those!"

"We figure," Macy explained, "that the girl had a caller. She gave him a drink—"

"The cigar means it was a man. A man she knew, or she wouldn't have had a drink with him dressed in that flimsy nightie," Rankin said.

"Yeh? Some of the tomatoes you run around with on your off time would—" Macy gestured broadly. "Sorry, ma'am. Anyway, we figure that this visitor puffs on his cigar and drinks his drink and then—"

"And then he pulls the shotgun out of his vest pocket and shoots his hostess smack in the face, is that it?" Miss Withers sniffed very dubiously. "Obliging of him to leave fingerprints. By the way, you're welcome to take mine, although I don't drink, smoke cigars, or shoot shotguns."

Rankin guffawed. "Oh, they're not women's prints. Mostly just fragments, but we got a complete thumbprint on one of the glasses, and it was a big one, even for a man. Too bad that dame's husband is in jail back East, or this would be duck soup."

"A man with black market connections," pointed out Miss Withers, "could arrange to have someone commit murder for him."

Macy shrugged. "Well, ma'am, we'll look into all that at the proper time. Let's go downtown." He led the way out through the back door, then stopped short. "What were you

199

doing here in the kitchen when you came in?" he demanded curtly.

"Looking for clues. You can tell a lot about a person by her garbage can, and her shelves. Notice the ham, and biscuit dough, and cans of black-eyed peas? A hearty eater, that girl. And if you'll look in her garbage—"

"I don't see any sense in pawing through old orange rinds and coffee grounds," Macy protested.

"That's the point. There weren't—"

But he hurried her along to the battered sedan which had been parked in the alley. Macy drove around to the front and down the street, while Officer Rankin looked after them wistfully from a front window. "Guess this is the first time Rankin's been squeamish about being left alone with a blonde," Macy said as they drove.

The schoolteacher was staring back toward the lonely cottage. "If I were you I shouldn't worry too much about his solitude," she said.

"Why not?"

"Because I just saw a man step out from behind a billboard across the street heading for the cottage."

Macy drove on automatically for half a block, and then made a quick U-turn which bumped Miss Withers severely against the door. They roared up the street again, brakes screeching as they stopped. "If you're playing tricks—" Macy warned.

But then he saw the cottage door open. They hurried in, Miss Withers no more than three feet behind, and found Rankin rolling on the floor in an undignified but very realistic wrestling match. His opponent turned out to be a pale, unshaven gentleman of about thirty, dressed in a neat, dark, pin-strip suit which had mopped up a great deal of dust from Eileen Travis's floor.

Seeing that the odds were now three to one against him, he stopped wrestling. But he wasn't talking.

"I do believe it's Mr. George Travis!" Miss Withers exclaimed. And as they all stared at her, she continued: "Elementary. The pallor of his face is the typical night-club tan of Manhattan. The clothing suggests Brooks Brothers. Besides, if you will notice the signet ring on his finger, you'll see the initials 'G T.' "

The stranger didn't deny it. "I want to see my wife . . .

200

alone. That's why I waited until I thought you'd gone. Where's Eileen?'

"In here," Macy said softly, and showed him. "This is just the way the cleaning woman found her this morning. Not pretty, huh?"

Travis came out of the bedroom looking pale around the gills. "I—I flew out here to see her," he admitted. "I walked in and this hot-head jumped me. I didn't know she was dead."

"You know it now," Macy said. "Let's go. All of us."

"You're not going to leave her alone like that?" Travis protested.

"She won't mind," Rankin told him. "You worry about yourself."

The house was locked up tight, with a note on the door to the coroner which read "Back in twenty minutes" and they all rode downtown in the police car. Nobody did any talking, although Miss Withers wished that she could be alone with Travis for a moment. He looked like a sulky schoolboy, and she knew how to handle them. Once at the station a mousy but excited little secretary was called in to take down his statement that he had just got off the Los Angeles plane, that he had come out here in an effort to get his wife to postpone the divorce until after his trial, and that he knew nothing about her murder.

"I risked forfeiting my bond just to talk to her," he went on. "Not that it would have done much good. She was bitter because I made her sell most of her jewels to raise cash so I could hang on to my property. She figured this was her chance to get even. Eileen had a rotten temper—no maid ever stayed with her more than a month, and she even went after one of them with a riding crop."

"Okay, okay," Macy said. "We're holding you. Not for murder, not yet. But if you're wanted in New York—" They took him away.

Miss Withers confidently expected the same fate, but the officers only took her fingerprints, made a few notes, and let her go. "Don't leave town, though," Rankin warned her.

Macy smiled. "Try the Mesa—it's a pretty fair hotel."

Miss Withers nodded, and went to La Mesa. In a little corner room, ornamented with a spittoon and a reproduction of "The End of the Trail" showing a dejected redskin on a more dejected cayuse, she sat herself down and thought her

201

own thoughts. Finally there came a knock at the door.

She opened it, facing a slick-haired young man who introduced himself as "Larry Koontz—I work down at the Wheel of Fortune." Miss Withers told him that she had not come to town to gamble—

The young man winked at her, lighted a cigarette, and said that he knew very well why she had come to town. "You're out here on this Travis case," he said. "You represent her family—"

"Do I?"

"Sure, I know. I got connections. You want to know the real lowdown?"

"Curiosity," admitted Miss Withers, "is my besetting sin."

"Huh? Well, anyway, I got the dope. I met Eileen down at the place I work. I'm a sort of shill—that means I play the dice games with the house money whenever there's a lull at the table. I can tell you all you want to know—" here he licked his thin lips—"if I get mine. I figure two grand would be about right."

Miss Withers had to admit that she was not in a position to lay any such honorarium on the line. He smiled. "You could get it from her folks, couldn't you?"

"I don't know. I'd have to have some idea—"

Mr. Koontz pondered. Then he opened his mouth, but before he could say anything, the telephone interrupted. The schoolteacher answered it, to hear the voice of the desk clerk. "Two gentlemen to see you."

"Sorry, but I'm busy at the moment," she said.

"They're on their way up. It's the police."

"Police? But—"

Miss Withers heard the door close, and when she looked around Mr. Koontz had disappeared. She had barely time to adjust her hair and assume an innocent expression, when Detectives Macy and Rankin came into the room. They looked grimly unpleasant. "Now don't tell me you found that my fingerprints matched those on the murder gun!"

They didn't tell her anything. "We want to know why you got into town yesterday and only went out to the Travis girl's apartment this afternoon," Rankin demanded.

"Very simple. I hadn't her address, only the phone number. It took some time to get any information out of the telephone company." She sniffed. "If you gentlemen would turn your suspicions upon Mr. George Travis—after all, he could have committed the murder last night, driven back to Los Angeles, and then flown in on the first plane this morning."

"We thought of that," Macy said wearily.

"But his prints didn't match the ones on the gun and glasses," Rankin finished.

"Fingerprints!" retorted Miss Withers scornfully. "Police put so much faith in technicalities like that that they forget to study motives and personalities. Not to speak of wedding rings."

They both stared at her. "Come, come!" Miss Withers chided, "Don't tell me you didn't notice that the ring you took from the dead girl's finger was too wide for the mark it was supposed to have left!"

"Go on," Macy said.

"You might start wondering why somebody took a narrow wedding ring off Eileen's finger and put on a wide one," the schoolteacher snapped. "In my opinion the girl wasn't wearing her own wedding ring while she was here waiting for her divorce. Or else—" Here she stopped short. "If it's not asking too much, could you tell me whether or not you've officially announced the murder of Eileen Travis?"

They shook their heads.

"Then," continued Miss Withers, "I suggest that you don't. Give out the story that the body has tentatively been identified as somebody else—any girl on your list of missing persons. You can always issue a corrected statement later."

Macy nodded. "So the killer will think he got the wrong girl maybe?"

Miss Withers smiled. "Sometimes it helps to toss a monkey wrench into the machinery."

"Could be, if Sheriff Kehoe will go for the idea." Macy seemed friendlier now. "You know, ma'am, we phoned New York about you, and they said at Centre Street that once in a while you made a lucky guess."

"Bless Inspector Piper's black Irish heart," murmured Miss Withers. Then she shrugged. "Well, here's another guess. Do you know a man named Larry Koontz, who is a shill at the Wheel of Fortune?"

Macy frowned and shook his head, but Rankin brightened. "Sure we do, Tom. That's Molly's husband—the girl who works in the sheriff's office. They busted up over some dame, and she's been crying her eyes out."

"Really? Things like that make me resigned to my state of single blessedness. Do you know where Mr. Koontz lives?"

They didn't, but said that they could easily find out. "We'll give you a ring," Macy promised.

Alone again, Miss Withers went down to dinner, came back again, and finally was in the midst of giving her hair its requisite hundred strokes preparatory for bed when the call came.

"Hello? Hello, Detective Rankin? Well, did you find Mr. Koontz's address?"

"Why, yes, ma'am, we did." There was an unpleasant overtone in the voice of Detective Rankin. "He was living out at the Iris Apartments. But he moved—a few minutes ago. Or rather, they moved him. Over to Callahan's Mortuary."

"*What?*"

"Acting on your tip, Macy and I went out there. The door was open, the lights were all on, and there was Koontz in the kitchenette with an ice-pick between his shoulder blades."

There was a moment of silence. "Oh, dear!" said Miss Withers.

"Oh dear is right. You can say the rest at the station. We're downstairs, so get a move on."

Miss Withers moved, getting into her dress again and taking two aspirins, fancying that this might be a hectic night. Neither Macy nor Rankin had much to say on the way to the station. "It seems odd to me that none of the neighbors heard or noticed anything," the schoolteacher finally offered.

"Lady, nobody in this town is ever home between ten o'clock and two or three in the morning. The visitors are playing, and the natives are working in the joints." Rankin pulled the car up outside police headquarters. In spite of all the haste Miss Withers found herself cooling her heels in a shabby outer office for some time.

At last the inner door opened and she was beckoned inside, where she faced Detectives Macy and Rankin, a beak-nosed sexagenarian with a sheriff's star pinned to the front of his Stetson, and a thin, freckled woman with red eyes whom she recognized as the one who had transcribed her statement earlier that day. "This is Molly Koontz," the sheriff said. "Ma'am, suppose you tell us why you were so interested in her late husband just before he got stabbed."

204

"Gladly," answered the schoolteacher, "if you'll answer a question for me, or have Mrs. Koontz answer it." Taking silence for consent, she told of her brief meeting with the shill who worked at the Wheel of Fortune, and who had had so little good fortune himself. "He knew the answer to all this, or he thought he did," she concluded.

The sheriff nodded noncommittally. "Now," said Miss Withers, "it's my turn. Forgive me, Mrs. Koontz, for prying into your family troubles but I understand that you and your husband separated over another girl."

"Girl! You mean girls. Larry played the field."

"Was one of those women Eileen Travis?"

Molly Koontz shrugged. "I dunno. We broke up a couple of months ago. Only we stayed in touch, sort of. Larry used to take me to dinner now and then, or borrow a few dollars when he got to gambling."

"Well, can you name any girl he was interested in?"

"No—only there was one little number who kept phoning him—one of those southern girls who say 'honey-chile' and 'lil ol' me.' Her name was Thelma something."

"Thelma Pringle," Detective Rankin put in. "She's on our Missing Persons list."

"Maybe," Molly said. "I can tell you one thing. Any girl Larry went for was on the *zoftig* side—you know, plump. And well-dressed. Larry went for the dressy ones."

Sheriff Kehoe yawned and stood up, signaling that the session was concluded. "By the way," pressed Miss Withers, "did anyone happen to check Koontz's fingerprints with those on the murder gun?"

"We did," Macy said. "And they weren't. But the prints on the icepick matched the prints on the shotgun and glasses."

"Of course!" Miss Withers cried. "Then—" But the sheriff gestured, and she found herself propelled toward the door by Macy.

"Thanks for trying to help," he said, as he led her down the hall, unlocking the door of another office. "You better spend the night here. That couch in the corner isn't too bad."

"But you can't—"

"Lady, whenever a cop hears anybody say anything about 'you can't do this to me!' he just laughs. Now take it easy. Maybe you'll go to sleep and dream up a solution to this case." He started out, then came back to remove a spare .38 pistol

205

and a pair of handcuffs from the desk drawer. He indicated the door of the washroom, and went out, locking the door firmly from the outside.

Miss Hildegarde Withers sat herself down indignantly upon the rickety couch, and then caught sight of the telephone on the desk. She lifted the receiver and said, "I want to call New York City, collect!"

But the operator, stationed at a switchboard somewhere in the building, said genially but firmly, "Take it easy, ma'am. Tomorrow is another day."

"Really!" Miss Withers slammed down the phone. Leaving the harsh overhead light burning, she flung herself down on the couch, closing her eyes in order to concentrate better.

In her mind's eye she saw the partially-smoked cigar which had left no ashes in the tray, the thin white line around the dead girl's finger. She saw the two whisky-stained glasses, the Scotch bottle, the shotgun, the icepick planted between the dapper shoulders of the man who thought he knew two thousand dollars' worth about the crime. But these clues kept mixing themselves up with other things that didn't matter, like the dead cactus around the adobe cottage, the black-eyed peas in the kitchen, the garbage can without any orange rinds, the golf clubs with the heads in their neat socks, the nylon hose, and the wedding ring. . . .

Then she jerked awake at the sound of rapping at the door. She realized that she had a stiff neck and that daylight surprisingly filled the room. But the puzzle was all neatly solved. She knew the name of the murderer—and why. It was as easy as that. She was smiling pleasantly when she opened the door to Detective Macy.

"Mornin', ma'am," he said. "After you get fixed up a little, could you join us in the sheriff's office, please? Somebody we want you to meet." He waited patiently while Miss Withers washed her face and did what she could to straighten her hair. Then he led the way down the hall.

"When did the Travis woman give herself up?" the schoolteacher asked.

Macy stopped dead in his tracks. "How'd you know that?"

"Isn't it obvious? It was clear from the beginning that it was not her body in the bedroom, in spite of the New York clothes. The girl who lived in that cottage had stocked the kitchen with the makings of meals preferred south of the

Mason-Dixon line. New Yorkers breakfast on coffee and orange juice, and there was no sign of an orange or an orange peel in the place."

Macy nodded. "I get it. Well, Eileen Travis read about the murder in the Los Angeles papers last night, and she hopped in her car and drove up here. She confessed—"

"Not to the murders?"

Macy laughed jovially. "No, ma'am. But here we are. Come in."

Sheriff Kehoe still sat at his desk, with his Stetson on the back of his head. Officer Rankin leaned against the window, and in the one comfortable chair sat a lovely, lush girl in a bright purple jacket and flannel slacks.

"Mrs. Travis," said the sheriff, half-arising, "this is the lady your mother hired to look you up and see if you were all right."

Eileen said coolly, "You may tell mother that I'm fine."

"Are you?" asked Miss Hildegarde Withers. "I wonder."

"We're sorry, Miss Withers, that we had to keep you here all night," the sheriff went on. "But we didn't want any more killings, and the New York police asked us to take special care of you."

"Thank you so much. And now, what is all this about Mrs. Travis's confession?" Miss Withers beamed brightly at them all.

"I simply admitted," Eileen burst forth, "that I'd taken a cottage here to establish legal residence, and then hired a girl I met in a gambling house to live there in my name."

"A girl with a southern accent, named Thelma Pringle?"

Eileen nodded. "I knew it wasn't strictly legal, but I didn't want to be stuck here when I could be in Los Angeles. And besides, I had good reason to believe that George would stop at nothing to keep me from getting my decree—to keep me from being able to testify against him legally later on."

"You said 'stuck here'?" questioned the sheriff ominously.

"I didn't mean that." Eileen flashed her soft dark eyes at him. "It's just that I don't gamble, and I love ocean swimming. . . ."

"We got pools," the sheriff said glumly. He looked at Detective Macy. "Better get George Travis up here, right away."

Eileen was open-mouthed. "You mean my husband is actually in town? Then that proves—"

Sheriff Kehoe wasn't listening to her. "And ask Molly to come in with her notebook," he called after the departing detective. There was a long, tense period of waiting, during which Miss Withers saw that Officer Rankin was having difficulty in keeping his eyes off Eileen's slim, bare, brown ankles.

Finally George Travis, even more disheveled and unshaven than before, was ushered into the room. He glared morosely at his wife.

"Hello, George," she said, in a low voice that dripped with acid. "Isn't it a shame that your hired hoodlum shot the wrong girl?"

Travis said nothing, but sank down quickly on a hard chair, his head in his hands. A moment later Detective Macy came in with Molly, who was still puffy-eyed. But she had her pencil and notebook.

"Now that we are all here, nice and cosy-like," began the sheriff, "we'll start at the beginning and see if we can straighten this out."

"I suggest," Miss Withers interrupted pleasantly but firmly, "that we start at the end instead. It will save a lot of time. You see, I know who the murderer is."

She met their blank stares with a bright smile. "It all came to me when I was asleep."

"Dreams, yet!" Detective Rankin muttered softly.

But the schoolteacher had the floor. "It's obvious that Mr. Koontz was killed to cover up the first murder, so when we solve the killing of Thelma Pringle we solve them both. Shall we take up the most important clue—the cigar?"

Rankin moved as if to silence her, but Detective Macy was nodding slowly, and the sheriff made no move. "The cigar," went on Miss Withers, "was obviously a plant. It was left as a false clue, having been smoked beforehand. Moreover, the killer was not used to cigars, for he forgot to remove the band and he held it in his lips, like a cigarette, leaving no teeth marks as real cigar smokers do. I've watched Inspector Piper, back home, mangle a cigar so that I didn't know if he was chewing or smoking it."

The sheriff nodded, looking at his own well-filled ashtray. "Moreover," Miss Withers continued, "Thelma Pringle was not killed by mistake, in place of Eileen here. She was killed by somebody who knew her and who wanted her dead. She was shot in the face with a shotgun, either by someone who

208

wanted to spoil her looks or who wanted to prevent identification, at least temporarily—"

There was a brief period of silence, broken when Molly Koontz dropped her pencil and had to grope for it.

"Now look here," the sheriff said, "you're trying to tell us that the killer walked in with a shotgun, had a drink with the girl, and then—"

"The drinks could have been set up afterward," Miss Withers pointed out. "There was a distinct reek of whisky in the garbage."

"But the girl would have yelled for help if she saw somebody come at her with a shotgun," Detective Rankin put in.

"Who would have heard her? The murder was committed at an hour when almost everybody in Las Vegas is away from home. I have my own theory as to how the gun came into the house. It could have been butt-down in a golf bag, with a golf-club stocking over the muzzle. But never mind that for a moment. The point is—*the murderer of Thelma Pringle was a woman!*"

"A woman who left a man's full-size fingerprints?" Rankin argued.

"Some women have large hands." Miss Withers looked at Molly Koontz, who had forgotten to take notes. The woman suddenly jumped to her feet.

"I didn't do it, I didn't! You can take my prints—"

"Relax, Molly," the sheriff said. "We already got 'em off the compact in your desk, and you didn't do it."

"I wasn't suggesting that she did," Miss Withers said, "even though her husband had been mixed up with Thelma Pringle. However, I think that they got the idea of blackmail separately. You see, the murder was well planned—designed to throw an even heavier weight of guilt on George Travis. The killer did not know that Travis was out on bond, but she did know that if a body identified as that of his wife was found in Las Vegas, he would be suspected of having instigated the murder. Even if the identity of the corpse came to light, it would still appear that his agents had merely struck down the wrong woman. Only one person had a motive to involve George Travis in *more* trouble than he was already in—and that person came into the cottage with a shotgun and killed the girl who was trying to blackmail her, thus killing two birds with one stone."

"Very neat," the sheriff said. "But if you're—"

"I certainly am," Miss Withers cried breathlessly. "Eileen Travis, I accuse you of a double murder."

It should have been a rousing climax, but it fell flat as a pancake. Eileen was shaking her head, almost pityingly. Macy's expression was sorrowful, and Rankin was almost laughing. The sheriff smiled a weary, patient smile. "All done, ma'am?"

"Isn't—isn't that enough?"

"Plenty. Very ingenious, too. Only I think that you ought to know, ma'am, that when she came in Mrs. Travis insisted we take her fingerprints, and they don't match the ones on the gun, glasses, or ice-pick!"

Miss Withers felt slightly faint. "But they *have* to!" she protested.

"Officer Rankin here is our fingerprint expert," the sheriff said. "He's read all the books."

Rankin beamed.

"But there must be some mistake!" cried Miss Withers.

"There is, and you've made it." The sheriff looked at the big silver watch the size of a teacup. "Miss Withers, there's a plane out of here at nine o'clock, which gives you just half an hour. Macy, you see that she gets placed and on that plane and out of my hair!"

Sheriff Kehoe was standing up now, his voice rising to a deep baritone roar. Miss Withers, the bitter taste of defeat in her mouth, backed hastily out of the door.

There was a long silence. The sheriff sat down again, lighted a cigar, and mopped his forehead. "Now, like I said, we'll start at the beginning, and see if we can straighten this out. You first, Mrs. Travis. We'll take your statement, and Molly will type it out so you can sign it and go."

Eileen spoke carefully and slowly, for some time. Her statement was in the typewriter when the telephone on the sheriff's desk rang shrilly. He picked it up. "Kehoe. What? Oh, Macy. What's the matter, did you let her miss the plane?"

There was a short pause, and then the sheriff heaved a deep sigh of relief. "Good, good. I'm glad you reported—it's a load off my mind." He started to hang up, and then jammed the instrument against his ear "What? What final request?"

The others in the room all strained their ears, but they could hear only a jumble of sounds from the other end of the line. At last the sheriff put down the phone, and said, "Rankin!"

"Yes, sheriff?"

"You're supposed to be our fingerprint expert. This case is at a dead end because we can't find any suspect whose prints fit those on the murder weapons and the drinking glass. Tell me, is there any way a person could deliberately leave false prints?"

The burly young detective swallowed. "There—there's a photographic process on gelatin, but it's easy to detect because it doesn't leave pore marks. . . ."

But the sheriff wasn't listening. He turned slowly toward Eileen Travis, who still leaned back in the one easy chair, her bare brown ankles crossed, a cigarette dangling from her full lush mouth. She stared back at him, letting the ashes fall to the floor.

"Mrs. Travis," he asked with ceremonious politeness, "would you mind very much if I asked you to take off your shoes?"

She opened her mouth, but no words came.

"It's been suggested by the lady who just left," continued Sheriff Kehoe, "that fingers are not the only portions of the human body that have distinctive skin patterns. With your permission—or without it—we'd like to take your *toeprints!*"

THE GARDEN OF
FORKING PATHS

BY JORGE LUIS BORGES

Jorge Luis Borges was born in Buenos Aires, Argentina, on
August 24, 1899, and educated in Switzerland. Until about
1930, his main creative medium was poetry, but in the
next ten years he virtually abandoned it for the short nar-
rative. His first story translated into English originally
appeared in the August 1948 issue of *Ellery Queen's Mystery Magazine*. In his early fifties, he became almost totally
blind, but he continues to write and lecture all over the
world. In 1976, he received a special award from the
Mystery Writers of America for his contribution to detective fiction.

ON PAGE 252 of Liddell Hart's *History of the World War* you may read that an offensive of thirteen British divisions supported by 1400 pieces of artillery, planned against the Serre-Montauban line for July 24, 1916, was postponed until the morning of the 29th.

The torrential rains, Captain Liddell Hart adds in a note, were responsible for this delay, an insignificant one in any case.

The following statement—dictated, reread, and signed by Dr. Yu Tsun, former professor of English in the *Hochschule* at Tsingtao, casts an unsuspected light over the entire affair. The first two pages of the statement are missing.

. . . and I hung up the receiver. As soon as I had done so, I recognized the voice which had answered in German. It was that of Captain Richard Madden. The presence of Madden in Viktor Runeberg's flat meant the end of our projects and—though this seemed, or should have seemed, of secondary importance to me—likewise the end of our lives. It meant that Runeberg had been arrested, or murdered.* Before that day's sun should set, I would incur the same fate.

Madden was relentless. Or rather, circumstances compelled him to be relentless. An Irishman in the English service, a man accused of apathy and perhaps of treason, could hardly fail to seize gratefully upon this miraculous chance to uncover, capture, and possibly kill two agents of the German Reich.

I went up to my room. Absurdly I locked the door and threw myself down on the narrow iron cot. Through the window I saw the roofs I had always seen and the clouded sun of six o'clock. It seemed incredible that this day, so like all others, should be the day of my inevitable death. No premonitions, no symbols . . . My father was long dead, it was

---

*An hypothesis at once repulsive and ridiculous. The Prussian spy Hans Rabener, *alias* Viktor Runeberg, used his automatic to attack Captain Richard Madden, who carried a warrant for his arrest. In self-defense Madden was obliged to inflict the wounds which resulted in the spy's death.—*Editor's Note.*

long ago that I was a child in the symmetrical garden of Hai Feng; but was I to die—and now? Then I reflected that all things happen to a man in the precise instant of now. Centuries pile upon centuries and only in the now can things happen; men innumerable fill the sea, the earth, the air, and all that really happens happens to me. . . .

The almost intolerable memory of Madden's horse-like face cut short these wanderings. In the midst of my hatred and terror (the terror no longer signifies, now that I have made a fool of Richard Madden, now that my throat longs for the noose), I remembered that this tumultuous and doubtless happy warrior had no suspicion that I possessed the Secret—the name of the precise location of the new British artillery station on the Ancre. A bird streaked across the gray sky and blindly I translated it into an airplane and this airplane into many that streaked through the French sky and annihilated the artillery station with vertical bombs. If my mouth, before a bullet destroyed it, could cry the name of that location so loudly that it might be heard in Germany . . . My human voice was weak. How could it reach the ear of the Chief? The ear of the sickly, hateful man who knew nothing of Runeberg and me save that we were in Staffordshire and that he vainly waited for word from us, sitting in his arid office in Berlin, endlessly nosing through newspapers. . . .

I said aloud, "I must flee." I arose soundlessly, in a useless perfection of silence, as though Madden were already on my trail. Something—perhaps merely the vanity of proving my helplessness—made me look through my pockets. I found what I knew I would find: the American watch, the nickel chain with the square charm, the key ring with the useless and compromising keys to Runeberg's flat, the wallet, a letter which I decided to destroy at once (and did not destroy), a cigar, two shillings and a few coppers, the red-and-blue pencil, the handkerchief, the revolver with one bullet. Absurdly I weighed it in my hand to give me courage. Vaguely I thought that a pistol shot could be heard over a long distance. In ten minutes my plan was complete. The telephone directory gave me the name of the only individual capable of transmitting my message; he lived in the suburb of Fenton, less than half an hour away by train.

I am a cowardly man. Now I can say it, now that I have carried out a plan the peril of which none can deny. I know

214

the terror of that plan. I did not do it for Germany; I care nothing for a barbarous country which imposed upon me the humiliation of being a spy. Besides I know of one Englishman—an unassuming man—who to me ranks no whit below Goethe. I talked with him for not over an hour, but during that hour he was Goethe . . . I did this thing because I felt that the Chief held in scorn those of my race, the innumerable ancestors who flow together in me. I wished to prove to him that a man with yellow skin could save his armies. Moreover, I wanted to escape Captain Madden. At any moment his hands and his voice would pound against my door. I dressed silently, bade myself farewell in my mirror, and left the house.

It was a short distance to the station, but I thought it wiser to take a cab. I argued that I ran less risk of being recognized; actually it was because in the deserted street I felt visible and infinitely vulnerable. I remember that I told the driver to stop a little before the main entrance. With difficulty I forced myself to get out casually, slowly; I was going to the village of Ashgrove but I bought a ticket for a station farther along the line. The train would leave in a very few minutes, at 8:50. I hurried; the next train was not until 9:30. There was almost no one on the platform. I looked over the coaches; I remember a few working men, a woman in mourning, a young man absorbed in the *Annals* of Tacitus, a wounded and happy soldier. At last the train pulled out. A man pursued it vainly to the edge of the platform. I recognized Captain Richard Madden. Shattered, trembling, I shrank into the opposite corner of the compartment, away from the terrifying window.

I passed from this shattered state to an almost abject contentment. I told myself that the duel had begun and that I had won the first encounter by thus frustrating—even if for only forty minutes, even if by a caprice of fate—the attack of my adversary. I argued that this least of victories foreshadowed the total victory. I argued that it was not so small a triumph, since but for this precious difference presented to me by the timetable I should now be imprisoned or dead. I argued (no less sophistically) that my cowardly contentment proved me a man capable of carrying out the adventure successfully. From this weakness I drew forces that were not to desert me.

215

I foresee that man will give himself over with each day to more atrocious enterprises; soon there will be only warriors and bandits. To them I leave this counsel: *He who undertakes an atrocious enterprise must imagine that he has already accomplished it, must impose upon himself a future no less irrevocable than the past.* That was my course, while my eyes (the eyes of a man already dead) noted the liquidity of that day, which was perhaps the last, and the diffusion of the night.

The train ran smoothly through rows of ash trees. It stopped almost in the open country. No one called the name of the station. "Ashgrove?" I asked some children on the platform. "Ashgrove," they replied. I got off.

A lamp lit up the platform, but the children's faces remained in the zone of shadow. One boy asked me, "Are you going to Dr. Stephen Corbie's?" Without waiting for my answer another said, "The house is a long way off, but you won't get lost if you take the road to the left and turn to the left at every crossroads." I tossed them a coin (my last), went down a few stone steps, and entered the lonely road. Slowly I followed it. It was of unpaved earth; the branches mingled overhead, the low circular moon seemed to accompany me.

For one instant I thought that Captain Madden had in some manner realized my desperate intention. I soon understood that that was impossible. The advice always to turn to the left reminded me that such was the standard procedure for reaching the center of certain mazes. I have some knowledge of mazes; not for nothing am I the descendant of that Ts'ui Pên who was governor of Yunnan but renounced temporal power to write a novel which was to be yet more all-embracing than the Hung Lu Meng and to construct a maze in which no man might find his way. Thirteen years he devoted to these ill-assorted labors, but the hand of a stranger murdered him and the novel made no sense and no man found the maze.

Beneath English trees I meditated on this lost maze: I imagined it inviolate and perfect on the secret summit of some mountain; I imagined it erased by rice fields or sunk beneath water; I imagined it infinite, no longer constructed of octagonal kiosks and twisting paths, but of rivers and provinces and kingdoms . . . I thought of a maze of mazes, a labyrinth of labyrinths, one sinuous waxing labyrinth that

216

should include the past and the future and in some manner involve the stars.

Absorbed in these illusory images, I forgot the fate which pursued me. I felt myself, for a certain space of time the abstract perceiver of the world. The limpid living countryside, the moon, the dying body of the evening worked upon me, and the slope of the road eliminated any possibility of weariness. The evening was intimate and infinite. The road descended and forked among the dimmed meadows. A shrill syllabic music drew near and faded in the shifting wind, swaddled in leaves and distance. I thought that a man may be the enemy of other men, at other moments of other men, but not of a country: not of fireflies, words, gardens, watercourses, sunsets.

Thus I arrived before a tall and rusty gate. Through its grille I made out a grove of poplars and a small house. I understood suddenly two things, the first trivial, the second all but incredible: the music came from the house and the music was Chinese. This was why I had accepted it so fully and with so little curiosity. I do not recall whether there was a bell or whether I knocked. The music continued to sparkle.

But from the depth of the little house a lantern drew near, a lantern which sent out its rays to ring the trunks of the poplars, a paper lantern which had the shape of a drum and the color of the moon. A tall man bore it. I could not see his face; the light blinded me. He opened the gate and said slowly in my own language, "I observe that the pious Hsi P'êng has undertaken to correct my solitude. You wish no doubt to see the garden?"

I recognized the name of one of our consuls. Disconcerted, I repeated, "The garden?"

"The garden of forking paths."

Something stirred in my memory. With unaccountable certainty, I said, "The garden of my ancestor Ts'ui Pên."

"Your ancestor? Your illustrious ancestor? Come in."

The damp path zigzagged like those I knew in childhood. We entered a library of Eastern and Western books. I recognized, bound in yellow silk, certain manuscript volumes of that Lost Encyclopedia edited by the Third Emperor of the Luminous Dynasty but never printed. The gramophone record revolved near a bronze phoenix. I remember too a porcelain jar of the Rose Family and another, many centuries

217

older, of that blue which our craftsmen copied from the Persian potters.

Stephen Corbie was watching me with a smile. He was, as I said, very tall, sharp-featured, gray-eyed, gray-bearded. There was something of a priest about him, and also something of a sailor. Later he told me that he had been a missionary in Tientsin "before I sought to become a Sinologue."

We seated ourselves, I on a long low divan, he with his back to the window and to the tall round clock. I calculated that I had an hour before the arrival of my pursuer, Captain Madden. My irrevocable resolve could wait.

"The fate of your ancestor Ts'ui Pên," said Stephen Corbie, "was astonishing. He was governor of his native province, learned in astronomy, in astrology, and in the unwearying exegesis of the canonical books, a master of chess, a famous poet and calligrapher—and all this he abandoned to compose a book and a maze. He renounced the pleasures alike of tyranny and of justice, of his well-populated couch, of banquets and even of learning; and for thirteen years he shut himself up in the Pavilion of Limpid Solitude. On his death his heirs found nothing save chaotic manuscripts. His family, as you are perhaps aware, wished to have these burned; but his executor—a Taoist or Buddhist monk—insisted on their publication."

"We of the race of Ts'ui Pên," I replied, "continue to curse that monk. The publication was an absurd enterprise. The book is a shapeless accumulation of contradictory drafts. I have examined it somewhat: in Chapter Three the hero dies, in Chapter Four he is alive. As for Ts'ui Pên's other undertaking, the maze . . ."

"Here is the maze," he said, indicating a tall, lacquered desk.

"A marble maze!" I exclaimed. "A labyrinth in miniature . . ."

"A labyrinth of symbols," he corrected me. "An invisible labyrinth in time. It has fallen to my lot, English barbarian that I am, to unveil this diaphanous mystery. After more than a hundred years the details are lost irrevocably; but one may conjecture the course of events. Upon one occasion Ts'ui Pên announced: 'I am retiring to write a book.' Upon another: 'I am retiring to construct a maze.' Everyone thought of two undertakings; no one imagined that the book and the maze were one. The Pavilion of Limpid Solitude stood, let us say, in the center of a rather intricate garden; this fact may have suggested a physical labyrinth. Ts'ui Pên died. In all the widespread lands that were his no man could find the maze. The chaos of the novel suggested to me that book *itself* was the maze. Two circumstances gave me the correct solution to the problem. One: the curious legend that Ts'ui Pên had proposed to construct a labyrinth strictly infinite in its extension. The other: a fragment of a letter upon which I chanced."

Corbie rose. For a moment he turned his back to me and opened a drawer in the desk of black and gold lacquer. He returned with a sheet of once-crimson paper. Now it was pink and fragile and creased. Ts'ui Pên had been justly celebrated for his calligraphy. With excitement, without comprehension, I read the words which a man of my blood had traced with his minute brush: *I leave to the various futures (and not to all) my garden of forking paths.*

Wordlessly I returned the paper. Corbie continued:

"Before I unearthed this letter, I had constantly asked myself how a book could be infinite. I could imagine no other method than that of a cyclic, a circular volume. A volume whose last page should be identical with the first, thus possibly continuing indefinitely. I remembered too that night which stands in the center of the Thousand and One Nights, when Queen Scheherazade (by some magical aberration of the copyist) begins to relate word for word the story of the Thousand and One Nights, incurring the danger of arriving once more at the night in which she tells the story of the Nights, and thus continuing to infinity. I conceived also an hereditary work, transmitted from father to son, to which each new generation should add a chapter or correct with pious care the pages of its ancestors.

"These conjectures served to entertain me; but no one of them seemed to correspond, even remotely, to the contradictory chapters of Ts'ui Pên. In this perplexity I received from Oxford the latter which you have examined. I paused, naturally, at the phrase: *I leave to the various futures (and not to all) my garden of forking paths.* Almost instantly I understood: the garden of forking paths was the chaotic novel; the phrase, *the various futures (and not all)*, suggested to my mind a forking, a bifurcation, not in space, but in time. Another survey of the work confirmed this theory. In all other works of fiction, a character confronted with various alternatives chooses one and eliminates the others. In this novel the character chooses—simultaneously—all of them. He thus *creates* varying futures, varying times, which in their turn likewise proliferate and fork. From this arise the 'contradictions' of the novel.

"Fang, let us say has a secret; an unknown man raps at the door; Fang resolves to kill him. Naturally, this situation may resolve itself in several possible manners: Fang may kill the intruder, the intruder may kill Fang, both may survive, both may perish, and so on. In the works of Ts'ui Pên, *all* these resolutions occur; each one is the point of departure for further forkings. Upon occasion the paths of this maze converge: for example, you arrive at my home; but in one of the possible pasts you are my friend, in another my enemy. If you will tolerate my incurable accent, we shall read a few pages."

In the vivid circle of lamplight his face was unquestionably that of an old man; but there was something unbreakable about it, even immortal. He read, with slow precision, two versions of the same epic chapter. In the first, an army marches toward battle across a barren mountain; the horror of the rocks and shadows causes them to hold their lives cheap and they gain an easy victory. In the second, the same army passes through a palace where a festival is in progress; the glittering battle seems to them a continuation of the festival and they gain an easy victory. With seemly veneration I listened to these ancient narratives, perhaps less admirable in themselves than because my blood had conceived them and because a man of a remote Empire had restored them to me in the course of a desperate adventure in a Western isle. I remember the last words, repeated in each version like a hidden commandment: *Thus did the heroes fight, peace in their noble hearts and violence in their swords, resolved to kill and to die.*

From that moment on I felt about me and within me an invisible, intangible swarming. Not the swarming of the divergent, parallel, ultimately coalescing armies, but an agitation at once more inaccessible and more intimate, which the armies in some manner prefigured. Stephen Corbie continued:

"I do not believe that your illustrious ancestor was playing

220

an idle game with his variations. I do not find it plausible that he should sacrifice thirteen years in the infinite execution of a rhetorical experiment. In your country the novel is a subsidiary form of literature; in his time it was even a contemptible one. Ts'ui Pên was a novelist of genius, but he was also a man of letters who assuredly did not consider himself a mere novelist. The evidence of his contemporaries demonstrates (and his own life confirms) his leanings toward the metaphysical, the mystical. Philosophical debate usurps a large portion of the novel. From other sources I know that of all problems none so perturbed and beset him as the abysmal problem of Time. And yet, that is the *only* problem which does not figure in the pages of *The Garden*. Not once does he employ even the very character which means Time. How do you acount for this deliberate omission?"

I advanced various solutions, none of them satisfactory. We discussed them, and at last Stephen Corbie said:

"In a riddle the answer to which is 'chess,' what is the one forbidden word?"

I reflected a moment and answered, "The word *chess*."

"Precisely," said Corbie. "*The Garden of Forking Paths* is a vast riddle, or parable, whose meaning is Time; that recondite cause forbids the mention of the word. Always to omit a word, to seek refuge in inept metaphors or blatant periphrases, is perhaps the most emphatic method of stressing that word. It is the tortuous method preferred, in each meandering of his indefatigable novel, by the oblique Ts'ui Pên. I have collated hundreds of manuscripts, I have corrected the errors introduced by the carelessness of copyists, I have conjectured the plan of this chaos, I have reestablished (I believe) the primordial order, I have translated the entire work —constantly struck by the fact that the translation never once necessitated the use of the word *time*. The explanation is obvious: *The Garden of Forking Paths* is an image, incomplete but not inaccurate, of the universe as Ts'ui Pên conceived it.

"Your ancestor differed from Newton and Schopenhauer in not believing in one uniform and absolute Time. He believed in an infinite series of Time, in a waxing, dizzying web of times, divergent, convergent, and parallel. This network of times which draw near each other, fork out of each other, cut across each other, or know nothing of each other for

221

centuries—these times embrace *all* possibilities. In most of these times we do not exist. In some you exist and I do not; in others I but not you; in yet others, both of us. In this time a favorable fate has granted that you enter my house; in another, you found me dead as you crossed the garden; in another, I am saying these very words, but I am an illusion, a phantom."

"In all times," I pronounced, not without a tremor, "I offer you my gratitude and veneration for your remaking of the garden of Ts'ui Pên."

"Not in all," he murmured smiling. "Time forks forever toward innumerable futures. In one of them I am your enemy."

Once more I felt that swarming of which I spoke. It seemed to me that the moist garden outside the house was infinitely saturated with invisible personages. And all of them were Corbie and I, vowed to other secrets, laden with other tasks, shaped in other forms in other dimensions of time. I raised my eyes; the tenuous nightmare dissolved. In the yellow and black garden there was only one man; but that man was coming toward me down the path and he was Captain Richard Madden.

"The future exists already," I said, "but I am your friend. May I look at the letter again?"

Corbie rose. The tall old man opened the drawer of the tall desk; for a moment he turned his back on me. I had the revolver ready. I fired with the utmost care; Corbie fell immediately, without a word. I swear that his death was instantaneous, a lightning-stroke.

The rest is unreal and insignificant. Captain Madden burst in and arrested me. I have been sentenced to hang. And I have won abominably; I have communicated to Berlin the secret name of the city which they must attack. They bombed it yesterday; I read that in the very papers which presented the English people with the puzzle of why the learned Sinologue Stephen Corbie should have been murdered by a stranger, Yu Tsun. The Chief has deciphered this puzzle. He knows that my problem was how to indicate (across the uproar of the war) the city called Corbie and that *I found no other solution save to murder a man of that name.*

He does not know (no one can know) my unspeakable regret and weariness.

THE LADY AND THE TIGER

BY JACK MOFFITT

Jack Moffitt was born in 1901 in Kansas City, Missouri. He attended the University of Missouri, then worked for the *Kansas City Star,* where his witty movie reviews won wide attention. He moved to Hollywood in 1941 and wrote more than forty feature films for Paramount, Warner Brothers, M-G-M, and other major studios. He was married in 1930 and had two daughters. For more than ten years he wrote a political column for the *Los Angeles Herald Express.* He died on December 4, 1969. "The Lady and the Tiger," his solution to Frank R. Stockton's great enigma "The Lady, or the Tiger?" appeared in the September 1948 issue of *Ellery Queen's Mystery Magazine.*

You may find it faintly ridiculous that I, Charles Sevier, a stout and fortyish researcher working in Rome at the Vatican Library, should be in love with a woman who has been dead two thousand years.

This strange infatuation was brought about by the most prosaic of instruments—Frank R. Stockton's short story, "The Lady, or the Tiger?" which was published in 1884, sixteen years before my birth.

During the intervening years I doubt if there has been a single literate American who has not attempted to answer the riddle, which Mr. Stockton propounded in words which I have taken the liberty to abridge:

"In olden times there lived a semi-barbaric king, whose ideas, though polished and sharpened by the progressiveness of distant Latin neighbors, were still large, florid and untrammeled.

"When one of his male subjects was accused of a crime, public notice was given that on an appointed day, the man's fate would be decided in the King's Arena. Here the prisoner faced two doors, exactly alike and side by side. It was the obligation of the person on trial to open one of these doors. He was subject to no guidance or influence. He could open either he pleased.

"If he opened one, there came out a hungry tiger.

"But if he opened the other, there came forth a lady, the most suitable to his years and station that the King could select from among his subjects, and to this lady he was immediately married, amid appropriate ceremonies.

"Sometimes the tiger was behind one door, sometimes the other. Chance was the only arbiter.

"Now the ruler had a daughter as blooming as his most florid fancies, and with a soul as fervent and imperious as his own. As is usual, in such cases, she was the apple of his eye, and was loved by him above all humanity. But among the King's courtiers was a young man who was handsome and brave to a degree unsurpassed in all this kingdom, and the princess loved him with an ardor that had enough of barbarism in it to make it exceedingly warm and strong.

"This love affair moved on happily for many months, until one day the King happened to discover its existence. He did not hesitate nor waver. The youth was immediately cast into prison, and a day was appointed for his trial in the King's Arena.

"As the youth advanced toward the doors, his eyes were fixed upon the princess, who sat to the right of her father. Had it not been for the barbarism in her nature it is probable she would not have been there. But her intense and fervid soul would not allow her to be absent.

"Possessed of power, influence and force of character, she had succeeded in doing what no other person had ever done—she had managed to learn the secret of the doors. She knew in which of the rooms was the tiger, and in which the lady.

"She also knew who the lady was—and she hated her. The girl was lovely, but she had dared to raise her eyes to the loved one of the princess. With all the savagery transmitted to her through long lines of barbaric ancestors, the King's daughter hated the woman who blushed and waited behind that silent door.

"She trembled as her lover turned and looked at her. His eye met hers as she sat there, with features paler and whiter than any in the vast ocean of anxious faces that surrounded her. And he saw instantly that she knew behind which door crouched the tiger, and behind which stood the lady.

"He had expected her to know it.

"Then his quick and anxious glance asked the question: 'Which?' It was as plain to her as if he shouted it from where he stood. The question was asked in a flash; it must be answered in another.

"Her right arm lay on the cushioned parapet before her. She raised her hand and made a slight, quick movement toward the right. No one but her lover saw her. Every eye but his was fixed on the arena.

"He turned, and with a firm and rapid step, walked across the empty space. Every heart stopped beating, every breath was held, every eye was fixed immovable upon that man.

"Without the slightest hesitation, he went to the door on the right and opened it.

"Now, the point of the story is this: Did the tiger come out of that door, or did the lady?"

I had heard that Stockton had obtained the idea for his story from a Roman Catholic antiquarian in the city of Rome; so it is small wonder that I determined to solve the riddle when, after several years as a researcher in the Library of Congress, I was sent to introduce a modern cataloguing system in the Vatican Archives. The immediate purpose of my employment was to search for a long-lost letter supposed to have been written by Pontius Pilate. But I had plenty of time for private research.

After considerable study I decided that Stockton's king could have been none other than Herod Antipas, who ruled Judea under the supervision of the Roman Governor, Pontius Pilate. He was the only eastern monarch who owned an arena, which his father had built after the Roman pattern, but he also had a daughter—or rather a step-daughter—of whom he was unnaturally and inordinately infatuated.

This girl was the Princess Salome.

The logic fitted. I felt that I had identified two of the characters in Stockton's story. But it was not until I found the cracked and yellowed parchment, covered with Hebrew characters and written in a sprawling, girlish hand, that I was certain of it. For this letter was written by the girl who had waited behind the second door.

To the High Priest, Caiaphas; from his daughter, Miriam.
Beloved Father,

How can I tell you how much I love you? I know that you must be ashamed of me because all Jerusalem now knows that I love the Greek youth, Jason. I know you will feel humiliated—almost defiled—to see me married to him, by a pagan ritual, before all the people in the King's arena tomorrow. Yet I know that even now, despite your sorrow and your humiliation, you are praying to our one true God to defend Jason and asking the Lord to lead him to the door behind which I will be waiting.

I know that you are doing this, in spite of your conviction that Jason is shallow and ambitious—one of those youths who came swaggering out of Alexandria to seek his fortune at the court of Herod. And I feel that you are praying for Jason, even though you dislike him, because you abominate murder and because you have always been a just and merciful man.

Oh, dear! It is dreadful to be young! It seems odd to remember that I didn't want to go with you to Herod's palace

226

on that day last autumn—when I first met Jason. For weeks I'd heard you and Grandfather discussing the arrogance of Pontius Pilate who had displayed the eagles of his legions on the fortress of Antonia, overlooking the Temple courtyard. Of course, I'd been taught to regard graven images as sacrilegious, but I wondered why older people made such a fuss about things.

When you decided that the family should ask Herod to intercede, I pretended to have a headache. But I didn't fool you. You said the visit would seem more tactful and more friendly if the whole family went along. I was amused to see, when we arrived at the palace, that your strategy had not fooled Herod any more than mine had fooled you. His chamberlain led you and Grandfather away to the King's audience chamber, while the rest of us were sent to wait for you in one of the private courtyards.

As soon as my little brothers saw the fountain splashing in the center of the palace, they rushed toward it squealing and laughing.

I tried to get them interested in the pictures in the floor of the courtyard. They were mosaics showing the fall of Troy. I told as much of the pagan story as I thought was good for them.

But you know Nathan. He can't sit still for more than a minute.

"Look!" he shouted, "I'll bet I can jump all around this place and never put my foot on anything but the women!"

This wasn't easy. There were many more warriors in the mosaic floor than there were goddesses. Nathan missed on the third jump. But he had started a game. Soon the whole place was filled with hopping children, wobbling and tottering as they leaped from Minerva to Aphrodite to Helen, and so on. I know it was childish, but it really was fun. So, just to keep them quiet, I pulled up my dress above my knees and joined in.

And then I heard someone laughing.

Dearest heavens! I could have died! A man had entered the courtyard—a tall, lithe man wearing sandals of silver leather and a tunic and cloak of green silk.

He laughed and said, "Who are you?"

You can imagine how confused I was as I dropped my skirts and tried to brush the hair out of my eyes. It was too awful for a grown-up woman to be caught like this by a member of the court, playing a ridiculous childish game. After all, I am fourteen years old.

"Who are you?" he repeated, coming toward me. "Surely you must have a name—is it Daphne? Or Thetis? Are you a dryad? Or a nymph?"

I was afraid the stranger might laugh at me when I told him who I was. But he didn't. He bowed and replied courteously. "You must come with me, Miriam," he said. "I have been commanded to bring you to the princess."

I wasn't so sure I should go. But the young man kept laughing and assuring us that he was repeating a royal order—until I finally let him lead me away through the maze of splendid corridors.

I couldn't find anything to say as I walked beside him, listening to his easy conversation. He told me that his name was Jason and that he had lived in Rome and Alexandria. He was the most interesting man I had ever met.

Finally, we came to a larger courtyard, where Salome idled beneath a pinkish awning, surrounded by many courtiers. Youths and maidens from all over the world were there—Greeks and Arabians and officers from the Roman garrison, and even a number of young Jews—though these were unlike any Jews I had seen before. Their cheeks were shaved and they wore Greek or Roman clothing.

Salome was a surprise. She didn't look at all like the kind of girl who could have caused the death of the young preacher whom the country people called the Baptist. She wore no veils or oriental draperies. Her gown was simple and Grecian, with the skirt folded into many soft pleats that concealed but outlined her small and doll-like figure. I had seen her mother, Herodias, in a procession once, and I had expected the daughter to have the same stately figure and proud eyes.

But Salome was a kitten. She had a little heart-shaped face and large and limpid brown eyes and she had learned how to use them.

"You are late, Jason," she said reproachfully, "our treasure hunt is over. Only you have returned empty-handed."

"You are wrong, Princess," said Jason, leading me forward, "you told me to bring you a Hebrew Diana—and I have."

"This is ridiculous!" Salome's pink small lips were pouting. "You knew I meant a statue."

228

"Did you, Princess? How could you? You know the Hebrews have made no images since the days of the Golden Calf. But it pleases you to demand the impossible of me."

"If I do, it is because you think you are so clever! Right now you feel quite proud of yourself!"

"Proud, yes. But not conceited." I felt my face burning as he held up my hand and slowly turned me around. "Praxiteles himself would be proud of the golden girl that I have brought."

"All you Greeks seem to think of gold in connection with women!" The milk-white Salome seemed to resent my olive skin. "To call this little thing a Diana is ridiculous."

"Let me go!" I struggled to free my wrist. "I despise every one of you!"

"No!" Jason's strong hands gripped my elbows as he lifted me up on a bench. "I didn't bring you here to be insulted! We'll show this princess that her taste is as bad as her manners! Hold your head up—you are the High Priest's daughter —you are as good as any of them!"

His voice was harsh, as though he were fighting a duel in which I was his weapon. I was trembling and overwrought, but I held up my head and tried to stare defiantly back at Salome, even though I was blinking back the tears.

"Observe the slender strength of her neck line!" he cried, as he snatched up a silver bow from the loot of the treasure hunt. "And have you noticed the supple gracefulness of her figure? Diana has come to life again!"

He fitted an arrow to the bow and placed it in my hands. The arrow was aimed straight at Salome. But she didn't flinch. There was a brooding hatefulness in her eyes.

"There!" said Jason, stepping back as I held the pose. "Is she not even more lovely than Diana? Can any of you say that the Diana of Epheseus has half her beauty? Answer me!"

"Well, it theems to me—" lisped the Greek called Philo, with a nervous glance at Salome.

"I'm not asking Greeks!" snapped Jason. "I am asking the Romans! What do you say, Galba?"

It was clever of him. The Romans loved to show their disdainful independence of Herod's provincial entourage. A slow grin spread over the youthful face of Galba. He passed his big hand over his close-cropped hair.

"By Jupiter! You're right," he said. "I have wasted incense before the statue of Ephesus, but I'd sacrifice my very sword and armor for the Diana we have here!"

All the other Roman officers were quick to agree with him. The courtiers chimed in too. I heard myself praised and complimented in a dozen accents, and my skin tingled with pleasure, just as it had flinched and trembled a few minutes before. It was glorious to be defended and admired.

And then I heard King Herod's smooth chuckle and saw him coming across the courtyard, followed by you and Grandfather.

"By Aphrodite!" he said. "Jason, it seems that you have found a jewel in my threadbare little country. I am very pleased."

I don't remember the rest of that day very clearly. All I remember is the horrible trip home. Grandfather Annas said that I had done something monstrous. It was a shameful thing for the daughter of the High Priest to pose as a pagan goddess before a throng of infidels.

I had little appetite for the dinner old Anna kept urging me to eat. She just can't forget that I no longer need a nurse. I went up on the roof and gazed out through the twilight toward the Mount of Olives. A great sense of poignancy welled up in me. I felt so lonely that it hurt. Then I heard you behind me.

"My dear," you said, "I know it is hard for you to believe but once, a long, long time ago, I was young too. I try to remember those times."

"Yes, Father," I replied looking out across the mystic Valley of Kidron.

You crossed the floor and stroked my hair. "We must have patience, Miriam," you said, "the heroes of our nation have always been men of the spirit—men who combined courage with inspiration. In our bitterest days they come to us—these men who live gloriously close to God. There have always been such men."

"Where are they now?" I asked.

"I do not know, child," you answered musingly. "But people tell of certain men in Galilee—there is the oldtime ring of greatness in much that I have heard of them."

Before you could go on, there was a pounding at the door and a voice: "Open in King Herod's name!"

I think, for all your dignity, Father, you were as frightened as I was as we stood, close together in the passage, and heard the officer tell us that I was to become a lady-in-waiting to Salome, and go with the court to Herod's winter palace at Tiberias.

No child knows how much it loves a parent until the time comes to leave home. Do you remember how melancholy the first autumn rains were when you took me to the Gennot Gate to join the royal caravan?

The trip was a lonely one. None of the women paid any attention to me. And I'd seen nothing of Jason. Shortly before dawn on the last day, I heard one of the camel men exclaim: "Tiberias!" and I poked my head through the curtains to get my first look at our destination.

It was a strange and wonderful sight that lay spread out before us in the fresh-washed air of the morning. The sun was just breaking through the clouds beyond the solemn dome of Mount Tabor and the light flashed back from the Sea of Galilee—really only a large lake—as though from a silver shield.

As I watched, there was a thunder of hoofs and a chariot swept past—a chariot drawn by four deep-chested, black-maned Arabians. Jason held the reins. He wore a tight tunic of orange-colored leather and an orange cape streamed back from his shoulders. He was a flame flashing down from the hills upon the black city of Tiberias.

Later, I was glad to see that Herod's palace wasn't so gloomy once you were inside. The rooms were bright with rich hangings and imported marbles. I was given a pretty little chamber at one end of the women's building. The King himself came with his royal housekeeper to see that I was comfortable. My only worry was that the balcony window could be reached from a nearby cedar. But, of course, I didn't complain. The King might have thought I was silly.

Some of the dresses that had been provided for me were positively indecent. You could see right through them. The others made of heavier materials had their skirts split too far above the knee. I was glad old Anna had taught me to sew, and that I'd brought my needle kit. With a little work I could make some of them look modest.

I had plenty of time. Neither Salome nor the Queen ever sent for me. Day after day I had nothing to do except work on my dresses and try new ways of fixing my hair.

Some weeks later I found Jason seated beside me at the

231

first of the King's banquets. I suppose I shouldn't say "seated." The guests reclined on long couches placed by the banquet table. Jason lounged by my side. I wasn't used to this fashion and was embarrassed.

But Jason made me feel at ease. He was smiling and very respectful. Even after the seventh course, when the wine was flowing much too freely and the party was getting a good deal worse than rowdy, he drank sparingly and never once touched me.

Salome didn't drink much either. She reclined across the room from us, between her mother and stepfather. I felt a little disloyal and unpatriotic for noticing that the King was getting tipsy. He laughed too loud and kept whispering things into the Princess's ear.

I would have thought that the Queen might have protected her daughter, but Herodias ignored her husband and kept her eyes fixed coldly on the entertainers, giving no encouragement to the suggestive dancers and their off-color songs. Though a member of the same mongrel clan as Herod, she conducted herself with the calm diginty of a Jewish matron.

Time and again I saw Salome's brown eyes look appealingly across the room to Jason. She seemed to envy us. And in spite of the way she'd neglected me, I felt sorry for her.

"Never feel sorry for a beautiful woman," replied Jason, when I mentioned this to him. "They know how to look out for themselves."

"My! Haven't you grown sophisticated and cynical!" I tried to speak mockingly, like one of the court ladies.

He turned to me and said, "I was born a slave but I might have been a prince—one of the rulers of the Roman world— if it hadn't been for a woman even more beautiful than Salome."

"A slave! You are teasing me! I don't believe it!"

"Even though I was born a slave," he said, "I am not a complete impostor. My father was a nobleman. He served on Marc Antony's flagship at the Battle of Actium."

"I don't care who you are, Jason—you don't have to tell me!"

He drank wine and stared morosely toward Salome. "My father became a slave and I was born in slavery because of the vanity of a woman. There was no reason for Cleopatra to be in that battle. Marc Antony begged her to stay ashore. But

232

she was very brave as long as the enemy galleys were on the other side of the horizon and she knew she looked very pretty in her armor. She wanted to be a sea queen and inspire the men!"

Jason spat upon the pavement and exclaimed, "To think that such vanity could have changed the fate of the world! At the height of the battle Cleopatra's ships turned and ran—and do you know why they ran?"

"I have heard that it was because Octavius, who opposed her, used his catapults to throw great glass globes filled with serpents and that when the globes broke on Cleopatra's decks, she became terrorized of the serpents—"

"That's not the real reason. Cleopatra wasn't afraid of snakes. She deserted Antony because she suddenly decided that it would be safer to win Octavius with her charms than to meet him in battle. And because of her cowardice, Marc Antony killed himself and my father was captured and reduced to slavery. Octavius forced him to become a gladiator."

He stopped abruptly as though he'd decided that he had talked enough. So this was the background of this seemingly gay man. He was the son of a slave and a gladiator.

Herodias was following her drunken husband from the room and Salome was picking her way among the sodden revelers toward the great arch that led to the moonlit gardens. She paused on the threshold and looked back toward us. And for the first time she was smiling.

"It is getting late," Jason told me, "You had better go to your room."

There was nothing to do but obey him.

After that it became apparent that the King had ordered Jason to be my escort at all court functions. But he didn't obey very often. It was exasperating to have him send an excuse, accompanied by some rich present, at the last moment.

Once the young people got up an excursion, with a picnic lunch and chariots, to hear a country preacher who addressed a great multitude on Mount Tabor. This preacher was quite the rage. The people told marvelous tales about him and even the court circle regarded him as a new sensation. I wondered if he was one of the men of Galilee whom you had mentioned. But I never found out. Jason didn't invite me, so I stayed with Salome and Herod and Herodias. After the scandal about the Baptist, they weren't much interested in country preachers.

Some weeks later, when the moon was waning, Herod gave an elaborate fête in the palace gardens. The grounds were illuminated by Greek fire thrown into the waters of the fountains. The floating flames transformed the black basins into gigantic lamps, and in this flickering glare Italian contortionists and acrobats and tight-rope walkers performed.

At first I was shocked by their nakedness. But Jason, seated beside me in the shadows, said that instead of scorning the poor mountebanks, I should pity them. For all we knew, he said, these boys and girls might be the children of aristocrats, or even of the Emperor. In Rome, he told me, unwanted children were left out in the hills for the wolves to eat and sometimes these abandoned creatures were found by human wolves—vagabonds and criminals who took them home and trained them for strange and evil callings.

"I can't understand your world," I said. "It is a terrible place! No Jewish mother could abandon her babies to such a life. No matter how low she had fallen."

"I know," he whispered. "My mother couldn't leave me out on the hill either—even though she tried to. It might have been better if she had."

Somehow I knew that I must comfort this man in his terrible gnawing misery. It was what God had put me in the world for. I put my hands on his cheeks and kissed him.

Then he was on his feet, pulling me up to him. His strong arm was around me as he led me into the shadows. He was returning my kiss—on my lips, my throat, my shoulders—and his kisses were fierce and hard.

"Darling, oh, my darling!" I cried, clinging to him. "You needn't be so fierce—so hurried—I will never run away from you—never!"

He paused and looked at me, and his arms were a tight circle around my body.

"Don't you see?" I said. "You need never be lonely again, ever—it doesn't matter what you've been—"

"You're wrong! It's the only thing that matters!" His arms grew slack and his voice was bitter. "I started as a piece of human garbage—left out on a Roman junk pile—and all my life has been a struggle to keep from going back there."

The fierceness had gone out of him. He sank to the ground

234

with his face turned toward the distant fountains, where the children's bodies glittered above the flickering fire.

"I never knew my mother," his words came moodily. "I hardly knew my father. The only clear memory I have of him is of one night—when I must have been about twelve. I was seated beside him at a great banquet in the barracks of the gladiators. The air was foul with the fumes of torches and there was a great deal of noise.

"Most of the gladiators were roaring drunk; guzzling liquor and gorging themselves until they vomited—trying to forget that they might die the next day. Others scarcely touched the heaping tables, because they hoped to be more fit in the arena. Some, too stupid or calloused to care what happened, tumbled on the floor with the slave women provided for their convenience.

"My father sat at a small table with an older gladiator named Longinus—a man whose life my father once had spared in the arena. They kept me on the bench between them.

"As the night wore on, he placed his hand behind my head and forced me to look at the hoggish couples who wallowed on the floor. 'Look, my son,' he said, with a mirthless smile. 'Look and see how you were created! Your mother was just such a drab as these!'

"I remember that I began to cry. And people stopped to stare at us. A child was the one thing they didn't expect to see at a gladiators' banquet. Longinus growled to my father to shut up. The scene was horrible.

"But my father continued in a low, intense voice. 'I am telling the boy this so that he may remember his destiny when I am gone! I didn't know his mother—I couldn't have told her from any of the other slatterns. The one time I embraced her, I was drunk. But, by the Gods, she remembered me! I shall never forget the dumb look that was on her face when she came to the barracks with her baby. I saw adoration there, not for me, but for the child—for you, son!'

"He told me that my mother had left me out on the hill, as she had left her previous children. But something nagged at her stupid mind and told her that she could not let the child of a prince die that way. So she went back to the hill and brought me to my father.

"And as he held me in his arms, my father felt that the ignorant trull was right. She had inspired him.

"His thick-skinned sword-hand gripped my shoulder as he told me all this and he said, 'I can only find freedom through you, my son! My blood in you can be a prince again! And this I demand of you, that no matter what happens—whether I live or die—that you shall fight by every method to reclaim our lost greatness!' "

Jason repeated his father's words in a voice that was low but excited, the tone he always used when he spoke of how important he might have been. Now his voice went flat.

"My father died the next day. He had been matched against Longinus. It was an honest fight. It had to be, or both men would have been thrown to the lions. Suddenly, though he had suffered no wound, my father collapsed upon the sand. I guess his heart gave out, after the long years of fighting. As I watched, his feeble arm went up in the gesture that asked for mercy. He wanted to live because of me.

"Longinus looked toward the Emperor. But Tiberius reached out a brawny arm and pointed his thumb—down.

"I saw the pleading look on Longinus' face. He hesitated. There were tears on his cheeks. The arena attendants were running forward to split my father's skull with mallets—the death reserved for a coward.

"Longinus' sword flashed down."

Jason had finished his story. The last of the flaming fountains flickered into darkness. We heard Herod ordering the servants to light the torches. I held Jason close and tried to comfort him. But when the flares were ignited, he moved away.

A few days later he was my escort when Herod took the court to his race course outside the city. Now he seemed to be trying to forget everything he had confided. His robes were rich and perfect. His eyebrows had been thinned and his smile was aloof and distant as he glanced toward the royal box, where Salome sat beside her stepfather.

In each race the colors of the charioteers were the same—white, red, blue, and green. Jason explained that these identified the four great racing syndicates in Rome. Herod favored the blue because that was the faction of the reigning emperor.

"I want to bet on the whites," I told Jason.

"Why?" he asked. "The blue is the best bet, but if you want a good long shot, go on and choose the red. It is an exciting color."

"But the whites are your horses!" I said. "I saw you drive them into the city."

His face clouded as he replied, "They are not my horses!" He spoke with undue vehemence. But I continued to smile at him. I knew what I had seen.

"Look, Miriam!" he cajoled. "The white hasn't a chance! They are older than the others, and the horse on the inside trace has a bowed tendon."

"Nevertheless, I want to bet on them!"

"All right," he shrugged. "At least, you'll get good odds."

Perhaps I imagined it, but as the chariots paraded past, I thought a slight signal passed from Jason to the charioteer in white.

I know you don't know much about racing, Father, so I'll try to explain to you. The two center horses are harnessed to the tongue of the chariot, while the outside animals run in leather shafts called traces. On the white chariot the outside horse was in a long trace so that he ran far out from his teammates. He wasn't pulling, he was running free and independently. And his long trace made a leather barrier across the track so that no other chariot could pass.

It was the first time this trick had been seen in Palestine. The shouts from the grandstands were deafening. At first, people thought there had been an accident and that the outside horse had broken his harness. But soon the air was filled with the excited frenzy of those who had backed the white and the curses of those who had bet on the other colors. Then everybody forgot money in their amazement at the skill of the thing. The outside horse swept around the track, keeping close to the outside railing—and the other chariots didn't try to pass for fear of getting entangled and turned over.

Of course, the white won! I turned excitedly to Jason.

"These provincial drivers are amateurs," he shrugged scornfully. "If this race had been run in Rome all the chariots would have had long traces. The green would have run into the white so that the blue could get through. Afterwards the drivers would have shared in the winning purse—and the Emperor's favor."

"But what of the drivers? They wear the ends of the reins wrapped around their bodies—wouldn't such crack-ups be dangerous?"

"Of course," he replied indifferently. "If they were quick,

they might cut themselves free with their daggers—or they might be killed. That's the chance you take in Rome."

The odds had been twenty to one. I won almost fifty silver shekels, even after the bookmaker had taken his commission.

I soon discovered that, even at Herod's court, a girl can have many friends after she's won fifty shekels. It was astonishing how many of the court ladies were short on spending money. They came to me for little loans—which they never paid back; and by way of compensation, they included me in their conversation, most of which was catty—if not positively evil. They seldom came right out and said anything vicious. But they were full of hints and innuendoes. According to them, the King was in love with Salome.

"And, my dear, his interest isn't entirely fatherly," one of them giggled.

I didn't like to hear this, even though I felt it might be true. The King's attitude toward Salome was anything but decorous. Still, the thing they hinted at was perfectly monstrous—and I doubted if even Herod, who had defied the Law by taking his brother's wife, would pile incest on incest by now making love to his stepdaughter.

"Whatever the King may lack," I said, "He is still our King —and the only protection we have from the Romans. And, as long as we are members of his household, we owe him our loyalty and our patriotism."

"Listen to her silly preaching!" laughed an Athenian girl named Enid. "Of all people! If Herod wasn't in love with Salome, little Miriam wouldn't be here!"

I didn't like this Enid. She had a long jaw that kept her from being pretty, so she tried to attract attention to her figure. To make sure of this, she walked with her hips thrust out in a most preposterous and vulgar way. She had borrowed more from me than the others. Maybe that was why she was always giving me digs.

"What do you mean?" I flared.

"Oh, please, Miriam!" She glanced over her shoulder at her hips with an air of exaggerated patience and languor. "You of all people shouldn't be naive! Don't you realize that the King brought you here to keep Jason away from Salome?"

"You are absolutely insane!" I retorted. "I never heard of anything so stupid! The King is the King! If he doesn't like Jason, he can send him away!"

"What a dull little thing you are! Herod isn't rude to one who's been favored by Pontius Pilate!"

"But how do I fit into his plans?"

"Darling, are you actually asking me to tell you? I was hoping we could be more delicate. Why do you think the King gave you this lovely room with a window—so accessible from the gardens?"

"Get out!" My face was flaming. "Get out! I won't answer your filthy accusations! I never want to see any of you again!"

Enid strutted toward the door, followed by the others. Their steps were insolent and leisurely.

"All right, we'll go, my dear. There's no need to be shrill. After all, it isn't our fault that the King's plan miscarried—and that the Greek prefers Salome. He never goes near you except when he is commanded, and even then he scarcely dares speak—he's so afraid of Salome. No wonder you're jealous!"

When they were gone I threw myself on the couch and cried. I wished I could go back home to Jerusalem. I longed for a life that was clean and decent. The court and everyone in it was hateful. I wanted you, father. I wanted to crawl in your lap, like a little girl, and to forget everything.

But that afternoon we were ordered to accompany the King to the famous mineral hot baths, south of the city.

I sent word that I was still too ill to go to the baths. But they refused to accept my excuses. Queen Herodias herself came to persuade me. Her attitude was almost motherly, and she was so serene and dignified that it was hard to argue with her. She said the baths were good for all sorts of ailments and were bound to make me feel better. Furthermore, she said that the King had sent her to tell me that Jason was waiting. I wondered if she knew that she and I were both pawns in his love game. But I didn't dare ask. I was too discouraged to do anything but submit. I let her take my hand and lead me out to Jason's chariot.

He was driving the Arabians and he looked very handsome. At once he began his amiable chatter.

"Please," I said. "There is no need to be charming. I know that you are with me only because of the King's orders."

His look was pained. "Miriam, you don't understand—"

"I think I do. Your father was a slave and you are a slave—a slave to your ambitions."

I wanted to hurt him. The anger flushed up behind his sunburn. He lashed the horses and the chariot spun forward ahead of the rest of the procession. He didn't rein until we had reached the baths.

"Miriam," he said. "You have to believe me!"

"Why should I? I know that you have lied to me. You even told me that these horses weren't yours!"

"In a way, they aren't," he said. "These horses were the property of the White Syndicate. I took them from Rome with me when I retired from racing."

"You stole those horses?" I made my voice scornful. "You *are* dishonest—and more foolhardy than your reckless nature seems capable of being."

"Well, why not!" he exclaimed. "They're my luck! Longinus apprenticed me to a charioteer after my father died, and I won two hundred and thirty-nine victories with these horses in the Circus Maximus. They made me a millionaire!"

"But you are not satisfied with being a millionaire! You must have the love of a princess, even though you have to share that love with her stepfather! You are as evil as they are!"

He restrained me as, trembling with anger, I started to leave the chariot.

"Please, Miriam!" he begged. "I know you have good reason to be angry. But doesn't the fact that I let my horses win for you mean anything? I had planned to keep that trick up my sleeve."

"I don't doubt it! And I still don't know why you became so generous—I don't want your pity! And I don't want your favors!" I flung myself out of the chariot.

The rest of the royal procession was driving up just then. Salome looked hatefully at me and even the Queen seemed irritated. But Herod was smiling and bland. We went into the baths.

I was relieved to see that the men's and women's quarters were separate. I hadn't known what to expect. As soon as we were in the women's section, Salome and the others threw their clothes off. I found a dark spot in a corner of the steam room and tried to be inconspicuous. The Queen had a pitcher of wine brought to her. It was the first time I had seen her drink. She explained that she did this to increase her perspiration. After a while she and her favorites played ball with a sphere stuffed with feathers. They caught it with their right hands and threw it with their left. Soon the Queen and an Abyssinian girl grabbed for the ball at the same time, and began to wrestle for it.

I clutched a towel around myself and tried to stay out of their way, as they grunted and strained in their efforts to throw each other. But they kept bumping into me and I had the feeling that these accidents were deliberate.

Finally I got away—only to face new tormenters. Salome and her girls were rushing around the room, rolling light metal hoops. I did my best to avoid them. But inevitably, Salome ran her hoop across my feet.

"Excuse me!" she would cry mockingly—then hit me with the stick she used to guide the hoop. "Oh, I'm sorry!" she would laugh.

The other girls were quick to take up the game. No matter where I went, they came toward me screeching, "You clumsy slattern! Get out of our way!"

I was so angry I forgot I didn't have any clothes on. I wanted to hit Salome and pull her hair and throw her on the pavement—even if the other girls all fought on her side. I knew I would be punished, but I didn't care. You can endure just so much. I wrested the stick from her hand and aimed a blow at her.

But before it could land, the other girls surrounded me and with shrieks and shouts, bore me through the great bronze doors to the plunge. They threw me in and leaped in after me. The water was hot. It smelled of sulphur and had a bitter, salty taste. I was ducked several times, then suddenly they let me alone and I crawled out and got dressed. The others, by now, were splashing in the showers or being massaged by the serving women. I slipped out of the building, without waiting for this.

A peasant woman with some donkeys was passing. I asked her to take me back to Tiberias. The road was dusty and the donkeys slow.

It wasn't long before my skin started itching and my eyes watering. From my sandals to my headband, I was feverish. I felt so ill I hardly noticed that a chariot was overtaking us. Jason swung the horses across the path of the donkeys.

"Get down!" he shouted. "Get down, you little fool!"

He was out of the chariot, reaching strong hands up to me.

"You poor little thing, I know what they did to you at the baths—"

"Don't touch me!" One of his arms was beneath my knees, the other around my shoulders. He carried me toward a thicket at the side of the road. The bewildered peasant woman made no effort to stop him. Beneath the shadows of gnarled olive trees the air was close and heavy with the fragrance of blossoming almonds. I could hardly breathe.

"Take off your clothes." He put me down beside a little stream. "You must bathe in fresh water."

"No—!" I backed away from him.

"You little idiot, don't you see their treacherous scheme? If you don't bathe in fresh water after the sulphur plunge, your skin will become blotched and hideous." He gripped my shoulders and shook me roughly. "I'll not have your beauty marred—you are the loveliest thing I've ever seen! Do as I tell you or I'll strip you and throw you in!"

As though reading my thoughts, he suddenly relaxed. His smile was gentle, and his voice tender.

"Don't be afraid. I'll go back down the path and wait."

He kissed my forehead and turned back into the bushes beneath the dark trees.

The brook was cool and refreshing. I lay back on the soft sand and let the waters rush over me. The ripples moved caressingly. All the discomfort and the fever was washed away. A sweet and dreamy lassitude overcame me. I wondered if he was watching from the depths of the thicket. But I didn't think so.

And then I wondered why he didn't come. Perhaps he only protected me as a child is protected. Was this another of his pitying favors? If a man really loved a woman, he could not stay away from her.

There was a stir in the undergrowth. Enid and the simpering Greek, Philo, stood looking at me.

"Oh, excuse us!" tittered Enid. "We saw Jason's chariot, so we sneaked in to see what he was up to. Of course, we didn't dream—!"

She turned as she saw Jason coming toward her.

"Thorry to dithturb your little idyl," lisped Philo.

Jason threw a stone and the intruders ran laughingly into the thicket. We both knew they'd make a malicious scandal of what they had seen as soon as they got back to Tiberias.

242

While Jason turned his back, I put my clothes on and we drove home in worried silence.

That night I didn't go to the dining hall for supper. And no one came to persuade me. As soon as it was dark, I took a dark cloak and what money I had left and slipped out through a side gate. Staying close to the walls in the dark streets, I headed for the fishing quarter at the shores of the Sea of Galilee.

The fishermen's nets, on drying racks, looked like acres of delicate lace in the moonlight. Shadowy figures were removing them. The sky was threatening and we were close to the season of spring rains.

I approached a slight, aristocratic-looking young man who was struggling rather clumsily to fold up some of the nets. He listened sympathetically as I told him that I was the daughter of Caiaphas, the High Priest, and that I had to get home to Jerusalem.

"It is a dangerous journey," he said with a kindly smile. "A desperate journey for a young girl. After the waters of the Galilee enter into the Jordan, the course is swift and tortuous. And the eastern shore is peopled with savage Bedouins—"

"I know! But anything is better than Tiberias! If I stay here I'll surely die! I'll pay you anything!"

"It isn't the pay." There was a deprecating smile on his fine Jewish features. "It is just that I am not a boatman. My name is Matthew—I used to be a tax gatherer. So you see, I have not been trained to do anything very useful."

He turned and pointed to a camp fire farther up the beach, where a number of men sat around the flames.

"But some of my friends are fishermen, very good fishermen—Peter and Andrew and James. Our Master teaches us that we must love our neighbors as ourselves—so I am sure that they will help you."

"Oh, if they only would!"

He hurried away toward the camp fire. Something about the man had given me reassurance and a certain feeling of hope.

And then from among the shadows and the foamy nets, I saw Jason's tall figure before me. I turned toward the boats drawn up on the sand. I didn't want to talk to him.

"Don't go, Miriam!"

243

"I have to—you shouldn't have followed me—"

"If you go, I must go with you. I will be your boatman."
He took my hand. "Whither thou goest, I shall go—thy people shall be my people, and thy god, my god."

"Please, don't mock me! Leave me alone!"

"I can never do that, dearest! God knows I have tried not to love you. I was a slave to ambition as you said—but now, I have forgotten everything—but you."

"If I could only believe you!"

The silvery moonlight, through the thick, scudding clouds, cast an uneven causeway across the waters. The far shores of Galilee, the savage shores, were wrapped in beckoning mystery.

"Come!" Jason lifted me into a boat and pushed it into the water. With a hasty movement he picked up the sweep and poled us out of the shallows.

I lay back against the rough wood and looked up toward the dappled heavens. Why did I always surrender? I seemed to have no will when Jason was near me. Still, if he was telling the truth, if he really loved me—

"Was Salome angry?" I asked.

"Furious! She made a terrible scene!"

"Are you sure that you want to leave her? That you don't love her?"

"Love! That woman doesn't know what it is to love! For months she has kept me dangling—simply playing with me."

"It is hard to believe that any woman could do that to you, Jason. You seem so sure of yourself."

"She is a princess," he said bitterly. "And the stakes were high. I learned to gamble when I was a charioteer. Herod is a worthless puppet. Everyone in Rome despises him and Salome is of royal blood. Her husband would be in a position to guarantee the Eastern empire. He might become emperor himself when Tiberius dies—"

"You dreamed of that!"

"Why not! I have a fortune and so has Salome. The throne will be sold by the Praetorian Guard—the palace troops control the empire. But all that is forgotten. Let's not talk about it any more."

I didn't want to talk. I was too happy. Jason raised the sail and gusts of wind propelled us southward. He came forward and lay beside me. We looked up at the changing sky.

Then, without warning, the squall broke upon us. The sail was split with a roar like a bull. Shredded canvas whipped in the wind as the boat was lashed by the fury of the spring rains.

Jason scrambled to the sweep, struggling awkwardly to keep us from the trough of the waves. I was drenched as I fought to take in the whipping fragments of the tattered sail. Then the whole keel shivered as the craggy nose of a concealed rock forced its way through the splintering wood. The waves closed over us and I felt Jason's arm around me. I sank into a swirl of thunder and darkness.

How long it lasted I will never know exactly. After a time my mind struggled toward consciousness—only to slip back to oblivion again. In these rare, half-lucid moments it seemed that I was again in my room in Herod's palace. Once I seemed to see Jason's face bending over me and feel his hand behind my head. A cup was pressed to my lips and I heard him say, "Drink, Miriam, dearest, you must get strong and well for my sake."

Finally the fever left me and I returned to the consciousness of a bright, sunshiny day. It hadn't been a hallucination. Outside the windows of my room in the palace the trees were in full blossom. But my chamber had the untidiness of a sickroom. I crawled from beneath the covers and looked at myself in the steel mirror. It was a thin, drawn face that looked back at me. I rang for the serving maid, but she did not come.

Finally, trembling and pausing to rest at frequent intervals, I managed to wash myself and dress in clean clothes. Then, supporting myself with a hand against the wall, I faltered out into the corridors. There was a littered, deserted look to the halls. The serving women, in untidy dress, gossiped in slatternly clusters. When I talked to them their looks were bold and insolent and their words just barely courteous. They told me that Herod and the entire court had returned to Jerusalem to celebrate the holidays.

I returned to my room to find one of the lesser servants—a girl about as old as I am—putting my gold hairpins in her hair. When she saw me, she made a guilty movement and knocked over the alabaster lamp—the one that Jason had given me. It smashed upon the floor.

I was so angry I snatched a girdle from the wardrobe and began to whip her with it. She dropped to her knees and whined for mercy.

"Stop sniveling!" I said. "And tell me what has happened. Take me to Jason!"

"He has gone—on the day after the Princess and the women's caravan left for Jerusalem, Enid came back here with a message for Jason."

"And?"

"It seemed to disturb him. He had not left your side since the night of the great storm. He put on his traveling cloak. Then he threw it aside. He walked in the gardens, hour after hour. He called for his chariot, then he returned it to the stables. It was not the first message the Princess had sent to him, but he had rejected all the others with curses. Now after many black looks he called for the chariot again and drove away toward Jerusalem."

"And the message?"

The servant whimpered that she did not know any more. So I ordered her to leave me.

Dear God! Was I never to be sure of him? Had Salome capitulated? Had her message said that she would marry him? And had this last surrender been too great a temptation?

I had to know. I got my faded cloak from the wardrobe. My silver still was secure in the secret pocket of the lining. Hurrying to the beach, I asked for the former tax gatherer, Matthew.

"He isn't here," a surly old fisherman told me. "He and his crowd have gone to Jerusalem for the Passover. Bad luck to them!"

"Why do you say that? Matthew seemed kind."

"Oh, yes," the fisherman grumbled. "Very kind. I took my son, Reuben, to Capernaum to be cured of blindness. But on the night we went there, this Matthew and his Master came to Tiberias. That was the miracle—the evil miracle! We missed each other—for no reason at all!"

"This may have been meant to test you!" I was saying anything in an effort to influence him. "You should follow these Galileans. Take your son to Jerusalem! By boat you can be there for the holidays!"

"By boat?" Such a journey had not occurred to him. I kept on talking and offered him silver. He took the money, but it was his love for his boy that decided him.

My thoughts raced ahead as we left the clear waters of Galilee and rushed through overhanging jungles, made lush and foul by the recent floods of the Jordan.

Despite the skill of the fisherman, the boat sometimes stuck on a sandbar. When this happened, he and I would go over the side. The sand eddied around our feet as we pushed the boat back into deeper current. At last the boat whirled into the shallows and I saw the crested helmets of the Romans at the post house. With the last of my silver I bribed an officer to take me up to Jerusalem on the crupper of his horse. We entered the city by the Double Gate. The streets were filled with people shouting hosannahs and waving palm branches. Through the crowd I caught a glimpse of Matthew in a little group of men. They were gathered around a Man wearing a colored robe, who was seated upon a donkey. And for an instant I thought I saw you, Father, standing on the outer stairs of the Temple, smiling approval toward these men.

But this was just a confused impression. Before I could identify you, the cavalryman turned his horse into one of the side streets leading to Herod's palace.

Galba was the officer in charge at the Portal of the Stairs. "Where is Jason?" I demanded. "Take me to him at once!"

"I'm afraid I can't do that, ladybird. You see, Jason has been arrested—the King caught him in Salome's boudoir."

My heart was leaden with conflicting sorrows. It was quite clear that Jason had betrayed me. He had left me to go to Salome. But hope dies so hard! I still didn't want him to suffer. There must be some explanation for his contradictory behavior.

Late at night I awakened when I heard someone fumbling at the lock on my door. Salome came in. She was flushed and agitated as she blurted: "That swine! That insufferable swine! My stepfather has condemned Jason to the arena! But you, you can save him—"

I mistrusted her and anything she might tell me. It would be best to question her carefully. I asked: "For what has he been condemned?"

"Herod has charged him with violating the sanctity of the women's quarters—with having gone to your room at night in the palace at Tiberias!"

"You know that is a lie!" I cried

247

She made no answer. Her shadow fluttered against the walls like a great moth as she strode up and down past the brazier.

"You have brought him to this!" I burst out angrily. "It is all your doing! He didn't leave Tiberias with the court—he stayed with me—until you lured him away with that wretched note you sent by Enid! What did you say in it?"

"I had no pride—only envy," she said finally. "After I'd seen him in your sickroom in Tiberias, nursing you, I knew I had to have him even though he didn't love me. So I sent Enid back to tell him that I'd marry him and run away with him to Alexandria."

I spoke harshly to keep back the tears. "Well, you succeeded! Your bargain must have appealed to him—he abandoned me and went to you!"

"He came to me," her face was averted, "to refuse my offer of marriage." She gave me a quick look from the corner of her eyes. "And to tell me he'd never love anyone but you. That's why he was with me when Herod caught us."

"Then why didn't you intercede for Jason? Why didn't you tell Herod the truth?"

"I did." Her laugh was mirthless. "I begged too hard—I told Herod that I loved Jason and for that I must be humiliated by being forced to sit in the arena and see Jason choose between the tiger and the lady *when he knows that you will be the lady behind one door!*"

"But why will *I* be there?"

"Herod could scarcely accuse the Greek of seducing *me*, his stepdaughter! He has shifted the whole scandal to you. So I shall have to sit there and watch the man I love being married to my rival—to you!"

"But suppose there isn't any marriage?" I could scarcely pronounce the words. "Suppose Jason chooses the door that frees the tiger? There is that terrible chance!"

Salome's smile was sly and determined. "That's why I have come here. Chance is going to be eliminated. You and I are going to cheat Herod. We will save Jason."

"Oh, Salome, how?"

"We will save him because we both love him. I am going to give him to you."

My voice was choking. "Oh, Salome, I have been so wrong about you!"

She brushed my embrace aside. "I'm not doing this for you.

248

I've thought of a way to save him—because I can't see him die."

It was three nights ago that we had this conversation. We talked far into the morning. Before she left, I had forgiven Salome all her former slights and cruelties. For she had shown me how to save Jason. I wonder if I could be as self-sacrificing as she. Her love for him is so great that she is willing that he shall marry me—since she says she knows he loves me and that we will be happy together.

I kissed her as we parted.

Since then I have spent my time writing this long letter to you. I know that it contains many things that ordinarily a daughter would not write to a father. But I have tried to be absolutely truthful, because I want you to know, dearest Father, that in spite of all the doubts and troubles I have gone through, I have done nothing that was wrong.

It is growing late and I am tired. Soon it will be morning. They will come and dress me in a bridal gown. My draperies will be arranged with many golden brooches. They will place flowers in my arms and the flame-colored veil of a Roman bride over my hair. And they will leave me in that little room, next to the room where they will have placed the tiger.

As soon as I am alone, I will take one of the golden brooches from my garment. I will open one of my veins with it and let my blood run from beneath the crack in the door, out onto the stone pavements of the dark corridor beneath the seats of the arena.

Before Salome takes her seat beside her stepfather, she will slip down into this corridor. She will see the blood and she will know in which room I am waiting. And she will signal to Jason to open my door.

I am happy, Father, despite my dreadful weariness. I hope that you will forgive me everything that has been reckless and foolish. I am a woman now, but still a little girl. How I wish that I could curl up in your lap and go to sleep! I am tired, but so contented and joyful—I must rest and be beautiful for my beloved. All my dreams will come true tomorrow.

Thus ended the letter of Miriam to her father. As I labored over its translation, this Jewish girl of twenty centuries ago became very real to me. I gave all my time to researches concerning Miriam. I had to learn what had happened to her.

The answer was found in the long-sought-for letter of Pontius Pilate to Tiberius. The first paragraph made it obvious that this originally had been dispatched to the Emperor as an explanation of Miriam's manuscript. But during the centuries they had become separated. Pilate's supplement was written in Latin upon two sheets of parchment. The first page read:

"To His Imperial Majesty, Tiberius Caesar, from Pontius Pilate, Procurator of Judea:

"May the Gods preserve Your Majesty! I forward the enclosed document to the Imperial Archives because it has some bearing upon Imperial policy in the Near East.

"As stated in previous reports, the High Priest (to whom the enclosed letter is addressed) has shown great stubbornness in refusing to cooperate in the matter of disposing of a certain Galilean preacher regarded by Your Majesty's Government as a dangerous malcontent. The High Priest was impervious to bribes, and even threats failed to coerce him into making the desired accusations which would enable Rome to crucify the Galilean and still place responsibility for the deed on the Jews.

"But now I am happy to inform Your Majesty that the whole matter has been satisfactorily resolved. Caiaphas is a broken man. His will has been completely shattered (indeed, I doubt if he can any longer be considered sane) and he is quite incapable of offering any further resistance.

"His transformation was brought about, quite unexpectedly, yesterday, when the Greek, Jason, was forced to choose between the lady and the tiger in Herod's Arena. I watched Caiaphas very closely when he made his appearance, as Herod had ordered, in the royal box. His bearing was dignified and aloof. I almost found myself wishing that this well-controlled man was a Roman.

"One of our secret agents had intercepted a letter which the girl, Miriam, had written to her father; so that Caiaphas had no way of knowing that his daughter was guiltless of Herod's implications. His trust in her evidently was based upon blind faith.

"Herod looked a trifle embarrassed as he turned to me and asked if I wanted to double my bet on the Greek's chances for survival. Of course, I did. Since I had read Miriam's letter, I felt I was betting on a sure thing. I even smiled to myself as, from the corner of my eye, I saw the Princess make her signal to the Greek to open the right-hand door.

"But I was a fool to trust Salome. The Greek, with his sense of the dramatic, started to pull back the portal very slowly. When it was open about a foot, we saw the sunlight fall on the striped hide and the blinking eyes of the tiger. The Greek seemed doomed. An automatic device made it impossible to push those doors shut, once either of them had started to open.

"But the Greek acted with the speed of lightning. As soon as he glimpsed the tiger, he stepped back and pulled open *both* doors. Now he was protected—wedged in the small space between the two open portals—as secure as if he had a big oak shield on each arm.

"The tiger, a finer specimen than any you'd see in Rome, advanced through the doorway on the right.

"And almost simultaneously, the girl, Miriam, looking pale but smiling beneath her bridal veil, came through the doorway on the left.

"For a few seconds the beast and the woman looked at each other. There was no sound in the amphitheater, except her father's sobbing.

"It was the fastest thinking I had ever seen. I did well to bet on the Greek."

The paper fell from my hand. All the injustice and cruelty of the world seemed summed up in Jason's contemptible strategem.

I read the second page. Pilate had added the following postscript to his message.

"Despite the Greek's adroitness I'm sure Your Majesty will agree that this Jason was too clever to be permitted to survive. His plot to marry Salome and seize the throne was a definite menace to Roman policy in Palestine and to Your Majesty's security. Since the man was the son of a slave and was not a Roman citizen, it was not difficult to charge him with the theft of the White Syndicate's horses and to condemn him, along with another thief and the Galilean preacher, to be crucified. He admitted under the torture that he had adopted the name of 'Jason' because of its romantic connotations. His real name was Gestos. He was the last of the three to die, and though his sufferings were excruciating, he did not ask for forgiveness."

A STUDY IN WHITE

BY NICHOLAS BLAKE

Nicholas Blake was born Cecil Day Lewis in Ballintogher, Ireland, on April 27, 1904. He was educated in England and graduated from Oxford, where with W. H. Auden and Stephen Spender he launched the "new" poetry of the 1930s. He taught school until 1935, when he retired to writing. In 1968 he was named Poet Laureate. Seventeen of the twenty crime novels he wrote as Nicholas Blake were about his amateur detective, Nigel Strangeways. He reviewed the detective story for *The Spectator* for many years and described it as "the folk myth of the 20th century." He died in 1972.

"SEASONABLE WEATHER FOR the time of year," remarked the Expansive Man in a voice succulent as the breast of a roast goose.

The Deep Chap, sitting next to him in the railway compartment, glanced out at the snow, swarming and swirling past the window-pane. He replied:

"You really like it? Oh, well, it's an ill blizzard that blows nobody no good. Depends what you mean by seasonable, though. Statistics for the last fifty years would show—"

"Name of Joad, sir?" asked the Expansive Man, treating the compartment to a wholesale wink.

"No, Stansfield, Henry Stansfield." The Deep Chap, a ruddy-faced man who sat with hands firmly planted on the knees of his brown tweed suit, might have been a prosperous farmer but for the long, steady, meditative scrutiny which he now bent upon each of his fellow-travelers in turn.

What he saw was not particularly rewarding. On the opposite seat, from left to right, were a Forward Piece, who had taken the Expansive Man's wink wholly to herself and contrived to wriggle her tight skirt farther up from her knee; a desiccated, sandy, lawyerish little man who fumed and fussed like an angry kettle, consulting every five minutes his gold watch, then shaking out his *Times* with the crackle of a legal parchment; and a Flash Card, dressed up to the nines of spivdom, with the bold yet uneasy stare of the young delinquent.

"Mine's Percy Dukes," said the Expansive Man. "P.D. to my friends. General Dealer. At your service. Well, we'll be across the border in an hour and a half, and then hey for the bluebells of bonny Scotland!"

"Bluebells in January? You're hopeful," remarked the Forward Piece.

"Are you Scots, master?" asked the Comfortable Body sitting on Stansfield's left.

"English outside"—Percy Dukes patted the front of his gray suit, slid a flask from its hip pocket, and took a swig— "and Scotch within." His loud laugh, or the blizzard, shook the railway carriage. The Forward Piece giggled.

"You'll need that if we run into a drift and get stuck for the night," said Henry Stansfield.

"Name of Jonah, sir?" The compartment reverberated again.

"I do not apprehend such an eventuality," said the Fusspot. "The stationmaster at Lancaster assured me that the train would get through. We are scandalously late already, though." Once again the gold watch was consulted.

"It's a curious thing," remarked the Deep Chap meditatively, "the way we imagine we can make Time amble withal or gallop withal, just by keeping an eye on the hands of a watch. You travel frequently by this train, Mr.—?"

"Kilmington. Arthur J. Kilmington. No, I've only used it once before." The Fusspot spoke in a dry Edinburgh accent.

"Ah, yes, that would have been on the seventeenth of last month. I remember seeing you on it."

"No, sir, you are mistaken. It was the twentieth." Mr. Kilmington's thin mouth snapped tight again, like a rubber band round a sheaf of legal documents.

"The twentieth? Indeed? That was the day of the train robbery. A big haul they got, it seems. Off this very train. It was carrying some of the extra Christmas mail. Bags just disappeared, somewhere between Lancaster and Carlisle."

"Och, deary me," sighed the Comfortable Body. "I don't know what we're coming to, really, nowadays."

"We're coming to the scene of the crime, ma'am," said the expansive Mr. Dukes. The train, almost dead-beat, was panting up the last pitch towards Shap Summit.

"I didn't see anything in the papers about where the robbery took place," Henry Stansfield murmured. Dukes fastened a somewhat bleary eye upon him.

"You read all the newspapers?"

"Yes."

The atmosphere in the compartment had grown suddenly tense. Only the Flash Card, idly examining his fingernails, seemed unaffected by it.

"Which paper did you see it in?" pursued Stansfield.

"I didn't." Dukes tapped Stansfield on the knee. "But I can use my loaf. Stands to reason. You want to tip a mail-bag out of a train—get me? Train must be moving slowly, or the bag'll burst when it hits the ground. Only one place between

254

Lancaster and Carlisle where you'd *know* the train would be crawling. Shap Bank. And it goes slowest on the last bit of the bank, just about where we are now. Follow?"

Henry Stansfield nodded.

"O.K. But you'd be balmy to tip it off just anywhere on this God-forsaken moorland," went on Mr. Dukes. "Now, if you'd traveled this line as much as I have, you'd have noticed it goes over a bridge about a mile short of the summit. Under the bridge runs a road: a nice, lonely road, see? The only road hereabouts that touches the railway. You tip out the bag there. Your chums collect it, run down the embankment, dump it in the car they've got waiting by the bridge, and Bob's your uncle!"

"You oughta been a detective, mister," exclaimed the Forward Piece languishingly.

Mr. Dukes inserted his thumbs in his armpits, looking gratified. "Maybe I am," he said with a wheezy laugh. "And maybe I'm just little old P.D., who knows how to use his loaf."

"Och, well now, the things people will do," said the Comfortable Body. "There's a terrible lot of dishonesty today."

The Flash Card glanced up contemptuously from his fingernails. Mr. Kilmington was heard to mutter that the system of surveillance on railways was disgraceful, and the guard of the train should have been severely censured.

"The guard can't be everywhere," said Stansfield. "Presumably he has to patrol the train from time to time, and—"

"Let him do so, then, and not lock himself up in his van and go to sleep," interrupted Mr. Kilmington, somewhat unreasonably.

"Are you speaking from personal experience, sir?" asked Stansfield.

The Flash Card lifted up his voice and said, in a Charing Cross Road American accent, "Hey, fellas! If the gang was gonna tip out the mail-bags by the bridge, like this guy says—what I mean is, how could they rely on the guard being out of his van just at that point?" He hitched up the trousers of his loud check suit.

"You've got something there," said Percy Dukes. "What I reckon is, there must have been two accomplices on the train—one to get the guard out of his van on some pretext, and the other to chuck off the bags." He turned to Mr. Kilmington, "You were saying something about the guard lock-

255

ing himself up in his van. Now if I was of a suspicious turn of mind, if I was little old Sherlock H. in person"—he bestowed another prodigious wink upon Kilmington's fellow-travelers—"I'd begin to wonder about you, sir. You were traveling on this train when the robbery took place. You went to the guard's van. You *say* you found him asleep. You didn't by any chance call the guard out, so as to—?"

"Your suggestion is outrageous! I advise you to be very careful, sir, very careful indeed," enunciated Mr. Kilmington, his precise voice crackling with indignation, "or you may find you have said something actionable. I would have you know that, when I—"

But what he would have them know was to remain undivulged. The train, which for some little time had been running cautiously down from Shap Summit, suddenly began to chatter and shudder, like a fever patient in high delirium, as the vacuum brakes were applied: then, with the dull impact of a fist driving into a feather pillow, the engine buried itself in a drift which had gathered just beyond the bend of a deep cutting.

It was just five minutes past seven.

"What's this?" asked the Forward Piece, rather shrilly, as a hysterical outburst of huffing and puffing came from the engine.

"Run into a drift, I reckon."

"He's trying to back us out. No good. The wheels are slipping every time. What a lark!" Percy Dukes had his head out of the window on the lee side of the train. "Coom to Coomberland for your winter sports!"

"Guard! Guard, I say!" called Mr. Kilmington. But the blue-clad figure, after one glance into the compartment, hurried on up the corridor. "Really! I *shall* report that man."

Henry Stansfield, going out into the corridor, opened a window. Though the coach was theoretically sheltered by the cutting of this windward side, the blizzard stunned his face like a knuckleduster of ice. He joined the herd of passengers who had climbed down and were stumbling towards the engine. As they reached it, the guard emerged from the cab: no cause for alarm, he said; if they couldn't get through, there'd be a relief engine sent down to take the train back to Penrith; he was just off to set fog-signals on the line behind them.

The driver renewed his attempts to back the train out. But what with its weight, the up-gradient in its rear, the icy rails, and the clinging grip of the drift on the engine, he could not budge her.

"We'll have to dig out the bogeys, mate," he said to his fireman. "Fetch them shovels from the forward van. It'll keep the perishers from freezing, anyhow." He jerked his finger at the knot of passengers who, lit up by the glare of the furnace, were capering and beating their arms like savages amid the swirling snow-wreaths.

Percy Dukes, who had now joined them, quickly established himself as the life and soul of the party, referring to the grimy-faced fireman as "Snowball," adjuring his companions to "Dig for Victory," affecting to spy the approach of a herd of St. Bernards, each with a keg of brandy slung round its neck. But after ten minutes of hard digging, when the leading wheels of the bogey were cleared, it could be seen that they had been derailed by their impact with the drift.

"That's torn it, Charlie. You'll have to walk back to the box and get 'em to telephone through for help," said the driver.

"*If* the wires aren't down already," replied the fireman lugubriously. "It's above a mile to that box, and uphill. Who d'you think I am, Captain Scott?"

"You'll have the wind behind you, mate, anyhow. So long."

A buzz of dismay had risen from the passengers at this. One or two, who began to get querulous, were silenced by the driver's offering to take them anywhere they liked if they would just lift his engine back onto the metals first. When the rest had dispersed to their carriage, Henry Stansfield asked the driver's permission to go up into the cab for a few minutes and dry his coat.

"You're welcome." The driver snorted: "Would you believe it? 'Must get to Glasgow tonight.' Damn ridiculous! Now Bert—that's my guard—it's different for him: he's entitled to fret a bit. Missus been very poorly. Thought she was going to peg out before Christmas; but he got the best surgeon in Glasgow to operate on her, and she's mending now, he says. He reckons to look in every night at the nursing home, when he goes off work."

Stansfield chatted with the man for five minutes. Then the guard returned, blowing upon his hands—a smallish, leathery-faced chap, with a noticeably anxious look in his eye.

"We'll not get through tonight, Bert. Charlie told you?"

"Aye. I doubt some the passengers are going to create a rumpus," said the guard dolefully.

Henry Stansfield went back to his compartment. It was stuffy, but with a sinister hint of chilliness, too: he wondered how long the steam heating would last: depended upon the amount of water in the engine boiler, he supposed. Among the wide variety of fates he had imagined for himself, freezing to death in an English train was not included.

Arthur J. Kilmington fidgeted more than ever. When the guard came along the corridor, he asked him where the nearest village was, saying he must get a telephone call through to Edinburgh—most urgent appointment—must let his client know, if he was going to miss it. The guard said there was a village two miles to the northeast; you could see the lights from the top of the cutting; but he warned Mr. Kilmington against trying to get there in the teeth of this blizzard—better wait for the relief engine, which should reach them before nine P.M.

Silence fell upon the compartment for a while; the incredulous silence of civilized people who find themselves in the predicament of castaways. Then the expansive Mr. Dukes proposed that, since they were to be stuck here for an hour or two, they should get acquainted. The Comfortable Body now introduced herself as Mrs. Grant, the Forward Piece as Inez Blake; the Flash Card, with the over-negligent air of one handing a dud half-crown over a counter, gave his name as Macdonald—I. Macdonald.

The talk reverted to the train robbery and the criminals who had pepetrated it.

"They must be awfu' clever," remarked Mrs. Grant, in her singsong Lowland accent.

"No criminals are clever, ma'am," said Stansfield quietly. His ruminative eye passed, without haste, from Macdonald to Dukes. "Neither the small fry nor the big operators. They're pretty well subhuman, the whole lot of 'em. A dash of cunning, a thick streak of cowardice, and the rest is made up of stupidity and boastfulness. They're too stupid for anything but crime, and so riddled with inferiority that they always give themselves away, sooner or later, by boasting about their crimes. They like to think of themselves as the

258

wide boys, but they're as narrow as starved eels—why, they haven't even the wits to alter their professional methods: that's how the police pick 'em up."

"I entirely agree, sir," Mr. Kilmington snapped. "In my profession I see a good deal of the criminal classes. And I flatter myself none of them has ever got the better of me. They're transparent, sir, transparent."

"No doubt you gentlemen are right," said Percy Dukes comfortably. "But the police haven't picked up the chaps who did this train robbery yet."

"They will. And the Countess of Axminister's emerald bracelet. Bet the gang didn't reckon to find that in the mail-bag. Worth all of twenty-five thousand pounds."

Percy Dukes' mouth fell open. The Flash Card whistled. Overcome, either by the stuffiness of the carriage or the thought of twenty-five thousand pounds worth of emeralds, Inez Blake gave a little moan and fainted all over Mr. Kilmington's lap.

"Really! Upon my soul! My dear young lady!" exclaimed that worthy. There was a flutter of solicitude, shared by all except the cold-eyed young Macdonald who, after stooping over her a moment, his back to the others, said, "Here you—stop pawing the young lady and let her stretch out on the seat. Yes, I'm talking to you, Kilmington."

"How dare you! This is an outrage!" The little man stood up so abruptly that the girl was almost rolled onto the floor. "I was merely trying to—"

"I know your sort. Nasty old men. Now, keep your hands off her. I'm telling you."

In the shocked silence that ensued, Kilmington gobbled speechlessly at Macdonald for a moment; then, seeing razors in the youth's cold-steel eye, snatched his black hat and brief-case from the rack and bolted out of the compartment. Henry Stansfield made as if to stop him, then changed his mind. Mrs. Grant followed the little man out, returning presently, her handkerchief soaked in water, to dab Miss Blake's forehead. The time was just 8:30.

When things were restored to normal, Mr. Dukes turned to Stansfield. "You were saying this necklace of—who was it? —the Countess of Axminister, it's worth twenty-five thousand pounds? Fancy sending a thing of that value through the post! Are you sure of it?"

259

"The value? Oh, yes." Henry Stansfield spoke out of the corner of his mouth, in the manner of a stupid man imparting a confidence. "Don't let this go any further. But I've a friend who works in the Cosmopolitan—the company where it's insured. That's another thing that didn't get into the papers. Silly woman. She wanted it for some big family do in Scotland at Christmas, forgot to bring it with her, and wrote home for it to be posted to her in a registered packet."

"Twenty-five thousand pounds," said Percy Dukes thoughtfully. "Well, stone me down!"

"Yes. Some people don't know when they're lucky, do they?"

Duke's fat face wobbled on his shoulders like a globe of lard. Young Macdonald polished his nails. Inez Blake read her magazine. After a while Percy Dukes remarked that the blizzard was slackening; he'd take an airing and see if there was any sign of the relief engine yet. He left the compartment.

At the window the snowflakes danced in their tens now, not their thousands. The time was 8:55. Shortly afterwards Inez Blake went out; and ten minutes later Mrs. Grant remarked to Stansfield that it had stopped snowing altogether. Neither Inez nor Dukes had returned when, at 9:30, Henry Stansfield decided to ask what had happened about the relief. The guard was not in his van, which adjoined Stansfield's coach, towards the rear of the train. So he turned back, walked up the corridor to the front coach, clambered out, and hailed the engine cab.

"She must have been held up," said the guard, leaning out. "Charlie here got through from the box, and they promised her by nine o'clock. But it'll no' be long now, sir."

"Have you seen anything of a Mr. Kilmington—small, sandy chap—black hat and overcoat, blue suit—was in my compartment? I've walked right up the train and he doesn't seem to be on it."

The guard pondered a moment. "Och aye, yon wee fellow? Him that asked me about telephoning from the village. Aye, he's awa' then."

"He did set off to walk there, you mean?"

"Nae doot he did, if he's no' on the train. He spoke to me again—juist on nine, it'd be—and said he was awa' if the relief didna turn up in five minutes."

"You've not seen him since?"

260

"No, sir. I've been talking to my mates here this half-hour, ever syne the wee fellow spoke to me."

Henry Stansfield walked thoughtfully back down the permanent way. When he passed out of the glare shed by the carriage lights on the snow, he switched on his electric torch. Just beyond the last coach the eastern wall of the cutting sloped sharply with the track. Although the snow had stopped altogether, an icy wind from the northeast still blew, raking and numbing his face. Twenty yards farther on his torch lit up a track, already half filled in with snow, made by several pairs of feet, pointing away over the moor, towards the northeast. Several passengers, it seemed, had set off for the village, whose lights twinkled like frost in the far distance. Stansfield was about to follow this track when he heard footsteps scrunching the snow farther up the line. He switched off the torch; at once it was as if a sack had been thrown over his head, so close and blinding was the darkness. The steps came nearer. Stansfield switched on his torch, at the last minute, pinpointing the squat figure of Percy Dukes. The man gave a muffled oath.

"What the devil! Here, what's the idea, keeping me waiting half an hour in that blasted—?"

"Have you seen Kilmington?"

"Oh, it's you. No, how the hell should I have seen him? Isn't he on the train? I've just been walking up the line, to look for the relief. No sign yet. Damn parky, it is—I'm moving on."

Presently Stansfield moved on, too, but along the track towards the village. The circle of his torchlight wavered and bounced on the deep snow. The wind, right in his teeth, was killing. No wonder, he thought, as after a few hundred yards he approached the end of the trail, those passengers turned back. Then he realized they had not all turned back. What he had supposed to be a hummock of snow bearing a crude resemblance to a recumbent human figure, he now saw to be a human figure covered with snow. He scraped some of the snow off it, turned it gently over on its back.

Arthur J. Kilmington would fuss no more in this world. His brief-case was buried beneath him; his black hat was lying where it had fallen, lightly covered with snow, near the head. There seemed, to Stansfield's cursory examination, no mark of violence on him. But the eyeballs started, the face was

261

suffused with a pinkish-blue color. So men look who have been strangled, thought Stansfield, or asphyxiated. Quickly he knelt down again, shining his torch in the dead face. A qualm of horror shook him. Mr. Kilmington's nostrils were caked thick with snow, which had frozen solid in them, and snow had been rammed tight into his mouth also.

And here he would have stayed, reflected Stansfield, in this desolate spot, for days or weeks, perhaps, if the snow lay or deepened. And when the thaw at last came (as it did that year, in fact, only after two months), the snow would thaw out from his mouth and nostrils, too, and there would be no vestige of murder left—only the corpse of an impatient little lawyer who had tried to walk to the village in a blizzard and died for his pains. It might even be that no one would ask how such a precise, pernickety little chap had ventured the two-mile walk in these shoes and without a torch to light his way through the pitchy blackness; for Stansfield, going through the man's pockets, had found the following articles —and nothing more: pocketbook, fountain pen, handkerchief, cigarette case, gold lighter, two letters, and some loose change.

Stansfield started to return for help. But only twenty yards back he noticed another trail of footprints, leading off the main track to the left. This trail seemed a fresher one—the snow lay less thickly in the indentations—and to have been made by one pair of feet only. He followed it up, walking beside it. Whoever made this track had walked in a slight right-handed curve back to the railway line, joining it about one hundred and fifty yards up the line from where the main trail came out. At this point there was a platelayers' shack. Finding the door unlocked, Stansfield entered. There was nothing inside but a coke brazier, stone cold, and a smell of cigar smoke. . . .

Half an hour later, Stansfield returned to his compartment. In the meanwhile, he had helped the train crew to carry back the body of Kilmington, which was now locked in the guard's van. He had also made an interesting discovery as to Kilmington's movements. It was to be presumed that, after the altercation with Macdonald, and the brief conversation already reported by the guard, the lawyer must have gone to sit in another compartment. The last coach, to the rear of the guard's van, was a first-class one, almost empty. But in one of its compartments Stansfield found a

262

passenger asleep. He woke him up, gave a description of Kilmington, and asked if he had seen him earlier.

The passenger grumpily informed Stansfield that a smallish man, in a dark overcoat, with the trousers of a blue suit showing beneath it, had come to the door and had a word with him. No, the passenger had not noticed his face particularly, because he'd been very drowsy himself, and besides, the chap had politely taken off his black Homburg hat to address him, and the hat screened as much of the head as was not cut off from his view by the top of the door. No, the chap had not come into his compartment: he had just stood outside, inquired the time (the passenger had looked at his watch and told him it was 8:50); then the chap had said that, if the relief didn't turn up by nine, he intended to walk to the nearest village.

Stansfield had then walked along to the engine cab. The guard, whom he found there, told him that he'd gone up the track about 8:45 to meet the fireman on his way back from the signal-box. He had gone as far as the place where he'd put down his fog-signals earlier; here, just before nine, he and the fireman met, as the latter corroborated. Returning to the train, the guard had climbed into the last coach, noticed Kilmington sitting alone in a first-class compartment (it was then that the lawyer announced to the guard his intention of walking if the relief engine had not arrived within five minutes). The guard then got out of the train again, and proceeded down the track to talk to his mates in the engine cab.

This evidence would seem to point incontrovertibly at Kilmington's having been murdered shortly after nine P.M., Stansfield reflected as he went back to his own compartment. His fellow-passengers were all present now.

"Well, did you find him?" asked Percy Dukes.

"Kilmington? Oh, yes, I found him. In the snow over there. He was dead."

Inez Blake gave a little, affected scream. The permanent sneer was wiped, as if by magic, off young Macdonald's face, which turned a sickly white. Mr. Dukes sucked in his fat lips.

"The puir wee man," said Mrs. Grant. "He tried to walk it then? Died of exposure, was it?"

"No," announced Stansfield flatly, "he was murdered."

This time, Inez Blake screamed in earnest; and, like an

263

echo, a hooting shriek came from far up the line: the relief engine was approaching at last.

"The police will be awaiting us back at Penrith, so we'd beter all have have our stories ready." Stansfield turned to Percy Dukes. "You, for instance, sir. Where were you between eight-fifty-five when you left the carriage, and nine-thirty-five when I met you returning? Are you sure you didn't see Kilmington?"

Dukes, expansive no longer, his piggy eyes sunk deep in the fat of his face, asked Stansfield who the hell he thought he was.

"I am an inquiry agent, employed by the Cosmopolitan Insurance Company. Before that, I was a Detective Inspector in the C.I.D. Here is my card."

Dukes barely glanced at it. "That's all right, old man. Only wanted to make sure. Can't trust anyone nowadays." His voice had taken on the ingratiating, oleaginous heartiness of the small business man trying to clinch a deal with a bigger one. "Just went for a stroll, y'know—stretch the old legs. Didn't see a soul."

"Who were you expecting to see? Didn't you wait for someone in the platelayers' shack along there, and smoke a cigar while you were waiting? Who did you mistake me for when you said, 'What's the idea, keeping me waiting half an hour?'"

"Here, draw it mild, old man." Percy Dukes sounded injured. "I certainly looked in at the huts: smoked a cigar for a bit. Then I toddled back to the train, and met up with your good self on the way. I didn't make no appointment to meet—"

"Oo! Well I *must* say," interrupted Miss Blake virtuously. She could hardly wait to tell Stansfield that, on leaving the compartment shortly after Dukes, she'd overheard voices on the track below the lavatory window. "I recognized this gentleman's voice," she went on, tossing her head at Dukes. "He said something like: 'You're going to help us again, chum, so you'd better get used to the idea. You're in it up to the neck—can't back out now.' And another voice, sort of mumbling, might have been Mr. Kilmington's—I dunno—sounded Scotch anyway—said, 'All right. Meet you in five minutes: platelayers' hut a few hundred yards up the line. Talk it over.'"

"And what did you do then, young lady?" asked Stansfield.

"I happened to meet a gentleman friend, farther up the train, and sat with him for a bit."

"Is that so?" remarked Macdonald menacingly. "Why, you four-flushing little—!"

"Shut up!" commanded Stansfield.

"Honest I did," the girl said, ignoring Macdonald. "I'll introduce you to him, if you like. He'll tell you I was with him for, oh, half an hour or more."

"And what about Mr. Macdonald?"

"I'm not talking," said the youth sullenly.

"Mr. Macdonald isn't talking. Mrs. Grant?"

"I've been in this compartment ever since, sir."

"Ever since—?"

"Since I went out to damp my hankie for this young lady, when she'd fainted. Mr. Kilmington was just before me, you'll mind. I saw him go through into the guard's van."

"Did you hear him say anything about walking to the village?"

"No, sir. He just hurried into the van, and then there was some havers about its no' being lockit this time, and how he was going to report the guard for it."

"I see. And you've been sitting here with Mr. Macdonald all the time?"

"Yes, sir. Except for ten minutes or so he was out of the compartment, just after you'd left."

"What did you go out for?" Stansfield asked the young man.

"Just taking the air, brother."

"You weren't taking Mr. Kilmington's gold watch, as well as the air, by any chance?" Stansfield's keen eyes were fastened like a hook into Macdonald's, whose insolent expression visibly crumbled beneath them.

"I don't know what you mean," he tried to bluster. "You can't do this to me."

"I mean that a man has been murdered, and when the the police search you, they will find his gold watch in your possession. Won't look too healthy for you, my young friend."

"Naow! Give us a chance! It was only a joke, see?" The wretched Macdonald was whining now, in his native cockney. "He got me riled—the stuck-up way he said nobody'd ever got the better of him. So I thought I'd just show him—I'd have given it back, straight I would, only I couldn't find him

265

afterwards. It was just a joke, I tell you. Anyway, it was Inez who lifted the ticker."

"You dirty little rotter!" screeched the girl.

"Shut up, both of you. You can explain your joke to the Penrith police. Let's hope they don't die of laughing."

At this moment the train gave a lurch, and started back up the gradient. It halted at the signal-box, for Stansfield to telephone to Penrith, then clattered south again.

On Penrith platform Stansfield was met by an inspector and a sergeant of the County Constabulary, with the police surgeon. Then, after a brief pause in the guard's van, where the police surgeon drew aside the guard's black off-duty over-coat that had been laid over the body, and began his pre-liminary examination, they marched along to Stansfield's compartment. The guard who, at his request, had locked this as the train was drawing up at the platform and was keeping an eye on its occupants, now unlocked it. The inspector entered.

His first action was to search Macdonald. Finding the watch concealed on his person, he then charged Macdonald and Inez Blake with theft. The inspector next proceeded to make an arrest on the charge of wilful murder. . . .

Whom did the Inspector arrest for the murder of Arthur J. Kilmington?

You have been given no less than eight clues by the author; these eight clues should tell you, by logical deduction, not only the identity of the murderer but also the motive of the crime and the method by which it was committed.

We urge you accept the author's challenge before going further, and when you have interpreted the eight clues, compare your solution with Mr. Blake's, which now follows.

The inspector arrested the guard for the wilful murder of Arthur J. Kilmington.

Kilmington's pocket had been picked by Inez Blake, when she pretended to faint at 8:25, and his gold watch was at once passed by her to her accomplice, Macdonald. Now Kilmington was constantly consulting his watch. It is inconceivable, if he was not killed till after 9 P.M., that he should not have missed the watch and made a scene. This point was clinched by the first-class passenger who had said that

266

a man, answering to the description of Kilmington, had asked him the time at 8:50: if it had really been Kilmington, he would certainly, before inquiring the time of anyone else, have first tried to consult his own watch, found it gone, and reported the theft. The fact that Kilmington neither reported the loss to the guard, nor returned to his original compartment to look for the watch, proves he must have been murdered *before he became aware of the loss*—i.e., shortly after he left the compartment at 8:27. But the guard claimed to have spoken to Kilmington at 9 P.M. Therefore the guard was lying. And why should he lie, except to create an alibi for himself? This is Clue Number One.

The guard claimed to have talked with Kilmington at 9 P.M. Now, at 8:55 the blizzard had diminished to a light snowfall, which soon afterwards ceased. When Stansfield discovered the body, it was buried under snow. Therefore Kilmington must have been murdered *while the blizzard was still raging*—i.e., some time before 9 P.M. Therefore the guard was lying when he said Kilmington was alive at 9 P.M. This is Clue Number Two.

Henry Stansfield, who was investigating on behalf of the Cosmopolitan Insurance Company the loss of the Countess of Axminster's emeralds, reconstructed the crime as follows:

Motive: The guard's wife had been gravely ill before Christmas: then, just about the time of the train robbery, he had got her the best surgeon in Glasgow and put her in a nursing home (evidence of engine-driver: Clue Number Three). A guard's pay does not usually run to such expensive treatment: it seemed likely, therefore, that the man, driven desperate by his wife's need, had agreed to take part in the robbery in return for a substantial bribe. What part did he play? During the investigation the guard had stated that he had left his van for five minutes, while the train was climbing the last section of Shap Bank, and on his return found the mail-bags missing. But Kilmington, who was traveling on this train, had found the guard's van locked at this point, and now (evidence of Mrs. Grant: Clue Number Four) declared his intention of reporting the guard. The latter knew that Kilmington's report would contradict his own evidence and thus convict him of complicity in the crime, since he had locked the van for a few minutes to throw out the mail-bags himself, and pretended to Kilmington that he had been asleep (evidence of Kilmington himself) when the latter knocked at the door. So Kilmington had to be silenced.

Stansfield already had Percy Dukes under suspicion as the organizer of the robbery. During the journey Dukes gave himself away three times. First, although it had not been mentioned in the papers, he betrayed knowledge of the point on the line where the bags had been thrown out. Second, though the loss of the emeralds had been also kept out of the Press, Dukes knew it was an emerald *necklace* which had been stolen: Stansfield had laid a trap for him by calling it a bracelet, but later in conversation Dukes referred to the "necklace." Third, his great discomposure at the (false) statement by Stansfield that the emeralds were worth £25,000 was the reaction of a criminal who believes he has been badly gypped by the fence to whom he has sold them. Dukes was now planning a second train robbery, and meant to compel the guard to act as accomplice again. Inez Blake's evidence (Clue Number Five) of hearing him say, "You're going to help us again, chum," etc., clearly pointed to the guard's complicity in the previous robbery: it was almost certainly the guard to whom she had heard Dukes say this, for only a railway servant would have known about the existence of a platelayer's hut up the line, and made an appointment to meet Dukes there; moreover, if Dukes had talked about his plans for the next robbery, on the train itself, to anyone *but* a railway servant suspicion would have been incurred should they have been seen talking together.

Method: At 8:27 Kilmington goes into the guard's van. He threatens to report the guard, though he is quite unaware of the dire consequences this would entail for the latter. The guard, probably on the pretext of showing him the route to the village, gets Kilmington out of the train, walks him away from the lighted area, stuns him (the bruise was a light one and did not reveal itself in Stansfield's brief examination of the body), carries him to the spot where Stansfield found the body, packs mouth and nostrils tight with snow. Then, instead of leaving well alone, the guard decides to create an alibi for himself. He takes his victim's hat, returns to train, puts on his own dark, off-duty overcoat, finds a solitary passenger asleep, masquerades as Kilmington inquiring the time, and strengthens the impression by saying he'd walk to the village if the relief engine did not turn up

268

in five minutes, then returns to the body and throws the hat beside it (Stansfield found the hat only lightly covered with snow, as compared with the body: Clue Number Six). Moreover, the passenger noticed that the inquirer was wearing blue trousers (Clue Number Seven). The guard's regulation suit was blue; but Duke's suit was gray, and Macdonald's a loud check—therefore, the masquerader could not have been either of them.

The time is now 8:55. The guard decides to reinforce his alibi by going to intercept the returning fireman. He takes a short cut from the body to the platelayers' hut. The track he now makes, compared with the beaten trail towards the village, is much more lightly filled in with snow when Stansfield finds it (Clue Number Eight): therefore, it must have been made some time after the murder, and could not incriminate Percy Dukes. The guard meets the fireman just after 8:55. They walk back to the train. The guard is taken aside by Dukes, who has gone out for his "airing," and the conversation overheard by Inez Blake takes place. The guard tells Dukes he will meet him presently in the platelayers' hut: this is aimed to incriminate Dukes, should the murder by any chance be discovered, for Dukes would find it difficult to explain why he should have sat alone in a cold hut for half an hour just around the time when Kilmington was presumably murdered only one hundred and fifty yards away. The guard now goes along to the engine and stays there chatting with the crew for some forty minutes. His alibi is thus established for the period from 8:55 to 9:40 P.M. His plan might well have succeeded, but for three unlucky factors he could not possibly have taken into account —Stansfield's presence on the train, the blizzard stopping soon after 9 P.M., and the theft of Arthur J. Kilmington's watch.

THE CAT'S-PAW

BY STANLEY ELLIN

Stanley Ellin was born on October 6, 1916, in Brooklyn,
N.Y. After graduating from Brooklyn College he married
his classmate, Jeanne Michael, and was employed as a
boilermaker's apprentice, a steelworker, a dairy farmer,
and a teacher before turning to the writing of fiction. His
first published work was "The Specialty of the House,"
one of *Ellery Queen's Mystery Magazine*'s most distinguished "first" stories. Since then, his reputation as a
writer has been absolute. He has won two Edgars for best
short story of the year and one for best novel. In 1975 he
won Le Grand Prix de Littérature Policière for his
novel, *Mirror, Mirror on the Wall*.

THERE WAS LITTLE TO CHOOSE among any of the rooms in the boarding house in their dingy, linoleum-floored, brass-bed-steaded uniformity, but the day he answered the advertise-ment on the *Help Wanted* page, Mr. Crabtree realized that one small advantage accrued to his room: the public tele-phone in the hallway was opposite his door, and simply by keeping an ear cocked he could be at the instrument a mo-ment after the first shrill warning ring had sounded.

In view of this he closed his application for employment not only with his signature, but with the number of the tele-phone as well. His hand shook a little as he did so; he felt party to a gross deception in implying that the telephone was his personal property, but the prestige to be gained this way, so he thought, might somehow weight the balance in his favor. To that end he tremorously sacrificed the unblemished principles of a lifetime.

The advertisement itself had been nothing less than a miracle. *Man wanted*, it said, *for hard work at moderate pay. Sober, honest, industrious former clerk, age 45-50 preferred. Write all details. Box* 111; and Mr. Crabtree, peering incred-ulously through his spectacles, had read it with a shuddering dismay at the thought of all his fellows, age 45-50, who might be seeking hard work at moderate pay, and who might have read the same notice minutes, or perhaps, hours, before.

His answer could have served as a model Letter of Appli-cation for Employment. His age was forty-eight, his health excellent. He was unmarried. He had served one single firm for thirty years; had served it faithfully and well; had an admirable record for attendance and punctuality. Unfor-tunately, the firm had merged with another and larger; re-grettably, many capable employees had to be released. Hours? Unimportant. His only interest was in doing a good job no matter the time involved. Salary? A matter entirely in the hands of his prospective employer. His previous salary had been fifty dollars per week, but naturally that had come after years of proved worth. Available for an interview at any time. References from the following. The signature. And then, the telephone number.

271

All this had been written and rewritten a dozen times until Mr. Crabtree had been satisfied that every necessary word was there, each word in its proper place. Then, in the copperplate hand that had made his ledgers a thing of beauty, the final draft had been transferred to fine bond paper purchased toward this very contingency, and posted.

After that, alone with his speculations on whether a reply would come by mail, by telephone, or not at all, Mr. Crabtree spent two endless and heart-fluttering weeks until the moment when he answered a call and heard his name come over the wire like the crack of doom.

"Yes," he said shrilly, "I'm Crabtree! I sent a letter!"

"Calmly, Mr. Crabtree, calmly," said the voice. It was a clear thin voice which seemed to pick up and savor each syllable before delivering it, and it had an instant and chilling effect on Mr. Crabtree, who was clutching the telephone as if pity could be squeezed from it.

"I have been considering your application," the voice went on with the same painful deliberation, "and I am most gratified by it. Most gratified. But before calling the matter settled, I should like to make clear the terms of employment I am offering. You would not object to my discussing it now?"

The word *employment* rang dizzily through Mr. Crabtree's head. "No," he said, "please do."

"Very well. First of all, do you feel capable of operating your own establishment?"

"My own establishment?"

"Oh, have no fears about the size of the establishment or the responsibilities involved. It is a matter of some confidential reports which must be drawn up regularly. You would have your own office, your name on the door, and, of course, no supervision directly over you. That should explain the need for an exceptionally reliable man."

"Yes," said Mr. Crabtree, "but those confidential reports . . ."

"Your office will be supplied with a list of several important corporations. It will also receive subscriptions to a number of financial journals which frequently make mention of those same corporations. You will note all such references as they appear, and, at the end of each day, consolidate them into a report which will be mailed to me. I must add that none of this calls for any theoretical work or literary treatment. Accuracy, brevity, clarity: those are the three measures to go by. You understand that, of course?"

"Yes, indeed," said Mr. Crabtree fervently.

"Excellent," said the voice. "Now, your hours will be from nine to five, six days a week, with an hour off at noon for lunch. I must stress this: I am insistent on punctuality and attendance, and I expect you to be as conscientious about these things as if you were under my personal supervision every moment of the day. I hope I do not offend you when I emphasize this?"

"Oh, no, sir!" said Mr. Crabtree. "I . . ."

"Let me continue," the voice said. "Here is the address where you will appear one week from today, and the number of your room"—Mr. Crabtree without pencil or paper at hand pressed the numbers frantically into his memory—"and the office will be completely prepared for you. The door will be open, and you will find two keys in a drawer of the desk: one for the door and one for the cabinet in the office. In the desk you will also find the list I mentioned, as well as the materials needed in making out your reports. In the cabinet you will find a stock of periodicals to start work on."

"I beg your pardon," said Mr. Crabtree, "but those reports . . ."

"They should contain every single item of interest about the corporations on your list, from business transactions to changes in personnel. And they must be mailed to me immediately upon your leaving the office each day. Is that clear?"

"Only one thing," said Mr. Crabtree. "To whom—where do I mail them?"

"A pointless question," said the voice sharply, much to Mr. Crabtree's alarm. "To the box number with which you are already familiar of course."

"Of course," said Mr. Crabtree.

"Now," said the voice with a gratifying return to its original deliberate tones, "the question of salary. I have given it a good deal of thought, since as you must realize, there are a number of factors involved. In the end, I let myself be guided by the ancient maxim: a good workman is worthy of his hire—you recall those words?"

"Yes," said Mr. Crabtree.

"And," the voice said, "a poor workman can be easily dispensed with. On that basis, I am prepared to offer you fifty-

273

two dollars a week. May I take it that that is satisfactory?"

Mr. Crabtree stared at the telephone dumbly and then recovered his voice. "Very," he gasped. "Oh, very much so. I must confess I never . . ."

The voice brought him up sharply. "But that is conditional, you understand. You will be—to use a rather clumsy term—on probation until you have proved yourself. Either the job is handled to perfection, or there is no job."

Mr. Crabtree felt his knees turn to water at the grim suggestion. "I'll do my best," he said. "I most certainly will do my absolute best."

"And," the voice went on relentlessly, "I attach great significance to the way you observe the confidential nature of your work. It is not to be discussed with anyone, and since the maintenance of your office and supplies lies entirely in my hands there can be no excuse for a defection. I have also removed temptation in the form of a telephone which you will *not* find on your desk. I hope I do not seem unjust in my abhorrence of the common practice where employees waste their time in idle conversation during working hours."

Since the death of an only sister twenty years before, there was not a soul in the world who would have dreamed of calling Mr. Crabtree to make any sort of conversation whatsoever; but he only said, "No, sir. Absolutely not."

"Then you are in agreement with all the terms we have discussed?"

"Yes, sir," said Mr. Crabtree.

"Any further questions?"

"One thing," said Mr. Crabtree. "My salary. How . . ."

"It will reach you at the end of each week," said the voice, "in cash. Anything else?"

Mr. Crabtree's mind was now a veritable log-jam of questions, but he found it impossible to fix on any particular one. Before he could do so, the voice said crisply, "Good luck, then," and there was the click which told him his caller had hung up. It was only when he attempted to do the same that he discovered his hand had been clenched so tightly around the receiver that it cost him momentary anguish to disengage it.

It must be admitted that the first time Mr. Crabtree approached the address given him, it would not have surprised

274

him greatly to find no building there at all. But the building was there, reassuring in its immensity, teeming with occupants who packed the banks of elevators solidly, and, in the hallways, looked through him and scurried around him with efficient disinterest.

The office was there too, hidden away at the end of a devious corridor of its own on the very top floor, a fact called to Mr. Crabtree's attention by a stairway across the corridor, which led up to an open door through which the flat gray of the sky could be seen.

The most impressive thing about the office was the CRABTREE'S AFFILIATED REPORTS boldly stenciled on the door. Opening the door, one entered an incredibly small and narrow room made even smaller by the massive dimensions of the furniture that crowded it. To the right, immediately inside the door, was a gigantic filing cabinet. Thrust tightly against it, but still so large that it utilized the remainder of the wall space on that side, was a huge, old-fashioned desk with a swivel chair before it.

The window set in the opposite wall was in keeping with the furniture. It was an immense window, broad and high, and its sill came barely above Mr. Crabtree's knees. He felt a momentary qualm when he first glanced through it and saw the sheer dizzying drop below, the terrifying quality of which was heightened by the blind, windowless walls of the building directly across from him.

One look was enough; henceforth, Mr. Crabtree kept the bottom section of the window securely fastened and adjusted only the top section to his convenience.

The keys were in a desk drawer; pen, ink, a box of nibs, a deck of blotters, and a half-dozen other accessories more impressive than useful were in another drawer; a supply of stamps was at hand; and, most pleasant, there was a plentiful supply of stationery, each piece bearing the letterhead, *Crabtree's Affiliated Reports,* the number of the office, and the address of the building. In his delight at this discovery Mr. Crabtree dashed off a few practice lines with some bold flourishes of the pen, and then, a bit alarmed at his own prodigality, carefully tore the sheet to minute shreds and dropped it into the wastebasket at his feet.

After that, his efforts were devoted wholly to the business at hand. The filing cabinet disgorged a dismayingly large file of publications which had to be pored over, line by line, and Mr. Crabtree never finished studying a page without the harrowing sensation that he had somehow bypassed the mention of a name which corresponded to one on the typed list he had found, as promised, in the desk. Then he would retrace the entire page with an awful sense of dallying at his work, and groan when he came to the end of it without finding what he had not wanted to find in the first place.

It seemed to him at times that he could never possibly deplete the monstrous pile of periodicals before him. Whenever he sighed with pleasure at having made some headway, he would be struck with the gloomy foreknowledge that the next morning would find a fresh delivery of mail at his door and, consequently, more material to add to the pile.

There were, however, breaks in this depressing routine. One was the preparation of the daily report, a task which, somewhat to Mr. Crabtree's surprise, he found himself learning to enjoy; the other was the prompt arrival each week of the sturdy envelope containing his salary down to the last dollar bill, although this was never quite the occasion for unalloyed pleasure it might have been.

Mr. Crabtree would carefully slit open one end of the envelope, remove the money, count it, and place it neatly in his ancient wallet. Then he would poke trembling exploratory fingers into the envelope, driven by the fearful recollection of his past experience to look for the notice that would tell him his services were no longer required. That was always a bad moment, and it had the unfailing effect of leaving him ill and shaken until he could bury himself in his work again.

The work was soon part of him. He had ceased bothering with the typed list; every name on it was firmly imprinted in his mind, and there were restless nights when he could send himself off to sleep merely by repeating the list a few times. One name in particular had come to intrigue him, merited special attention. *Efficiency Instruments, Ltd.* was unquestionably facing stormy weather. There had been drastic changes in personnel, talks of a merger, sharp fluctuations on the market.

It rather pleased Mr. Crabtree to discover that with the passage of weeks into months each of the names on his list had taken on a vivid personality for him. *Amalgamated* was steady as a rock, stolid in its comfortable success; *Universal* was highpitched, fidgety in its exploration of new techniques; and so on down the line. But *Efficiency Instruments, Ltd.* was Mr. Crabtree's pet project, and he had, more than once, nervously caught himself giving it perhaps a shade more attention than it warranted. He brought himself up sharply at such times; impartiality must be maintained, otherwise . . .

It came without any warning at all. He returned from lunch, punctual as ever, opened the door of the office, and knew he was standing face to face with his employer.

"Come in, Mr. Crabtree," said the clear, thin voice, "and shut the door."

Mr. Crabtree closed the door and stood speechless.

"I must be a prepossessing figure," said the visitor with a certain relish, "to have such a potent effect on you. You know who I am, of course?"

To Mr. Crabtree's numbed mind the large, bulbous eyes fixed unwinkingly on him, the wide, flexible mouth, the body, short and round as a barrel, bore a horrifying resemblance to a frog sitting comfortably at the edge of a pond, with himself in the unhappy role of a fly hovering close by.

"I believe," said Mr. Crabtree shakily, "that you are my employer, Mr. . . . Mr. . . ."

A stout forefinger nudged Mr. Crabtree's rib playfully. "As long as the bills are paid, the name is unimportant, eh, Mr. Crabtree? However, for the sake of expedience, let me be known to you as—say—George Spelvin. Have you ever encountered the ubiquitous Mr. Spelvin in your journeyings, Mr. Crabtree?"

"I'm afraid not," said Mr. Crabtree miserably.

"Then you are not a playgoer, and that is all to the good. And if I may hazard a guess, you are not one to indulge yourself in literature or the cinema either?"

"I do try to keep up with the daily newspaper," said Mr. Crabtree stoutly. "There's a good deal to read in it, you know, Mr. Spelvin, and it's not always easy, considering my work here, to find time for other diversions. That is, if a man wants to keep up with the newspapers."

The corners of the wide mouth lifted in what Mr. Crabtree hoped was a smile. "That is precisely what I hoped to hear you say. Facts, Mr. Crabtree, facts! I wanted a man with a single-minded interest in facts, and your words now as well as your application to your work tell me I have found him in you. I am very gratified, Mr. Crabtree."

Mr. Crabtree found that the blood was thumping pleasantly through his veins. "Thank you. Thank you again, Mr. Spelvin. I know I've been trying very hard, but I didn't know whether . . . Won't you sit down?" Mr. Crabtree tried to get his arm around the barrel before him in order to swing the chair into position, and failed. "The office is a bit small. But very comfortable," he stammered hastily.

"I am sure it is suitable," said Mr. Spelvin. He stepped back until he was almost fixed against the window and indicated the chair. "Now I should like you to be seated, Mr. Crabtree, while I discuss the matter I came on."

Under the spell of that commanding hand Mr. Crabtree sank into the chair and pivoted it until he faced the window and the squat figure outlined against it. "If there is any question about today's report," he said, "I am afraid it isn't complete yet. There were some notes on *Efficiency Instruments* . . ."

Mr. Spelvin waved the matter aside indifferently. "I am not here to discuss that," he said slowly. "I am here to find the answer to a problem which confronts me. And I rely on you, Mr. Crabtree, to help me find that answer."

"A problem?" Mr. Crabtree found himself warm with a sense of well-being. "I'll do everything I can to help, Mr. Spelvin. Everything I possibly can."

The bulging eyes probed his worriedly. "Then tell me this, Mr. Crabtree: how would you go about killing a man?"

"I?" said Mr. Crabtree. "How would I go . . . I'm afraid I don't understand, Mr. Spelvin."

"I said," Mr. Spelvin repeated, carefully stressing each word, "how would you go about killing a man?"

Mr. Crabtree's jaw dropped. "But I couldn't. I wouldn't. That," he said, "that would be murder!"

"Exactly," said Mr. Spelvin.

"But you're joking," said Mr. Crabtree, and tried to laugh, without managing to get more than a thin, breathless wheeze through his constricted throat. Even that pitiful effort was cut short by the sight of the stony face before him. "I'm terribly sorry, Mr. Spelvin, terribly sorry. You can see it's not the customary . . . it's not the kind of thing . . ."

"Mr. Crabtree. In the financial journals you study so assiduously you will find my name—my own name—repeated endlessly. I have a finger in many pies, Mr. Crabtree, and it always prods the plum. To use the more blatant adjectives, I am wealthy and powerful far beyond your wildest dreams—granting that you are capable of wild dreams—and a man does not attain that position by idling his time away on pointless jokes, or in passing the time of day with hirelings. My time is limited, Mr. Crabtree. If you cannot answer my question, say so, and let it go at that!"

"I don't believe I can," said Mr. Crabtree piteously.

"You should have said that at once," Mr. Spelvin replied, "and spared me my moment of choler. Frankly, I did not believe you could answer my question, and if you had it would have been a most disillusioning experience. You see, Mr. Crabtree, I envy, I deeply envy, your serenity of existence where such questions never even enter. Unfortunately, I am not in that position. At one point in my career, I made a mistake, the only mistake that has ever marked my rise to fortune. This, in time, came to the attention of a man who combines ruthlessness and cleverness to a dangerous degree, and I have been in the power of that man since. He is, in fact, a blackmailer, a common blackmailer who has come to set too high a price on his wares, and so must now pay for them himself."

"You intend," said Mr. Crabtree hoarsely, "to kill him?"

Mr. Spelvin threw out a plump hand in protest. "If a fly rested in the palm of that hand," he said sharply, "I could not find the power to close my fingers and crush the life from it. To be blunt, Mr. Crabtree, I am totally incapable of committing an act of violence, and while that may be an admirable quality in many ways, it is merely an embarrassment now, since the man must certainly be killed." Mr. Spelvin paused. "Nor is this a task for a paid assassin. If I resorted to one, I would most assuredly be exchanging one blackmailer for another, and that is altogether impractical." Mr. Spelvin paused again. "So, Mr. Crabtree, you can see there is only one conclusion to be drawn: the responsibility for destroying my tormentor rests entirely on you."

"Me!" cried Mr. Crabtree. "Why, I could never—no, never!"

"Oh, come," said Mr. Spelvin brusquely. "You are working yourself into a dangerous state. Before you carry it any further, Mr. Crabtree, I should like to make clear that your failure to carry out my request means that when you leave this office today, you leave it permanently. I cannot tolerate an employee who does not understand his position."

"Not tolerate!" said Mr. Crabtree. "But that is not right, that is not right at all, Mr. Spelvin. I've been working hard." His spectacles blurred. He fumbled with them, cleaned them carefully, replaced them on his nose. "And to leave me with such a secret. I don't see it; I don't see it at all. Why," he said in alarm, "it's a matter for the police!"

To his horror Mr. Spelvin's face turned alarmingly red, and the huge body started to shake in a convulsion of mirth that rang deafeningly through the room.

"Forgive me," he managed to gasp at last. "Forgive me, my dear fellow. I was merely visualizing the scene in which you go to the authorities and tell them of the incredible demands put upon you by your employer."

"You must understand," said Mr. Crabtree; "I am not threatening you, Mr. Spelvin. It is only . . ."

"Threatening me? Mr. Crabtree, tell me, what connection do you think there is between us in the eyes of the world?"

"Connection? I work for you, Mr. Spelvin. I'm an employee here. I . . ."

Mr. Spelvin smiled blandly. "What a curious delusion," he said, "when one can see that you are merely a shabby little man engaged in some pitiful little enterprise that could not possibly be of interest to me."

"But you employed me yourself, Mr. Spelvin! I wrote a letter of application!"

"You did," said Mr. Spelvin, "but unfortunately the position was already filled, as I informed you in my very polite letter of explanation. You look incredulous, Mr. Crabtree, so let me inform you that your letter and a copy of my reply rest securely in my files should the matter ever be called to question."

"But this office! These furnishings! My subscriptions!"

"Mr. Crabtree, Mr. Crabtree," said Mr. Spelvin shaking his head heavily, "did *you* ever question the source of your weekly income? The manager of this building, the dealers in supplies, the publishers who deliver their journals to you were no more interested in my identity than you were. It is, I grant, a bit irregular for me to deal exclusively in currency sent through the mails in your name, but have no fears for me, Mr. Crabtree. Prompt payments are the opiate of the businessman."

"But my reports!" said Mr. Crabtree who was seriously starting to doubt his own existence.

"To be sure, the reports. I daresay that the ingenious Mr. Crabtree, after receiving my unfavorable reply to his application, decided to go into business for himself. He thereupon instituted a service of financial reports and even attempted to make *me* one of his clients! I rebuffed him sharply I can tell you (I have his first report *and* a copy of my reply to it) but he foolishly persists in his efforts. Foolishly, I say, because his reports are absolutely useless to me; I have no interest in any of the corporations he discusses, and why he should imagine I would have is beyond my reckoning. Frankly, I suspect the man is an eccentric of the worst type, but since I have had dealings with many of that type I merely disregard him, and destroy his daily reports on their arrival."

"Destroy them?" said Mr. Crabtree stupefied.

"You have no cause for complaint, I hope," said Mr. Spelvin with some annoyance. "To find a man of your character, Mr. Crabtree, it was necessary for me to specify *hard work* in my advertisement. I am only living up to my part of the bargain in providing it, and I fail to see where the final disposition of it is any of your concern."

"A man of my character," echoed Mr. Crabtree helplessly, "to commit murder?"

"And why not?" The wide mouth tightened ominously. "Let me enlighten you, Mr. Crabtree. I have spent a pleasant and profitable share of my life in observing the human species, as a scientist might study insects under glass. And I have come to one conclusion, Mr. Crabtree, one above all others which has contributed to the making of my own success. I have come to the conclusion that to the majority of our species it is the function that is important, not the motives, nor the consequences.

"My advertisement, Mr. Crabtree, was calculated to enlist the services of one like that; a perfect representative of the type, in fact. From the moment you answered that advertisement to the present, you have been living up to all my expectations: you have been functioning flawlessly with no thought of either motive or consequence.

281

"Now murder has been made part of your function. I have honored you with an explanation of its motives; the consequences are clearly defined. Either you continue to function as you always have, or, to put it in a nutshell, you are out of a job."

"A job!" said Mr. Crabtree wildly. "What does a job matter to a man in prison! Or to a man being hanged!"

"Oh, come," remarked Mr. Spelvin placidly. "Do you think I'd lead you into a trap which might snare me as well? I am afraid you are being obtuse, my dear man. If you are not, you must realize clearly that my own security is tied in the same package as yours. And nothing less than your permanent presence in this office and your steadfast application to your work is the guarantee of that security."

"That may be easy to say when you're hiding under an assumed name," said Mr. Crabtree hollowly.

"I assure you, Mr. Crabtree, my position in the world is such that my identity can be unearthed with small effort. But I must also remind you that should you carry out my request you will then be a criminal and, consequently, very discreet.

"On the other hand, if you do not carry out my request—and you have complete freedom of choice in that—any charges you may bring against me will be dangerous only to you. The world, Mr. Crabtree, knows nothing about our relationship, and nothing about my affair with the gentleman who has been victimizing me and must now become my victim. Neither his demise nor your charges could ever touch me, Mr. Crabtree.

"Discovering my identity, as I said, would not be difficult. But using that information, Mr. Crabtree, can only lead you to a prison or an institution for the deranged."

Mr. Crabtree felt the last dregs of his strength seeping from him. "You have thought of everything," he said.

"Everything, Mr. Crabtree. When you entered my scheme of things, it was only to put my plan into operation; but long before that I was hard at work weighing, measuring, evaluating every step of that plan. For example, this room, this very room, has been chosen only after a long and weary search as perfect for my purpose. Its furnishings have been selected and arranged to further that purpose. How? Let me explain that.

"When you are seated at your desk, a visitor is confined to the space I now occupy at the window. The visitor is, of course, the gentleman in question. He will enter and stand here with the window *entirely open* behind him. He will ask you for an envelope a friend has left. This envelope," said Mr. Spelvin, tossing one to the desk. "You will have the envelope in your desk, will find it, and hand it to him. Then, since he is a very methodical man (I have learned that well), he will place the envelope in the inside pocket of his jacket— and at that moment one good thrust will send him out the window. The entire operation should take less than a minute. Immediately after that," Mr. Spelvin said calmly, "you will close the window to the bottom and return to your work."

"Someone," whispered Mr. Crabtree, "the police . . ."

"Will find," said Mr. Spelvin, "the body of some poor unfortunate who climbed the stairs across the hallway and hurled himself from the roof above. And they will know this because inside that envelope secured in his pocket is not what the gentleman in question expects to find there, but a neatly typewritten note explaining the sad affair and its motives, an apology for any inconvenience caused (suicides are great ones for apologies, Mr. Crabtree) and a most pathetic plea for a quick and peaceful burial. And," said Mr. Spelvin, gently touching his fingertips together, "I do not doubt he will get it."

"What," Mr. Crabtree said, "what if something went wrong? If the man opened the letter when it was given to him. Or . . . if something like that happened?"

Mr. Spelvin shrugged. "In that case the gentleman in question would merely make his way off quietly and approach me directly about the matter. Realize, Mr. Crabtree, that anyone in my friend's line of work expects occasional little attempts like this, and, while he may not be inclined to think them amusing, he would hardly venture into some precipitous action that might kill the goose who lays the golden eggs. No, Mr. Crabtree, if such a possibility as you suggest comes to pass, it means only that I must reset my trap, and even more ingeniously."

Mr. Spelvin drew a heavy watch from his pocket, studied it, then replaced it carefully. "My time is growing short, Mr. Crabtree. It is not that I find your company wearing, but my man will be making his appearance shortly, and matters must be entirely in your hands at that time. All I require of you is this: when he arrives, the window will be open." Mr. Spelvin

thrust it up hard and stood for a moment looking apprecia-
tively at the drop below. "The envelope will be in your desk."
He opened the drawer and dropped it in, then closed the
drawer firmly. "And at the moment of decision, you are free
to act one way or the other."

"Free?" said Mr. Crabtree. "You said he would ask for the
envelope!"

"He will. He will, indeed. But if you indicate that you
know nothing about it, he will quietly make his departure,
and later communicate with me. And that will be, in effect, a
notice of your resignation from my employ."

Mr. Spelvin went to the door and rested one hand on the
knob. "However," he said, "if I do *not* hear from him, that
will assure me that you have successfully completed your term
of probation and are to be henceforth regarded as a capable
and faithful employee."

"But the reports!" said Mr. Crabtree. "You destroy
them . . ."

"Of course," said Mr. Spelvin, a little surprised. "But you
will continue with your work and send the reports to me as
you have always done. I assure you, it does not matter to me
that they are meaningless, Mr. Crabtree. They are part of a
pattern, and your adherence to that pattern, as I have already
told you, is the best assurance of my own security."

The door opened, closed quietly, and Mr. Crabtree found
himself alone in the room.

The shadow of the building opposite lay heavily on his desk.
Mr. Crabtree looked at his watch, found himself unable to
read it in the growing dimness of the room, and stood up to
pull the cord of the light over his head. At that moment a
peremptory knock sounded on the door.

"Come in," said Mr. Crabtree.

The door opened on two figures. One was a small, dapper
man, the other a bulky police officer who loomed imposingly
over his companion. The small man stepped into the office,
and with the gesture of a magician pulling a rabbit from a hat,
withdrew a large wallet from his pocket, snapped it open to
show the gleam of a badge, closed it, and slid it back into his
pocket.

"Police," said the man succinctly. "Name's Sharpe."

Mr. Crabtree nodded politely. "Yes?" he said.

"Hope you don't mind," said Sharpe briskly. "Just a few questions."

As if this were a cue, the large policeman came up with an efficient-looking notebook and the stub of a pencil, and stood there poised for action. Mr. Crabtree peered over his spectacles at the notebook, and through them at the diminutive Sharpe. "No," said Mr. Crabtree, "not at all."

"You're Crabtree?" said Sharpe, and Mr. Crabtree started, then remembered the name on the door.

"Yes," he said.

Sharpe's cold eyes flickered over him and then took in the room with a contemptuous glance. "This your office?"

"Yes," said Mr. Crabtree.

"You in it all afternoon?"

"Since one o'clock," said Mr. Crabtree. "I go to lunch at twelve and return at one promptly."

"I'll bet," said Sharpe, then nodded over his shoulder. "That door open any time this afternoon?"

"It's always closed while I am working," said Mr. Crabtree.

"Then you wouldn't be able to see anybody going up that stair across the hall there."

"No," replied Mr. Crabtree, "I wouldn't."

Sharpe looked at the desk, then ran a reflective thumb along his jaw. "I guess you wouldn't be in a position to see anything happening outside the window either."

"No, indeed," said Mr. Crabtree. "Not while I'm at work."

"Now," said Sharpe, "did you *hear* something outside of that window this afternoon? Something out of the ordinary, I mean."

"Out of the ordinary?" repeated Mr. Crabtree vaguely.

"A yell. Somebody yelling. Anything like that?"

Mr. Crabtree puckered his brow. "Why, yes," he said, "yes, I did. And not long ago, either. It sounded as if someone had been startled—or frightened. Quite loud, too. It's always so quiet here I couldn't help hearing it."

Sharpe looked over his shoulder and nodded at the policeman who closed his notebook slowly. "That ties it up," said Sharpe. "The guy made the jump, and the second he did it he changed his mind, so he came down hollering all the way. Well," he said, turning to Mr. Crabtree in a burst of confidence, "I guess you've got a right to know what's going on here. About an hour ago some character jumped off that roof

285

right over your head. Clear case of suicide, note in his pocket and everything, but we like to get all the facts we can."

"Do you know," said Mr. Crabtree, "who he was?"

Sharpe shrugged. "Another guy with too many troubles. Young, good-looking, pretty snappy dresser. Only thing beats me is why a guy who could afford to dress like that would figure he has more troubles than he can handle."

The policeman in uniform spoke for the first time. "That letter he left," he said deferentially, "sounds like he was a little crazy."

"You have to be a little crazy to take that way out," said Sharpe.

"You're a long time dead," said the policeman heavily.

Sharpe held the doorknob momentarily. "Sorry to bother you," he said to Mr. Crabtree, "but you know how it is. Anyhow, you're lucky in a way. Couple of girls downstairs saw him go by and passed right out." He winked as he closed the door behind him.

Mr. Crabtree stood looking at the closed door until the sound of heavy footsteps passed out of hearing. Then he seated himself in the chair and pulled himself closer to the desk. Some magazines and sheets of stationery lay there in mild disarray, and he arranged the magazines in a neat pile, stacking them so that all corners met precisely.

Mr. Crabtree picked up his pen, dipped it into the ink-bottle, and steadied the paper before him with his other hand.

Efficiency Instruments, Ltd., he wrote carefully, *shows increased activity . . .*

LACRIMAE RERUM

BY EDMUND CRISPIN

Edmund Crispin is the pseudonym of Bruce Montgomery. He was born on October 2, 1921, and educated at Oxford. Since the age of 14 he has been a pianist, organist, conductor, and composer. After a period (1944-1953) during which he wrote detective novels and a collection of short stories, many featuring Oxford professor Gervase Fen, he wrote no more in the genre until the 1970s. He has edited a number of anthologies, including science fiction, and written film scripts, radio plays, and the musical scores of many British films. He is the mystery-fiction reviewer for *The Sunday Times* (London) and lives in Devon.

"You CHATTER ABOUT 'the perfect crime,'" said Wakefield irritably, "but you seem incapable of realizing that it isn't a topic one can *argue* about at all. One can only pontificate, which is irrational and useless."

"Have some more port," said Haldane.

"Well, yes, I will. . . . The perfect murder, for instance, isn't known to be a murder at all; it looks like natural death, and no suggestion of foul play ever enters anyone's mind. Only the *imperfect* murders are *known* to be murders. And consequently, to argue about 'the perfect murder' is to argue about something which you cannot, by definition, prove to exist."

"Your logic," said Gervase Fen, "isn't exactly impeccable."

Wakefield gazed at him stonily. "What's wrong with my logic?" he demanded.

"Its major premise is wrong. You've gone astray in defining the perfect murder."

"I have n— How have I gone astray?"

"The sort of thing you suggest—the apparently natural death—has one serious disadvantage from the murderer's point of view."

"And that is?" Wakefield leaned forward across the table. "That is?"

"At the risk of boring you all, I could illustrate it." Gervase Fen glanced at his host and his fellow guests, who nodded a vinously emphatic approval; only Wakefield, who hated losing the conversational initiative, showed any sign of restiveness. "What I have in mind is a murder which was committed several years before the war—the first criminal case, as it happens, with which I ever had anything to do."

"Quite a distinction for it," Wakefield muttered uncivilly into his wine glass.

"No doubt. And it was certainly the most daring and ingenious crime I've ever encountered."

"They all are," said Wakefield.

"It succeeded, did it?" Haldane interposed rather hurriedly. "That is to say, the criminal wasn't discovered or punished?"

"Discovered," said Fen, "but not punished."

288

"You mean there was no case against him?"

"There was a cast-iron case; conclusive proof, followed by a circumstantial confession. But the police couldn't act on it."

"Oh, well," said Wakefield disgustedly, "if all you mean is that he escaped to some country he couldn't be extradited from—"

Gervase Fen shook his head. "That isn't at all what I mean. The murderer is at the present moment living quite openly almost next door to New Scotland Yard."

There was a general stir of interest.

"I don't see how that's possible," Wakefield said sourly.

"And you never will," Haldane told him, "if you don't stop talking and give us a chance to hear about it. . . . Go on, Gervase."

"The murder I mean," said Fen, "is the murder of Alan Pasmore, in 1935."

"Pasmore the composer?" Wakefield asked.

"Yes."

"I remember it caused quite a commotion at the time," said Haldane thoughtfully. "And then it all seemed suddenly to fade out, and one heard no more about it."

Fen chuckled. "The authorities were over-precipitate," he explained, "and naturally they were anxious that their shortcomings shouldn't be advertised. Hence the conspiracy of silence. . . .

"Pasmore and his wife were living at Amersham, in Bucks. He was forty-seven at the time of his death, and at the height of his reputation; though since then he's sunk almost completely into oblivion, and nowadays his stuff's hardly ever performed.

"His wife, Angela, was a good deal younger—twenty-six, to be exact. Attractive, intelligent, competent. As well as seeing to it that his house was kept like a new pin, she acted as his secretary. There was plenty of money—his, not hers. No children. Three servants. Superficially, it seemed quite a successful marriage, as marriages go.

"On the afternoon of October second, 1935, two visitors came to tea.

"One was Sir Charles Frazer, the conductor, who lived only a few miles away. The other was a wholly unimportant young man called Beasley, who worked at an insurance office in the City. Both of them, it appears, were to some extent infatuated with Angela Pasmore. Sir Charles was there by invitation; Beasley just 'dropped in.' And neither of them was pleased to find the other there, since at tea-time, if she were at home at all, you could be sure of having Angela to yourself. Her husband always worked from two to six in the afternoon, and had his tea alone in the study upstairs.

"At four o'clock, then, tea was served in the downstairs drawing room to Angela, to Sir Charles, and to Beasley. Five minutes later the afternoon mail arrived. It was taken from the postman at the front door by Soames, the manservant, who carried it straight to the drawing room and gave it to Angela. It consisted of a card for Soames, several letters and cards for Angela, and a single typewritten envelope for Pasmore. This last Angela immediately opened. She glanced through the letter inside and then handed it, with a slight grimace, to Sir Charles."

"And why," Wakefield inquired, "did she do that?"

"The letter," Fen continued unperturbed, "was from another conductor—Paul Brice, to be specific. He was in Edinburgh (where, as it was afterwards proved, this letter had been posted on the previous afternoon), and there, at the Usher Hall in two days' time, he was scheduled to conduct the Hallé Orchestra in a concert whose program included Pasmore's symphonic poem *Merlin. Merlin* was at this date quite a new work. It had had only one performance so far, under Sir Charles Frazer at the Queen's Hall. And since the score was tolerably complicated, Brice wanted advice from the composer on a good many points of interpretation.

"That was what his letter was about. I've seen it, and it consisted of a long list of things like: *'At 3 after C, can I relax tempo in the bar and a half before the Bb entry?'* and: *'At 5 before Q, string accompaniment and clarinet solo are both marked p, but clarinet doesn't come through; pp accompaniment would blur harmonic texture; can clarinet play mf?'* and: *'At 7 after Y, do you want the più mosso as in the exposition?'* There were, I think, at least two dozen such queries. Conductors aren't normally so conscientious, but Brice and Pasmore were lifelong friends, and Brice took Pasmore's music rather more seriously than its actual merits warranted.

"You will understand now"—and Fen eyed Wakefield with a certain severity—"why Angela should show this letter to Sir Charles. Having conducted the first and only performance of the work in question, he might be expected to be interested. He read the letter attentively, commenting, uncharitably one gathers, on Brice's artistic perceptivity. Then he gave it back to Angela.

"She in turn handed it to Soames, who was still hovering in the background, and told him to take it up to her husband with his tea, which by immutable custom was served to him at four fifteen. This he did, testifying subsequently that at four fifteen Pasmore was alive, uninjured, and in every way normal.

"At four twenty Angela excused herself to her two visitors and left the drawing-room—in order, as she asserted later, to 'powder her nose.' Beasley and Sir Charles remained together, making mistrustful small talk, until at half-past four she returned. She then stayed with them up to a quarter to five, when—as she'd previously warned them—she was engaged to drive her cook, Mrs. May, to the Chesham Cottage Hospital to visit her son, who had recently smashed himself to bits in a motorcycle accident. Beasley and Sir Charles weren't much pleased at being superseded by this work of mercy, but there was nothing they could do about it; so, with Angela, they left the drawing room and went out into the hall. Here she asked them to wait while she went up to her bedroom, whose door was clearly visible at the head of the stairs. And I'd better emphasize at this point, to save futile racking of your brains, that both men saw her go straight into this room, and that both were prepared to swear she couldn't have entered any other room upstairs, let alone the study, without their knowing."

"There being, of course"—Haldane picked up his glass and stared pensively at it before drinking—"no means of communication between the bedroom and the study."

"None whatever; care was taken to establish that. Moreover, Angela wasn't, according to Sir Charles and Beasley, in the bedroom for more than a minute at most. Emerging from it, she ran straight downstairs, went to the clothes closet in the hall, disappeared into it for a few seconds, departed to the kitchen to fetch Mrs. May, returned with her immediately, took a coat from the clothes closet and put it on, and finally shepherded Mrs. May and Sir Charles and Beasley to the front door. Outside, she said goodbye to the two men and got into the car with Mrs. May. And from then on she was with Mrs.

291

May continually, in the car or at the hospital, until at least twenty minutes after her husband's body was found.

"All of which boils down to this: that if Pasmore was killed by his wife, she could only have done it between four twenty and four thirty, the time during which she was away from the drawing room.

"It was Soames who found the body, when at six o'clock—again in accordance with immutable custom—he took whisky and water up to the study for Pasmore's preprandial drink. There proved, on investigation, to be nothing in the immediate circumstances of the crime that could help the police. Pasmore had been stabbed in the back while sitting at his desk, and had died instantaneously. The weapon was an eighteenth-century Venetian stiletto which hung normally over the study mantelpiece. There had been very little bleeding. The room had not been disturbed, and nothing, so far as could be discovered, was missing. There were no fingerprints on the weapon, and none in the room except such as were to be expected: the servants', Angela's, the dead man's. The police doctor arrived on the scene too late to be able to state the time of death with any certainty; 'probably between four and five' was the most he could say. A cookie had been eaten and a cup of tea drunk, Pasmore's prints being on the cup; and he had been killed, according to the *post-mortem* findings, between five and fifteen minutes after consuming these things. But since there was no evidence as to *when* he had consumed them—whether immediately after being brought the tea-tray, or later—that didn't help, either.

"In short, the police had uncommonly little to work on; all the same, within three days Angela was under arrest.

"Only a very brief investigation had been needed to reveal the fact that the marriage was not as successful as on the surface it appeared; that, not to be longwinded about it, Pasmore's *ménage* was on the rocks. Angela had committed adultery with some worthless poltroon whose name I can't now remember, Pasmore had found out, and Pasmore was determined on divorcing her—had, indeed, actually taken the preliminary steps towards doing so. His fortune was considerable; divorce would have put it permanently beyond Angela's reach; and so it was clear that she had motive enough for killing him. There was opportunity, too—those ten minutes during which she had been absent from the drawing room.

292

Questioned about whether she'd entered her husband's study during that time, she denied doing so. And that was fatal, since it happened that both Soames and a maidservant had seen her do so. . . . Mind you, all the evidence against her was circumstantial; there wasn't nor apparently could there be, any conclusive *proof* of guilt. But circumstantial evidence is quite commonly hanging evidence, and the police were perfectly justified in making the arrest. In due course the indictment was sanctioned by the Department of Public Prosecutions, and Angela, reserving her defense, was committed for trial at the Assizes.

"She pleaded not guilty, admitting, in the witness-box, that she *had* entered Pasmore's study, but stating that she left him alive and well—'writing a letter; I don't think he'd started his tea'—after a couple of minutes' casual coversation about household matters. The prosecution's case being on the thin side, the defense had reasonable hopes of an acquittal; and but for Angela's own behavior in the witness-box, they would have been fairly confident of it. Unfortunately, however, she blustered and contradicted herself and told transparent lies and in general made a very poor impression. What would have happened if the trial had run normally to its end, one doesn't know. And the question is academic, since it didn't run normally to its end. At almost the last possible moment, when the judge was on the point of starting his summing-up, the prosecution quite unexpectedly entered a plea of *nolle prosequi;* new evidence had emerged, it was stated, which conclusively established the prisoner's innocence. The judge had no alternative but to direct the jury to bring in a verdict of not guilty; the jury obeyed; and Angela Pasmore was acquitted of her husband's murder.

"You'll have guessed that the 'new evidence' had to do with Brice's letter. What actually happened, during the final day of the trial, was this:

"Angela remembered something which, she said, had been completely driven out of her mind by her husband's death, by the investigation, and by her own arrest—namely, the existence of a reply by Pasmore to that letter from Brice which had arrived by the afternoon post. It was Pasmore's habit to put letters which he wanted mailed on the dressing table in her bedroom (the servants, by the way, corroborated this). And on going up to her bedroom, just prior to leaving the house with Mrs. May, she had found this reply there, had put it in an envelope and addressed it, and had taken it down-stairs in her pocket, transferring it at once to the pocket of her outdoor coat, which was hanging in the clothes closet in the hall. Thereafter (I continue to quote her own account of the matter), she not only forgot to post it—as one does oc-casionally forget to post letters—but also forgot, in the even-tual confusion and distress, that the thing had ever existed. And presumably it was still in the pocket of her coat.

"All of this Angela communicated to her counsel. And he, naturally, wasn't slow to see the importance of it. *If* Brice's letter had not reached Pasmore till four fifteen, as it probably hadn't; *if* he had written a reply to it; *if* that reply had taken him more than fifteen minutes to write, as it probably had—then Angela could not have murdered him, since the only opportunity *she* had had was between four twenty and four thirty.

"Someone was sent off post-haste to Amersham. The letter was found. Handwriting experts were unanimous in agreeing that Pasmore had written it—that no part of it was forged. Tests established the fact that the absolute minimum time required to write it must have been twenty minutes. As to its content, that was a *seriatim* answer to Brice's queries, such as Pasmore could only have produced with the details of those queries in front of him. The arrival of Brice's letter by the afternoon mail was sworn to beyond the possibility of contra-diction by the postman, by Soames, by Beasley, and by Sir Charles. And Brice was emphatic that by no conceivable means could Pasmore have become acquainted with the questions about *Merlin* prior to the arrival of the letter.

"You see what all this evidence added up to: Pasmore couldn't have been killed before twenty-five to five at the earliest; and therefore it was not Angela who killed him."

Finishing his port, Fen lit a cigarette.

"As for myself," he went on after a moment's consideration, "I had no personal contact with the affair until after the trial was over. I read about it more or less attentively in the papers, and that was all. But about a week after Angela's acquittal I was dining with the Chief Constable of Bucking-hamshire, and he, knowing I had a lay interest in criminology, showed me the dossier of the case. Most of it was just repeti-tion and expansion of what I already knew. There was also, however, a complete typewritten copy of Pasmore's letter to Brice. And something in the last paragraph of that letter struck me as being ever so slightly odd. . . .

"The bulk of the thing, as I've told you, was simply a point-by-point reply, impersonal and business-like in tone, to Brice's queries. The final paragraph, though, ran like this:

Forgive me if I don't write more. I'm in the middle of scoring Ariadne *(with a concert on my next-door neighbor's wireless—lacrimae rerum!—to help me along) and am anxious, as you know, to get it done as quickly as possible. Good luck to the performance—I'm sorry I can't be there. Yours—*and so forth.

"Well, the police had, of course, checked this business of the concert; and Pasmore's neighbor's radio had, in fact, been on between three thirty and four forty-five. So far, so good. But *'lacrimae rerum'*—somehow that particular tag was wrong in that particular context. One's neighbor's radio is often tiresome, no doubt. But one doesn't use, as a comment on it, a phrase intended to express the profound, essential melancholy of all human activities—and more, of existence itself; the nuisance is too trivial and localized. And it occurred to me, as a consequence of this disparity, that *'lacrimae rerum'* might carry some specialized meaning for Brice and Pasmore—might in effect be a sort of private joke. Luckily, Brice was conducting at Oxford three or four days later, and I was able to make contact with him and ask him about it. And my notion turned out to be right. Brice and Pasmore had been at school together, had been close friends there, united in a passionately earnest devotion to music—a devotion whose naïveté occasionally bordered on the ludicrous. And on one occasion, when they had been listening together to Tchaikowsky's Sixth Symphony, Pasmore had remarked, in solemn, awe-struck tones: *'Lacrimae rerum,* Paul; it sums up the whole tragedy of humankind.' Brice had been much amused by this pretentious gloss on the music, and thereafter *'lacrimae rerum'* had been often used between them as a means of referring to that particular work.

"So naturally I went away and hunted through back numbers of *The Radio Times* until I found the program of the concert which had been broadcast on the afternoon of Pasmore's murder. It consisted of two works, the Walton Symphony followed by the Tchaikowsky Sixth; and there was no

295

difficulty in calculating that the Tchaikowsky must have begun at about a quarter past four and gone on until the end of the concert at a quarter to five. All quite straightforward, you see: no discrepancy with the suggestion that Pasmore's reply to Brice had been written more or less immediately after receiving Brice's letter at four fifteen.

"There I might have left it, but for the chance that I was lecturing in Amersham a week or so later, and, having an hour or so to spare, decided to go and interview Pasmore's neighbor—he of the radio. He turned out to be a pleasant little man—something to do with the Home Office, I fancy—and naturally enough he still remembered the events of the crucial afternoon quite clearly. He'd had that concert on all right, from beginning to end, but beyond that there didn't seem to be anything of value he could tell me. And I was on the point of leaving, in a welter of civilities, before he quite unexpectedly let the cat out of the bag.

" 'Of course, the police questioned me about it,' he said, 'and even though that wasn't till several weeks afterwards, I had no difficulty in recalling the concert—partly, no doubt, because of the change in the program.'

"I must have looked as though I'd seen a ghost. 'Change?' I echoed.

" 'Why, yes. For some mysterious reason of their own they played the Tchaikowsky first and the Walton second.'

"And they had. I checked with the BBC, and it was true. Owing to some kind of mismanagement, the orchestral parts of the Walton hadn't been in the studio at the start of the concert, and the Tchaikowsky had had to be played while the Walton parts were searched for. Therefore, the Tchaikowsky —'lacrimae rerum'—had *finished* at four o'clock; and therefore, if the reference in the final paragraph meant anything at all, Pasmore's letter to Brice had been completed by four o'clock."

Fen chuckled suddenly. "And given that, it didn't really require much thinking to deduce how Angela's alibi had been contrived. The police, as I discovered, had worked it all out for themselves—but not, unfortunately, until after the acquittal."

Fen paused, and Haldane shook his head. "I'm afraid that for my own part—"

"Oh, come . . . Brice's letter had been posted in Edinburgh

on the previous afternoon. It arrived at Amersham, of course, by the *morning* post on the day of the murder. Angela opened it—I've mentioned that she acted as Pasmore's secretary—and saw in it her opportunity. She destroyed the envelope in which it arrived, made a note of Brice's queries, typed a fresh envelope, inserted the letter, stamped, and *posted it again.* She could thus be fairly sure of its arriving a second time, in the presence of the invited and infatuated Sir Charles, by the afternoon post. And in the meantime she went to her husband and said something like this:

" 'Brice rang up from Edinburgh while you were out. He's written you a letter about *Merlin,* but it struck him that it might possibly not arrive soon enough for your reply to reach him in time for the final rehearsal. I've made a note of his queries, and if you write off to him some time this afternoon, that should be all right.'

"Pasmore would believe this—why shouldn't he?—and the reply to Brice would be written. And all that Angela had to do after that was to destroy the notes she'd made of Brice's queries and the envelope, typed by herself and with a local postmark on it, in which Brice's letter arrived at the house for the second time. Between four twenty and four thirty, of course, she entered Pasmore's study and killed him."

There was a brief, astonished silence; then: "Brilliant!" Haldane exclaimed. "Really brilliant . . . only"—his enthusiasm waned slightly—"there are a lot of things which *could* have gone wrong. Pasmore might just have omitted to write the reply; or it might not have been long enough—though I suppose that in view of the number of queries it was bound to be fairly long; or it might have contained some very definite reference to the hour of day at which it was being written."

"Yes, yes, I know all that," said Fen. "But you must realize that all these possible accidents and possible flaws in the scheme have one thing in common: if they were going to happen at all, they would happen *before the murder.* So if anything had gone wrong, Pasmore would quite simply not have been killed—not on that day, and in that particular way."

"I suppose she missed the point of *'lacrimae rerum,'* " said Haldane at last. "Interpreted it as just a general comment on neighbors' radios . . . She'd read the letter, of course, before killing Pasmore."

Fen nodded. "Certainly she would. It's to be presumed that Pasmore put it in her bedroom about four o'clock, and that she read it there, at twenty past four, before going to the study and killing him . . . I don't know why I say 'presumed.' By Angela's own admission that's what in fact happened. I wrote to her, you see—at considerable risk of a libel action—and by return post she sent me congratulations on my perspicuity and a circumstantial account of the crime."

"But look here," said Wakefield with sudden energy, "you can't possibly maintain that she arranged for Pasmore's letter to be her alibi and then *forgot* about it."

"Of course she didn't forget. She only pretended to—that was the whole point of her scheme. We're back where we started, you see; this is where the business of 'the perfect crime' comes in. Your murder which looks like natural death —well, it's satisfactory up to a point; but the murderer can never be *quite* sure that one day, perhaps years after, some accident may not reveal the truth and send him to the gallows. His only road to absolute immunity from punishment is to be tried and acquitted, for it's a basic principle of English Common Law that *nemo debet bis vexari*—that no one may be tried a second time for the same offense. Angela *wanted* to be tried, in order that she might be acquitted and live afterwards in perpetual immunity. Hence, Pasmore's letter was 'forgotten' until the right moment for its use arrived. Angela took a great deal of risk, of course. But it worked out very nicely for her in the end."

"Well, I consider it's abominable," said Haldane with disgust.

"There are those"—Gervase Fen spoke very mildly—"who would maintain that such injustices are invariably rectified at a higher court."

"Ah." Wakefield sat up abruptly. "And why do they maintain that? They maintain it because they believe the Universe to be subject to Laws, and they believe that because the phenomenal flux, without the concept of Order, is psychologically intolerable. Aldous Huxley—"

"Have some more port," said Haldane.

DOUBLE EXPOSURE

BY BEN HECHT

Ben Hecht was born in New York City on February 28, 1893. He began writing for the Chicago *News* and published stories in the *Little Review* and *Smart Set*. His first novel, *Erik Dorn* (1921), made use of his 1918-19 experience as a Berlin reporter. In 1923 he began his own newspaper, the *Literary Times*. He collaborated with Charles MacArthur on two plays, *The Front Page* and *Twentieth Century*, both of which were made into successful films. They also wrote the 1939 scenario for *Wuthering Heights*. His autobiography, *A Child of the Century*, was published in 1954. He died in 1964.

DR. HUGO HANDED ME a newspaper as I entered his Park Avenue apartment, and said, "Sit down and read that story. I'm in a rotten situation and I need some advice."

Under the headline, "Bride Slays Noted Psychiatrist on Honeymoon," the story related the shooting of Dr. Caleb Mudie in a Miami Beach Hotel. The photographs illustrating this unhappy event revealed a middle-aged, baldish man with thick eyebrows, and a voluptuous young dancer in long black hose. Her heavy lips were parted in what seemed to be a mood of chronic delight.

"Quite a tale," I said.

"Full of inaccuracies," Dr. Hugo said. "Mudie was not a psychiatrist. He was a neurologist. And not remotely noted. Except for stupidity. A man of even the most rudimentary intelligence seldom gets himself murdered on a honeymoon. Will you have a drink and make yourself comfortable—and control your desires to interrupt and shine in my eyes as a literary man of great astuteness? I know you are. That's why you're here. I have a story to tell you—a rather curious story— in which I may be the villain and not the hero, as I like to imagine myself. In addition to giving me advice you'll decide that, too, of course."

Dr. Hugo handed me my drink and I nodded with some irritation at my tall and unctuous host and his master-mind mannerisms. There was, as always, a gentle smile of triumph and derision on his once-handsome face—a face that reminded me of an expensive but overused handkerchief. It was a smile that said, "Life is a scurvy business—but let's pretend it isn't."

I had never been able to decide whether Dr. Hugo was an eminent psychiatrist or a rogue with a vocabulary. His wit seemed too sharp for a medical man and I shuddered at the prospect of ever becoming his patient. It would be like confiding one's symptoms to a blackmailer. There was, however, a soiled sort of charm about the man. His mop of rumpled graying hair managed somehow to signal fellowship as well as chicanery. It was a fellowship that made me nervous, for it was like being winked at by the Devil.

"The story," said Dr. Hugo, "begins some time ago. The deceased bridegroom and I interned together and shared an office when we started practice. It took me five years to shake loose of him. He was inclined to embrace his betters like a squid—with eight arms. A medical charlatan and a human cypher but with enough conceit to have served a dozen geniuses. Among his strongest convictions was the fancy that he was irresistible to women." Dr. Hugo looked tenderly at the murder headline. "A fancy," he added, "that has now been permanently canceled.

"You never met Felicia," he went on. I shook my head. "A woman of great animal charm," he said, "with a paranoid temper hidden in her childlike smile. As her recent activity testifies. I shall do everything I can, of course, to see that she is not punished for her misconduct."

"That's going to a bit difficult," I said, "judging from that story."

"Not at all," Dr. Hugo said. "I shall take the witness stand in her defense when the time comes. I doubt if any jury will convict her—any more than you will—after hearing me out."

An air of hidden, antic excitement came into his words as he continued.

"You see, I could have prevented Caleb's murder. A few words to Felicia before the mismated couple took off on their macabre honeymoon, and the pompous little man would still be alive. But Caleb outwitted me. He left a day earlier than he had announced. He didn't want me saying those few words to Felicia. Who knows, perhaps I was silent because I foresaw what might happen. Being very much in love with Felicia myself, it would have been quite a clever thing to let him go off and be murdered by her, now, wouldn't it? An interesting way of disposing of a rival, don't you think? With no legal responsibility attached and—" Dr. Hugo chuckled. "I'm afraid I'm boasting," he resumed. "I'll put it this way: I am certainly not displeased to lose Caleb as a friend or patient."

"I didn't know he was a patient of yours," I said. "What was his trouble?"

"There was nothing wrong with him at all," said Dr. Hugo. "Such deficiencies as Dr. Mudie possessed are not for the art of medicine. Not even I know of any cures for a blatant and slobbering ego. But I have a number of doctors of his sort who bring me fake neuroses for treatment. Their sole object is to pick my brain and misuse some of my wisdom on their own unfortunate patients.

301

"In Caleb's case, however, the brain-picking was mutual. I kept myself informed, while analyzing him, on the progress of his courtship of Felicia. Of course, he was eager enough to help me along there. The foolish fellow imagined that he had stolen Felicia from me and that the details he had to offer of their growing love were coals of fire. Like all stupid men he hated his betters even while robbing them. But let me assure you, he was committing no robbery. Felicia had been stolen from me a full year ago."

Dr. Hugo sighed and allowed me to observe a spasm of pain in his soiled and clever eyes.

"A man can lose a woman like Felicia again and again," said Dr. Hugo, "and still remain in love with her. She belongs to that rare type of female whose allure is not dependent on virtue, and whose charms, in fact, seem only refreshed by their misuse. They lie and cheat and vow eternal love all in one breath. And, somehow, remain as innocent as children playing games. Yes," Dr. Hugo sighed, "to know Felicia is to mistrust her, forgive her, and desire her forever.

"You may wonder," he continued, "how so unappetizing a fellow as Dr. Mudie ever made any headway with our exotic Felicia. The answer, I'm afraid, is that Felicia was the kind of Venus who could never scorn a worshipper with an incense pot. I say 'was' because I'm sure her present troubles have cured her of this failing."

Dr. Hugo drank, then studied the story of his rival's murder for a moment, his eyes turning mockingly to the dead man's photograph as he continued.

"Yes, to Felicia a man in love with her was like a new dress. She couldn't resist trying it on, however unbecoming it might be; trying it on, strutting a bit, and then discarding it. The poor child was too giddy with this game-playing to know that Caleb was a hair shirt rather than a new dress. I could have told her, but warning Felicia of danger was always a waste of time. She would much rather love what she shouldn't—which is, perhaps, the reason she once loved me.

"As for Caleb, from the moment he fell in love with her— I call it love because this is after office hours—his single, blinding purpose was to make her as miserable and unhappy as possible. He did this by dumping a psychotic jealousy on her which should have thoroughly revolted her. Of course, it

302

didn't. Women are usually fascinated by a jealous man. He inspires them with a sense of their powers which a civilized fellow like myself, seldom does. And he adds spice and danger to their deceptions.

"And also," Dr. Hugo smiled, "Caleb's grubby jealousies took Felicia's mind off her true troubles. These were considerable. She was still in love with the man who had stolen her from me. Desperately in love, as usually happens to women like Felicia when they find a man they can't have entirely. The drawback is usually a wife in the background."

Dr. Hugo paused and added in a quiet, dramatic voice: "You've heard of Hans Wienerz, of course?"

"No," I said.

Dr. Hugo frowned.

"Really?" he said. "Don't you read the papers?"

"Who is he?" I asked.

"Hans Wienerz, the concert violinist," he said. "He had his day in the press only recently."

"I don't go to violin concerts," I said. "I seldom read the papers when I'm writing. And Hans Wienerz is unknown to me."

"This is a little unexpected," Dr. Hugo smiled. "I shall have to introduce Hans to you—in full. He is an important part of my story—and another reason for doubting whether I'm its villain or its hero. Mr. Wienerz, who stole Felicia's love from me, was one of those storm-tossed husbands who are always married to the wrong woman. He was a thick-necked, glowering fellow with an empty skull who could play the violin superbly. A sort of Golem with electric fingers. He detested Madam Wienerz but nothing could induce him to leave her. He explained to Felicia that his wife had vowed to kill him if he ever abandoned her for another woman and, of course, this was all Felicia had to know to become a slave of love. Something she couldn't have—a wife in the background with a gun—a lovelorn oaf who couldn't dispel the situation in words—and a violin that sang to her out of Heaven. I couldn't very well compete with so wondrous a scenario, so I did the next best thing—retired gracefully and waited hopefully.

"You can see why I didn't mind Dr. Mudie's idiotic courtship." Dr. Hugo smiled. "It was, in fact, a sort of comic relief. For while she was vowing love eternal and fidelity ever-

303

lasting to Caleb's lunatic jealousies, I knew Felicia's heart was with her fiddler. She had given him up for the time because of his refusal to brave his wife's threat of gunplay and run away with her. But her eyes always filled with tears at his name and she sneaked off to his concerts and followed him in the streets like a creature in a trance."

Dr. Hugo paused and looked at me with a curious, unspoken insistence. He had a hypnotic trick of compelling the right questions in a listener and I heard myself saying, vaguely:

"I'm waiting for Dr. Mudie to discover that Felicia loved another."

"That he did," Dr. Hugo said.

"As part of your treatment of his neurosis, I imagine," I said.

"Oh, no, I didn't tell him." Dr. Hugo looked mockingly at me.

"Who did?" I asked.

"Madam Wienerz," he answered. "She was being treated by Dr. Mudie for severe headaches."

"Really," I said. "That's rather odd—finding Madam Wienerz a Mudie patient. As a writer I always frown on coincidence."

"It wasn't coincidence," Dr. Hugo said. "I sent Madam Wienerz to Caleb. Which is one of the things that worries me." His voice grew mocking again. "For you may decide that I was responsible for what happened. Knowing Madam Wienerz, through my own sorrows, and knowing Dr. Mudie, it might seem to you that I arranged and precipitated the Wienerz tragedy in order to rid myself of rival Hans."

"I see," I said. "Felicia no longer loves the fiddler."

"No, I don't think she does," Dr. Hugo said. "At least, I hope not. And if she does, I don't think it matters any more."

Dr. Hugo was enjoying some sort of joke, and he continued:

"Caleb hadn't any idea of Madam Wienerz's place in his life or of Felicia's place in Madam's. He knew only that she suffered from very bad headaches and that she believed they were caused by her worry over her husband. She suspected that he had resumed his attentions to the woman who had already once ruined their marriage.

"On her third visit Caleb discovered that his hysterical

patient carried a gun in her purse, and this seemed to excite him, for he told me about it. He seemed fascinated by a type of jealousy obviously superior to his own. Well," Dr. Hugo smiled, "a week later the fat was in the fire. Dr. Mudie, who was always more gossip than medico, asked Madam Wienerz if she knew the name of her rival. And Madam gave him quite an answer, as you may imagine. She said the Other Woman was a wanton dancing girl named Felicia Gauer.

"Caleb brought me the news the same evening. He fumed for an hour. I was a scoundrel; Felicia was a monster. How long had I known? He saw through my sending Madam Wienerz to him. He should have suspected any largesse from me—which was true. I would as soon have thought of sending a patient to a phrenologist as to Caleb Mudie.

"I listened, refused to answer questions, and let him shout himself hoarse. He left finally and I imagined I knew what was going to happen. Felicia, trapped by Caleb's windfall of information, would undoubtedly admit the truth—or part of it—and the ungainly romance between the two would be over. You may well imagine I had no objection to such a finale."

"I can't see how it could make much difference to you, one way or another," I said. "There would still be Mr. Wienerz—as a rival. In fact," I looked intently at Dr. Hugo's clever face, "I don't see the point or purpose of your sending Madam Wiernez to him. It isn't like you to go in for pointless malice." Dr. Hugo was silent. "Or were you more jealous of Dr. Mudie than you've let on?"

"I never had any interest in Mudie or jealousy of him," Dr. Hugo said. "He was a nuisance and a fool. It was Hans Wienerz who stood between me and my happiness."

"What happened—to Wienerz?" I asked slowly.

"Caleb laid a deep plot," said Dr. Hugo, "which he kept from me until it was over. Although you only have my word for that. If you are suspecting me as the villain of this story, it might well be that Caleb discussed his plot with me—even that I may have put the plot in his mind. He's no longer here to offer his version. You will therefore have to be content with mine.

"Caleb persuaded Madam Wienerz that he could prove that her jealousy was groundless, that he could convince her of that fact. He would call her husband to his office and question him, and Madam Wienerz could be hidden in a closet of his office, with the door ajar, and listen to her husband's answer.

"Three days later Caleb called on me late at night." Dr. Hugo smiled at my staring interest. "He had a newspaper in his hand—with a headline much like this one." Dr. Hugo tapped the newspaper in his lap. "It contained a story of the fatal shooting of Hans Wienerz by his demented wife, Stella Wienerz. The gunplay had taken place in the office of Dr. Caleb Mudie that afternoon."

"You weren't too surprised, I hope," I said.

"I am never surprised by anything," Dr. Hugo said. "I listened to our diabolic Caleb without batting an eye. He was very smug about his murder by proxy—and he recited his little plot in full.

"Hans Wienerz had come to his office and Caleb, acting as a scientist interested only in saving Madam Wienerz's sanity, had questioned him. Did he know that uncertainty was destroying his wife's health? There was only one cure for Madam's headaches—the truth. If he—Dr. Mudie—knew the truth he would know how to treat Madam—how to soothe her, what methods to pursue. And he promised the glowering and distracted Hans that the truth—whatever it was—would go no further than his office.

"Please," Dr. Hugo smiled at my staring, "it was Mudie who said these things, not I."

"He seems suddenly a very clever man," I said.

"Jealousy has that effect on people, sometimes," Dr. Hugo said. "It sharpens their wits."

"Wienerz told the truth?" I asked.

"Yes," Dr. Hugo said. "He said that Madam's suspicions were well founded—that, in fact, he was running off with Felicia as soon as her show closed—in two weeks.

"And at this point," Dr. Hugo sighed, "Madam Wienerz came out of the closet and fired five bullets into the body of her truth-telling husband. He died instantly. The widow was removed a few days later to an institution for the criminally insane."

"Dr. Mudie seems to have committed a perfect crime," I said, "with your slight aid."

"Yes, that was Caleb's attitude," said Dr. Hugo. "He was very amused at my dilemma. I could not inform against him.

306

Not because—as you suggest—I had helped him polish off his rival, Hans (I should say our rival, I suppose), by sending the homicidal wife to him for treatment. But for the much simpler reason that he had only to deny what I said—and I would be held up to scorn as a publicity-seeking psychiatrist who was trying to betray a patient, to boot."

"And you couldn't tell Felicia the truth, either," I said, "without losing her forever."

"It is pleasant to be understood." Dr. Hugo smiled. "You are quite right—Felicia believes me a very clever man. She would very likely fancy I had arranged the murder of her fiddler and in her first grief over his death develop a hatred against me from which she might never recover. I decided to wait until Felicia's tears subsided—and the story would be less a shock to her. At which time, of course, it might not be necessary to tell her anything. For winning Felicia back from Dr. Mudie presented no problem to me. Hans had been the problem. And Hans was gone."

Dr. Hugo sighed.

"I waited too long, however," he said. "For when Caleb visited me again two weeks later, he had married Felicia that morning. You must believe me when I tell you that I had not anticipated this move.

"The bridegroom was flushed and garrulous. He told me Felicia didn't know he had found out the truth about her and Hans. She had cried for a week after Hans's death and despite Caleb's public connection with the fiddler's name, she pretended she had never even heard it. She explained her grief by telling Caleb her brother had been killed in an accident.

"Felicia's duplicity didn't surprise me. Lies are the finery of the female mind. A woman dislikes being caught in the truth as much as she does being found without her make-up on, her hair uncombed, and her stockings down.

"But Caleb was a bit of a revelation. I hadn't expected so much cunning or so much hatred in him of Felicia. All his long-standing loathing of women was now concentrated on Felicia—and his plot to break her down and utterly destroy her personality."

Dr. Hugo smiled.

"I shall make all this very clear on the witness stand," he said. "I shall tell the jury how Dr. Mudie enjoyed the situation, how he gloated over Felicia's feeling of guilt for her lover's death."

He paused, then resumed wryly:

"I pointed out to Caleb that that was why she had married him—as a species of atonement. She wanted to punish herself for having destroyed Hans by loving him. And what greater punishment could a woman inflict on herself than becoming Mrs. Mudie?

"Caleb laughed at my indignation. He said he was going to see to it that Mrs. Mudie's atonement was a thorough one. He was going to tell her that he knew all about her lies and deceptions. He was going to make her confess her love for the dead Hans. And he was going to prove to her that it was her own lying soul that had killed him. In short, our Caleb was going to unmask Felicia and put an end to her dual nature. He was going to make her spit out the truth of her abominable betrayal of himself and of the dead man. He was going to make her atone for all her sins—by bringing them into the open. When he got through with her, said Caleb, there would be left a different Felicia—a made-over Felicia who would never again dare to lie or to fool a man.

"I asked him when he intended to start this campaign of torture and Caleb answered me smugly that he was going to continue as her honeymooning dupe on the boat. They were leaving the next day. And, said he, when they had reached their hotel and were all unpacked, in Miami, he would then start his inquisition."

Dr. Hugo tapped the headline from Miami and added:

"Caleb's reform movement backfired rather quickly. Of course, I could have prevented all that by talking to Felicia—as I told you. And I intended to—the next morning. Knowing Felicia as I do, I could have made a good guess as to how she would react under torture. Very much as she did. But they left that night. Caleb had fooled me about the time of the boat departure."

"That surprises me a little," I said. "Caleb fooling you. It would have been the first thing I'd have thought of—that he wasn't going to let you talk to Felicia."

Dr. Hugo looked at me blandly.

"Perhaps I was too distressed," he said.

"What advice do you want from me?" I asked.

"I wanted to ask if you thought my marrying Felicia before

308

her trial would lessen my effectiveness as her witness. But I've decided for myself while talking to you. It will be better if I wait."

Dr. Hugo poured drinks and sat, glass in hand, looking into the fireplace. His eyes were half-closed and he was waiting for a verdcit, from me. For he had obviously put himself on trial before me and confessed to having murdered two men, so deftly and so cunningly that no punishment could ever be meted out to him by the law.

But had he really done these murders, I wondered. It could be that he was merely boasting of how subtle and clever a man he was and laying claim to two perfect crimes as proof of his vast superiority to the human race and all its institutions. Such a boast would be in keeping with the Hugo character. But so would the boast of murder. Dr. Hugo would want someone to know how brilliant he had been in disposing of his two rivals. His ego would demand the applause of someone fully aware of his cunning. There have been criminals who actually confessed to real crimes for no other reason than that.

I was weighing the matter when the doorbell rang. A telegram was delivered.

Dr. Hugo opened it slowly, studied it, and then handed it to me.

I read:

"Darling. Thanks. I need you. Hurry. All my love. Felicia."

Dr. Hugo smiled at me.

"I knew that would be her answer," he said. "To know the souls of others is the great sport of living. Would you care to come to the station with me? I am all packed. You see, I already have a reservation on the midnight train to Miami."

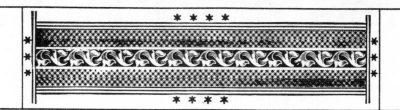

THE ARROW OF GOD

BY LESLIE CHARTERIS

Leslie Charteris was born Leslie Charles Bowyer Lin on May 12, 1907, in Singapore. In his one year at Cambridge University he read every book on crime he could find and in 1928 published the first Simon Templar novel, *Meet the Tiger*. He has been a policeman, prospected for gold, driven a bus, fished for pearls, tended bar, toured with a carnival, and played professional bridge in a London club. He is a good horseman, has a pilot's license, and has been a columnist for *Gourmet* and a Hollywood scriptwriter. But his most phenomenal success is Simon Templar, The Saint, whose stick-figure trademark is Charteris' own sketch.

ONE OF SIMON TEMPLAR's stock criticisms of the classic type of detective story is that the victim of the murder, the reluctant spark-plug of all the entertaining mystery and strife, is usually a mere nonentity who wanders vaguely through the first few pages with the sole purpose of becoming a convenient body in the library by the end of Chapter One. But whatever his own feelings and problems may have been, the personality which has to provide so many people with adequate motives for desiring him to drop dead, is largely a matter of hearsay, retrospectively brought out in the conventional process of drawing attention to one suspect after another.

"You could almost," Simon has said, "call him a *corpus derelicti*. . . . Actually, the physical murder should only be the mid-point of the story: the things that led up to it are at least as interesting as the mechanical solution of who done it. . . . Personally, I've killed very few people that I didn't know plenty about first."

Coming from a man who is generally regarded as almost a detective-story character himself, this comment is at least worth recording for reference; but it certainly did not apply to the shuffling off of Mr. Floyd Vosper, which caused a brief commotion on the island of New Providence in the early spring of that year.

Why Simon Templar should have been in Nassau (which, for the benefit of the untraveled, is the City of New Providence which is an island in the Bahamas) at the time is one of those questions which always arise in stories about him, and which can only be answered by repeating that he liked to travel and was just as likely to show up there as in Nova Zembla or Namaqualand. As for why he should have been invited to the house of Mrs. Herbert H. Wexall, that is another irrelevancy which is hardly covered by the fact that he could just as well have shown up at the house of Joe Wallenski (of the arsonist Wallenskis) or the White House—he had friends in many places, legitimate and otherwise. But Mrs. Wexall had some international renown as a lion hunter, even if her stalking had been confined to the variety which roars loudest in plush drawing rooms; and it was not to be expected that the advent of such a creature as Simon Templar would have escaped the attention of her salon safari.

Thus one noontime Simon found himself strolling up the driveway into what little was left of the life of Floyd Vosper. Naturally he did not know this at the time; nor did he know Floyd Vosper, except by name. In this he was no different from at least fifty million other people in that hemisphere; for Floyd Vosper was not only one of the most widely syndicated pundits of the day, but his books (*Feet of Clay; As I Saw Them;* and *The Twenty Worst Men in the World*) had all been the selections of one book club or another and still sold by the million in reprints. For Mr. Vosper specialized in the ever-popular sport of shattering reputations. In his journalistic years he had met, and apparently had unique opportunities to study, practically every great name in the national and international scene, and could unerringly remember everything in their biographies that they would prefer forgotten, and could impale and epitomize all their weaknesses with devastatingly pinpoint precision, leaving them naked and squirming on the operating table of his vocabulary. But what this merciless professional iconoclast was like as a person, Simon had never heard or bothered much to wonder about.

So the first impression that Vosper made on him was a voice, a still unidentified voice, a dry and deliberate and peculiarly needling voice, which came from behind a bank of riotous hibiscus and oleander.

"My dear Janet," it said, "you must not let your innocent admiration for Reggie's bulging biceps color your estimate of his perspicacity in world affairs. The title of All-American, I hate to disillusion you, has no reference to statesmanship."

There was a rather strained laugh that must have come from Reggie, and a girl's clear young voice said: "That isn't fair, Mr. Vosper. Reggie doesn't pretend to be a genius, but he's bright enough to have a wonderful job waiting for him on Wall Street."

"I don't doubt that he will make an excellent contact man for the more stupid clients," conceded the voice with the measured nasal gripe. "And I'm sure that his education can cope with the simple arithmetic of the Stock Exchange, just

312

as I'm sure it can grasp the basic figures of your father's Dun and Bradstreet. This should not dazzle you with his brilliance, any more than it should make you believe that you have some spiritual fascination that lured him to your feet."

At this point Simon rounded a curve in the driveway and caught his first sight of the speakers, all of whom looked up at him with reserved curiosity and two-thirds of them with a certain hint of relief.

There was no difficulty in assigning them to their lines—the young redheaded giant with the pleasantly rugged face and the slim pretty blonde girl, who sat at a wrought-iron table on the terrace in front of the house with a broken deck of cards in front of them which established an interrupted game of gin rummy, and the thin stringy man reclining in a long cane chair with a cigarette holder in one hand and a highball in the other.

Simon smiled and said: "Hullo. This is Mrs. Wexall's house, is it?"

The girl said, "Yes," and he said: "My name's Templar, and I was invited here."

The girl jumped up and said: "Oh, yes. Lucy told me. I'm her sister, Janet Blaise. This is my fiancé, Reg Herrick. And Mr. Vosper."

Simon shook hands with the two men, and Janet said: "I think Lucy's on the beach. I'll take you around."

Vosper unwound his bony length from the long chair, looking like a slightly dissolute and acidulated mahatma in his white shorts and burnt chocolate tan.

"Let me do it," he said. "I'm sure you two ingénues would rather be alone together. And I need another drink."

He led the way, not into the house but around it, by a flagged path which struck off to the side and meandered through a bower of scarlet poinciana. A breeze rustled in the leaves and mixed flower scents with the sweetness of the sea. Vosper smoothed down his sparse gray hair; and Simon was aware that the man's beady eyes and sharp thin nose were cocked towards him with brash speculation, as if he were already measuring another target for his tongue.

"Templar," he said. "Of course, you must be the Saint—the fellow they call the Robin Hood of modern crime." ....

"I see you read the right papers," said the Saint pleasantly.

"I read all the papers," Vosper said, "in order to keep in

313

touch with the vagaries of vulgar taste. I've often wondered why the Robin Hood legend should have so much romantic appeal. Robin Hood, as I understand it, was a bandit who indulged in some well-publicized charity—but not, as I recall, at the expense of his own stomach. A good many unscrupulous promoters have also become generous—and with as much shrewd publicity—when their ill-gotten gains exceeded their personal spending capacity, but I don't remember that they succeeded in being glamorized for it."

"There may be some difference," Simon suggested, "in who was robbed to provide the surplus spoils."

"Then," Vosper said challengingly, "you consider yourself an infallible judge of who should be penalized and who should be rewarded."

"Oh, no," said the Saint modestly. "Not at all. No more, I'm sure, than you would call yourself the infallible judge of all the people whom you dissect so definitively in your books and columns."

He felt the other's probing glance stab at him suspiciously and almost with puzzled incredulity, as if Vosper couldn't quite accept the idea that anyone had actually dared to cross swords with him, and moreover might have scored on the riposte—or if it had happened at all, that it had been anything but a semantic accident. But the Saint's easy inscrutable poise gave no clue to the answer at all; and before anything further could develop there was a paragraphic distraction.

This took the form of a man seated on top of a truncated column which for reasons best known to the architect had been incorporated into the design of a wall which curved out from the house to encircle a portion of the shore like a possessive arm. The man had long curly hair that fell to his shoulders, which with his delicate ascetic features would have made him look more like a woman if it had not been complemented with an equally curly and silken beard. He sat cross-legged and upright, his hands folded symmetrically in his lap, staring straight out into the blue sky a little above the horizon, so motionless and almost rigid that he might easily have been taken for a tinted statue except for the fluttering of the long flowing white robe he wore.

After rolling with the first reasonable shock of the apparition, Simon would have passed on politely without comment, but the opportunity was irresistible for Vosper to display his virtuosity again, and perhaps also to recover from his momentary confusion.

"That fugitive from a Turkish bath," Vosper said, in the manner of a tired guide to a geek show, "calls himself Astron. He's a nature boy from the Dardanelles who just concluded a very successful season in Hollywood. He wears a beard to cover a receding chin, and long hair to cover a hole in the head. He purifies his soul with a diet of boiled grass and prune juice. Whenever this diet permits him, he meditates. After he was brought to the attention of the Western world by some engineers of the Anglo-Mongolian Oil Company, whom he cured of stomach ulcers by persuading them not to spike their ration of sacramental wine with rubbing alcohol, he began to meditate about the evils of earthly riches."

"Another member of our club?" Simon prompted innocuously.

"Astron maintains," Vosper said, leaning against the pillar and giving out as oracularly as if the object of his dissertation were not sitting on it at all, "that the only way for the holders of worldly wealth to purify themselves is to get rid of as much of it as they can spare. Being himself so pure that it hurts, he is unselfishly ready to become the custodian of as much corrupting cabbage as they would like to get rid of. Of course, he would have no part of it himself, but he will take the responsiblity of parking it in a shrine in the Sea of Marmora which he plans to build as soon as there is enough kraut in the kitty."

The figure on the column finally moved. Without any waste motion it simply expanded its crossed legs like a lazy tongs until it towered at its full height over them.

"You have heard the blasphemer," it said. "But I say to you that his words are dust in the wind, as he himself is dust among the stars that I see."

"I'm a blasphemer," Vosper repeated to the Saint, with a sort of derisive pride combined with the ponderous bonhomie of a vaudeville oldtimer in a routine with a talking dog. He looked back up at the figure of the white-robed mystic towering above him, and said: "So if you have this direct pipeline to the Almighty, why don't you strike me dead?"

"Life and death are not in my hands," Astron said, in a calm and confident voice. "Death can only come from the hands of the Giver of all Life. In His own good time He will strike you down, and the arrow of God will silence your mockeries. This I have seen in the stars."

"Quaint, isn't he?" Vosper said, and opened the gate between the wall and the beach.

Beyond the wall a few steps led down to a kind of Grecian courtyard open on the seaward side, where the paving merged directly into the white sand of the beach. The courtyard was furnished with gaily colored lounging chairs and a well-stocked pushcart bar, for which Vosper immediately headed.

"You have visitors, Lucy," he said, without letting it interfere with the important work of reviving his highball.

Out on the sand, on a towel spread under an enormous beach umbrella, Mrs. Herbert Wexall rolled over and said: "Oh, Mr. Templar."

Simon went over and shook hands with her as she stood up. It was hard to think of her as Janet Blaise's sister, for there were at least twenty years between them and hardly any physical resemblances. She was a big woman with an open moley face and patchily sunbleached hair and a sloppy figure, but she made a virtue of those disadvantages by the cheerfulness with which she ignored them. She was what is rather inadequately known as "a person," which means that she had the personality to dispense with appearances and the money to back it up.

"Good to see you," she said, and turned to the man who had been sitting beside her, as he struggled to his feet. "Do you know Arthur Gresson?"

Mr. Gresson was a full head shorter than the Saint's six foot two, but he weighed a good deal more. Unlike anyone else that Simon had encountered on the premises so far, his skin looked as if it was unaccustomed to exposure. His round body and his round balding brow, under a liberal sheen of oil, had the hot rosy blush which the kiss of the sun evokes in virgin epidermis.

"Glad to meet you, Mr. Templar." His hand was soft and earnestly adhesive.

"I expect you'd like a drink," Lucy Wexall said. "Let's keep Floyd working."

They joined Vosper at the bar wagon, and after he had started to work on the orders she turned back to the Saint and said: "After this formal service, just make yourself at home. I'm so glad you could come."

"I'm sure Mr. Templar will be happy," Vosper said. "He's a man of the world like me. We enjoy Lucy's food and liquor, and in return we give her the pleasure of hitting the society columns with our names. A perfectly businesslike exchange."

"That's progress for you," Lucy Wexall said breezily. "In the old days I'd have had a court jester. Now all I get is a professional stinker."

"That's no way to refer to Arthur," Vosper said, handing Simon a long cold glass. "For your information, Templar, Mr. Gresson—Mr. Arthur *Granville* Gresson—is a promoter. He has a long history of selling phony oil stock behind him. He is just about to take Herb Wexall for another sucker; but since Herb married Lucy he can afford it. Unless you're sure you can take Janet away from Reggie, I advise you not to listen to him."

Arthur Gresson's elbow nudged Simon's ribs.

"What a character!" he said, almost proudly.

"I only give out with facts," Vosper said. "My advice to you, Templar, is, never be an elephant. Resist all inducements. Because when you reach back into that memory, you will only be laughed at, and the people who should thank you will call you a stinker."

Gresson giggled, deep from his round pink stomach.

"Would you like to get in a swim before lunch?" Lucy Wexall said. "Floyd show him where he can change."

"A pleasure," Vosper said. "And probably a legitimate part of the bargain."

He thoughtfully refilled his glass before he steered Simon by way of the veranda into the beachward side of the house, and into a bedroom. He sat on the bed and watched unblinkingly while Simon stripped down and pulled on the trunks he had brought with him.

"It must be nice to have the Body Beautiful," he observed. "Of course, in your business it almost ranks with plant and machinery, doesn't it?"

The Saint's blue eyes twinkled.

"The main difference," he agreed good-humoredly, "is that if I get a screw loose it may not be so noticeable."

As they were starting back through the living room, a small birdlike man in a dark and (for the setting outside the broad picture window) incongruous business suit bustled in by another door. He had the bright baggy eyes behind rimless

317

glasses, the slack but fleshless jowls, and the wide tight mouth which may not be common to all lawyers, bankers, and business executives, but which is certainly found in very few other vocations; and he was followed by a statuesque brunette whose severe tailoring failed to disguise an outstanding combination of curves, who carried a notebook and a sheaf of papers.

"Herb!" Vosper said. "I want you to meet Lucy's latest addition to the menagerie which already contains Astron and me—Mr. Simon Templar, known as the Saint. Templar—your host, Mr. Wexall."

"Pleased to meet you," said Herbert Wexall, shaking hands briskly.

"And this is Pauline Stone," Vosper went on, indicating the nubile brunette. "The tired businessman's consolation. Whatever Lucy can't supply, she can."

"How do you do," said the girl stoically.

Her dark eyes lingered momentarily on the Saint's torso, and he noticed that her mouth was very full and soft.

"Going for a swim?" Wexall said, as if he had heard nothing. "Good. Then I'll see you at lunch shortly."

He trotted busily on his way, and Vosper ushered the Saint to the beach by another flight of steps that led directly down from the veranda. The house commanded a small half-moon bay, and both ends of the crescent of sand were guarded naturally by abrupt rises of jagged coral rock.

"Herbert is the living example of how really stupid a successful businessman can be," Vosper said tirelessly. "He was just an office boy of some kind in the Blaise outfit when he got smart enough to woo and win the boss's daughter. And from that flying start he was clever enough to really pay his way by making Blaise Industries twice as big as even the old man himself had been able to do. And yet he's dumb enough to think that Lucy won't catch on to the extracurricular functions of that busty secretary sooner or later—or that when she does he won't be out on a cold doorstep in the rain. . . . No, I'm not going in. I'll hold your drink for you."

Simon ran down into the surf and churned seawards for a couple of hundred yards, then turned over and paddled lazily back, coordinating his impressions with idle amusement. The balmy water was still refreshing after the heat of the morning, and when he came out the breeze had become brisk enough to give him the luxury of a fleeting shiver as the wetness started to evaporate from his tanned skin.

He crossed the sand to the Greek patio, where Floyd Vosper was on duty again at the bar in a strategic position to keep his own needs supplied with a minimum of effort. Discreet servants were setting up a buffet table. Janet Blaise and Reg Herrick had transferred their gin rummy game and were playing at a table right under the column where Astron had resumed his seat and his cataleptic meditations—a weird juxtaposition of which the three members all seemed equally unconscious.

Simon took Lucy Wexall a martini and said with another glance at the tableau: "Where did you find him?"

"The people who brought him to California sent him to me when they had to leave the States. They gave me such a good time when I was out there, I couldn't refuse to do something for them. He's writing a book, you know, and of course he can't go back to that dreadful place he came from, wherever it is, before he has a chance to finish it in reasonable comfort."

Simon avoided discussing this assumption, but he said: "What's it like, having a resident prophet in the house?"

"He's very interesting. And quite as drastic as Floyd, in his own way, in summing up people. You ought to talk to him."

Arthur Gresson came over with an hors d'oeuvre plate of smoked salmon and stuffed eggs from the buffet. He said: "Anyone you meet at Lucy's is interesting, Mr. Templar. But if you don't mind my saying so, you have it all over the rest of 'em. Who'd ever think we'd find the Saint looking for crime in the Bahamas?"

"I hope no one will think I'm looking for crime," Simon said deprecatingly, "any more than I take it for granted that you're looking for oil."

"That's where you'd be wrong," Gresson said. "As a matter of fact, I am."

The Saint raised an eyebrow.

"Well, I can always learn something. I'd never heard of oil in the Bahamas."

"I'm not a bit surprised. But you will, Mr. Templar, you will." Gresson sat down, pillowing his round stomach on his thighs. "Just think for a moment about some of the places you have heard of, where there is certainly oil. Let me mention them in a certain order: Mexico, Texas, Louisiana, and the recent strike in the Florida Everglades. We might even include Venezuela in the south. Does that suggest anything to you?"

"Hm-mm," said the Saint thoughtfully.

"A pattern," Gresson said. "A vast central pool of oil somewhere under the Gulf of Mexico, with oil wells dipping into it from the edges of the bowl, where the geological strata have also been forced up. Now think of the islands of the Caribbean as the eastern edge of the same bowl. Why not?"

"It's an interesting theory," said the Saint.

"Mr. Wexall thinks so too, and I hope he's going into partnership with me."

"Herbert can afford it," intruded the metallic sneering voice of Floyd Vosper. "But before you decide to buy in, Templar, you'd better check with New York about the time when Mr. Gresson thought he could dig gold in the Catskills."

"Shut up, Floyd," said Mrs. Wexall, "and get me another martini."

Arthur Gresson chuckled in his paunch like a happy Buddha.

"What a guy!" he said. "What a ribber. And he gets everyone mad. He kills me!"

Herbert Wexall came down from the veranda and beamed around. As a sort of tacit announcement that he had put aside his work for the day, he had changed into a sport shirt on which various exotic fish were depicted wandering through vines of seaweed, but he retained his business trousers and business shoes and business face.

"Well," he said, inspecting the buffet and addressing the world at large. "Let's come and get it whenever we're hungry."

As if a spell had been snapped, Astron removed himself from the contemplation of the infinite, descended from his pillar, and began to help himself to cottage cheese and caviar on a foundation of lettuce leaves.

Simon drifted in the same direction, and found Pauline Stone beside him, saying: "What do you feel like, Mr. Templar?"

Her indication of having come off duty was a good deal more radical than her employer's. In fact, the bathing suit which she had changed into seemed to be based more on the

French minimums of the period than on any British tradition. There was no doubt that she filled it opulently; and her question amplified its suggestiveness with undertones which the Saint felt it wiser not to challenge at that moment.

"There's so much to drool over," he said, referring studiously to the buffet table. "But that green turtle aspic looks pretty good to me."

She stayed with him when he carried his plate to a table as thoughtfully diametric as possible from the berth chosen by Floyd Vosper, even though Astron had already settled there in temporary solitude. They were promptly joined by Reg Herrick and Janet Blaise, and slipped at once into an easy exchange of banalities.

But even then it was impossible to escape Vosper's tongue. It was not many minutes before his saw-edged voice whined across the patio above the general level of harmless chatter:

"When are you going to tell the Saint's fortune, Astron? That ought to be worth hearing."

There was a slightly embarrassed lull, and then everyone went on talking again; but Astron looked at the Saint with a gentle smile and said quietly: "You are a seeker after truth, Mr. Templar, as I am. But when instead of truth you find falsehood, you will destroy it with a sword. I only say, 'This is falsehood, and God will destroy it. Do not come too close, lest you be destroyed with it.' "

"Okay," Herrick growled, just as quietly. "But if you're talking about Vosper, it's about time someone destroyed it."

"Sometimes," Astron said, "God places his arrow in the hand of a man."

For a few moments that seemed unconscionably long nobody said anything; and then before the silence spread beyond their small group the Saint said casually: "Talking of arrows —I hear that the sport this season is to go hunting sharks with a bow and arrow."

Herrick nodded with a healthy grin.

"It's a lot of fun. Would you like to try it?"

"Reggie's terrific," Janet Blaise said. "He shoots like a regular Howard Hill, but of course he uses a bow that nobody else can pull."

"I'd like to try," said the Saint, and the conversation slid harmlessly along the tangent he had provided.

After lunch everyone went back to the beach, with the

321

exception of Astron, who retired to put his morning's meditations on paper. Chatter surrendered to an afternoon torpor which even subdued Vosper.

An indefinite while later, Herrick aroused with a yell and plunged roaring into the sea, followed by Janet Blaise. They were followed by others, including the Saint. An interlude of aquatic brawling developed somehow into a pick-up game of touch football on the beach, which was delightfully confused by recurrent arguments about who was supposed to be on which of the unequal sides. This boisterous nonsense churned up enough sand for the still freshening breeze to spray over Floyd Vosper, who by that time had drunk enough to be trying to sleep under the big beach umbrella, to finally get the misanthropic oracle back on his feet.

"Perhaps," he said witheringly, "I had better get out of the way of you perennial juveniles before you convert me into a dune."

He stalked off along the beach and lay down about a hundred yards away. Simon noticed him still there, flat on his face and presumably unconscious, when the game eventually broke up through a confused water-polo phase to leave everyone gasping and laughing and dripping on the patio with no immediate resurge of inspiration. It was the last time he saw the unpopular Mr. Vosper alive.

"Well," Arthur Gresson observed, mopping his short round body with a towel, "at least one of us seems to have enough sense to know when to lie down."

"And to choose the only partner who'd do it with him," Pauline added vaguely.

Herbert Wexall glanced along the beach in the direction that they both referred to, then glanced for further inspiration at the waterproof watch he was still wearing.

"It's almost cocktail time," he said. "How about it, anyone?"

His wife shivered, and said: "It's going to blow like a son-of-a-gun any minute. Let's all go in and get some clothes on first—then we'll be set for the evening. You'll stay for supper of course, Mr. Templar?"

"I hadn't planned to make a day of it," Simon protested diffidently, and was promptly overwhelmed from all quarters.

He found his way back to the room where he had left his clothes without the benefit of Floyd Vosper's chatty courier

service, and made leisured and satisfactory use of the fresh-
water shower and monogramed towels. Even so, when he
sauntered back into the living room, he almost had the feeling
of being lost in a strange and empty house, for all the varied
individuals who had peopled the stage so vividly and vigor-
ously a short time before had vanished into other and unknown seclusions and had not yet returned.

He lighted a cigarette and strolled idly towards the picture
window that overlooked the veranda and the sea. Everything
around his solitude was so still, excepting the subsonic suggestion of distant movements within the house, that he was
tempted to walk on tiptoe; and yet outside the broad pane of
plate glass the fronds of coconut palms were fluttering in a
thin febrile frenzy, and there were lacings of white cream on
the incredible jade of the short waves simmering on the
beach.

He noticed, first, in what should have been a lazily sensual
survey of the panorama, that the big beach umbrella was no
longer where he had first seen it, down to his right outside the
pseudo-Grecian patio. He saw, as his eye wandered on, that it
had been moved a hundred yards or so to his left—in fact, to
the very place where Floyd Vosper was still lying. It occurred
to him first that Vosper must have moved it himself, except
that no shade was needed in the brief and darkening twilight.
After that he noticed that Vosper seemed to have turned over
on his back; and then at last as the Saint focused his eyes he
saw with a weird thrill that the shaft of the umbrella stood
straight up out of the left side of Vosper's scrawny brown
chest, not in the sand beside him at all, but like a gigantic pin
that had impaled a strange and inelegant insect—or, in a
fantastic phrase that was not Simon's at all, like the arrow of
God.

Major Rupert Fanshire, the senior Superintendent of
Police, which made him third in the local hierarchy after the
Commissioner and Deputy Comissioner, paid tribute to the
importance of the case by taking personal charge of it. He was
a slight pinkish blond man with rather large and very bright
blue eyes and such a discreetly modulated voice that it commanded rapt attention through the basic effort of trying to
hear what it was saying. He sat at an ordinary writing desk in
the living room, with a Bahamian sergeant standing stiffly be-

side him, and contrived to turn the whole room into an office in which seven previously happy-go-lucky adults wriggled like guilty schoolchildren whose teacher has been found libelously caricatured on their blackboard.

He said, with wholly impersonal conciseness: "Of course, you all know by now that Mr. Vosper was found on the beach with the steel spike of an umbrella through his chest. My job is to find out how it happened. To start with, the topography suggests that the person responsible came from, or through, this house. I've heard all your statements, and all they seem to amount to is that each of you was going about his own business at the time when this might have happened."

"All I know," Herbert Wexall said, "is that I was in my study, reading and signing the letters that I dictated this morning."

"And I was getting dressed," said his wife.

"So was I," said Janet Blaise.

"I guess I was in the shower," said Pauline Stone.

"I was still working," said Astron. "This morning I started a new chapter of my book—in my mind, you understand. I do not write by putting everything on paper. For me it is necessary to meditate, to feel, to open flood-gates in my mind, so that I can receive the wisdom that comes from beyond the—"

"Quite," Major Fanshire assented politely. "The point is that none of you have alibis, if you need them. You were all going about your own business, in your own rooms. Mr. Templar was changing in the late Mr. Vosper's room—"

"I wasn't here," Arthur Gresson said recklessly. "I drove back to my own place—I'm staying at the Fort Montagu Beach Hotel. I wanted a clean shirt. I drove back there, and when I came back here all this had happened."

"There's not much difference," Major Fanshire said. "Dr. Rassin tells me we couldn't establish the time of death within an hour or two, anyway. . . . So the next thing we come to is the question of motive. Did anyone here," Fanshire said almost innocently, "have any really serious trouble with Mr. Vosper?"

There was an uncomfortable silence, which the Saint finally broke by saying: "I'm an outsider, so I'll take the rap. I'll answer for everyone."

The Superintendent cocked his bright eyes.

"Very well, sir. What would you say?"

"My answer," said the Saint, "is—everybody."

There was another silence, but a very different one, in which it seemed, surprisingly, as if all of them relaxed as unanimously as they had stiffened before. And yet, in its own way, this relaxation was as self-conscious and uncomfortable as the preceding tension had been. Only the Saint, who had every attitude of the completely careless onlooker, and Major Fanshire, whose deferential patience was impregnably correct, seemed immune to the interplay of hidden strains.

"Would you care to go any further?" Fanshire asked.

"Certainly," said the Saint. "I'll go anywhere. I can say what I like, and I don't have to care whether anyone is on speaking terms with me tomorrow. I'll go on record with my opinion that the late Mr. Vosper was one of the most unpleasant characters I've ever met. I'll make the statement, if it isn't already general knowledge, that he made a specialty of needling everyone he spoke to or about. He goaded everyone with nasty little things that he knew, or thought he knew, about them. I wouldn't blame anyone here for wanting, at least theoretically, to kill him."

"I'm not exactly concerned with your interpretation of blame," Fanshire said detachedly. "But if you have any facts, I'd like to hear them."

"I have no facts," said the Saint coolly. "I only know that in the few hours I've been here, Vosper made statements to me, a stranger, about everyone here, any one of which could be called fighting words."

"You will have to be more specific," Fanshire said.

"Okay," said the Saint. "I apologize in advance to anyone it hurts. Remember, I'm only repeating the kind of thing that made Vosper a good murder candidate. . . . I am now specific. In my hearing he called Reg Herrick a dumb athlete who was trying to marry Janet Blaise for her money. He suggested that Janet was a stupid juvenile for taking him seriously. He called Astron a commercial charlatan. He implied that Lucy Wexall was a dope and a snob. He suggested that Herb Wexall had more use for his secretary's sex than for her stenography, and he thought out loud that Pauline was amenable. He called Mr. Gresson a crook to his face."

"And during all this," Fanshire said, with an inoffensiveness that had to be heard to be believed, "he said nothing about you?"

"He did indeed," said the Saint. "He analyzed me, more or less, as a flamboyant phony."

"And you didn't object to that?"

"I hardly could," Simon replied blandly, "after I'd hinted to him that I thought he was even phonier."

It was a line on which a stage audience would have tittered, but the tensions of the moment let it sink with a slow thud.

Fanshire drew down his upper lip with one forefinger and nibbled it inscrutably.

"I expect this bores you as much as it does me, but this is the job I'm paid for. I've got to say that all of you had the opportunity, and from what Mr. Templar says you could all have had some sort of motive. Well, now I've got to look into what you might call the problem of physical possibility."

Simon Templar lighted a cigarette. It was the only movement that anyone made, and after that he was the most intent listener of them all as Fanshire went on: "Dr. Rassin says, and I must say I agree with him, that to drive that umbrella shaft clean through a man's chest must have taken quite exceptional strength. It seems to be something that no woman, and probably no ordinary man, could have done."

His pale bright eyes came to rest on Herrick as he finished speaking, and the Saint found his own eyes following others in the same direction.

The picture formed in his mind: the young giant towering over a prostrate Vosper, the umbrella raised in his mighty arms like a fantastic spear and the setting sun flaming on his red head, like an avenging angel, as he thrust downwards with all the power of those herculean shoulders . . . and then, as Herrick's face began to flush under the awareness of so many stares, Janet Blaise suddenly cried out: "No! No—it couldn't have been Reggie!"

Fanshire's gaze transferred itself to her curiously, and she said in a stammering rush.: "You see, it's silly, but we didn't quite tell the truth, I mean about being in our own rooms. As a matter of fact, Reggie was in my room most of the time. We were—talking."

The Superintendent cleared his throat and continued to gaze at her stolidly for a while. He didn't make any comment. But presently he looked at the Saint in the same dispassionately thoughtful way that he had first looked at Herrick.

Simon said calmly: "Yes, I was just wondering myself

326

whether I could have done it. And I had a rather interesting thought."

"Yes, Mr. Templar?"

"Certainly it must take quite a lot of strength to drive a spike through a man's chest with one blow. But now remember that this wasn't just a spike, or a spear. It had an enormous great umbrella on top of it. Now think what would happen if you were stabbing down with a thing like that?"

"Well, what would happen?"

"The umbrella would be like a parachute. It would be like a sort of sky anchor holding the shaft back. The air resistance would be so great that I'm wondering how anyone, even a very strong man, could get much momentum into the thrust. And the more force he put into it, the more likely he'd be to lift himself off the ground, rather than drive the spike down."

Fanshire digested this, blinking, and took his full time to do it.

"That certainly is a thought," he admitted. "But damn it," he exploded, "we know it was done. So it must have been possible."

"There's something entirely backwards about that logic," said the Saint. "Suppose we say, if it was impossible, maybe it wasn't done."

"Now you're being a little ridiculous," Fanshire snapped. "We saw—"

"We saw a man with the sharp iron-tipped shaft of a beach umbrella through his chest. We jumped to the natural conclusion that somebody stuck it into him like a sword. And that may be just what a clever murderer meant us to think."

Then it was Arthur Gresson who shattered the fragile silence by leaping out of his chair like a bouncing ball.

"I've got it!" he yelped. "Believe me, everybody, I've got it! This'll kill you!"

"I hope not," Major Fanshire said drily. "But what is it?"

"Listen," Gresson said. "I knew something rang a bell somewhere, but I couldn't place it. Now it all comes back to me. This is something I only heard at the hotel the other day, but some of you must have heard it before. It happened about a year ago, when Gregory Peck was visiting here. He stayed at the same hotel where I am, and one afternoon he was on the beach, and the wind came up, just like it did today, and it picked up one of those beach umbrellas and carried it right

327

to where he was lying, and the point just grazed his ribs and gave him a nasty gash, but what the people who saw it happen were saying was that if it'd been just a few inches the other way, it could have gone smack into his heart, and you'd've had a film star killed in the most sensational way that ever was. Didn't you ever hear about that, Major?"

"Now that you mention it," Fanshire said slowly, "I think I did hear something about it."

"Well." Gresson said, *"what if it happened again this afternoon, to someone who wasn't as lucky as Peck?"*

There was another of those electric silences of assimilation, out of which Lucy Wexall said: "Yes, I heard about that." And Janet said: "Remember, I told you about it! I was visiting some friends at the hotel that day, and I didn't see it happen, but I was there for the commotion."

Gresson spread out his arms, his round face gleaming with excitement and perspiration.

"That's got to be it!" he said. "You remember how Vosper was lying under the umbrella outside the patio when we started playing touch fotball, and he got sore because we were kicking sand over him, and he went off to the other end of the beach? But he didn't take the umbrella with him. The wind did that, after we all went off to change. And this time it didn't miss!"

Suddenly Astron stood up beside him; but where Gresson had risen like a jumping bean, this was like the growth and unfolding of a tree.

"I have heard many words," Astron said, in his firm gentle voice, "but now at last I think I am hearing truth. No man struck the blasphemer down. The arrow of God smote him, in his wickedness and his pride, as it was written long ago in the stars."

"You can say that again," Gresson proclaimed triumphantly. "He sure had it coming."

Again the Saint drew at his cigarette and created his own vision behind half-closed eyes. He saw the huge umbrella plucked from the sand by the invisible fingers of the wind, picked up and hurled spinning along the deserted twilight beach, its great mushroom spread of gaudy canvas no longer a drag now but a sail for the wind to get behind, the whole thing transformed into a huge unearthly dart flung with literally superhuman power—the arrow of God indeed. A fantastic, an almost unimaginable solution; and yet it did not have to be imagined because there were witnesses that it had almost happened once before. . . .

Fanshire was saying: "By Jove, that's the best suggestion I've heard yet—without any religious implication, of course. It sounds as if it could be the right answer!"

Simon's eyes opened on him fully for an instant, almost pityingly, and then closed completely as the true and right and complete answer rolled through the Saint's mind like a long peaceful wave.

"I have one question to ask," said the Saint.

"What's that?" Fanshire said, too polite to be irritable, yet with a trace of impatience, as if he hated the inconvenience of even defending such a divinely tailored theory.

"Does anyone here have a gun?" asked the Saint.

There was an almost audible creaking of knitted brows, and Fanshire said: "Really, Mr. Templar, I don't quite follow you."

"I only asked," said the Saint imperturbably, "if anyone here had a gun. I'd sort of like to know the answer before I explain why."

"I have a revolver," Wexall said with some perplexity. "What about it?"

"Could we see it, please?" said the Saint.

"I'll get it," said Pauline Stone.

She got up and left the room.

"You know I have a gun, Fanshire," Wexall said. "You gave me my permit. But I don't see—"

"Neither do I," Fanshire said.

The Saint said nothing. He devoted himself to his cigarette, with impregnable detachment, until the voluptuous secretary came back. Then he put it out and extended his hand.

Pauline looked at Wexall, hesitantly, and at Fanshire. The Superintendent nodded a sort of grudging acquiescence. Simon took the gun and broke it expertly.

"A Colt thirty-eight Detective Special," he said. "Unloaded." He sniffed the barrel. "But fired quite recently," he said, and handed the gun to Fanshire.

"I used it myself this morning," Lucy Wexall said cheerfully. "Janet and Reg and I were shooting at the Portuguese men-of-war. There were quite a lot of them around before the breeze came up."

"I wondered what the noise was," Wexall said vaguely.

"I was coming up the drive when I heard it first," Gresson said, "and I thought the next war had started."

"This is all very int'resting," Fanshire said, removing the revolver barrel from the proximity of his nostrils with a trace of exasperation, "But I don't see what it has to do with the case. Nobody has been shot—"

"Major Fanshire," said the Saint quietly, "may I have a word with you, outside? And will you keep that gun in your pocket so that at least we can hope there will be no more shooting?"

The Superintendent stared at him for several seconds, and at last unwillingly got up.

"Very well, Mr. Templar." He stuffed the revolver into the side pocket of his rumpled white jacket, and glanced back at his impassive Bahamian sentinel. "Sergeant, see that nobody leaves here, will you?"

He followed Simon out on to the veranda and said almost peremptorily: "Come now, what's this all about?"

It was so much like a flash of a faraway Scotland Yard Inspector that the Saint had to control a smile. But he took Fanshire's arm and led him persuasively down the front steps to the beach. Off to their left a tiny red glowworm blinked low down under the silver stars.

"You still have somebody watching the place where the body was found?" Simon asked.

"Of course," Fanshire grumbled. "As a matter of routine. But the sand's much too soft to show any footprints, and—"

"Will you walk over there with me?"

Fanshire sighed briefly, and trudged beside him. His politeness was dogged but unfailing. He was a type that had been schooled from adolescence never to give up, even to the ultimate in ennui. In the interests of total fairness he would be game to the last yawn.

He did go so far as to say: "I don't know what you're getting at, but why *couldn't* it have been an accident?"

"I never heard a better theory in my life," said the Saint equably, "with one insuperable flaw."

"What's that?"

"Only," said the Saint, very gently, "that the wind wasn't blowing the right way."

Major Fanshire kept his face straight ahead to the wind and

said nothing more after that until they reached the glowworm that they were making for and it became a cigarette-end that a constable dropped as he came to attention.

The place where Floyd Vosper had been lying was marked off in a square of tape, but there was nothing out of the ordinary about it except some small stains that showed almost black under the flashlight which the constable produced.

"May I mess up the scene a bit?" Simon asked.

"I don't see why not," Fanshire said doubtfully.

Simon went down on his knees and began to dig with his hands, around and under the place where the stains were. Minutes later he stood up, with sand trickling through his fingers, and showed Fanshire the mushroomed scrap of metal that he had found.

"A thirty-eight bullet," Fanshire said, and whistled thinly through his teeth.

"And I think you'll be able to prove it was fired from the gun you have in your pocket," said the Saint. "Also you'd better have a sack of sand picked up from where I was digging. I think a laboratory examination will find that it also contains fragments of bone and human flesh."

"You'll have to explain this to me," Fanshire said quite humbly.

Simon dusted his hands and lighted a cigarette.

"Vosper was lying on his face when I last saw him," he said, "and I think he was as much passed out as sleeping. With the wind and the surf and the soft sand it was easy for the murderer to creep up on him and shoot him in the back. But the murderer didn't want you looking for guns and comparing bullets. The umbrella was the inspiration. I don't have to remind you that the exit hole of a bullet is much larger than the entrance. By turning Vosper's body over, the murderer found a hole in his chest into which it couldn't have been too difficult to force the umbrella shaft—thus obliterating the original wound and confusing everybody in one simple operation."

"Let's get back to the house," said the Superintendent abruptly.

After a while, as they walked, Fanshire said: "It's going to feel awfully funny, having to arrest Herbert Wexall."

"Good God!" said the Saint, in honest astonishment. "You weren't thinking of doing that?"

Fanshire stopped and blinked at him under the still distant light of the uncurtained windows.

"Why not?"

"Did Herbert seem at all guilty when he admitted he had a gun? Did he seem at all uncomfortable—I don't mean just puzzled, as you were—about having it produced? Was he ready with the explanation of why it smelled of being quite recently fired?"

"But if anyone else used Wexall's gun," Fanshire pondered laboriously, "why should they go to such lengths to make it look as if no gun was used at all, when Wexall would obviously have been suspected from the very first?"

"*Because it was somebody who didn't want Wexall to take the rap,*" said the Saint. "Because Wexall is the goose who could still lay golden eggs—but he wouldn't do much laying on the end of a rope, or whatever you do to murderers here."

The Superintendent pulled out a handkerchief and mopped the perspiration off his face.

"My God," he said, "you mean you think Lucy—"

"I think we have to go all the way back to the prime question of motive," said the Saint. "Floyd Vosper was a nasty man who made dirty cracks about everyone here. But his cracks were dirtiest because he always had a wickedly good idea what he was talking about. Nevertheless very few people become murderers because of a dirty crack. Very few people kill other people on points of principle. Vosper called us all variously dupes, phonies, cheaters, and fools. But since he had roughly the same description for all of us, we could all laugh it off. There was only one person about whom he made the unforgivable accusation. . . . Now shall we rejoin the mob and finish up?"

"You'd better do this your own way," Fanshire muttered almost inaudibly.

Simon Templar took him up the steps to the veranda and back through the French doors into the living room, where all eyes turned to them in deathly silence.

"A paraffin test will prove who fired that revolver in the last twenty-four hours, aside from those who have already admitted it," Simon said, as if there had been no interruption. "And you'll remember, I'm sure, who supplied that very handy theory about the Arrow of God doing away with Vosper."

332

"Astron!" Fanshire gasped.

"Oh, no," said the Saint, a little tiredly. "He only said that God sometimes places his arrow in the hands of a man. And I feel quite sure that a wire to New York will establish that there is actually a criminal file under the name of Granville, with fingerprints and photos that should match Mr. Gresson's —as Vosper's fatally elephantine memory remembered. . . . That was the one crack he shouldn't have made—mentioning Granville as Gresson's middle name—because it was the only one that was more than gossip or shrewd insult, the only one that could be easily proved, and the only one that had a chance of upsetting an operation which was all set—if you'll excuse the phrase I use—to make a big killing."

Major Fanshire fingered his upper lip and looked at Simon Templar inquiringly, as if for guidance.

"I don't know," he began; and then, as Arthur Granville Gresson began to rise like a floating balloon from his chair, and the ebony-faced sergeant moved to intercept him like a stolid, well-disciplined automaton, he knew.

DUST TO DUST

By WILBUR DANIEL STEELE

Wilbur Daniel Steele was born on March 17, 1886, in Greensboro, N.C. He attended the University of Denver, where his father was professor of Biblical Literature, and studied painting at the Museum of Fine Arts in Boston, the Académie Julien in Paris, and the Art Students' League in New York. Joining the artists' colony in Provincetown, Mass., he tried his hand at writing a Cape Cod story, which was published in *The Atlantic* in 1912. In 1919 he received the first O. Henry award for writing short stories of outstanding excellence. His stories are notable for their variety of background, their ingenuity, and their grasp of psychopathology.

THE DAY NEWT LEXX buried his wife Ruby there was a fair attendance at the graveside. Considering the circumstances. It was haying time in Connecticut and good haying weather. Of Candlebrook's four burying grounds the one at Willis Hill is the most remote, six miles out from the Center, and the least tended, being of late years little used. For a long while the woods have been creeping back about it. The buildings of seven farms were once in view from that field above the Willis Hill road. Today the mourners could see but one roof, the old Willis place itself. When Ruby Willis had been born there, it was painted and prosperous. It had been far from that for years now, since the old folks died and Ruby and her do-nothing husband returned there to squat in squalor. A fit lair for a dumb animal like Newt.

Two things lay behind the comparatively large turnout this afternoon; curiosity and respect. Respect not for Ruby, long since forgotten even of pity. Respect for Ruby's sister Pearl. Pearl Tomasson's house was the best in the Center and her husband was manager of the Hartford Deposit's branch bank in Titusport across the river. And that was where curiosity came in. Day before yesterday his cashier had up and shot himself. So, today, would Will Tomasson show up here at the grave of his wife's sister, or would he be busy otherwheres? Hear of a cashier's suicide and you'll think right away of a shortage, bank examiners, and so on.

But curiosity had another side here today, even more titillating to minds of a morbid turn. It is said of a man that he buries his wife. Here it was no mere figure of speech. Trapping furs and potting protected deer won't keep a good-for-nothing fed. Newt had to take on a cash chore now and then; he was one of the town's two gravediggers. To a man of thinner hide it might have occurred to call on the other in this case. But not to Newt. All forenoon he had spent in sinking the hole. Now, once the rest were gone, he would take off the decent dark suit of her husband's which Pearl had sent with the caustic plea that he wear it, put on his overalls, and shovel the earth back in.

That he had been moved by the plea and worn the suit

surprised no one more than it did Pearl. She had realized the minute she had sent it what a slap in the face the act might seem. (Not that she cared as to that.) But no; she had seen so little of him in so long, she had almost forgotten that Newt was incapable of being insulted. He had been so much the feared and admired as a boy, by so much the top bully in all things muscular, and his face so handsome, he had never had to worry what was gibe and what was flattery. He had never had to listen when others talked, or laugh when they laughed, or wash his neck to make the girls yearn.

One more thing Pearl realized in anger today: Newt **Lexx** hadn't had to suffer, as others have to. In the eighteen years since he was seventeen he had not suffered any growth or any change. The same dull handsome face, lineless as a new-pulled turnip. Same old uncut haircut crawling down his neck's soiled nape. And the build. Newt and Will Tomasson had once been of much the same proportions. Now Will's coat was so scant across Newt's chest it wouldn't button, and Will's vest and pants-belly hung on him like a bag. Could it be that that was Newt's reason for wearing it here and now, deliberately to slap Pearl back? Pearl couldn't believe, though, his brain was bright enough for that.

All the same she got to wishing Will were here to see and be hurt, his pompous self-love infuriated. Serve him right for getting out of attending Ruby's funeral. Oh, yes, she knew, the cashier and the books, the whole plaguy upset. But then, being plagued and upset was nothing new with Will; he had been in a dirty temper for months now, it seemed to his wife in her righteous indignation. Her neuralgic pains increased while the minister's prayer ran on.

She mustn't think of the prayer so, as too long drawn out. She must think only of her loss, only of Ruby. Not as of lately but as of long ago. Ruby the golden, lush and slow and loving peacefulness. No spine. It hadn't been Ruby's fault that Newt **Lexx** had changed his mind and taken her of the two. "Ashes to ashes"; here was the hour meet for forgiveness and a tear. Ruby, beloved sister . . .

Newt, the unspeakable animal . . . Will, the weak sneak. Yes, sneak. He would be here if he could "possibly make it, even late." Oh, yes? As if the ordeal weren't even worse for Pearl than for him. The eyes of these townspeople peering between the pious fingers at their brows to see how she and

Newt were taking it. For they knew the whole of it, of course. Knew it was not her fault or Ruby's fault or Will's fault that Ruby was the wife Newt was burying and Pearl the lady of a banker's house, with a cook and a cleaning-woman and activities and nerves and pains.

"Dust to dust."

Pearl had been terrified lest something prompt Newt to see her to her car, in which she had come accompanied by an elderly spinster cousin from East Center. But then when he never budged, just stood there as if unconscious of her and the others' existence, contemplating the hole, the earth-pile and the shoveling to do, then it was like Pearl to be doubly furious with him. Turning back from halfway to the cars, she begged God for words to hurt him with. Something supercilious.

She looked him up and down. "Those clothes of Will's."

"I'll change them before I go at it." As stupid as that.

"Why bother? Certainly my husband won't be wanting them back."

"O.K."

Was there no club so cruel it would dent that skull? She thought wildly of asking what was his charge for the grave-digging; she wanted to pay. But hopelessness tied her tongue. As she rejoined her cousin Hattie at the car she saw Newt getting a shovel and overalls from behind a neighboring gravestone, on which he had hung Will's coat and vest.

Hers was the last car; many of those ahead had disappeared when she turned out into the road below. It was a wonder she could drive. Agony stabbed along her shoulderblades. Her head was about to split, when she suddenly forgot it and braked the car, peering in the mirror. Back beyond the graveyard turn-in, parked off the road among some sumacs below the wall's far corner, was Will's cream-and-green coupe. It was plain it had come in from the road's other end, the ferry.

So? He would get there, if "even late," would he? Hooey! *Deliberately* late. And park down there, unobtrusively, until she, his wife, and all the others had departed. Why? Pearl's mind was capable of vast leaps; the kind of mind that "something tells," as she was fond of putting it.

Why? So he could go up there to Ruby's grave, all by his precious self, alone. Like a moping poet. His remembrances

337

too sacred and too lorn for the eyes of people and Pearl to look upon. Those people and this wife whom he had hoodwinked into supposing him merely another tired businessman, his only troubles money troubles, no hidden depths. As was Pearl's way, she "saw it all" in "one bitter flash." Alone with his dead love, alone at last.

Fit to do murder, Pearl's first impulse was to back the car down there, roaring, honking. But she thought just in time, with a nasty delight, of how far from alone with Ruby Will was due to find himself, the widower busy shoveling. Pearl drove on, her fingers blue-white on the wheel.

She determined she wouldn't go home; let Will get there and do the waiting. Maybe the worrying. But after an hour at her cousin's house in East Center she decided she would go but not say a word to Will, just look at him. But then the blow; Will wasn't home yet. The cook said there'd been three phone calls, wanting Mr. Tomasson to call Titusville 121 the minute he was in. She had told them, the first one, about the funeral.

Titusville 121. The bank. Anxiety began to temper Pearl's rage. It couldn't mean, could it, something bad would happen to Will? As bad as losing his position? Merely because help he had hired had turned out dishonest? Absurd! But where *was* Will? Supposing she'd been all wrong about his parking in that queer place. Out of gas, a flat tire, or something. And her not stopping to find out.

Pearl got her car and drove back out the Willis Hill road, alert to wave Will down if she met him. She had passed the Larns farm, half a mile short of the graveyard, when she overtook Newt Lexx, afoot, carrying a jack.

"Get in," she told him. "He's got a flat?"

"And no jack. I come for the loan of Larn's."

"Where did you leave him? At the car?"

"Nope. Up there."

"Alone?" Here was fury back again. "With my sister?"

Newt gaped, like a dull one bewildered. "Ruby? She's dead. . . . Look, there's another car there by it. Looks like Bontree's police car."

It was not Lieutenant Bontree but a sober civilian with him who came to where Pearl stopped at the turn-in. Mr. Curtaine, from the bank's home office at Hartford. Anxious, most anxious, to contact Tomasson.

"Wh-what for?" It was Pearl's nerves and sight of the police car.

Curtaine smiled in reassurance. Mrs. Tomasson wasn't, please, to mind Bontree; it was simply that he had kindly offered the lift. They had just arrived, via the ferry, to find Mr. Tomasson's car, with a flat tire, but no Mr. Tomasson.

"Up there." Newt indicated the wall above the road as he started with the jack for the cream-and-green coupe.

Pearl said it was just a step, they could walk. "It's my sister we buried today. My husband meant to attend, but as you know, with all this bank business, it seems that he arrived too late. And now, this tire." Pearl took pains with every syllable, such was her state of mind by now. Bontree at their heels. There was no reason Bontree shouldn't come along, having nothing else to do. But policemen always started Pearl's imagination working.

Though it was full dusk even in the open of the burying ground, there was enough light to show that Will Tomasson wasn't there. Around the grave, three-quarters filled in, the long grass still lay flat where the feet of the mourners had pressed it. Bontree left a wake as he waded through the stuff to the wall above the road to hail down to Newt. "Tell him to come up here," Curtaine called after the policeman.

It was too much for Pearl. "Mr. Curtaine. What do you want of Will? I mean, so—in such a rush."

Women, so jumpy where their men folks are concerned; Curtaine had to smile. All that was wanted of her husband, he assured Pearl, was to get him back to the bank, "all hands to the pumps," a long night's work. After a long day's work? Unfortunately, yes. At the day's end it had seemed to be settled that the shortage was a moderate figure, little over thirty-five hundred. The cashier's widow, broken down, had admitted knowledge of about that much. Everything, so far as the cash went, seemed to check. Everything finished, good night. It was only afterwards, when the examiner's man decided to stay on and take one routine look into the securities account, that the thing blew wide open. No wonder the cashier had killed himself. Not only robbing the bank; two-timing his wife as well. No, there was no knowing as yet— that was where Tomasson's knowledge of the files was needed —but that thirty-five-hundred cash loss was already beginning to look like a drop in the bucket. And now Tomasson—not

339

that it was Tomasson's fault he was unfindable quickly—but Mrs. Tomasson could see how exasperating . . .

Pearl could see.

Newt, coming up with Bontree, couldn't see, of course. All this to-do over Will not there. Probably got tired waiting. Thumbed a ride, likely enough; there'd been cars by. Very likely, Pearl hastened to agree. Probably home by now. Well, that was that. They were preparing to go when Bontree said wait, his eyes on Newt. Newt had turned and was studying the woods where they went up from the eastern, rearward, end of the field. "Just a minute," said Bontree to the others quietly.

It was Bontree's business to know people's makeups. The side of Newt Lexx which was mentally arrested and emotionally closed Bontree knew as well as anyone did. But he knew there was another side, a smart one, purely sensory. Newt's eyes, ears, even his nose; Bontree had seen them at work, in the woods. Which of these was attentive now Bontree couldn't have said. And Newt didn't say. He lifted his voice and called, "Will?" After a moment, when nothing came of it, he picked up his shovel from the ground.

It had affected Curtaine, nevertheless. "I get a feeling of something somehow queer. Mr. Lexx, tell me. You say he came up here to get you to shift his tire. Yes?"

Newt turned his shovel end for end. "No, I didn't."

"I mean, I gathered that. What *did* he say? Or do?"

"Nothing. Stood around, watched me shovel. Till by and by."

"By and by—what?"

"He says he wanted to pay me for the digging, five dollars."

Pearl jumped in, avid. "And what did *you* say to *that?*"

"I said it was eight." Of the hearers Curtaine alone felt no queasy turning of the stomach. He was yet unaware that this was the buried woman's husband speaking. "Will only had a ten, so he says if I go down, shift his wheel, we'll call it right. So that's how come."

With a thumb Newt prepared to clean the blade of his shovel. He desisted almost right away and looked at the thumb. Curtaine's anxiety to get going began to show as temper. But again Bontree said wait.

Having rubbed the thumb with a finger, Newt looked at the grave. He dropped the shovel, turned, bent over the dwindled dirt pile, felt it here and there as if for variations of freshness. Again he returned and studied the soil in the grave.

Bontree spoke. "Look, Newt, was Tomasson carrying anything?"

Newt shook his head, engrossed. "Except one of these leather what-you-call-ems."

"Briefcase?" That was Curtaine.

And Bontree: "And there's more dirt in there than there was when you left, Newt? . . . Give me that shovel."

Newt fended off angrily the policeman's hand, took the shovel and himself stepped down in. That gesture of violence, that betrayal of some resentment, some sense at last of this being his wife's grave, not just anybody's, for Tom, Dick and Harry to be monkeying with; Pearl's mind was too intent on this revelation to catch up quickly with the others' minds, the implication of the act, the dreadful thing impending.

It wasn't long. The narrow, shallow box of japanned metal had been covered by barely two inches of hasty soil down there. "After he saw us coming," Bontree surmised. "Wouldn't you say, Newt?"

Newt didn't say. Hunch, anger, discovery; the episode was finished for Newt with his stepping out of the grave, so it seemed. He propped his shovel, spat on a hand, surveyed the pile, his familiar stupid self again. "How about it?" he asked of Bontree.

Bontree waited on Curtaine, busy some paces distant riffling the box's contents; bearer bonds (it was later to be known) in the amount of over thirty-three thousand dollars; inevitably to have been held against a suicide's account, had it not been for dull Newt's wild-animal shrewdness.

Curtaine pocketed the box and said to Bontree: "Let's go. I've a theory we'll find him long since home, cozy and innocent."

"Unless," said Bontree, eying the rise of woods which Newt had eyed, "unless he *was* there, watching, and saw us find it. Eh, Newt?"

"Nope. I heard it since then, and it's Larn's heifer he lost last night." Newt spat on his other hand. "How about it?"

"Go ahead, fill in, finish up. And say nothing, as if nothing was out of ordinary. Mind, Newt, I mean that." Bontree went

341

to where Pearl sat frozen on a gravestone, the same on which were hung Will's loaned-out coat and vest of the afternoon. "We're going to have to ask you, Mrs. Tomasson, not to come along just yet. I'm sorry."

Curtaine was less civil. "And to make sure, we'll take her car keys with us."

"And either send them or bring them back in not too long; I'm sorry, Mrs. Tomasson." Bontree went with the bank man, leaving Pearl and Newt there in the falling night with Ruby. The numb, the dumb, and the dead.

Pearl could have sat in her car. But that would have meant rising from the stone and walking down there. Down, down, down. The rasp of gravelly earth on Newt's shovel measured time for a while; then it was the thud of his tamper methodical on the mounded sod. When it was done and he laid the tamper down, Pearl found her voice.

"What can they want of Will? They've got their money."

"Will? I have to laugh," said the man who never laughed. He shouldered his shovel and came toward Pearl. But it was only to pass her by, as she sprang to her feet, and walk on toward the field's rear, leaving a wake in the knee-high grass.

Along this Pearl found herself running, panting at his heels.

"What, Newt? Where you going, Newt? . . . Newt, stop, wait! I know. That was a lie, it wasn't a heifer. It was Will. And what's it to you?"

They came to the tumbled wall, thick-set with undergrowth beyond. Pearl grabbed at the trailing shovel blade and hurt her hand—that was all the good it did. Newt stepped on over.

"Very well then, Newt. Wherever you go, I'm going with you."

Newt turned, only his face visible in a frame of leaves.

"Go over to the house and wait. You're not coming in here."

"I'd like to know who'll stop me!"

"It's thick with copperheads."

"All the same—" Pearl's voice went, with that. To save her life she couldn't have stirred then.

It was nothing Newt did, of his will; it was something the woods did to him. Bontree could have told Pearl, at least a little, of the transfigurations apt to be undergone by this creature in the wilds with his own. Waiting for his brother fox to come inquiring or his sister quail to brush his hand;

in every feature the fox, the quail. But not even Bontree had seen what Pearl was face-to-face with now.

Suggestion helped, darkness helped, no doubt. The flattening of the brow, the flaring of the jaw-line, the narrowing of the neck, held away back, whiplike; these were of course pure illusion. But illusion resident in the head itself. And in the eyes, swaying ever so little as the head swayed, but unwinking, viperine, deadly.

"It's thick with copperheads."

The gap in the leaves was empty. No sound of twigs or feet. Only, presently, from a distance, Newt's voice saying: "Go over home."

Pearl remained frightened, almost literally, out of her wits.

Bontree was gone two hours. When he returned he was minus Curtaine and had another state car following. He noted the finished grave and, with his flash, followed the beaten track to the woods. Mrs. Tomasson's whereabouts was what puzzled him most. It occurred to him finally he'd best have a look at the Willis place. Leaving his fellows, he walked the hundred yards or so along the road, the ferry way, then down the thickly grown trail which had once been the lane.

The house was dark and looked dead. Bontree all but missed noting the deeper shadow that was a figure seated on the steps.

"Your husband hasn't shown up at home, Mrs. Tomasson. I presume you've guessed that. Where is Lexx?"

"I don't know."

"Up in the woods there? Looking for Mr. Tomasson?"

"I don't know."

It was natural the woman should be stunned, her world of comfort and respect shot to pieces, so shortly since, no warning. Yet it seemed to Bontree there was needed some added element to explain her guarded words and her stony stillness.

"Why are you here?" he tried next. "Waiting here."

Pearl's eyes sought somewhere to rest. They rested on the step beside her. "Here I was born. My and my sister's home, as girls."

"See here, Mrs. Tomasson, it isn't your home now. Why don't you go home and wait there?"

"He and I went together. Will and Ruby went together. We planned to take in Hamburg Fair one fair-time. I took

343

a stand: I wouldn't go with him unless he would get a coat and wear a necktie. He bought a coat and tie and put them on Will; Will daren't cross him. 'I hope they suit your taste to go to the fair with,' Newt said to me, him still in the same old dirty zipper. He went and took Ruby by a wrist and said, 'Me, I'm taking Ruby.' And you know Ruby, how she always hated having scenes and contentions."

"Now look, Mrs. Tomasson, please . . ."

"It's easy to think him dumber than he is. I shouldn't have sent him that suit of Will's today. And Will shouldn't have— Will's done a lot of things today he shouldn't have."

"Your keys are in your car."

"But he wore the suit. He took Will's pay. Could it be it was Will's taking advantage of Ruby's grave that way? I don't know."

"Or if you'd rather, I'll go along with you. Come."

But there was no stirring her. Ordinarily quick to argue and in a fever to be doing, now she was made of wood. Wood petrified.

It was after twelve, the moon up, when Newt came. He came by the back way; the first they heard of him was his voice inside the house, calling "Pearl?" He appeared, to Bontree's hail, descended the steps between the two, reposed himself among the dew-sodden weeds at the foot, looked at one and the other and then at the moon.

"Where have you been, Lexx? What doing? Tell me."

"Roving around. Here and there. Like I do."

Perhaps because he sat touching earth again; perhaps because his skin and hair still shone with the wet of the woods; not yet had he shaken off all his luster of animal excitation.

"Lexx. Why that lie about a heifer? Where is Tomasson?"

"You tell me." Newt lay back in the weeds, his head pillowed in his joined hands. "You tell me." He yawned, big and black. "When you find him."

"That's your line? Very well. Do you feel inclined to explain me this much? How came that tire flat? Blow-out? Puncture?"

"Unscrewed valve. Like you noted. The way it looks, Will seen me at work. Wanted to fix it somehow he could be alone up there with—"

"—Ruby." Miserable Pearl. The instant it had blurted from her, color swept her face, dark in the dim light.

344

Newt fixed his attention on her from his couch of earth.

"You look more like yourself, Pearl. Handsomer 'n I've seen you look for long. No fidgets, no aches, no pains."

Pearl tried to cry: "Don't say such things!" But somehow she couldn't utter. The sheen of the wild on the creature, the innocence of the beast in the appraising eyes; not even at the woods' edge up there had she felt so weak-as-water. Besides, what if what he'd said was true?

Bontree had supposed he'd known the thickness of Newt's skull and skin, until now. Now it was incredible, with a third party present.

"I been to blame, Pearl. I did you wrong. Ruby knew it. We talked it over many the time, me and Ruby. I oughtn't to left Will have you. I should have sent Will packing, and took the two of you. I'm man enough. And you'd have been the way Ruby was, healthy, happy."

Bontree felt fantasmal. And outraged. He was trying to find words when Newt settled his head back in his hands and shut his eyes. "Not tonight, Pearl; I'm tired. But come out soon; I want to talk with you." Within a minute—there was no artifice about it—the man slept.

The two black roads which, with the river, bound the district had been under patrol for two hours already— a routine measure. From Pearl's house, where he returned with her, Bontree took another step by telephone. He directed his station at Westbrook to send out a statewide teletype, describing Tomasson as wanted. He had more than a hunch, he felt the certainty, that this too was merely perfunctory.

A search was made of the woods next day, an area three miles square, the bulk of it to the east of Willis Hill. It couldn't be thoroughgoing; Bontree hadn't the men. It was as much by luck as anything that a shovel handle was espied protruding from the surface of shallow Saw Pond, less than a mile over the ridge from the graveyard.

Bontree went to Pearl Tomasson. This was now his third attempt at breaking through the torpor and listlessness which still seemed to wall the woman's memory away—whether naturally or deliberately he would have given much to know. He put it as a challenge; how came she to have forgotten to mention the shovel Lexx took with him?

That was so, she said; she had forgotten the shovel.

345

With that much he had Newt brought in to him at the station. Confronted with the shovel, Newt was unbothered.

"It's old. I got tired of carrying it. Threw it away."

"In Saw Pond, yes. Why in a pond? Why in water?"

"I threw it at a fish."

"I've a mind to hold you, Lexx. On suspicion of murder."

"Of who?"

Well, there remained only to go at it the hard way. Go through a triangular area of roughly fifteen square miles. Comb it inch by inch. End to end. This time for one thing specific: earth lately turned.

It took time to organize and to do. Upwards of fifty men in line, back and forth, strip by strip, like swaths of a mower. One would have sworn not an inch was missed. There's such a thing as making certainty dead certain.

Lastly they took the old house itself, Newt's house. And there the eight days' labor had its only pay. Not concealed, not even stowed away: Will Tomasson's empty briefcase.

"I found it. Just happened." Newt's hand caressed the thing. "Good piece of leather . . . Where? Over by Saw Pond. . . . Why?"

Two days later Bontree appeared at Pearl's house. "I am kicking myself," was his preface.

Pearl sat and said nothing to that. She didn't look at Bontree. Through it all her gaze was fixed beyond him, curiously apathetic yet curiously engrossed. (Later he discovered there was a mirror there.)

"I want you to think hard, Mrs. Tomasson. We've been going on the assumption that your husband has come by some bodily harm. I have anyhow, and I think you have. As we were meant to? I'm wondering."

If Bontree had thought to startle her, he had failed; Pearl seemed not even curious. For all the overturn of her world and the strain now two weeks borne, she appeared to have taken on flesh; flesh she could well do with. The old nerve-twitch was nearly gone from between her brows. And this fixed stillness of her gaze, once forever jumping here and there —it took Bontree's mind back to the moonlit Willis steps, her stony stillness.

"Think hard, Mrs. Tomasson, will you? Is there, or has there ever been, any reason you can conceive of, why Lexx would wish your husband success in getting clear away? Wish it enough, dumb as he is, to make a lot of bright people look a darn sight dumber? Think hard."

Pearl shook her head, no, her eyes still going past the officer.

"Unless," she said in the same half-minded way, "unless, as you heard him that night, his mistake not to take me too made him send Will packing. But what difference now, I can't see."

They were both silent for a minute. Bontree needed all of a minute. He got up then as if to leave, and he said: "By the way, what was it he said, about wishing you'd come out? He wanted to have a talk with you?"

"I'd be in terror," Pearl said, without a trace of it. She arose and went into the hall ahead of Bontree.

"You'd have no call to be. Your every minute there would be under surveillance, Mrs. Tomasson. I give you my word. I wouldn't suggest it, except that with you alone, something he might say, some little thing—"

"I'd be in terror." Pearl turned and walked up the stairs, leaving Bontree to let himself out, after a meditative minute.

Pearl went to her bedroom, shut the door, took a chair, and said for the third time: "I'd be in terror." She said it this time to the woman in the mirror; the chair she had taken was her dressing-table chair.

Strange woman in the mirror. Temples unhollowed, eyes unharassed, mouth relaxed, its lips inclined to fullness. Woman in her prime.

Pearl's mind was nothing if not conventional. It had dwelt in her body as her body had dwelt in Banker Will's house, content and careful to be looked up to. Will's last-minute turpitude should not be allowed to weigh a jot with the widow in her weeds, which is the way Pearl saw herself surely in her mind. That Will was dead her mind had accepted all in one instant, one look at Newt in the moonlight at the steps. A beast bedewed, gorged with prey, full length on the night earth, his upward scrutiny of her simple as any wild thing's. ("Handsomer n' I've seen you look for long, Pearl. No fidgets, no aches, no pains.") Bitterly to mourn the slain, savagely to hate the uncouth, unclean, stupid slayer; that was the orthodox thing to which Pearl's mind set itself, and set itself. But her brain and her blood were different entities. That was how it came that while her intellect was resolved

347

to grieve, her flesh paid no heed and went its own way, blooming. That was the terror of it.

It was growing dark when the phone rang. Lieutenant Bontree, from the station at Westbrook. He began with an uneasy brightness, as one conscious that the goodness of his news was not unmixed. Mrs. Tomasson could now forget all that about a talk with Lexx. Bontree's tardy hunch was soon proved right. Tomasson—yes—alive and in good health—in Buffalo. They—er—they expected to have him extradited and home by Friday. When yet Pearl had uttered no word he asked sharply if she was all right. Yes, she said. He forced his cheer again. One worry at least she could forget now. No call now to go through with "that little talk" with Lexx, the devil.

When Pearl had hung up, she sat unstirring for a while. It takes a while to get the dead back alive and the world back the way it was.

The way it was? Hardly! Extradited. Handcuffs? What was the worst she could expect for Will? Prison?

It came over Pearl in a sickening sweep; no, prison wasn't the worst. Supposing he were somehow to be freed, home, here in this room, there in that other of the twin beds. His name and his money gone. Nothing left of him but his soft, scrubbed, pale stomach to mound the blankets. By Friday!

Pearl became conscious of her own stomach; not so much a pain as a hollowness in the pit of it. How dared the doctors keep telling her it was nerves and nothing more! She went and frowned intently into the dark mirror to see if the wrinkle was coming back between her brows. All Will's doing, nobody's else. ("And you'd have been the way Ruby was, healthy, happy.") A shoulderblade twitched and set the old neuralgia stabbing. That was the last straw. That was more than Pearl would take, or need take, from Will, alive.

Pearl told the cook she was going to New London to a picture. Halfway out to Willis Hill she stopped the car, got a lipstick from the glove-compartment and did her mouth the best she could in the windshield mirror. Driving on then she passed the graveyard and the house lane and parked fifty yards beyond the latter.

There was a lamp in the sitting room, some of its light behind Newt when he opened the front door. He had on a pair of corduroy pants, no shirt, no shoes. It was summer.

"It's me," said Pearl. "You wanted a talk with me."

He came out on the steps and stood motionless for moments, wholly intent on the surrounding thickets. "Not out here. There's one of them there in the hazels. One up yonder. But I'm too deep for them. Will's too deep for them. Hold your hush and come inside."

Now was the time Pearl should have told him how wrong he was and how unlikely anyone was watching now. But Newt had taken her by a wrist, just as once he had taken Ruby by a wrist. Her heels clicking, his soles silent, he led her in, rearward along the hall to the blackness of the summer-kitchen.

There he said: "Not in the house. I don't like a house. Ruby never liked a house. Take your shoes off." He bent and did it for her, impatient of her hesitation. Ruin of stockings meant nothing to him. Pearl herself took off her stockings.

Her feet had long forgotten the chill and prickle of going barefoot. Luckily, once out the back door, the going was slow business. Three or four steps, and the shadow ahead of her halted, and Pearl must halt each time and stand and wait. She had to think back to earliest memory to believe that to the end of the wagonshed could be so long a journey. And to think that here and now she could put a stop to all this stealth by telling Newt of Will and Buffalo.

By and by they were in cover, leaves pressing on either side, though there was the feel of a path against Pearl's wincing soles. This was land familiar to her childhood, but no one could have been more utterly lost now than she. Still, though rarer, there were the halts to hearken. With each one a strange sense in Pearl grew stranger. Something knocking at the door of memory. When had she ever done just so before? But then there came one halt in a rift of the woods. In the starlight, after the pitch dark, Newt's act and attitude were for the first time clearly visible. Now she knew where she was.

There used to be an oak; yes, and there it still stood, to her left, dominating the tiny glade. And it was not she who had been coming up the path like this, that other time. She, the girl, had been lying out along one of the oak's great boughs, dreaming daydreams. And they had come so and halted and stood just so. He querying with eyes, ears, and nostrils one half the compass; she, the other half. Deer in Autumn. A buck and a doe. By and by he had beckoned with his antlers, all's well, and she had followed on.

Newt didn't go on. He beckoned Pearl and she went to him.

"Can't be alone together in a house, someway. Ruby and me, we always liked here."

He took Pearl by the back of her neck with his left hand. With the furry under-side of his right forearm he cleansed her mouth of the lipstick and he kissed her. He tossed her in the air and caught her and crushed her and kissed her. . . .

What wind there was came from the southwest; they could hear the Titusport town clock, across the river. Pearl heard it telling two. How could it have been so many hours? She might have wondered also how she could lie here supine, clasped hands pillowing her head, and never feel the leaf-mat sodden and clammy. But she didn't feel it, so she didn't wonder. She counted stars. Stretched beside her, Newt was halfway drowsing.

Pearl said: "Newt. My sending Will's suit out for you to wear—I hope you didn't think that I was trying—"

"That's all right."

"Anyway, forgive me, Newt."

"That's all right." Then after quite a while: "I can't forgive him, though, figuring to pay me for Ruby's grave." And after another while, something that sounded like gibberish to Pearl: "It's long too late."

But of course, Pearl thought it out. Newt too in his simple mind had accepted Will gone as Will dead. It was time now she should conquer her soul-and-body's lassitude and tell Newt.

But Newt had reared on his haunches beside her and was combing the angle of his nape with his fingers to rid it of grass-stems and rotted leaves.

What an animal.

He laid a hand on her. "Would you ever believe this, Pearl? You with me here alone, like you always have wanted. And same with him, the way he always wanted, alone together, him and her. Tell me if it ain't like a book."

Together in the after-life, of course he meant, Will and Ruby. Come, Pearl, come, come, tell him. . . . By and by . . .

It was nearly four when Pearl got in under the wheel and closed the door quietly. But then there came a sound of run-

350

ning feet and Lieutenant Bontree's face was in the window, haggard with anxiety. Sight of Pearl's dishevelment made it only more haggard.

"I shall never forgive either my men or myself, never! Mrs. Tomasson, tell me. Did you—have you suffered any harm?"

Impassive. Almost somnolent. "What do you mean harm?"

"I should be, probably shall be, broken for this. But will you believe me I had no faintest idea yesterday, when I misled you as to your husband's whereabouts and known safety —will you believe I had only in mind—Mrs. Tomasson, move over; I'll drive."

They had gone half a mile, far past the graveyard turn-in, before Pearl drew a hand over her eyes and spoke.

"What was it you said back there? Will's not alive?"

"I didn't say that. Not to our *knowledge*, I mean. I'm sorry."

Sorry, guilty, a blunderer, Bontree was still the policeman.

"If it's not too much to ask, Mrs. Tomasson. How did Lexx seem to react to the 'news'—your husband in Buffalo? What did he say?"

Pearl was listless. "I forgot to tell him."

That capped the anticlimax. Bontree would have time aplenty for self-razzing later. Not now. "Well, then," he pressed her, "anything he did say, any comment on the situation as it stands. Can you remember anything in particular Lexx said?"

"No, nothing."

(Nothing? "It's long too late," hadn't he said, in seeming gibberish? Hadn't he said: "And the same with him, the way he always wanted, alone together, him and her?")

Pearl said to Bontree: "Will you slow down, please. Stop the car."

When Bontree had done so Pearl sat on for awhile as still as death, gray of face in the gray light. Bontree felt his own face going the same color as he studied her.

He couldn't hold his breath forever. "Yes? Tell me. What?"

"I can't see how. But."

"What?"

"I'm going to ask you to do something, Bontree, quickly. Open up my sister's grave."

Then Pearl fainted.

351

There had been less than a foot-deep of soil on top of the coffin's pine encasement when the body of Will Tomasson was lowered there. Above the body another two feet had been shoveled in before the metal box was deposited, to be hidden in its turn by but few and hasty inches; time had been an element for Newt Lexx to think of.

Nothing would ever make Newt say. It is probable, however, his first intention was to leave the box there handy to recovery at some safe future time, had it not been for the unexpected coming and concern of the stranger, Curtaine, the police officer, Bontree, and Pearl, all in their innocence to bear down upon his over-simple, over-wary imagination. It is conceivable that Newt's disposal of Will was really, intellectually, an act of dullness. An act of instinct, pure and simple. A wild animal's wile.

The hail to the woods. The "dampness" of earth, on the shovel and on the pile. The dubious study of the grave's remaining depth. And to crown it, innocently, stupidly, seemingly, so to have passed up a treasuretrove that might have been his for the silence. Wealth and ease.

But what, after all, is future ease as compared with instant safety, to a fox, a quail, a deer? What are bearer bonds to a copperhead?